Sheila Norton lives in Chelmsford, Essex and part-time in Torquay, Devon. She worked for most of her life as a medical secretary, until retiring early to concentrate on her writing.

Sheila's first novel was published in 2003. Before starting to write novels, she had over a hundred short stories published in women's magazines.

Sheila enjoys hearing from readers and can be contacted through her website: www.sheilanorton.com, where you can also ask to be added to an email mailing list for updates about Sheila's books and writing life.

Sheila Norton

The Secret of Angel Cove

PIATKUS

PIATKUS

First published in Great Britain in 2022 by Piatkus

1 3 5 7 9 10 8 6 4 2

A CIP catalogue record for this book
is available from the British Library.

ISBN 978-0-349-42986-1

Typeset in Sabon by M Rules

Printed and bound in Great Britain by
Clays Ltd, Elcograf S.p.A.

Papers used by Piatkus are from well-managed forests
and other responsible sources.

Piatkus
An imprint of
Little, Brown Book Group
Carmelite House
50 Victoria Embankment
London EC4Y 0DZ

An Hachette UK Company
www.hachette.co.uk

www.littlebrown.co.uk

*For all my neighbours at our Devon home,
who have welcomed us and our family into the
community and become such good friends.*

A Saturday in September

I've woken up early. I really didn't want to – today of all days, the
first day of *the rest of my life*, as I've been thinking of it. I wanted
to sleep late from now on – every day if I like. I'll never again have
an alarm blaring at me, nagging me to get up, get dressed, hurry
to work, hurry to my patients and spend my busy days dressing
their wounds, giving them their vaccinations, checking their tem-
peratures, their pregnancies, their babies, the boils on their bums.
From today, I'm not a senior practice nurse any more. I'm retired.

'Are you awake, Joy?' Terry mutters as he turns over next
to me. Always seems a pointless question, really. 'Did you hear
that noise?'

'Mm,' I say, yawning. 'What was it?'

'I don't know.' He throws off the duvet and goes across to the
window, peering behind the curtain. There's never much to see.
Just the sky, the sea, the changing seasons measured by the dawn
and dusk. Daylight now: it leaks into the bedroom, showing the
specks of dust floating gently in the air. The thought occurs to
me – and I dismiss it quickly – that I'll have no excuse, now, for
dodging the housework.

Terry stretches and shrugs as he lets the curtain fall again.

'I'll make a cup of tea, shall I – now I'm up?'

'Mm. Thanks.'

I wonder if I can grab another five minutes' sleep while he's doing it. I hear him pad downstairs, hear the kettle being filled – but almost immediately, he's coming back up, the sound of his surprise arriving before he does:

'It's next door! A removal van! They're moving in. Did you know?'

I open my eyes, struggle to sit up. 'Really? No, I didn't – how would I know?'

'It's that young couple, the ones who came to view the house earlier in the summer,' he says.

'Oh, the ones with the little boy? That'll be nice.'

'Didn't see the boy. But yes, them.' He turns to go back downstairs. 'Tea, then?'

'Thanks.' I lie back against the pillows, thinking how good it'll be, after living next to an empty house for nearly a year, to have neighbours again. The house was rented for a long while, a succession of neighbours coming for just long enough to get to know them before they moved on again. Then, last year, the landlord decided to sell, but not until he'd had the whole place redecorated, which seemed a bit crazy to me, as surely any buyers would want to do up the house to their own taste.

'It had probably been neglected for so long,' Terry had pointed out, 'that it desperately needed it. And he'd have wanted to maximise his profit.'

So here we are: on the very day that I begin the rest of my life, I get new neighbours to share it with. I hope they're going to be friendly.

It would be difficult, living here, if you had neighbours you didn't like. Numbers One and Two, Smugglers' Cottages, are the only two houses here at Angel Cove. They're a pair of Victorian brick-built semis, overlooking the sea, backing onto the beach. The cove is a tiny, perfectly U-shaped inlet at the end of the lane that leads up to Bierleigh village, about a mile away. Either side of Smugglers' Cottages, the woods rise steeply away towards Bierleigh in one direction, and Angel Head in the other. It's impossible to live in one of the cottages without your lives becoming entwined with those of the people next door. We share the decking area at the back of our houses, where we have washing lines, outdoor tables and chairs. The beach is our back garden. We put our bins out in the same place – the turning area where the lane ends outside our houses and becomes the footpath through the woods. The bin lorry can just about make it, doing a tight three-point-turn there before heading back up the single-track lane to Bierleigh.

Up till now, with Terry and I both working full-time in different towns – Terry in his office in Dartmouth, me in one of the GP surgeries in Totnes – we've never become particularly close to any of the succession of temporary residents in Number Two cottage. We've been here more than thirty years; we bought Number One, Smugglers' Cottages, when it was the original small, two-bedroomed house. Next door is still like that, but we've added a two-storey extension to our side; we reached the point after a few years here when we could afford something bigger, but we just didn't want to move away. We'd never find anywhere else that matched the location of Angel Cove.

'I'm going to ask if they'd like some tea or coffee,' I tell Terry later, after I've cleared up the breakfast things.

'OK,' he says without looking up from his laptop.

'It's Saturday,' I remind him, as if that's going to make any difference. 'The weekend.'

'Mm.'

He's started doing this recently: working at weekends, and in the evenings. I suppose he's just going through a busy period.

I go to knock on the back door of Number Two, introduce myself and make the offer of tea and coffee.

'Thanks so much,' says the young woman when I return with a tray of mugs and a plate of biscuits. She looks like she's in her early or mid-thirties; petite and slim, with long fair hair tied back off her face in a purple spotted scarf, a smut of dust on her nose and a tired look on her face. 'I'm Sara. And—' she indicates the tall, good-looking man carrying in a bundle of towels and bedding '—this is Rob. My ... um ... husband.'

Um ... husband? 'Pleased to meet you, Rob,' I say. 'Look, I don't want to get in your way, but if you need any help with anything at all, don't hesitate to give me – or my husband, Terry – a shout.'

'Thank you,' she says a bit gruffly.

Rob puts down his bundle and gives me a smile. 'Yes, thanks, Joy. Good to meet you. I'll be going to collect our little boy, Charlie, later. He's back in Plymouth with a friend while we get a bit straight here.'

'That's nice – I'll look forward to meeting him,' I say, returning the smile. 'This is a perfect place for children. I hope you'll be very happy here.'

'Thank you,' Sara says again, and she nods, squaring her shoulders and adopting a brisk, *better get on with* it expression, while Rob picks up the bundle again and follows one of the removal men upstairs.

I feel a bit dismissed. But, of course, they're busy, and moving house is exhausting.

'Well, give me a knock if you need anything, won't you,' I tell Sara, turning to leave.

I don't know if she will. She seems quite brisk and capable and I can't quite judge yet whether she's going to be friendly or not. But, we don't know the first thing about each other yet. And they'll be busy settling down at the moment. I think I'll give it a while before I disturb them again.

A few weeks later: Friday 5 October

It's a clear autumn day, a bit chilly but with a perfect blue sky and calm sea sparkling below us, and Sara and I are standing on top of Angel Head, the headland at one end of our cove, looking back along the coast. This is the first time we've got together properly since she moved in. I've seen her only occasionally, giving me a quick wave as she rushed in and out, taking her little boy to school and back. I haven't seen Rob at all; I presume he must be working long hours. Sara always looked so hurried and businesslike that I felt a little bit wary of her.

But this morning I bumped into her outside and we had a quick chat. She seemed more approachable than the impression I'd had of her so far. I told her I was going for a walk and I was pleasantly surprised that she asked if she could come with me. She says she likes walking, it's how she relaxes, taking a little time off from her work occasionally for that reason, and catching up after Charlie's asleep. So we've walked up here through the woods; I wanted to show off the view to her on a good day.

'Why do you think it's called Angel Cove?' she asks me now.

'I honestly have no idea,' I admit. 'I know there's a local legend about it – about an angel that's supposed to watch over the cove.

But I've never found out exactly how it all started.' I shrug. 'Some people say the angel protects the sea at the cove. They say bathing in the sea is lucky, and I've even heard it said that it's impossible to drown here.' I grin at her. 'I like swimming here myself, when it's warm enough, but I wouldn't want to put that to the test! It's nonsense, obviously, just some old legend. I've never got around to trying to find out exactly how it started.'

Never had time, to be honest. Never had time for anything – until now.

'I like things like that,' Sara says, nodding her head enthusiastically. 'It'd be nice to know what the story is. I'd be tempted to do some research on it if I had time.' She shrugs. 'But I need to keep to my deadlines.'

Sara works from home; she's told me she's a freelance book editor. She says she loves her work and can fit it around Charlie's school hours.

'Well, I could have a go at researching it myself,' I say. 'It *would* be interesting to try to find out more about it.'

The idea quite appeals to me, now I've started thinking about it.

'Perhaps there might be something online?' she suggests.

'Yes, I could try that first. Or the village library might have some local history books.'

'Let me know how you get on, won't you.' She smiles at me. 'Shall we finish the walk now? Do we go this way?'

'Yes, come on. It's downhill now.'

This next part of the path is quite gentle, and we reach the shingle beach at the bottom fairly quickly.

'It's deserted!' Sara says, staring around her.

'The only access down here is the way we've just come.' The red Devon cliffs stretching along the beach from here are steep and hazardous. 'There are rockfalls along there nearly every year,' I add, pointing to the scar of the most recent fall. 'The coast path

7

just here went into the sea a few years ago; it detours onto the road a bit further inland.'

'So we can't walk any further.' She looks disappointed. I get the impression she'd be up for a route-march. I like walking myself but I'm beginning to wonder if I'll keep up with her!

'Only along the beach and back, if you want to – but the tide's coming in. We can do plenty of different walks, though, other days, if you're up for it?'

'Yes, definitely, I'd like that. Thanks, Joy,' she says.

'Well, I'm enjoying it too. I didn't often get time to do this before I retired.'

We turn and start to walk back. The sun is beginning to peek out cautiously from behind the clouds, and a shaft of sunlight suddenly arrows its way across the sea, glinting the tips of the waves with sparkling diamonds.

We stand in silence for a moment, admiring the view.

'Beautiful!' Sara says. She gives a strange little chuckle. 'Well, if nothing else, my childhood dream has come true – I always did want to live by the sea.'

'If nothing else?' I query, a little taken aback.

At first I don't think she's going to reply. She shakes her head as if she's cross with herself.

'I've been an idiot,' she says finally, turning to look at me. 'The thing is, Rob and I always loved this part of the coast. We used to talk about how much we'd like to live here. So when I found this house, and Rob seemed so pleased about it . . . I know this is going to sound totally idiotic, but I somehow managed to deceive myself that he'd change his mind and settle back down here with me and Charlie after all.'

'Oh, Sara!' I stare at her. I feel stupid now. It should have been obvious – I haven't even seen Rob since their moving day. 'I'm sorry, I got totally the wrong impression. I thought perhaps Rob was working away—'

'No. *Playing* away would be more accurate,' she says with an attempt at a laugh.

'But you say you thought he might change his mind? When did you finally realise that he wouldn't?'

'Only on the day I moved in,' she says. She looks at me and gives a little self-deprecating snort. 'It was ridiculous; I should have known perfectly well he wasn't going to ditch Jade, his girl-friend. He's been seeing her for a year now, and when I found out, he actually told me he couldn't live without her. I was so stupid; I got taken in by the fact that Rob was still being fair and decent about everything, going on about staying friends, agreeing with everything I suggested about co-parenting Charlie. He came with me to look at properties . . . and, well, when we looked at this place, this house, he seemed so excited . . . '

She stops and shakes her head. 'I don't know whether to be angry with him, now, for . . . well, for being so bloody patronising, trying to keep me sweet and make it easier for him to get what he wanted, or angry with myself for being taken in by it!'

'You must have felt so let down when you realised,' I say.

'I was gutted,' she admits. 'I'd imagined this scenario where he suddenly said, when he helped me move in, that he'd realised what he was throwing away . . . Huh! He did help me, but the whole day, his eyes were constantly straying to his watch, and to his phone, thinking how soon he could go back to *her*.'

I think she's sounding incredibly strong, considering what she's telling me. Her face is pink with the indignation she obviously feels, or perhaps the frustration of having deluded herself. At the moment, our acquaintance is so new, I can't quite work her out, and I wonder if she's really as strong as she appears. Even her style of dressing seems to be promoting herself as a person who faces the world square on: today she's wearing purple jeans with a bright green sweater, and she has bold streaks of red in her blonde hair.

'But I'm OK, Joy,' she says firmly as we start to walk on. 'I can't deceive myself any more: it's over. He's living with Jade, in her flat, while they look for a place to buy together – their next step. The final step, I suppose ... apart from divorce.'

'Has that been mentioned?'

'No, but it's bound to be what he wants, isn't it? What *she's* going to want. And I can't let this ruin the rest of my life. I have to make a life for myself and Charlie now.'

'Good for you,' I say. 'And you're not on your own here, you know. If you want someone to talk to any time, just give me a shout. I'm always happy to stop for a quick cup of tea or coffee and a chat.'

I must admit, the occasional chat over a cuppa might help me too. Like most people of my age – sixty-five on my last birthday – I'd been looking forward to my retirement for some time before I finally took the plunge. My work had been exhausting me for longer than I cared to admit. I always used to drive home from work in a hurry, anxious to get indoors and start cooking dinner, pour myself a glass of wine, put the TV on and my feet up. But I'd also usually still be preoccupied by the day's events at the surgery. It was hard to put the patients out of my mind completely after I'd finished my day's work.

But I'll never have to rush anywhere again now, whether it's to fetch a defibrillator because of an emergency, or simply to make a cup of tea in a two-minute break between patients. I'm free! I'm still not sure what to do with all this freedom, but at the moment, I don't really care. I just want to take my time, gaze at the sea, and the autumn leaves in the woods, watch the squirrels in the trees and the seagulls swooping overhead, and remember why we love this place.

'We've always considered ourselves so lucky to live here,' I say out loud now to Sara as we finally arrive back at Smugglers'

Cottages. 'We like to think of the cove as one of South Devon's best kept secrets.'

'The beach certainly doesn't get crowded, does it,' she says.

'No. Not many holidaymakers come down here – there's nothing for them to do. No cafés, restaurants, public loos or anything. And the nearest pub, of course, is the Angel, up in the village. But we do get plenty of people from Bierleigh coming down to swim here during the summer.'

'Knowing they're safe from drowning?' Sara says, grinning at me. 'The Angel of the Cove protects them?'

'Well, you never know, there may be some truth in it.' I grin back. 'I'll see what I can do to find out.'

Saturday 6 October

'What are you going to do today?' Terry asks me as he's getting dressed. He asks me every day. It makes me feel a bit defensive. I feel like saying, I'm going to lie around all day doing nothing, if that's all right with him, just to see the expression on his face. But I can't bring myself to say it.

'I'm thinking I could go for another walk,' I say, 'but I don't suppose Sara will have time to join me again today – Charlie's home, and—'

'Yes, you need to be careful you don't intrude,' he says. 'Of course Sara's busy. She's got her work, and Charlie.'

'I know, Terry. I won't *intrude*, but going for walks together was Sara's idea. She's aware that sitting all day is bad for her.' I pause, and then go on, 'I keep warning *you* about it, don't I? You ought to do some stretching exercises, at least, if you haven't got time to get up and walk about a bit.'

He's bringing work home every night now. It seems odd that he's mostly been doing this since I retired – not that I'm reading anything into it. Well, I'm trying not to, anyway.

'I hope you're not going to start lecturing *Sara* with all your nursing advice.' He gives a little laugh, pretending he's joking, but the tone of his voice doesn't match the smile.

'I won't.' I stare back at him, hurt. Is that what he thinks of me? 'I'm just trying to help. She's just separated from her husband, and she's probably a bit lonely.'

To be honest, I'm not even sure whether that's true. Sara seems perfectly fine with being on her own, and more angry than upset about the situation. But I'm not ready to admit that maybe *I'm* feeling a bit lonely myself.

He turns to face me, just in his pants, with one arm in his shirt. 'OK. But I think you need to find interests of your own, too. As well as seeing Sara.'

I turn away from him, sitting on my side of the bed to pull my socks on.

'All I'm trying to do is be a good friend and neighbour,' I say, a bit sharply. 'I *am* getting some interests of my own too – give me a chance, OK? I've only been retired a few weeks.'

'Fair enough.'

'And in fact, I've already decided on another new interest,' I add.

'Go on?' he says. 'What's that?'

'I'm going to research the history of this cove. And the legend of the angel.'

'Oh! Well, good luck with that. I don't suppose there's much to discover but at least it'll keep you occupied.'

Occupied? Or out of his way? I'm beginning to wonder. Well, I'll show him! I *will* start to research the story of the Angel of the Cove. I'll bloody well start today.

After breakfast, I set up my laptop on the kitchen table and decide I'm not moving until I've made a start on this research. My first few Google searches for 'Angel Cove, Devon' don't result in anything beyond some descriptions of the location of the cove, several results referring to Bierleigh and review site listings of the Angel Inn. Something prompts me to go over to Facebook and, without much conscious thought, I put 'Angel Cove' into a search on there. Nothing. Sighing, I put in 'Bierleigh' instead and, to my surprise, it turns out there's a Bierleigh Facebook group. I don't use Facebook a lot, but even so, I'm surprised I never realised before that this existed. I suppose, having spent my life working in a different area, I don't know half of what goes on in the village here.

I request permission to join the group straight away, and by the time I've spent a bit of time on some more fruitless searches elsewhere, the admin of the Facebook group has already accepted me. I start reading recent posts but they're mostly from local people asking for recommendations for plumbers and tree surgeons. Scrolling down the feed, though, there are occasional posts about local history. Someone has posted old photos of their class at the village school back in the 1950s. And there are pictures, too, of Fore Street and the various shops and houses through the decades. I get sidetracked for a while by looking at these, and by reading some of the posts.

'Does anyone remember the name of the lady who ran the sweetshop back in the early seventies when I was at the village school?' someone asks. 'I remember her giving a bag of sweets to every child at Christmas.'

There are lots of replies. I find myself smiling, thinking what a nice tradition that must have been. I didn't live here myself in the early seventies. I was in my late teens then, doing my nurse training in Exeter, where I grew up. My memories of the seventies are largely bound up with the three-day week, power cuts, rubbish piling up in the streets when the binmen went on strike and – on the other hand – nights out in the city centre with the new friends I was making as a student nurse. I'd never been to Bierleigh, let alone Angel Cove. I'm not even sure I knew where it was.

I post a 'thank you' for being accepted, and over the course of the next hour or so there's a trickle of replies, welcoming me to the group. There are even a couple of posts from people who know me, asking how I am and seeming to be surprisingly pleased that I've joined this Facebook group. So, next I pose my question:

> I've been wondering if anybody knows anything at all about the legend behind the name of Angel Cove? Although I've lived here a long time, all I know is there's supposed to have been some story about an angel, people say it's lucky and you're not supposed to be able to drown here. Any info would be much appreciated.

I stop to make a coffee, and when I return to my laptop, to my surprise there are already a couple of responses to my question. One says:

> No idea, sorry.

Another says:

> Never knew there was a legend about it.

I wonder, somewhat uncharitably, why they bothered to reply if that's all they have to say. I can't believe how disappointed I'm feeling already. This is silly, I tell myself. I have to give it time. There's bound to be more responses in due course, and hopefully some of them might actually be helpful!

It's really warm this afternoon so I take my laptop outside to try some more research, but I soon become pleasantly distracted by watching little Charlie from next door as he jumps from one rockpool to the next, nimble as a goat. He's got a bucket in his hand,

and every now and then he squats to peer into a pool with the unhurried concentration of the very young. I can still remember the pleasure of being seven years old at the seaside. How it felt to be able to clamber over the rocks, as Charlie's doing now, in bare feet, without slipping, without fear, and to squat like that without making my legs ache, or lose my balance and topple into a rockpool!

He stands up, shading his eyes against the sun as he stares out to sea, and then turns and catches sight of me on our shared decking, and carries his bucket back up the beach.

'Hello, Charlie,' I say as he approaches. 'What have you found there?'

'Shells.' He jumps two at a time up the six wooden steps to the decking, sits down on the floor and rummages through his bucket. 'This is the best one,' he tells me solemnly, holding out a small pearly white shell, perfectly intact.

'It's very pretty. What sort of creature do you think lived in that?' I ask him.

'A fish. A very, very small one. He was very lonely and sad.'

'Why?'

'Because his mum lived in a different shell,' he says, looking at me in surprise that I should ask something so obvious. 'So did his dad, and all his friends.'

'Ah, I see. Good point.' I smile at him. 'Well, I'm glad we're not shellfish, then. You're right, it must be quite a lonely thing to be.'

'Me and my mummy are lonely too,' he goes on after a moment, still looking at the little shell in his hand. 'Now that we don't live with my daddy any more.'

What on earth do I say to this?

'I know, Charlie, it's difficult, isn't it? When things change, and we don't really like them.'

'I like being *here*,' he says. 'At the seaside. But I wish we still lived with my dad. And I wish I still went to my old school, with my friends.'

I want to say that I'm sure it'll soon get easier. That he'll get used to only seeing his dad on weekend visits. That his mum will manage to find more time for him, once she's more settled in their new home, and then he won't feel so lonely – wandering around out here on the beach on his own. And that he'll soon make friends at his new school. But although I don't know much about children, I'm sure they can tell when we're just saying what makes *us* feel better, even if it does nothing whatsoever to help them.

'Change is never easy,' I sympathise instead. 'But I find chocolate biscuits always seem to help.' I give him a smile. 'Would you like me to see if I've got any?'

He smiles back. 'Yes please.'

'Go in and ask Mummy if she's got time to join us. I'll make her a cup of tea, and – orange juice for you?'

'Thanks!' He jumps up and runs into his kitchen, calling for his mum.

'Want a cup of tea?' I call into the living room, where I know Terry will still be staring at his laptop, piles of paperwork on the table next to him.

'Thanks, love,' he calls back.

What the hell *is* going on with him? He insists he's just busy, but he seems so distracted all the time these days, staring at his phone or his laptop, frowning, miles away. Terry's an accountant, and he's always worked hard, always been busy – that's what you have to put up with when you're a partner in the business. But I'd hoped, to be honest, that once I retired, he might find a bit more time for *us*, to spend doing things together. Perhaps I was being naive. After all, it was my decision to take retirement at sixty-five, so it's true, it's up to me to keep myself occupied.

I head back outside with the drinks and biscuits on a tray.

17

Charlie's looking up in expectation of a chocolate biscuit, as Sara comes out to join us, wearing a bright pink shirt with cropped jeans.

'Hi, Joy,' she says, sitting down next to me. 'Thanks for this. Phew, it's hot! Just been up in the attic, putting some boxes of stuff out of the way. I might get straight some time next year at this rate!'

She's sounding bright and chirpy today, but perhaps it's all bravado. It's hard for me to imagine how she must feel. Terry and I have been married for nearly forty years, and our lives here have been pretty uneventful. Our only sadness was not having children to bring up here, to watch them play on the beach and swim in the sea, like Charlie will be doing.

'I've started the research about the cove this morning,' I tell her. 'And I've joined a local Facebook group, so I'm hoping someone on there might know something.'

'Ah, well done,' she says. 'I'm really looking forward to hearing what you find out.'

Perhaps she's just being polite. But she sounds so enthusiastic about it, as if it'll somehow make a huge difference to her ability to settle here, if I can discover the origin of the name. So I've got another reason to do it now. As well as proving something to Terry.

Monday 8 October

After Terry's left for work this morning, I open my laptop to the Bierleigh Facebook group's page again and I'm pleased to see there's now another response to my query. I read it without much hope, but, in fact, this is probably the most helpful thing I've found so far:

> Hello. Have you thought about contacting the
> Bierleigh Historical Society?

I didn't know there was one, but I'm surprised I haven't found any reference to it on any of my searches so far. The comment includes an email address which looks pretty official: *info@bierleighhistory.co.uk*

I thank the responder and immediately send off an email to the address – with a ridiculous feeling of excitement. And I'm thinking that when you get excited about contacting a local historical society that you never even knew existed, you begin to realise that your life has become . . . a little lacking in thrills lately!

After yesterday's sunshine, it's suddenly turned quite cold today. Autumn here is usually mild, but it can be unpredictable.

It's quite sheltered in the cove, but we do sometimes get blustery coastal winds, storms rushing in from the Atlantic, the colour of the sea turning from blue to grey in minutes. During a full-blown winter storm, the wind can whirl angrily around the confines of the cove, the waves crashing onto our decking, the rain beating against our windows.

I decide to walk up to Bierleigh Library this morning to look for some books on local history. I'm not particularly confident I'm going to find much but it's worth a try.

Bierleigh Library can only just about justify its name. It's not much bigger than the sitting room of an average house.

There are clearly labelled shelves for fiction on the left and non-fiction on the right, and although logistics prevent much of a selection, the library assistant, Julia, does her best. It takes me all of three seconds to browse the shelf marked 'Local History' – one second per book. The first book is by a local author, known to everyone here, who's only lived in Bierleigh for about a year and whose knowledge of the area is sadly reflected by that fact. Another of the books is about Dartmouth with – when I flick through it – absolutely no mention of Bierleigh or any of the other nearby villages. The third looks a bit more hopeful. *Bierleigh Through the Ages* at least has lots of black-and-white photos of the village in days gone by. I scroll down the index of chapters at the front, hoping to find something about Angel Cove, without any success. But I'll borrow the book anyway. It's surely got a mention in there somewhere.

After lunch, I sit down with *Bierleigh Through the Ages*. It's actually an interesting read. There's a blurry photo of the library/parish council building itself, when it was a house, with an old lady standing on the doorstep, holding a goat on a leash for some reason. Another picture shows the village school – almost completely unchanged from the outside. The most striking thing is how few buildings the village actually consisted of in some of the earliest pictures. There's a chapter about the village shops: originally, there were two – a general store and a butcher's. How far did people have to go to buy other things? What about fresh fruit and veg? I guess they all grew it themselves. The little house, still called 'The Old Forge', really was a forge back then, and the blacksmith is photographed here holding the reins of a big carthorse.

I already knew about the tiny ancient chapel, which fell out of use in the 1960s and has since been converted into a teashop. There's a nice story in the book about the people of the village building the chapel themselves so that they had somewhere to meet and worship together. It's still called 'Chapel Tearooms'. The much bigger church of St Mark, by the village green, wasn't built until later.

At last, towards the end of the book, I find a mention of Angel Cove, but it's pretty much a passing reference, at the beginning of a section about the village pub.

The Angel Inn, near the lower end of Fore Street, is a fine example of an eighteenth-century coaching inn, with many beautiful interior features including a huge brick fireplace and original oak beams. The name of the inn presumably derives from nearby Angel Cove, a tiny wooded inlet situated approximately one mile south-west of Bierleigh, approached by a single-track lane. The lane ends at this cove, and there are no facilities at any time of year. The coast further west is inaccessible except on foot. The origins of the name 'Angel' are unclear, although some local people talk of a legend concerning an angel which seems to have been forgotten over the ages. Angel Inn . . .

The author goes on to describe the pub's menu and the delights of its beer garden at some length. Perhaps he's related to the landlord. He certainly doesn't seem to care very much for Angel Cove! There aren't even any pictures of it. And he hasn't gone to any trouble to find out about the 'forgotten' legend. I'm disappointed, but not particularly surprised. I'm still hoping the Historical Society might be my best source of information.

The rain's stopped while I've been immersed in my reading, and it's turned half past three already. When I look out of the back door a few minutes later, Charlie's already home from school, sitting outside on the decking, arranging some of his shells and pebbles on the table.

'Hello!' I call to him. 'What are you up to?'

'I'm going to do a painting,' he tells me, standing back to look at his arrangement, head on one side.

'A still life? Of your shells and stones?'

'Yes. We did painting at school today.' He turns and gives me a smile. It transforms his face. 'Mrs Dudley said my picture was the best.'

'Oh, well done, Charlie. I liked collecting shells too, when I was about your age, when we had a day out at the seaside.'

'Did you have any brothers and sisters, when you were my age?' he asks.

'No. I was an only child, like you. Although I did have a cousin who felt like a sister.'

Pauline was only a year older than me, and lived just round the corner from me. It felt just like having a sister; we were really close – right up until her family, she and my aunt and uncle, emigrated to Australia when she was sixteen and I was fifteen. I cried for weeks. We kept in touch for years but, as these things do, our letters became less and less frequent as we got older. My aunt and uncle passed away years ago and I don't even know if Pauline still lives in Australia or not.

Charlie seems to be thinking about this for a few moments while he moves some more of his shells around.

'I wanted my mum to have another baby,' he says then, quite matter-of-factly. 'I'd like to have a brother. Or even a sister. But I don't think she wanted to have one. And she says she can't now anyway.'

I'm just wondering how to respond to this when he turns round again and gives me a very direct look.

'That's because of my daddy not living here,' he explains. 'You need a man and a woman to make a baby.'

I smile. 'Right. Yes, I see. Well, I'm sure your mummy will let you have friends here, to play. That'll be company for you.'

'I haven't got any friends,' he says with a shrug.

'Well, maybe not yet, as you've just started at a new school. But I'm sure you'll make friends soon, and they'll all want to come and play on the beach with you.'

He shrugs again. 'I'm going to get my paints now,' he says.

'All right. Let me see your painting when it's finished, won't you?'

'OK!' He gets up, heading for his back door, before looking back and adding, 'I might be an art teacher when I grow up. Like my daddy. Bye!' – and he's gone. But now I understand the interest in painting; of course, it's a link to his dad.

Tuesday 9 October

Sara comes outside this morning for a chat while I'm hanging some washing out, and I tell her about the book on Bierleigh village.

'So no mention of the angel?' she says.

'No. And I haven't found anything online yet, either,' I say. 'But I *have* joined a Bierleigh Facebook group, *and* I've contacted Bierleigh Historical Society. I'm waiting for a reply at the moment.' I shrug. 'Perhaps someone there might have some information. Oh!' I add, looking down in surprise as I feel something furry brush against my legs. 'Where has that cat come from? I haven't seen him around here before.'

'He's mine,' Sara says with a smile, turning to watch as the cat makes his way cautiously down the steps to the beach. 'I've only let him out today for the first time. You know, after moving house. I've been worried about him getting lost.'

'Yes, of course. I didn't realise you had a cat. I'm surprised I haven't heard him meowing.'

'He's a quiet boy,' she says. 'Luckily it didn't bother him much, being kept indoors. He's not the type to get agitated and start climbing up the windows. He just spent his entire time sleeping on the sofa!'

'Aw, yes, I can see he's a bit cautious about being out here for the first time. He's beautiful, though – lovely colours. What's his name?'

'Pumpkin. A bit silly, I know, but it kind of suits him. We got him as a kitten – about five or six years ago. I thought it would be good for Charlie, growing up with a pet for company.'

'Definitely,' I say. 'We always had cats when I was little. I was an only child too. But I can't have one now. Terry doesn't like cats.'

'Oh! I'd better keep Pumpkin away, then—'

'Don't worry. He's not allergic or anything like that. He just had a bad experience as a young child – a grumpy-natured cat attacked him, gave him a nasty bite, and he got such a bad infection from it that he ended up in hospital on intravenous antibiotics. He's not exactly *afraid* of cats, but he does tend to avoid stroking or cuddling them.'

'Childhood trauma can last a lifetime, can't it. Shame for you, though, if you like cats yourself. Well, you're very welcome to stroke and cuddle Pumpkin! I'm sure he'll appreciate that.'

'Thank you, so will I! Pumpkin's a lovely cat.'

We both watch him as he sits on the edge of the decking, washing himself. I'm hesitating now, after Terry's warning, but I decide to ask her anyway.

'Are you going to be busy this morning? Or can you fit in another short walk?'

'Yes, that'd be good. I'm ahead of my deadline now, so I can take an hour off and then get back to it later.'

'Great! We could walk the other way – along the beach and up the other side of the cove, if you like.'

We're both quiet when we set off. Sara's wearing boots today – huge black ones that look strangely at odds with her flowery dress and bright blue bomber jacket. We pick our way around the rocks and then climb the steep path at that end of the cove. On the flat grassy area at the top, called Harry's Plain, I persuade her to rest for a moment; again, she's been striding along with such enthusiasm that I'm struggling to keep up with her.

'Who's Harry?' she asks me.

'Old Harry. It's a euphemism for the devil.'

'Oh!' She looks a bit startled. 'I didn't realise. So, do you know what he's got to do with anything?'

'Not really, no, although I suppose it could be tied up with the angel story somehow. Everyone around here just seems to accept the names without too much thought – they've probably been the same for centuries. I've seen them marked on old maps. The steep path we're going to go down now is actually called Old Harry's Staircase.'

'Really? We'd better tread carefully, then!' she jokes as I lead the way. The path *is* like a staircase, too – narrow and steep, like a mini crevasse in the cliff. It always feels like we need a handrail to hold on to.

'It's just a gentle path uphill, from here,' I tell her once we've made it all the way down. 'Through some woods, into the village. Then we can walk back on the lane, if you like.'

'OK,' she says, and we set off up the path. 'This is nice. Thanks for suggesting it.'

'Well, I realise I'm a bit old to be company for you—' I begin. I'm still a little unsure where I stand with her. She's friendly enough, but she can be quite full on: quite blustery and loud, and I'm still trying to work out whether it's all an act or not. But she interrupts me straight away.

'Of course you're not! Look, I haven't got any other friends around here yet. The other parents at the school gates know each other really well already, and it's hard to break into their friendship groups. And anyway, I'm not bothered. I'd rather have your company.'

'Don't you miss your old friends from Plymouth?'

'No,' she says, bluntly. 'I thought I would, but already, I feel ... kind of *distanced* from them. My situation has changed so much, while theirs haven't. Their children – Charlie's old friends – are still at the same school, and the mums all still meet one morning a week for coffee, and one evening every fortnight for a girls' night out in the city centre.' She shrugs. 'Their lives don't seem to have any similarity to mine any more.'

'But didn't you confide in them when your marriage broke down? Weren't they sympathetic?'

'Yes, they all seemed shocked – horrified – when I told them. They said all the things you'd expect, about supporting me and *being there for me* – and, of course, they were all up in arms in solidarity about all men being lying, cheating bastards at heart. Even though none of their husbands or partners, to anyone's knowledge, was, in fact, a lying, cheating bastard at all. Only mine!' She guffaws with laughter about this, as if it's a joke.

'I suppose they meant well.'

'I know. But then they just got on with their lives, of course, with their own non-cheating husbands, and why wouldn't they? And now it feels like they don't just live twenty miles away in a city that I don't much care whether I ever visit again or not, but on another planet.'

'Well, you can carve out a new life for yourself and Charlie here. And you *will* make more friends, eventually. You'll find other mums in the same position as yourself – I'm sure of that.'

'I suppose so. But I'm not bothered.'

I turn to look at her as we continue on the path. She's got a fixed look of determination on her face as she marches along beside me. It's nice that she thinks of me as a friend, despite the age gap. People seeing us together could assume she's my daughter, I suppose, but if it doesn't matter to her, it certainly doesn't to me.

'I'm a bit short of friends myself,' I admit now. 'I know people in Bierleigh, of course, but I never really had time to make proper friends with them. My friends were my colleagues at work. But now I've left—'

'It probably won't be the same?' she finishes for me.

'No, I don't think it will. I won't be seeing them every day like before, and I won't intrude on them. They're so busy. I'm not going to forget how that feels.'

'Don't you have any family nearby?'

'No. Haven't really got any family at all, in fact, apart from Terry. Well, I do have one cousin, Pauline. We were very close as children but she emigrated to Australia with her family and—' I swallow '—we've gradually lost touch.'

I've found myself thinking more and more about Pauline since I retired. It feels like an awful thing to say, but during those years when I was so busy, she rarely entered my mind. Now, suddenly, it hurts to realise she's – as far as I know – the only living blood relative I have, and we don't even exchange Christmas cards any more. How did we let that happen?

We walk back through Bierleigh, while Sara's asking me about the village: what the various shops are like, and which ones I'd recommend. She asks about the Angel Inn, too, and I tell her it's really good. Terry and I have often had meals there together at weekends in the past. I suggest that perhaps Sara and I could have lunch there one day.

'Do you know what, Joy, I'd really like that,' she says. 'Great idea.'

I'm quite touched by her enthusiasm, and glad she seems to be so determined to take a positive attitude, to want to do something sociable and fun, despite her situation. But I still can't help wondering if she really feels so positive underneath the brave face. It must have been horrible, living in the same house as Rob for the past year, since he told her about his affair. Knowing about it – knowing about Jade, the girlfriend, especially as she was a teacher at the same school as him. I wonder what took them so long to make their separation a reality. Finding their new homes, I suppose, and Charlie's new school. Well, I hope it'll be easier for her to move on now that she's here, disruptive though the whole move must have been. I suppose I am starting to feel a bit motherly and protective towards her. She says she hasn't got parents any more; that's really sad. A mum would have been a support to her, with what she's going through, but she's told me both her parents have passed away. Well, she's got a friend now – albeit one twice her age.

After dinner this evening, Terry settles down with his laptop again. There's nothing much on TV; I choose an old film to watch but it's pretty boring so I pick up my phone to check my emails, and since I last looked, this afternoon, there's a reply from someone called Howard Hardcastle who says he's the chairman of the Bierleigh Historical Society – and reading between the lines, is pretty proud of the fact too. He explains that the society meets every Monday evening, and there's an AGM in July of every year, and that new members are welcome and should expect to be included on the Refreshments Rota (with capital letters). He tells me the cost of annual membership, which is ludicrously cheap, and which has to be paid by cheque, sent to his address, enclosing a stamped addressed envelope for a receipt. I get the impression Howard Hardcastle is historical in more ways than one – certainly too set in his ways to handle internet or phone payments. I'm surprised he even uses email. His email, in fact, is written in the formal manner of the mid-twentieth century, beginning with 'Dear Madam' and closing with 'Kind regards, Yours sincerely'. I can't help picturing him sitting at an old-fashioned writing desk, wearing a waistcoat and a watch on a chain, and using a quill and sealing wax. I also can't help reflecting ruefully that I didn't, in fact, even contact him to ask about joining his society, but to ask if they had any information about the Angel of the Cove. However, there's a PS at the end of the email, saying:

> In response to your query about the origin of the name Angel
> Cove, perhaps you'd like to attend one of our meetings, where –
> after the formal part of the evening – members normally mingle
> over refreshments, and discuss matters of interest.

So it seems it's a question of No Information Without Membership. I smile to myself, imagining the 'mingling over refreshments'. Well, I'll join anyway. It can't do any harm, and perhaps I'll even enjoy the meetings, as well as possibly learning something. You never know. In fact, I'll get my application sorted first thing in the morning.

Wednesday 10 October

I spend half an hour this morning searching for my chequebook, wondering when I last used it – who writes cheques these days? – and then another ten minutes finding envelopes. But finally my membership application is complete, and I decide I'll walk up to the village right now and pop it through the door of Howard Hardcastle himself, who apparently lives in a turning off Fore Street. It's dry today, chilly but bright. As I walk, I remind myself that this is the retirement I looked forward to for so long, and that I might feel strange and a bit aimless at the moment but that I'll soon get the hang of it, and joining a new club might be just what I need.

I didn't expect Terry to retire yet, just because I chose to. But I wasn't, either, anticipating him seeming to need to work even more, now, than he ever did before. I can't help wondering if he's trying to avoid spending any time with me at all. It feels a bit that way, but I'm probably just being paranoid. We've had so few proper conversations recently that it's hard, really, to know exactly what he's thinking or feeling most of the time. Does he think I've become boring, now I've stopped working? Is that why he keeps telling me I need to find myself some new interests? I guess retirement is

31

a strange thing to get used to: a relief, but, at the same time, a bit of a shock.

I've already reached the village, and it only takes a few more minutes to find Howard Hardcastle's house, in a little cul-de-sac called Chapel Close. I'd imagined from the persona I've invented for him, that he'd live in one of the first couple of cottages in this road, visible from Fore Street – old brick houses not dissimilar from ours at Angel Cove. But no, his house, number seventeen, is one of a development of very new bungalows a little further down the road. It's smart and attractive, with white walls, big windows, a wood-panelled front door and neat little front garden. I push my envelope through the letter box and, as I'm turning to walk back up the path, the door opens, making me jump almost out of my skin.

'Hello. Can I help you?' says a tall, silver-haired guy who's probably about my own age. He's got warm hazel-coloured eyes, which seem to sparkle behind his glasses.

'Oh!' I give a little laugh of embarrassment. 'Sorry, no, I just put an envelope through your letter box. This is the right house, I hope? For Howard Hardcastle?'

'That's me,' he says with a smile.

'Oh, er ... good!' My vision of him as an ancient, doddery recluse in a velvet smoking jacket dissipates into the mist. This man's slim and fit-looking, dressed in jeans, and a T-shirt bearing a 'Star Wars' slogan. 'Well, I've just delivered ... um ... my application to join the Historical Society. And my cheque,' I add quickly.

'Ah! Then you must be Joy Vincent of Angel Cove.' He holds out his hand. 'Pleased to meet you.'

'Likewise!' I shake his hand, and find myself laughing – partly at my own ridiculous assumptions about him, and partly in response to his cheerful, smiley manner.

'Sorry I couldn't help with your query,' he says. 'I haven't been living here too long, but I'm sure one of the other members might be able to throw some light on it for you. Some of them have lived around here since the dawn of creation, from what I can make out!'

I laugh again. 'It's possible I might know a few of them, in that case. I've been here for more than thirty years myself, although I—'

'Oops. I didn't mean any offence,' he says quickly.

'None taken.' I'm laughing again. Can't seem to stop myself – how embarrassing. 'I was going on to say that, in fact, I didn't spend much time around here till recently. I used to work in Totnes. Before I retired.'

'Ah. Retirement. It's a bit of a shock to the system, isn't it?' He nods at me, with a sympathetic look – as if I'd actually stood here and poured out all my innermost feelings to him. It feels quite unnerving, like I've taken off my clothes in front of him. The thought of this, of course, makes me feel even more unnerved. 'I only retired last year myself,' he goes on. 'Retired from banking, moved down here from Bristol, bought this brand-new bungalow with a view to starting a brand-new life, and then, well, didn't quite know how to start it. The brand-new life,' he adds, because I'm probably staring at him like an idiot, as if I'm not keeping up.

'But you're ... running the Historical Society already,' I protest.

'Yes. I joined it, because everyone – my daughter, my sons, even my grandkids – everyone back in Bristol – told me I needed to get a hobby, join something, go out and make new friends. Then, when I joined the society, I realised it was on its knees – as are most of the members, bless them! So at the AGM in July, when the previous chairman stepped down because of ill health, I offered to take over, and they nearly fell over themselves to accept me. I've spent all my time since then trying to update everything. They had a website, but it needed a lot of improvement. You're actually the first person to contact me since I took over, so I'm afraid I just sent you their standard membership-query email. Sorry, that needs updating too! And I didn't realise we weren't even set up to take membership

33

payments online. That's another thing I need to get sorted, but the other members are ... a little bit resistant to change, shall we say?'

'Well, I must admit I did think it all seemed a bit old-fashioned!' I say, giving him a conspiratorial grin.

'You're right, it is! I did add a paragraph to the end of that standard letter, though. To make it clear you're welcome to come along to a meeting, to try us out. Without feeling obliged to join.'

'Oh, I didn't realise ... I thought I'd have to join first. It's fine, though. It's not exactly expensive.'

'No.' He chuckles. He has the most attractive creases around his eyes when he laughs. 'But mark my words, you'll be strong-armed into the kitchen to help with the refreshments. Tea and biscuits seem to be the most popular part of the meetings.'

'That's fine by me.'

We both stop, suddenly looking at each other awkwardly now that we've run out of conversation.

'Well, anyway, shall I look forward to seeing you on Monday evening?' he says eventually. 'Seven o'clock, in the village hall?'

'Yes, definitely. See you then. Bye, um, Howard.'

'Bye, Joy.'

I'm halfway home before I realise I'm still smiling. It bothers me. Was I *flirting* there, with the – let's face it – rather attractive Mr Howard Hardcastle? Really? Have things become so unsatisfactory between me and Terry that I've actually started eyeing up other men? At my age? How ridiculous. My face is burning with embarrassment at myself as I walk down the lane. I don't need to flirt with another man. I just need to able to spend a bit of time occasionally with my husband. Or if nothing else, at least to have a proper conversation with him!

This evening I'm waiting, with dinner already cooking, as he walks in the front door.

'Hello!' I call out. 'How was your day? Want a pre-dinner drink while I dish up?'

He stops in the kitchen doorway, looking at me in surprise. 'Um, no, thanks. I'll just go up and get changed, then I'll put my laptop on charge ready for—'

'Do you *have* to work this evening, Tel? Can't we just . . . sit and have a chat together?'

'A chat?' He stares at me as if he's never heard of such a thing. 'I can't, love, not tonight. I've got to get these accounts finished.'

'But you're working every night now,' I point out, trying not to sound like I'm whining, or being critical – difficult though it is.

'It's just . . . a busy time. Sorry, love. Just the way it is,' he says, shrugging. 'Haven't you got things to occupy yourself with?'

I should stand my ground – tell him that whether I'm *occupied* or not isn't really the point. But he's already heading upstairs to change out of his office clothes. I start dishing up the dinner, banging the serving spoon against the plates in frustration, and when he comes back downstairs, he looks into the kitchen and stops with surprise.

'There's a cat outside the back door.'

I turn and look. So there is! And he's meowing as if he'd like to come in. I think, actually, if I opened the door, he would.

'It's Pumpkin,' I say. 'Sara's cat. He's pretty, isn't he? He's a calico.'

'What's calico?' he queries, frowning.

'White, black and orange. You don't know much about cats, do you?'

'Um, yes,' he says. 'I know enough to understand that they can put you in hospital, so I try to have as little to do with them as possible.'

'I know, love. But you won't have to. In fact, Sara's only just started letting him out. He's really cute.'

'*You* might think so, but he can keep away from me, thanks very much.'

I feel a pang as I watch Pumpkin pad off across the decking. Terry doesn't have to get involved with him, but I can. As Sara said, there's nothing to stop me making a fuss of him. The way things are going, I'll probably talk more to him than with my husband!

Monday 15 October

It was cold and wet at the end of last week, and all over the weekend, until this morning. I haven't seen much of Sara or Charlie but this afternoon, after school, they're outside, playing on the beach with his ball.

'Any luck with the research yet?' she asks eagerly as soon as she sees me.

'No. But I've joined the Bierleigh Historical Society now.' I think about telling her about meeting Howard Hardcastle, but the thought of it makes me feel too silly. 'I'm going to my first meeting this evening, so I'm hoping someone there might know something about the angel.'

'I hope you enjoy the meeting, then.'

Charlie comes running up the beach to join us.

'Hello, Joy,' he says. 'Guess what? I got a sustificate for my painting.'

'*Certi*ficate, Charlie,' Sara says, smiling.

'Wow, well done,' I tell him, pleased to see how happy he is. 'You're obviously a good little artist.'

'That's what my teacher said,' he says proudly. 'It's what my dad says too.'

'And he certainly knows what he's talking about, doesn't he!' Sara says. 'I hope you're going to take your certificate to show Daddy next weekend.'

''Course I will,' he says, brightening up. 'I can't wait!' he says to me. 'I'm going after school on Friday, and staying till Sunday. It'll be weird, though, 'cos Daddy doesn't live in our old house now, he lives in a flat. With . . . ' He glances at Sara, shifting awkwardly from foot to foot, and she gives him an encouraging nod. 'With Jade,' he finishes quietly.

'It's all right to talk about her, Charlie,' Sara says gently. 'But Daddy told you, didn't he, that she won't be there. She'll be visiting her parents for the weekend. Giving you both some space.' She turns to me and adds, 'This'll be his first weekend back with Rob. We wanted Charlie to have a few extra weeks here first, to settle a bit, but he'll normally be going on alternate weekends now.'

'Daddy says there's a bedroom for me in the flat,' Charlie says excitedly, 'with some new stuff in it for me. I don't know what. And he says, maybe not this time, but another time I go there, I can have one of my friends from my old school round to play.'

'That'll be something to look forward to, won't it?'

'Yes.' He grins. 'It'll be cool.'

I give Sara a sympathetic smile. It's going to be hard for her, I'm sure; but I'm also sure she's feeling pleased, as I am, to see Charlie looking happy.

I've already started cooking dinner this evening before I remember I've got to get ready to go to the Historical Society meeting – and then I start thinking once again about how giggly and silly I got, when I talked to Howard Hardcastle on his doorstep. I need to put that behind me if I'm going to enjoy the meetings. As well as perhaps helping me find out about the Angel of the Cove, this will hopefully give me the opportunity to meet some more people.

I eat my own dinner quickly, leaving Terry's meal on a plate for him to reheat in the microwave when he deigns to come home, and set off up the lane. It feels good to be out on my own, walking into the village with a sense of purpose. I decided against bringing my car. It's a dry, calm evening, and I'm well used to walking up and down this lane in the dark. There's never anyone about, and I know every bend, crack and pothole as if they're on a little map in my head. Even so, I do use the torch on my phone these days, just in case there's anything unexpected that I might walk into. Once I nearly fell over the carcass of a muntjac deer in the middle of the road, and more than once I've trodden on dead birds or rats, or skidded on a dollop of animal excrement.

Tonight, though, I reach the village hall without any dramas. It's already just a few minutes to seven when I push open the door, so I'm expecting to hear a buzz, if not a hubbub, of voices from the members gathered inside, but it's strangely quiet. There are a few people, with their backs to me, standing around a table near the stage, leafing through some papers, and three elderly ladies sitting on some of the chairs which have been placed in a semicircle facing the table, so nobody has seen me come in. Wondering whether the rest of the group are in the kitchen, already preparing tea and biscuits for 'mingling time', or even out the back in the toilets, I give a little cough to advertise my presence as I walk towards them all.

'Oh! Hello, Joy!' Howard Hardcastle has turned around and gives me a smile of welcome. 'Come and sit down; we're just finishing checking through the ... um, membership accounts.' He raises his eyebrows at me as he says this, as if we're sharing a secret. I presume he thinks it's totally unnecessary to be checking the 'membership accounts', and if the number of members I see here at present is any indication of their normal numbers, I think he's probably right. 'This is Joy Vincent, everyone,' he announces. 'A new member. Let's make her welcome.'

The three elderly ladies, who had been talking together, now look round at me too, and I realise I do, in fact, recognise them all, as they're long-time residents of the area, often to be found chatting in the village shops. But I need to be reminded of their names.

'Hello,' I say, giving them all a smile, as Howard introduces them.

'What are you doing here?' says Freda Jones – who I remember now, sadly, has quite advanced dementia.

'She's joining the society, Freda,' says Margaret Parmenter.

'What society?' says poor Freda, looking worried.

'Sorry!' Margaret mouths at me. 'She's a bit confused.'

'Don't worry.' I sit down next to Grace Unwin at the end of the row. These two ladies are both friends of Freda's and evidently keep an eye on her. The other two men standing at the table with Howard have looked up from their membership accounts now. One is a large, florid man of, I guess, about seventy, who I don't recognise. The other, Saul Messop, was celebrated last year as the oldest man in the village and the first ever of our small population (as far as anyone was aware) to turn a hundred. You'd never know it. He looks far sprightlier than the large man next to him, probably due to having worked on the farm at the top of the village ever since he was a boy and only retiring relatively recently.

'Y'all right, my lovely?' he directs at me now, with a toothless grin.

'I think you know everyone here, then,' says Howard, his eyes twinkling at me. 'Except possibly David.' He nods at the bigger man. 'Our treasurer.'

'Pleased to meet you,' I say. 'Um ... are there a lot of people missing tonight?'

Howard glances uneasily at David.

'No. There's only one who couldn't make it. Mrs French. She's in hospital, unfortunately, and—'

So there are only seven members. Eight now, including myself. And the average age must be about eighty. Well, on the bright side, if I can't find out anything about local history from a group of people of this vintage, I might as well give up. They've all lived through it!

David and Saul come and join us in the semicircle of chairs now, and Howard, remaining at the front of the group, speaks first, raising his voice for the benefit of ... well, almost everyone, really, since at least three of them appear to be wearing hearing aids.

'We're talking tonight about the village school through the ages,' he says, with which he, too, comes to sit down.

I gather this will be a casual sharing of memories rather than anyone presenting a talk. To be fair, it's interesting, too – perhaps all the more so for being informal, allowing each person to chip in with their own comments. Some of them have brought photos along, which are duly passed around. Of course, Saul's reminiscences are the most fascinating, as he recalls being at school back in the 1920s.

'We started school age five, and left at fourteen,' he says. 'That's when I started working in the fields full-time. I'd already been helping my dad and older brothers on the farm outside school hours, ever since I was old enough to be of any use. In class, we learned the alphabet and times tables by chanting them aloud. And we learned to write with chalk, on slates. We didn't get notebooks and pencils till we were good writers.' He chuckles. 'If we were naughty or didn't work hard enough, we got smacked on the hands with a ruler. I got the cane once, too, for pulling one of the girls' pigtails and pushing her over. She'd been kicking me under our desk all morning but I didn't tell the teacher that. Nobody liked a telltale.'

'It was the still the same in the 1940s,' says Margaret Parmenter. 'Very strict. If we asked to go to the toilet during lessons, we got told off because we should've gone at playtime. The toilets were outside, of course, and horrible. The boys used to climb up and try and look at us over the doors, so we tried not to need to go.'

'And we had evacuees here during the war, of course,' says Grace. 'The classrooms were too small, really, to have any extra pupils, but we had to squash up and have three at a desk instead of two. Some of them from London were very poor, even poorer than us. They came to school in ragged clothes and my teacher, Miss Grey, actually gave one little boy a jumper because he didn't have one and he was freezing in the winter. She must have used her own clothing coupons.'

I'm spellbound, listening to them all remembering their schooldays from so long ago. Their faces seem to have changed completely – their expressions relaxed and softened – as they look back in their minds to those years of their childhoods, when things were tough but uncomplicated, when they were young and carefree and didn't have arthritis, bad chests and poor eyesight, and didn't need walking sticks or hearing aids.

As soon as he's announced the tea break, Howard makes a beeline for me.

'Should I be helping in the kitchen?' I ask him, as Margaret and Grace head out there, after having made quite a performance of counting hands for four teas, two white coffees and one black.

'Next time you can, please – if you come next time?' he says. 'Have you enjoyed it so far? Sorry it's a bit ... rambling.'

'I've loved it,' I assure him. 'It's been fascinating. Much nicer than just listening to a talk.'

He smiles, looking pleased and relieved. 'Oh, good. We do have people giving us a talk occasionally, but because there aren't many of us, our subs don't cover their fees and I don't like asking the members to pay more. It'll be so good to have someone new joining us. We so badly need some fresh blood. Younger people like you.'

I laugh. 'I'm hardly *younger*!'

'Yes, you are. Younger than these others. Although—' he gives me that grin again '—to be fair, it's the older ones who have more interesting things to share. Historically. Especially as they've all lived here for a long time.'

'Definitely. And as it happens, I'm hoping to have a word with one or two of them. I'd like to ask whether anyone knows—'

'About the angel of Angel Cove? Of course – I hadn't forgotten, Joy. I've planned to bring this up after the break. We can have a little talk about it and see if anyone has any ideas. Would that be OK with you?'

'Oh, I wouldn't expect that – after all, I'm new here, and you must all have other things to discuss.'

'Not at all. They seem to enjoy a change of topic. We oldies have short attention spans, you know!'

'*You're* not an oldie!' I laugh, and then have to struggle to stop myself from blushing. For God's sake – since when did I talk to people in this silly coquettish voice?

'Officially geriatric. Sixty-five, to be exact.'

'Oh, me too!'

'Give over.' He looks me up and down. I definitely feel myself blushing now. 'You look ten years younger.'

'Yeah, yeah. I bet you say that to all the geriatric ladies!'

Fortunately, before this conversation can go any further, Margaret approaches us, followed by Grace, both walking slowly and carefully, in the manner of a little procession, each shakily bearing a tray – one with full cups, which rattle alarmingly on their saucers, the other with two plates of biscuits.

'Oh, let me help!' I say, going to take Margaret's tray from her.

'No, no – you're not on the refreshments rota tonight,' she says quite firmly. 'Just take your tea, please, and a biscuit from each plate. These are custard creams, and those are digestives.'

I thank her and do as I'm told, as does Howard, who catches my eye and gives me a little wink. I think I need to move on and talk to someone else. Urgently.

'OK, I'm going to have a chat to some of the others,' I tell him.

I finish my cup of tea while I have a quick talk with David about his role as treasurer – which he seems to take as seriously as if he were running the Bank of England. Then Howard calls the group together again and we go back to our seats.

'Right. I've got something interesting to run past you this evening,' he says, standing in front of the group again. 'Our new member, Joy, lives in one of the Smugglers' Cottages down at Angel Cove, and she's been trying to research the name – Angel – and find out whether anyone knows its origin. We understand there's a legend, but do any of you happen to know anything about it?'

Almost immediately, Freda gives a shout. 'That was my house. I lived there! Number two, Smugglers' Cottages.'

We all turn to look at her in surprise.

'You lived at Angel Cove, Freda?' I ask her.

'Yes, she did,' Margaret answers for her. 'When she was a girl.'

'Me and my sister,' Freda says. 'Chrissie. Little Chrissie. She's dead now.'

'Oh, I'm sorry to hear that,' I say automatically. I'm so intrigued, I'm desperate to keep her talking. But Howard gives me a warning glance, and I nod in response. Because of Freda's dementia, it's hard to know how much we can trust her memory, or her grasp on reality – or, come to that, how far it's fair to push her.

But Freda seems determined to tell us more.

'She got married,' she says, nodding to herself. 'I was her bridesmaid. Pink … pink dress, I wore. It was last year.' She hesitates, her certainty suddenly dissolving. 'Or was it the year before? I've got muddled again, haven't I?'

'It's all right, love,' Grace tells her gently. 'Don't worry.' She looks at me and adds: 'It's true, she often talks about her sister Chrissie.'

'Where's Chrissie now?' Freda says, looking more confused now. 'She's my little sister. I thought she was dead. I wore a pink dress, didn't I?'

'Let's drop it,' I say quietly to Howard. 'I don't want to upset her.'

I feel bad, now. But at the same time, I can't help feeling a tiny flutter of excitement. At least I've found a link, however tenuous, to Angel Cove in the past – and to Smugglers' Cottages. And just as Howard's about to move on to the next thing – to the amazement of all of us – Freda suddenly blurts out:

'There was an angel there, you know. At Angel Cove. Chrissie saw it. It was lucky; she was so lucky that she saw the angel.'

'When was this, Freda?' Howard asks her. 'When did she see the angel?'

But Freda's staring around the room again, asking Grace who she is, and what she's doing there. The moment has passed. Howard comes to sit down and instigates a little discussion among us all about whether anyone else has heard about the angel of Angel Cove, but nobody else knows anything, really, just the usual rumours about good luck; and by now, Freda's probably forgotten she mentioned it at all. But I can't help feeling, as I walk back along the dark lane to Smugglers' Cottages, that I'm a little closer to learning something. Even if it's only what happened to Freda's sister – and how she, apparently, came to see the Angel of the Cove!

February 1960: A Sunday afternoon

Philip and Chrissie were sitting on their favourite rock, the biggest, flattest-topped one, on the eastern fringe of their beach at Angel Cove. It was a cold, windy day, with threatening black clouds scudding across the sky, the sea the colour of school ink, and the angry incoming waves tipped with white foam. Philip had his arm protectively around his young girlfriend, whose pretty blonde head rested on his shoulder.

'They won't let us get married,' she said, her eyes filling with helpless tears. 'You know they won't, Phil.'

'They might,' he said, trying to sound more confident than he felt. He was eighteen now, a working man, a fisherman like his father – not a kid any more. He had to take charge, take control, look after her. 'If I speak to them, Chris, and explain the situation—'

'You can't!' she cried. 'You mustn't tell them I'm in the family way. They'll kill me!'

'They won't,' he said – although, in fact, he had his doubts. Chrissie's parents were terrifying; his own were strict enough, but hers made them seem like gentle pussycats by comparison. Mr and Mrs Jones might not actually kill their daughter, but it was possible they might kill him! 'They're going to find out, sooner or later. When you start getting bigger—'

She let out a little whimper of fear, and he held her closer again. He didn't blame her for being scared. He was scared himself, and after all, she was only fifteen. Below the age of consent. He suspected he could be taken to court, maybe even locked up – who knew? – for having made love to her. *Love*, he reminded himself firmly, swallowing hard to keep his fear under control. He loved Chrissie, and she loved him back. It wasn't as if he'd just taken advantage of her. They'd been sweethearts all their lives, they'd played together on this beach when she was still not much more than a baby and he'd been like a big brother to her, looking after her, holding her soft little hands while she paddled at the edge of the sea, helping her build sandcastles, teaching her how to catch crabs from the rock pools. He'd always preferred spending time with her to playing with his own two younger brothers, who were twins and tended not to need anyone other than each other. He'd loved her then, and he'd never stopped. He never would, no matter what her parents said. So he had to be brave and face them, didn't he?

'Maybe I should just tell Freda first,' Chrissie said. 'She might know what to do.'

Philip considered this carefully for a moment. Freda, Chrissie's big sister, was ten years her senior. She was a teacher at Bierleigh School but still lived at home because she was unmarried, which, at the age of twenty-five, made people think of her as an old maid. Chrissie didn't even think she'd ever had a boyfriend. Because of the age gap, the sisters weren't particularly close; in fact, Chrissie often said she felt like she had three parents. Philip suspected Freda had actually had her nose put out of joint when her pretty little sister was born, after being the only child for ten years, and she might still secretly resent her, even now.

'I don't know whether Freda would be very sympathetic,' he said.

'No. But I think I'd rather face her than my mum or dad.'

'Would you like me to talk to her?' he offered – and hated himself for the rush of relief he then felt when Chrissie said no, she ought to speak to her alone first. He'd never felt Freda seemed to like him – or his brothers – very much.

'She's gone to see her friend in the village. I'll tell her when she comes home this evening,' she said, wiping her eyes. 'Maybe she'll talk to Mum for me.'

'Or she might at least know what we can do about it,' Phil said, being careful to say *we* and not *you*. He actually had no idea what they could 'do about it', and felt ignorant and pathetic for not knowing. But he didn't want Chrissie to think it was her responsibility alone. He felt guilty enough for getting her into trouble. He'd been sure it would be all right – the first time. That was what he'd heard other lads say, anyway. Other lads who bragged and showed off about the various girls they'd had, girls they didn't even care about in the way he cared for Chrissie. *Why did it have to happen to us, and not* them? he asked himself bitterly. *It wasn't fair!*

'Come outside later and tell me what she says,' he suggested. 'I'll wait for you by the breakwater when the tide turns.'

'OK.' She glanced behind them; he realised she was checking that neither of her parents had come out of their cottage, where she'd left them sleeping off their Sunday dinner. Then she reached up and kissed him. 'I'll try to get her on our side,' she promised.

Philip knew she was trying to sound braver than she felt, and he loved her more than ever for it. He straightened his shoulders as he watched her get up from their rock and pick her way back across the beach. If Freda couldn't help, he would talk to his own parents, he decided. They'd be angry, but at least they might help.

They might be able to tell him what they could do. Whether they could get married without Chrissie's parents' consent. There had to be a way! He wasn't going to let her be an unmarried mother, no matter what. He'd never forgive himself for that.

Tuesday 16 October

Terry hasn't spoken to me since last night. He was furious when I got home from the Historical Society. Although I'd left him his dinner, I hadn't left a note, or messaged him to remind him where I was going; I'd stupidly thought I'd told him, and that he'd remember. Then during the evening, I'd missed two calls and three text messages from him – having turned the sound off on my phone for the duration of the meeting. By the time I turned it back on, I was halfway home, it was getting on for half past nine, and when I saw the messages demanding to know where I was, *I* was miffed. Why hadn't he remembered? Why didn't he take any notice of anything I told him? Why did he keep nagging me about getting hobbies, if he wasn't going to be interested when I told him about them?

Unfortunately, once the argument started, I began to realise that perhaps I didn't even tell him about it. And instead of graciously accepting that maybe I was in the wrong, I got on the defensive.

'Well, it's no wonder I don't tell you stuff, is it?' I said. 'We don't spend any time together, you don't talk to me at all apart from telling me to *keep myself busy* – in other words, keep out of your way.'

'Surely it's just common courtesy to say where you're going? What am I supposed to think when I get home and find you gone – the car still here, a dried-up meal on a plate – and you're not answering your phone?'

'Oh, so it's the meal you're most concerned about, is it? Well, it wouldn't have been dried up if you'd come home from work at a reasonable sort of time, like other people!'

And so it went on, and by the time I was calming down and beginning to wish I'd just apologised and admitted it wouldn't have hurt me to leave him a note, he was stomping off upstairs to bed and refusing to discuss it – or anything else – any further. Or since.

We never used to be like this. I can't believe how suddenly, since I retired, our relationship seems to have . . . let's face it . . . started to flounder. In the space of just a few weeks! Or am I fooling myself? Was it getting as bad as this *before* then, and I didn't notice – or mind – because I was busy myself? Were we, in fact, just rubbing along OK together because we hardly had any time to spare for each other anyway? Did I just not *realise*, before, how much work he brought home, how little we did together? It can't have happened overnight, after all. So how long *has* it been like this? How long have we had a rubbish marriage, without me even realising it? When exactly did we stop communicating properly? Or am I just overreacting?

When I look out of my back door this morning, I see Sara's already outside on the beach, walking up and down and hollering for her cat.

'Have you seen Pumpkin?' she shouts as soon as I open my back door.

'No. Not since yesterday, anyway; I gave him a stroke when I saw him out here in the afternoon. Why? Can't you find him?'

'No. He didn't come in last night. I hope it wasn't too soon to let him out. He still doesn't really know his way around. I didn't think he'd wander too far off.'

'I'm sure he won't. And you did the right thing, keeping him in for the first few weeks, so he should be fine now.'

'There was no sign of him when I called him for his dinner last night. I don't like him being out at night, especially now we're in a new area. When I went to bed, I left the cat flap unlocked. I was sure he'd be in when I got up this morning, but he still hasn't turned up.' She sighs and brushes her hair out of her eyes. 'Charlie didn't want to go to school. I had to persuade him that I'll find Pumpkin before he comes home.'

'Perhaps – because there was some more rain during the night – he found somewhere to shelter, and he's fallen asleep,' I say.

'Where, though? Where could he shelter?'

She's got a point. Apart from our two houses, there's nothing here – no sheds, garages, fences or even gardens. Nothing apart from . . .

'The woods?' I suggest. 'Perhaps he's climbed a tree and can't get down. I had a cat once who did that in our garden, when I was a kid, and my father had to get his ladder out to rescue her.'

'Good idea. I'll walk through there now and shout for him,' she says, turning to run back indoors. 'I'll just get my shoes on.'

'I'll come with you,' I suggest. 'With two of us looking, there'll be more chance of spotting him.'

Sara marches ahead of me as we walk into the woods, yelling for Pumpkin and rattling a packet of cat treats. She's worried, really worried to the point of seeming close to tears.

'Pumpkin's never done this before,' she says in between shout-ing his name. 'He's never strayed much further than our garden, back at the old house. This is all because of me having to move! All because of bloody Rob, dumping me for sodding Jade. It's his fault, all his fault everything's gone so wrong in my life.'

I follow her through the undergrowth, staring up into the

branches of the trees, watching and hoping for a flash of white, orange and black fur. *Come on, Pumpkin*, I think. *Where the hell have you got to?* It's such a shame to see Sara so upset, when up till now she's been so positive about everything – or at least, that's how she's appeared to me. If it was winter, the trees completely bare, he'd be so much easier to spot. As it is, he'd blend in only too well with the gold and rust colours of the autumn leaves. When we reach the stretch of beach at the other side of Angel Head, we both look up at the huge red cliffs.

'Could he have wandered this far?' Sara wonders aloud. 'What if he'd tried to climb up the cliff? What if he'd got stuck, or cut off by the tide?'

'I think he'd have run back into the woods,' I try to reassure her.

'Yes. He'd have been scared by the sea. He's not used to it yet.'

When we come to the other end of the woods we turn and walk back. Sara's still shaking the cat treats and calling, but I can hear the defeat in her voice.

'He might have turned up at home while we've been out,' I say hopefully. 'That would be just typical of a cat, wouldn't it? We're searching high and low, worrying about him, and he might have just snuck in through the cat flap and gone to sleep in his bed.'

We hurry the rest of the way back through the woods, both of us still calling, but there's still no sign of Pumpkin at the cottages.

Sara gives me an apologetic look as we part company. 'Thanks for your help, Joy. I know I've got myself into a state ... but it's just—'

'Just another thing that's gone wrong,' I say gently. 'I understand.'

'Yes. And I can't imagine how I'm going to tell Charlie, if Pumpkin's still missing when he comes home from school.' She sits down heavily on one of the wooden chairs. 'I wish I'd never had the damned cat flap put in. I wish I'd kept him as an indoor cat for longer. Or for ever!' She pauses, and adds, very quietly: 'I wish I'd never had to move here.'

I sit down next to her and put an arm around her. The big brave act has dropped a little, now.

'I know. Moving house is such an upheaval, even if the move was … for a *nice* reason. It's bad enough, what's happened to your marriage, isn't it, without all this upset. Settling Charlie in at school, and now, Pumpkin.'

'It's been tough,' she admits, swallowing hard.

'But you've been so brave and positive. This is just a setback. Look, I bet Pumpkin will come running back later on, maybe when Charlie gets in from school. Why don't you try to take your mind off it for now?'

'Yes. I do need to get on with some work. Thanks, Joy.'

This afternoon, I walk up to Bierleigh on my own, take back the Bierleigh library book and choose a couple of new novels, before walking up to the top of Fore Street and back, idly looking in shop windows. One of the last buildings at the far end of the street is the local vet's surgery. I've never even set foot inside here – not having any pets – but on an impulse I pop in now and wait for the receptionist to be free, pretending to read the posters on the wall about vaccinations and flea treatments while listening to a waiting patient, a young woman cuddling a tiny dog and talking to it in a sing-song voice as if it's a baby.

'Sorry to bother you,' I say when the receptionist has finished her phone call. 'I just wondered if you have any advice about finding lost cats.'

Even as I'm saying it, I realise how naive it sounds.

'Is the cat microchipped?' she asks.

'Um – I don't actually know,' I admit. 'It's my neighbour's cat, she's only recently moved here, but I presume—'

'Well, if it is chipped, your neighbour needs to contact the microchip database company to update her address, if she hasn't already done that. And we'd be happy to put up a notice, with a photo, on our noticeboard if she wants us to do that?'

'Oh, thank you. I'll suggest that to her.'

I walk home feeling pleased with myself, feeling that at least I'm trying to help. But perhaps I'm just jumping the gun? Hopefully, Pumpkin will have come back by now – and if not, Sara might have thought of those suggestions herself already.

I try calling on her but it's not until later in the afternoon that I see her outside.

'Charlie and I had another walk along the beach and through the woods,' she tells me, looking upset. 'Still no sign of Pumpkin.'

I tell her quickly about my visit to the vet's.

'Oh, thanks, Joy. Yes, he is microchipped,' she says, 'and it's a good point: I didn't update the microchip details with my new address. I just didn't think of it. I can't even remember what the website is, or the password – I think Rob set it up. I'll have to call him. I'll do that tonight.'

'And, just in case Pumpkin doesn't come back by the morning,' I add carefully, 'I'd be happy to take a photo of him down to the vet's, for their noticeboard. It might help?'

'Definitely. I'll print off a "missing" notice, with a picture on it. But I can take it to the vet's myself, or we can walk down there together, in the morning?'

'OK, that's a plan,' I agree. 'But I really hope he's back by then.'

Because I've just caught a glimpse of Charlie's sad little face. And I really want to see him smiling again.

Wednesday 17 October

'Any sign of Pumpkin yet?' I ask Sara this morning when she comes back from the school run.

She shakes her head. 'I've just left Charlie crying at school. It's heartbreaking.' She sighs.

'Oh dear, I'm so sorry. Shall we take your poster down to the vet's now, then?'

'Yes, definitely, if that's OK with you,' she agrees. 'We can search for him along the lane on the way.'

We walk slowly up the lane, looking behind hedgerows as we go. It's sad to see Sara so despondent, instead of striding off in the purposeful, brisk manner I've already become accustomed to. She's calling Pumpkin, every couple of steps along the way. If he's wandered this far, he'll definitely be lost and frightened.

Fortunately, there are only a couple of people waiting in the vet's. The receptionist is the same one as yesterday. I remind her about the missing cat, and she gives Sara a sympathetic look as she takes the 'missing' leaflet from her and looks at Pumpkin's photo.

'Ah, he's beautiful!' she says. 'Try not to worry. He can't have gone far. And if people find a lost cat, they do usually bring them in to us.'

'Did I hear someone's lost a cat?' says a man's voice.

Sara looks up sharply. The young man who's just spoken is halfway through a door at the back of reception, and he's stopped, staring at Sara – who's staring straight back.

'Oh. *You*,' she says quietly, in a deadly tone as if it's an accusation.

He's flushed to the roots of his reddish-blond hair.

'Hello, Sara,' he says, and for a moment they just continue to stare at each other, obviously lost for words.

'What are you doing ... I mean, why are you here?' she says, stumbling over her words.

He gives an awkward little laugh. He's a nice-looking young man, probably in his thirties – about the same age as her. 'I work here. I told you, didn't I? I'm a vet nurse now. I started here last month. Why are *you*—?'

Sara doesn't answer. Instead, she turns away abruptly and starts to head for the door. I give the receptionist and the young man both an apologetic shrug and start to follow her, trying to ignore the curious looks from other people in the waiting room.

'Sara – wait!'

The young man's come through the hinged part of the counter into the waiting room and is following us. Sara's reached the door now and is fumbling with the handle, her cheeks pink with ... surprise? Annoyance? I don't know.

'Sorry!' he says to me, flashing me a rather nice smile as he ducks past me to follow Sara through the door. 'Sara! Don't rush off. Come on, I'm as surprised as you are. I didn't know you were ... in this area.'

'Didn't you?' she replies crossly. She stops and turns to face him. I'm half in, half out of the door and would prefer not to be in the middle of this – whatever it is – but I'm now kind of stuck, and neither of them are taking any notice of me. 'Well, it seems a very strange coincidence. I told you I was moving, didn't I?'

'Yes, and I told you *I* was! I told you I'd gone back to college, trained as a vet nurse and was moving to take up this new job.'

'Well, I didn't know it was *here*,' she says truculently.

Whoever he is, I get the definite impression she'd have moved somewhere else, anywhere else if necessary, to avoid meeting up with him again!

'Um . . . ' I say, trying to squeeze myself past them without actually pushing either of them out of the way. 'Look, I'll go on ahead, shall I, Sara – see you at home?'

'No, I'm coming now.'

She turns away from him without so much as a goodbye, but he calls after us, an edge of desperation in his voice:

'But I was going to offer to help. Is it your cat that's missing?' He pauses and glances at me. 'Or yours? Sorry, I didn't mean to be rude,' he adds with that charming smile again. 'I'm Luke.'

'Oh, hello. Luke, I'm Joy. I, er, live next door to Sara,' I tell him. 'Well, no, it's Sara's cat, not mine. We've just given your receptionist a notice to put up, about him – Pumpkin.'

Sara's looking daggers at me. I presume I've said too much, or I shouldn't be talking to him at all. I stop, feeling flustered. Whatever this is all about, I don't want to fall out with her over it.

'Well, I'll certainly do whatever I can to help,' he says. He sounds genuine enough. There's real sympathy in his startlingly bright green eyes. 'I'm a cat lover myself. I hate to think of a little cat being lost.'

'Yes, well, thanks, but I think we'll manage,' Sara says, and once again she starts to walk away.

Luke doesn't try to stop her this time, but he watches her go, looking puzzled and – I think – a bit hurt. I feel quite sorry for him; but, of course, I don't know their history. I don't know why she feels so obviously hostile towards him.

'Thank you anyway,' I tell him quietly, as I turn to follow her.

She's walking at top speed back down Fore Street, swinging her arms, looking straight ahead of her. I don't even want to ask. I think I'll wait for her to tell me – if she wants to.

We're nearly home when she slows down – allowing me to catch up, and catch my breath – and says, with a sigh:

'Sorry, Joy.' She tries to smile at me, but it doesn't quite work. 'That was . . . very awkward, to put it mildly.'

'You don't like him, do you?' I say, stating the obvious.

'I have no feelings one way or the other,' she retorts. 'We just used to go to school together, that's all.'

'I see. Well, at least he said he'd like to help. It seemed quite genuine.'

'Maybe. But I'll manage without him. Pumpkin must be around here somewhere.' She swallows, tears suddenly coming to her eyes.

'It still hasn't been long,' I remind her, putting an arm round her. 'I bet he'll soon come trotting back.'

'Will he? I can hardly bear it, Joy. It's just not fair!' I sense that she's not just talking about Pumpkin's disappearance now. It seems meeting up with this Luke has somehow made her feel worse than she already did. 'It feels like . . . when life knocks you sideways,' she goes on, 'it doesn't just leave it there. It bloody well kicks you while you're down. And then it poos all over you.'

'Ah, come on, it'll be OK,' I say, giving her a hug. It's hard to know what else to say. I might have found her a bit full-on when I first met her, but this sudden descent into despair is all the sadder because of it. 'Look, how about I put a message about Pumpkin on the Bierleigh Facebook page? Do you think that might help?'

'Yes, it could do, couldn't it,' she agrees. 'Thanks, Joy. And if I email you a picture of Pumpkin, would you be able to download that and add it to the Facebook post? Do you need me to show you how? Or would it be easier if I sign up to the page myself?' she adds.

'No, I'm sure I can work that out,' I say. I've got nothing much else to do, after all.

'Thanks. Sorry, but I'm not feeling much like chatting today.'

'No, I don't suppose you are. You'll be better off throwing yourself into your work. Trying to take your mind off . . . things.'

'Yes. See you later.'

Terry seems to have calmed down by the time he comes home tonight, but it feels like neither of us really knows how to start talking again now, after the argument the other night. I dish up dinner, put the plates on the table and we both sit down to start eating, before he suddenly asks:

'So how's the new hobby coming on? The local history research? I presume that's why you've joined this club?'

'Good, thanks,' I say. At least he's making an effort. And I know I do owe him an apology. 'Look, I'm really sorry I didn't make sure you knew about it – Monday night.'

'Well, perhaps you're right, perhaps I forgot.' He shrugs. 'I've got other things on my mind, unfortunately.'

I feel like saying, *Yes, I've noticed* – but that wouldn't be fair, in the circumstances. He's being generous in sharing the blame for the row.

'Well, I think I've found a point of contact at the society,' I say. 'Where I might get some more information.' If I'm lucky. If she remembers anything else!

'Good,' he says. He doesn't ask any more, so I don't bother to elaborate. Instead, I ask him how things are going now with his work. I always ask, but he rarely says anything apart from the standard reply he gives me now, without looking up from his dinner:

'Busy.'

I'd like to say we're back on speaking terms. But it's not as if we do much speaking now anyway.

Thursday 18 October

This morning when I get back from buying bread in the village, Sara's outside in the lane, calling for Pumpkin again, her voice rising and falling above the noise of the wind that's blown up overnight.

'No luck yet?' I ask.

'No. I've already walked through the woods again this morning. I don't know what to do, now. I can't bear to think he's out here somewhere, crying, lost and on his own. I've got to keep trying.'

'Of course. I put the message and the photo on the Facebook page last night. So, together with the poster at the vet's, let's hope that does some good.'

'Yes, I hope so too. Well, I'd better get on with some work,' she goes on. 'It normally takes my mind off things, but it's not helping at the moment – I'm struggling to concentrate.'

And I'm struggling to find anything positive to say.

'Would you like to join me for a coffee?' I suggest. 'If you've got time.'

'Oh, go on then,' she says. 'If it's a quick one . . . Decaf for me, if you've got it, please. I'm trying to be healthy.' She sighs. 'I'm sorry, Joy, I'm not very good company at the moment, am I?'

'I understand. Come inside, Sara – it's too cold out here.'

I put the kettle on, and while we're waiting for it, I start to tell Sara a little about the Historical Society meeting, beginning with the members of the society. Before long, I've managed to make her laugh despite herself.

'So they're *all* older than you?' she says.

'Yes, apart from the chairman, Howard. And most of them are quite deaf. I have the definite impression some of them only go along for the tea and biscuits,' I chuckle. 'But they're a nice little group, I shouldn't be mean about them. Especially poor Freda who doesn't really understand where she is.'

As I'm making the coffee, I go on to explain that Freda and her family actually used to live in Sara's house when she was young.

'Oh, that *is* interesting!' she says, sitting up straight. 'Did she tell you anything about it? What it was like back then?'

'No. Unfortunately, as I said, her memories are very sporadic. And quite unreliable.'

I tell Sara about Freda's little sister, Chrissie, as she'd called her, and how Freda remembered being her bridesmaid when she got married.

'That seemed to be a nice memory for her,' I say. '*And* . . .' I pause dramatically as I put Sara's coffee down in front of her ' . . . she told us that Chrissie apparently saw the Angel of the Cove once. She said it was very lucky that she'd seen it.'

'Oh, wow, you've got a contact now – someone who might know more about the angel.'

'Well, not really, as I'm not sure how much I can believe. And I didn't like to push her. She tends to forget where she is and what she's doing, mid-sentence, and gets upset.'

'Ah, that's sad,' Sara says. 'Anyway, what's this Howard like – the only one who's younger than you?'

'Not younger. The same age, apparently. He's nice,' I add, deliberately looking away.

'Oh, really?' There's a smile in Sara's voice. 'How nice?'

'Oh, I didn't mean anything like that!' I say, feeling myself going a bit pink. 'I meant he seems friendly, that's all.'

She laughs. 'I was teasing you, Joy. But anyway, there's no harm in thinking he's nice, is there?'

'Maybe not,' I say with a shrug, and quickly changing the subject. 'Well, how's Charlie getting on at school now?'

We chat for a little longer, managing to avoid talking about Pumpkin for a while. She updates me about Charlie: about a new little friend at school who seems to be making him happier, and the weekend with his dad that he's looking forward to so much. By the time we part company I think she's cheered up a bit. She's going to get on with her work now, to keep herself from thinking about Pumpkin – while I decide, for no particular reason, to clean all the windows.

'Done anything interesting today?' Terry asks this evening. He's looking at his phone even while he's asking the same old question as always – whether I'm doing anything he'd consider worthwhile.

'Been busy cleaning the windows,' I say, a bit shortly.

'Right. Well, as long as you're keeping yourself busy, that's the most important thing.'

'Is it?' I retort, suddenly feeling riled with him. 'Why? Why is it so important to you that I keep myself busy? Would it bother you if I said I'd sat around all day reading a book? Or dozed on the sofa watching daytime TV? I *am* retired, you know. We're not *all* so completely self-defined by our jobs that we don't know how to relax and just be ourselves.'

'Whoa!' He actually takes a step back. 'Where is *this* coming from? What's wrong?'

'Nothing.'

I've run out of steam almost as soon as I boiled over. But it had been brewing for so long – my irritation at both his sudden descent into workaholism, and his constant dialogue about me having nothing to do, no serious purpose, my existence being somehow aimless and worthless now that I haven't got a label. Nurse. Accountant. Anything, other than Retired Person. What's wrong with being labelled simply as a *Person*? Perhaps I just haven't ever had time, before, to work out who, or what, I actually am. Perhaps I need to be left alone to find out, rather than constantly being urged to do something useful. I've *been* useful! Now I'd just like to ... I don't know ... *live*.

But even as I'm thinking this, I'm aware that I'm being silly, child-ish. Thinking about *finding myself*, like some ageing hippy going to live in a commune. Terry's still staring at me as if he's wondering if I'm about to start foaming at the mouth and speaking in tongues.

'Sorry,' I add, although I'm not, particularly. What's wrong with me? I wonder briefly whether we need a break from each other – we've never had one before, not even for a separate holiday, not even a weekend. Never wanted to. But it's not as if we see too much of each other, after all – he's only ever here for a few hours before we go to sleep at night! I feel bad for even wondering about it, wondering whether I'd like us to spend some time apart – espe-cially when I think of Sara, on her own and trying to be so brave about it. I suppose I ought to be grateful that Terry's still here, even if his very presence has started to make me feel peeved and hurt.

'Look, I'm sorry we argued the other night,' he says in a tired voice, obviously assuming I'm still feeling sore about that. 'But—'

'I know. It was my fault. I said I was sorry.'

'So what's the matter?'

I feel tempted to respond that *he's* the matter. That I'm fed up with being ignored, and that it seems he only notices me if I start to have a rant. But what's the point? He's already picked up his phone again.

'Nothing,' I say, again, with a sigh.

'Well, it's not like you to be so snappy.'

'Maybe it is, though,' I say, pretending to chuckle a bit. 'Maybe this is the real me. We don't really know who I am, yet, do we?'

But I don't think he's in the mood for a philosophical discussion. He frowns and turns away from me.

'What's for dinner?' he says. 'Can I smell apple sauce?'

'No.' I head off to start wondering what to cook. 'It's the window-cleaning spray.'

Friday 19 October

There's still no news about Pumpkin. Nothing on the Facebook page apart from several sympathetic messages from people saying they'll look out for him. No calls in response to the poster in the vet's surgery. I hate to say it, but I'm seriously beginning to wonder if he's going to turn up at all.

It's dry today, but overcast and gloomy-looking. I knock on Sara's back door and ask whether she'd like to have a walk today, or whether she's too busy.

'I'm not particularly busy,' she says. 'I can spread my work over the whole weekend. Charlie's going to his dad's. Rob's picking him up from school this afternoon.'

I look at her sympathetically. 'I bet it's going to feel strange without him.'

'Yes.' She hesitates for a moment and then goes on: 'How about we have that lunch together today – at the pub?'

I'm pleased and surprised; I didn't expect her to feel like it, but I guess she wants to take her mind off Charlie going to Rob's, as well as Pumpkin still being missing. We meet outside a little later, and it looks like she's made a huge effort, wearing more make-up than usual, heels, and a flamboyant bright pink jacket that I haven't seen before. I look down at my jeans and trainers and feel a bit dowdy. Retirement is making me lazy about my appearance – but then, who's going to notice me?

We chat cheerfully enough while we walk up to Bierleigh, and while we choose our food. I think she's making an effort with her mood, as well as her appearance, and I admire her for that even though it's pretty obvious she's really feeling miserable. We're just getting stuck into our meals when the door to the pub opens and – of all the people in the village – in comes Luke from the vet's. He's on his own, and he heads straight to the bar and orders a coffee and a sandwich before he even turns around and sees us.

'Oh. Hello again,' he says, coming over to our table.

'Hello,' Sara sighs, closing her eyes as if she wishes he'd disappear.

'I don't want to interrupt you, while you're eating,' he says to Sara. 'But I was going to call you later.'

'Call me?' Sara says, immediately sounding suspicious. 'Why?'

'Just about Pumpkin,' he says.

She sits up straight at once. 'Oh! Is there any news?'

'Not *exactly*.' He pauses, then goes on: 'But I think there's been a sighting. Someone who came into the vet's this morning for an appointment with her dog, saw the picture of Pumpkin on the wall. She said she's pretty sure he was the cat she saw one of her neighbours letting into her house a couple of days ago. I'm going to follow it up – call on the neighbour – on my way back to work after I've had some lunch.'

'Oh!' Sara gasps again. She doesn't seem to be able to say anything else.

'Don't get your hopes up yet,' he warns her. He gives her a smile. 'It might turn out to be another cat, but—'

'But if it *is* Pumpkin, you'll let us know right away, won't you?' I press him.

'Of course.' He glances at Sara again, and shifts from foot to foot, looking awkward, before adding, 'I wasn't sure if you'd changed your phone number – since you moved down here, I mean. But I saw it was the same on the poster.'

'Yes,' she says, her cheeks flushing as bright pink as her jacket. 'I've only got the mobile. No landline now.'

They nod at each other. 'Well, enjoy your lunch,' he says, and starts to walk away. 'I'll keep you informed.'

'Thank you, Luke,' she says quietly.

'Don't thank me yet,' he replies, gently. 'Until we know more.'

I make sure he's out of earshot, sitting at his own table, before I say: 'Well, fingers crossed. He seems very keen to help.'

'Yes.' She sounds non-committal, but she can't hide the light of hope that's come into her eyes now. Pumpkin's been spotted – or at least, we hope so. 'I can't help wondering, though,' she adds, almost to herself.

'Wondering what?'

'Well, it's just ... such a coincidence. *Him* turning up *here*. Getting himself involved in looking for *my* cat.'

'You said you were at school together? So ...' I hardly like to ask, as there's quite obviously something very odd between the two of them '... has it been a long time since you last saw him?'

She gives a little snort. I can't quite make out whether she's embarrassed, or disgusted by him. 'No, in fact we bumped into each other just before I moved down here.'

'Oh, right.'

I'm just trying to find another topic of conversation, to change the subject, when she suddenly glances over at Luke's table, where he seems to be engrossed in his sandwich, and goes on quietly, 'I've known him for ages, you see. We used to be best friends. We hung around together all the time.'

'Oh!' I stare at her. 'I'm . . . sorry, I got the impression you didn't like him. You were best friends back when you were at school?'

'Right from starting playgroup when we were three years old. Right through junior school and senior school. A group of us used to hang around together. Even after most of us went away to uni, we'd meet up in the holidays.'

She stabs a chip viciously with her fork, dips it in ketchup and puts it in her mouth, shrugging as she chews it.

'Then you lost touch?' I prompt her.

'Not right away. But eventually, yes. After we all started settling down – careers, marriage, kids, you know.'

'I see,' I say.

She doesn't seem to want to say any more, and I'm not going to press her. Instead, as we finish our lunch, I find myself talking about Terry. I didn't intend to, but once I start, I can't seem to stop, and before long I've spilled out all my worries to her – how he's not only working harder and longer now than ever before, but seems to be nagging me all the time about keeping myself busy and getting some hobbies. I even tell her about the arguments we've started having. When I run out of steam, I'm horrified with myself. What am I like? Sara *really* doesn't need me sounding off about my own issues – she has so much worse herself to contend with.

'Oh, Joy,' she's saying – but I interrupt her quickly before she can start giving me any unearned sympathy for my stupid outburst.

'No – I'm really sorry, I didn't mean to tell you all that. You've got enough worries of your own, for God's sake, and I'm just being daft, it's nothing serious.'

'But it's serious to you, isn't it, that's the point. You're worried.'

'But probably for no reason. Terry keeps telling me he's just really busy at the moment. We're fine, really. It's just me, imagining things . . . thinking he's bored with me, now I'm retired.'

'I'm sure that's not true!' She looks at me sympathetically. 'I imagine it takes time to get used to being retired, and yes, Terry's probably just extra busy, but he's being a bit thoughtless too.'

'Well, I suppose that's men for you!' I joke. 'Anyway, shall we have a coffee? Or would you like a dessert?'

'Oh, God, no dessert, thanks!' she says, patting her completely flat stomach as if she's massively overeaten. 'But maybe a cup of tea. I'll go and order.'

While she's at the bar, I see Luke – who's finished his lunch already – getting up and heading for the door. He turns to look over at our table as he goes, and gives me a little wave goodbye. Sara hasn't noticed – she has her back to him – but as she returns, she glances across at where he was sitting, looking surprised that he's gone.

'Hopefully he's gone straight to the house where someone thinks they saw Pumpkin,' I say, and she nods. 'And I'm sure he'll call you, one way or the other,' I add quietly. Because, whatever she says to the contrary, and even regardless of finding Pumpkin, I somehow think she would, really, *like* him to call her.

Saturday 20 October

I tap on Sara's back door this morning. I can't wait any longer to find out.

'Did you hear anything from Luke?' I ask anxiously.

She sighs. 'Yes. Sorry I haven't called to tell you, Joy, but I'm so upset about it . . .'

'What? It isn't . . . bad news, I hope?'

'Not exactly.' She holds the door open. 'Come in while I tell you. It looks like it's going to rain any minute.'

It does, too. Black clouds scudding across the sky, the sea grey and threatening in response.

'Sit down for a minute,' she says. 'Want a coffee?'

'No, I won't stay. I'm not interrupting your work, am I?' I add quickly.

It's nice and cosy in her kitchen. She's got the heating on, some washing drying on an airer next to the radiator, the radio playing quietly and her laptop open on the little kitchen table.

'No – it's fine, I'm just trying to keep myself occupied while Charlie's not here.' She pauses, and then goes on: 'Luke saw Pumpkin yesterday, at that house he went to. He says it was definitely him. Alive and well.'

'Oh, thank God!' I say, smiling. Then I stop, looking at her face. 'So, why . . . ?'

'Apparently the woman there tried to insist he belonged to her. But she hurried him out of sight, which she surely wouldn't do unless she was aware that he was someone else's cat.' Sara shakes her head. 'Well, of course she's bloody well aware! She's stolen him!'

'So, you need to get his microchip scanned, to prove it.'

'Exactly. That's what Luke told her, but needless to say, she wouldn't agree to take Pumpkin to the surgery for the check. In fact, she said she'd call the police if Luke didn't go away.'

'Well, if she did call the police, they'd agree that a microchip check would settle the issue.'

'Yes. Luke told her that too. He said even if she'd believed Pumpkin had been a stray, and had taken him in out of the kindness of her heart, the law would definitely not be on her side – she should have taken him straight to the vet first. He even warned her that she'd be committing a crime if she refused, and he'd have to report her. Apparently that scared her.'

'Good. So . . . where's Pumpkin now?'

Sara sighs again, raising her eyes to the ceiling in exasperation. 'The stupid woman had let him run out of her back door while they were talking.'

'Oh no!'

'Yes. I'm furious, and . . . well, I suppose I took it out on Luke. I was so disappointed, after having my hopes raised like that. I turned on him. Asked him how he thought it was good news, that he'd found my cat and promptly lost him again. I know, I know I was being unfair,' she says, seeing the look on my face. 'And I did feel bad then, because he went on to tell me he'd gone out into this woman's street and searched for Pumpkin himself. I suppose he did his best. I shouldn't have snapped at him.'

'To be honest, the woman who'd taken him in must be pretty stupid. Even if she *hadn't* known Pumpkin belonged to someone, she shouldn't have let him go outside until he knew his way around.'

'Exactly. Although ... Luke did say, he ended up thinking she might have learning difficulties, and that she genuinely seemed to believe it was OK to keep Pumpkin. Not that that makes me feel any better. As far as I'm concerned, she stole my cat, end of story.'

'So what happens now?' I ask. 'Is Luke going to go back again?'

'Yes. He says he'll keep looking, now we know he's somewhere around there. He's going back when he finishes work today. He hopes Pumpkin will find his way back to that same house again. He's been fed there, so it would be the natural thing to do. He told the woman – Lina, she's called – to contact the vet's if he does – and to keep him inside until one of us goes to collect him. He seems quite sure, now, that we're going to get him back.'

'Well, he's right: Pumpkin's bound to go back to her for food. And I reckon the threat of the police will have made that woman see sense. Don't give up, Sara.' I place my hand over hers. 'I'm sure he'll soon be back home, now.'

'Thanks. I know I should be glad he's been found alive and well, at least.' She sighs, closing her eyes for a second. 'I should be grateful to Luke.'

'Yes, it's good of him, isn't it? I mean, he didn't have to go to so much trouble.'

'I know,' she says. 'Well, OK, I *am* grateful, but ... let's just say I'm still not enjoying having him around. It wasn't ... what I expected, when I moved down here: to find out he's moved here too. I think we've both been so shocked at meeting up down here, it's made it ... uncomfortable. It's an unfortunate coincidence.'

'Fair enough.' I can't deny I'm puzzled. She says they'd been best friends for much of their lives, so something must have happened in the intervening years, after they went their separate ways, to explain why she's seemed so shocked and unhappy about them winding up in the same area again now.

She's looking up at the ceiling for a moment, like she's trying to decide whether to say any more. Then she just shakes her head, as if to dismiss her own thoughts, and goes on more cheerfully, 'Charlie called me earlier.' She smiles. 'He sounded so excited about being with his daddy again. He told me all about his bedroom in the apartment. Apparently, he has a desk with an *actual laptop* on it, and a shelf of books that Daddy knew he'd like, and some paints, and a new Lego set that makes an *actual* battleship. He told me all this in such a flurry of excitement that I couldn't help laughing. But after I'd wished him a nice weekend, I asked him to pass me over to Rob.'

'Did you think it was all too much?' I guess.

'Well, I did wonder about the *actual laptop*. But he said it's just his old one, and he's taken everything off it apart from a couple of games – innocuous ones, he said. And he's promised to keep Charlie to his screen-time limit, and he'll make sure it's turned off at bedtime.'

'So I guess that's fine?'

'Yes, of course. It's fair enough for Charlie to have a few treats when he goes to stay with his daddy. I just didn't want to think he'd bought a new laptop for him.'

'You're being very fair.'

'For Charlie's sake, I have to be. I managed to wait till we'd hung up before I started crying! So much for moving on,' she adds with a little shrug, and I find her honesty quite endearing now, considering all the courage she's been displaying up till now. 'The last thing Rob said was that he hoped I'd soon hear something about Pumpkin. Charlie hadn't even mentioned him. I'm glad he's got other things to take his mind off the situation.'

'Yes, that is good.' I get to my feet, stopping to focus on the pictures pinned to a cork board over the worktop. 'Are those Charlie's paintings? Aren't they wonderful? I love his shell pictures. And the beach scene! He really is quite talented.'

'I think so,' she says, smiling. 'I'm so proud of him. For how he's coping with this new start, too – better than I am, really.'

'Kids are adaptable. He'll be fine, I'm sure – and so will you, eventually.' I pause. 'I'll let you get on. But tell me if you hear any more, won't you?'

'I will. Thanks, Joy.'

Terry looks up at me questioningly when I go back indoors.

'Just been into Sara's,' I explain. 'Pumpkin – her cat – is still missing, but we think we know where he might be, now.'

'Right. Well, I hope she gets him back soon.' He looks away, seeming to consider his words carefully. 'I'm glad you've made friends with Sara, Joy. You probably needed the company. I've noticed lately that you do seem to be at a bit of a loose end.'

'I'm not at a loose end, Terry,' I say quietly. 'I'm just getting used to being retired.'

'But you quite obviously don't know what to do with yourself. So it's nice that you've made a new friend, so you can go for little walks and have nice little lunches out and so on. As well as your new little hobby, of course, with the local history—'

Little walks? Little lunches? My little hobby?

'You don't have to bloody patronise me!' I snap. Nice! I've gone from perfectly calm, through mild irritation, to full-blown fishwife in thirty seconds. 'I'm not a little housewife who needs a little hobby, I've been a career woman all my life, and I've just retired! I'm not apologising for retiring!'

I sit down next to him, sighing, far more annoyed with myself than I am with him.

'Sorry,' I say quickly, as he's staring at me in surprise, like he doesn't quite know how to deal with me now. 'Didn't mean to yell at you. But I don't need you to treat me like ... like a special needs child ... just because I don't have a job any more.'

'All right,' he says. 'Well, I'm sorry, too. I didn't mean to be patronising.'

Even as he's saying it, he's patting my hand in a way that could only be considered, in anybody's book, as patronising. I shrug him off. I still feel rattled, but more than anything, I feel sad and upset. We used to be so good together. Now it seems we're either like two complete strangers who barely talk to each other, or we're arguing over nothing. I've been blaming Terry for being so caught up with his work he couldn't be bothered to spend any time with me. But I don't know – perhaps it's me. Perhaps I really do need to sort myself out, find myself a new purpose in life. Or perhaps this is all just pointing to something more fundamentally wrong with our relationship. Perhaps we're just not compatible any more.

Monday 22 October

It's the school half-term holiday this week and at least the sun's shining this morning. I make a quick call on Sara to see if there's been any more news about Pumpkin. He's been missing for a week now.

'Well, Luke did call me this morning,' she says. 'Apparently he's been checking in with that Lina woman every day. She says she's *seen* Pumpkin in her garden, but she hasn't managed to get him back inside.'

'He's probably scared,' I point out. 'But he'll be hungry by now, too.'

'Yes. And ... well, it seems Luke's been walking up and down Lina's street, too, looking for him.'

'That's nice of him.' I can't help thinking how all of this is surely beyond the call of duty for Luke. And it's pretty obvious he's mostly doing it because it's for Sara.

'I'm trying not to say too much in front of Charlie,' Sara adds quietly.

'Of course. How was his weekend with his dad?'

'Oh, he had a great time. He was so excited to tell me all about it last night, when Rob brought him home. He was chatting nineteen to the dozen about his *second home*, his *new bedroom*, the laptop, the paintings he and Rob did together, the film they watched, the afternoon at the park, the pizza . . .'

'Was that a bit difficult for you?' I suggest gently, but she shakes her head.

'No. I was expecting him to be excited – fair enough. But it went on for so long, I made the mistake of suggesting Rob stayed for a coffee before driving back.' She shrugs. 'Well, I'll be honest, it wasn't a mistake: I *wanted* him to stay. I wanted to sit opposite him for a bit longer, and listen to him laughing at Charlie prattling on. Just . . . kind of pretending to myself, I suppose, that we were still a family. But, of course, all it achieved was that it hurt even more when he did leave.'

'That must have been tough.'

'Well, it was my own fault. But Charlie didn't even think to ask about Pumpkin until Rob was just about to leave. And, of course, when I told him he still wasn't back, he got really upset. He said, "He's run away, hasn't he! He's run away from home because he hates it here, he wants to go back to live with Daddy, and *so do I*!"'

'Oh dear. Do you think it was because he'd got overtired?'

'That's what Rob said. He did apologise for not bringing him back earlier, before he got tired and emotional. And I said not to worry, it wasn't his fault. But, to be honest, it is, isn't it? Everything is his fault – the break-up of our marriage, our family. Charlie being upset. Even my lovely cat going missing. It's all because of his *stupid infatuation*.'

'He must realise that, too,' I say.

'Yes, but do you know what? I was still sitting there looking at him, wishing he'd give me a hug, give me some bloody comfort. I can't understand why I still love him!'

'Well, you shared a life together, had a child together, of course all those feelings don't just suddenly evaporate,' I sympathise.

'I should hate him!' she retorts. 'I *want* to hate him, but there I was, like an idiot, wishing we were still a family, wishing things could be like they used to be.'

'It's understandable, Sara.'

'No, it isn't, because I know it can't *ever* be like it used to be. And I've promised myself I'd never take him back.' She stands up straighter and manages a smile, giving herself a little shake and changing the subject. 'Anyway, Joy, is it tonight you go to your Historical Society?'

'Yes.'

'I'll look forward to hearing about it tomorrow, then. Maybe what's-her-name – Freda? – might have another sudden burst of memory about the Angel of the Cove.'

'I hope so!' I agree with a smile.

I made a point, this morning, of reminding Terry about the meeting.

'I'll leave you a note, anyway,' I said. 'In case you forget. And your dinner will be on a plate.'

'OK. Have a good time,' he said, distractedly. I was tempted to say that, in fact, I was going to a wife-sharing party where we'd all be taking drugs and taking our clothes off, and see whether he even looked up from his phone screen, or just said, 'Have a good time,' again. But that would be childish . . . wouldn't it?

By this evening the weather's changed again and there's a fine, persistent drizzle in the air. I'm taking the car down to Bierleigh this time. I arrive quite early, and Howard's the only one already in the hall when I go in, so I help him to get the chairs out.

'What did you say we were going to be talking about tonight?' I ask him. 'Entertainment, wasn't it?'

'Yes, I suggested *entertainment through the ages*.' He shrugs. 'How people used to enjoy their spare time? The thing is, Joy, since I've taken over running the group, nobody else has come up with any suggestions about what to talk about each week. Nobody's ever disagreed with my ideas, either,' he adds with a grin. 'So I suppose that's something.'

'It's nice that they trust you to take the lead, then, isn't it?'

'Perhaps. But, on the other hand, I'm bound to run out of ideas pretty soon,' he says.

'Have any of them told you what they used to do before you took over?'

'Yes. Apparently, they just used to sit and chat about *the old days*. And once in a while somebody – usually one of the members themselves – gave a little talk about their own life. Even though they all knew everything about each other already!'

'Well, they must be glad they've got you choosing a theme now.'

'If you have any ideas, for God's sake let me know!' he says, and we both laugh.

But tonight's discussion is quite lively. It starts with Margaret telling us, firmly and a little crossly, that *in her day*, there really wasn't time for any such thing as entertainment, that it's a modern invention and people these days have far too much free time for their own good. She worked as a shop assistant at the village shop until she got married, she says – after which she never had a free moment to spare for herself.

'Did you work on Sundays?' Howard asks innocently.

'Of course not!' she exclaims, sounding scandalised. 'We all went to church.'

'What about the evenings?' David asks.

'Well, we didn't have television or anything like that. So the family used to go for walks together. Or, in the winter, we'd listen to the radio or sing along to my father playing the piano.'

'So that was your entertainment,' David dares to point out.

'Of course it wasn't *entertainment*!' she says with a sniff. 'We just knew how to *occupy* ourselves in those days.'

Howard clears his throat. 'Anyone else like to tell us how they used to ... er ... occupy themselves when they were younger?'

'Us men used to go down the Angel,' says old Saul with a cackle of laughter. 'And play dominoes or shove-ha'penny over a pint with our pals.'

'While your wives slaved away at home, no doubt,' says Margaret.

'No, my missus used to come too. She sat in the saloon bar with the other ladies. They used to put the world to rights over a few halves of stout. Loved a gossip, did my Mary.' He sighs and pauses for a moment before adding, ''Course, that was before she got the TB and died. She were only thirty-five.'

'Oh. Sorry to hear that,' we all mutter.

'How about you, Grace?' Howard asks Mrs Unwin. 'Did you, or your family, have any ways of amusing yourselves when you weren't working?'

'Oh yes,' she says. 'Every Sunday afternoon, in the summer, me and my Stanley used to take all the children down to Angel Cove with a picnic basket and a rug. The children used to play on the beach, and me and Stanley used to canoodle behind the breakwater—'

'Canoodle?!' squawks Margaret, looking shocked and offended. 'On the beach? On a *Sunday*?'

We're all, apart from poor Margaret, doing our best not to snigger now, but Howard wisely changes the subject, starting to talk, instead, about what everyone used to listen to on the radio. This starts a heated debate about when *The Archers* was first broadcast, and whether *Listen with Mother* was good for children or not. Saul begins to talk about dominoes again, telling us how there was a dominoes league in the Angel, and he won it three years running.

Through all of this, Freda remains silent, looking lost in

thought, until suddenly, just as everyone else seems to be running out of conversation, she sits up straight and announces:

'That was what *she* did. My poor sister. Canoodling on the beach. With that boy! Naughty girl, Chrissie, you got yourself into trouble, didn't you? Oh dear. So much trouble, wasn't there.'

There's a hush. Grace puts her arm around Freda, to comfort her, because she's now gone back to staring around the room, looking upset.

'All right, Freda, dear. Don't get yourself all worked up. I was talking about me and Stanley, not your sister, dear.'

'No. It was Chrissie. Chrissie and that Phil from next door. She told me all about it. I should have helped her, shouldn't I? But I was *jealous*, that was the truth of it. Jealous of my little sister.'

I'm holding my breath, hoping she'll say more, but at the same time not wanting her to upset herself. I want to know who *Phil* was, who lived next door. Next door, at Smugglers' Cottages? In my house? I don't like to ask ... but, to my surprise, Howard does.

'So did this boy live next door to you at Angel Cove, Freda?'

'Philip! Of course he lived next door. Ended up marrying my sister, didn't he? I was her bridesmaid. It was a pink dress!' she exclaims, suddenly looking around her with pleasure in her eyes. 'Always a bridesmaid, never a bride – that's what they said. And I never did get married, did I?' She looks confused again for a second, before shaking her head and saying, 'I lived with Doris. My friend. Where's Doris?'

It's so sad, the sudden switch from remembering the past, to forgetting the present. Of course, nobody talked openly, years ago, about why two women would want to live together, but I do remember some gossip when I first moved to the area. Freda's *friend*, Doris, passed away around ten years ago. Howard was telling me last week that Freda started to deteriorate a couple of years later. She now lives in a care home, and her weekly outings to these meetings, picked up and taken back by Margaret or Grace, are her special treats. I wonder if she wishes her life could have been different; that she *could* have been the bride instead of the bridesmaid; if she could have lived openly with Doris, as partners, and even – impossible though it would have seemed back then – married her?

We break for refreshments at this point, and I'm on the rota this time so I'm too caught up with helping David in the kitchen to think much more about it. As I carry the tray of teas and coffees around the group, Margaret Parmenter beckons me to one side. She's a nice woman, not usually as gruff and disapproving as she was earlier about people *entertaining* themselves!

'I saw how interested you were in what Freda was saying,' she begins.

'Well, it's just that I live in Smugglers' Cottages, so—'

'Of course. So I wondered if you realise Philip's actually still alive? Well, as far as I know, anyway.'

'The Philip who married Freda's sister?' I hesitate. I'm intrigued, of course, because of this couple having lived in our houses – mine and Sara's. And also because of Freda's comment last week about her sister seeing the angel. But really, am I just being nosy? I'm considering whether or not to ask Margaret if she knows where Philip lives now, when she goes on:

'They moved away, after they married – Philip and Christine. Somewhere up in North Devon. Freda told me about it, before she started to get so confused. But apparently, after Christine died – cancer, so sad – Philip moved back down here.'

'He's back in Bierleigh?'

'I'm not sure whether he's actually in Bierleigh, or one of the other villages around here. Not even sure that Freda knows, herself. But on the grapevine, I heard that he's gone into one of those apartment complexes for the elderly. He'd only be, let me see, probably about seventy-six or seventy-seven now. Maybe you can track him down, if you wanted to talk to him. His name's Sutton. Philip Sutton.'

I hesitate. 'Maybe I could. But it seems a bit cheeky, really.'

'Well, it's up to you – he can always say no! But I think it's perfectly understandable that you're interested. I can't offer any more help, unfortunately. I didn't live around here back then, when Freda and her sister, and Philip, were young, so I don't know what exactly happened – the *trouble* she talks about. Although it sounds like some kind of scandal, probably a pregnancy, I suppose.'

'Yes, it sounds like it,' I agree.

'Anyway, I'd better get back to Freda, but good luck with your ... little quest, my dear.'

My little quest. Is it really understandable that the story of these two young people – let alone the story of the angel! – is piquing my curiosity so much? After the break, I help David collect the cups and wash them up while the others reconvene, and when we join them again there's already an interesting discussion started about the various societies and clubs that have flourished, or not, over the years here in Bierleigh. I'm fascinated to hear about a choir – still going strong – that I didn't even know existed, and a drama group and marching band, both set up during the Second World War, to help keep people's minds off the horrors of wartime.

Howard catches up with me as I'm putting on my coat at the end of the meeting.

'It'll be more interesting during the spring and summer,' he says apologetically, 'when we can plan some outings. Last year we visited a couple of National Trust places. I hired us a minibus.'

'That sounds good. But I *am* finding it interesting,' I reassure him.

'Oh, I'm glad. It's good to have someone else, um, relatively young—' he gives a little chuckle '—in the group. I wondered whether you'd like to help me come up with more ideas for our meetings. I worry that we're not attracting any new members.'

'Well, it's difficult, I suppose. You wouldn't want to change things so much that it upsets all the current members.'

'That's my problem, exactly. It would be really helpful to have more of a chat at some point.'

'Yes, OK,' I say. 'If you think I can help.'

He looks at me thoughtfully for a moment and then blurts out suddenly: 'Would you like to come out for a drink with me one evening?'

The others have all left. He's holding the keys to the village hall, passing them from one hand to the other like a nervous tic, watching me, waiting for an answer. I can feel myself growing hotter and hotter.

'A drink?' I repeat, as if I've never heard of such a thing. 'Oh, well, look, I don't ... really think so. I mean, no, I'm sorry if I ...'

Sorry if I *what*? Let him think I was interested? Interested in what – just a drink, or ... *what*, exactly? What the hell did I think I was doing, giggling and smiling coyly at him like a schoolgirl?

'Um, I'm married!' I say, hearing the panic in my own voice as I turn away, heading towards the door. 'I'm sorry, I should have said.'

'I know you are.'

There's a hideous silence between us for a moment, before he goes on, quietly, talking to the back of my head, because I can't bring myself to turn back and face him: 'I just meant a drink and a chat about our meetings here. That's all.'

'Oh.' I swallow. My face is burning now. 'Yes, of course, well, I realise that. Well, maybe, um ... Anyway, I'd better run now. Bye.'

I drive home like a bat out of hell, and have to sit in my car outside the house for a few minutes to calm myself down before I go in and face Terry.

'Good time?' he asks without looking up from his laptop.

'Yes.' I head into the kitchen to pour myself a drink. I can't remember feeling this mortified since my knicker elastic broke when I was about eleven and my pants fell down around my ankles during a country dancing lesson. I'm not sure I'll be going back to the Historical Society next week now; I don't know how I'd be able to face Howard again. Despite how much I want to find out more about Christine and Philip, and what happened to them when they lived here in Smugglers' Cottages – it just doesn't seem worth the shame of facing Howard!

February 1960: Sunday evening

Philip waited for Chrissie by the breakwater, as he'd promised, until she managed to sneak out of the house that evening. She sat down next to him on the damp sand, holding his hand in the dark.

'Did you tell Freda about the baby?' he asked her softly.

'Yes.' She sounded as if she was trying to hold back the tears but almost choking on them. 'She wasn't any help at all. She was horrible to me, Phil! She called me horrible names. She said Mum and Dad will disown me, they'll send me away and make me give up the baby. She said it's no more than I deserve because I'm a slut and ... ' She stopped and shook her head. 'And I ought to drown myself.'

Philip pulled her closer and tried to kiss away the tears. He was furious, fuming to himself. How could Freda talk like that to her own sister? What was wrong with her? Chrissie had turned to her for *advice*!

'She's just jealous,' he said. 'She's an old maid who's never had a boyfriend. I don't know why we ever thought she'd be any help.'

'No. I wish I hadn't told her. Now she'll probably tell Mum and Dad, and she's right – they'll send me away! What on earth am I going to do?'

'I won't let them send you away. Let me talk to *my* parents. They might be more—'

'No! Phil, they won't help either. They might not be as angry as my parents but they'll just feel like they have to tell them, won't they?'

Philip lowered his head, trying not to cry himself. He was the man, here! And this was all his fault!

'I wish I'd never persuaded you to do it!' he muttered. 'I got carried away . . . I should never have . . .'

'You didn't persuade me,' she said quietly. 'You know that. I *wanted* to do it. Mum would say that it was up to me to say no, but I didn't want to. Freda's right, I'm a slut.'

'Don't say that!' he retorted. 'You're not! And I love you!'

'I love you, too,' she said, starting to cry again. 'Oh, Phil, why can't we just run away together? Go off somewhere on our own, live together, have the baby, be together for ever? We don't need anyone else. You're a fisherman, you can buy your own boat and—'

'With what?' he said sourly. 'The couple of pounds a week I get from Dad if the catch is good?'

She sighed and shrugged, and Philip reflected, as always, on how sweetly innocent she was in some ways. The economics of life were still slightly vague to her, as her parents had been persuaded by her teachers to allow her to stay on at school for another year, to take GCE exams because she was 'a bright girl'. *That* obviously wasn't going to happen now, he thought sadly – another thing he'd always blame himself for. He knew perfectly well that the strict headmistress of the girls' school Chrissie went to – whom she referred to as The Dragon – would never stand for the shame of having a pregnant girl in the school, lowering the tone and giving other girls wicked ideas. Her parents had had high hopes of her becoming a teacher like Freda; and Philip, who'd left school at fifteen without passing any exams, had felt so proud of her, so glad she wouldn't have to work in the fields, or in the fish market in Bierleigh. Now what hope was there for her to get a nice respectable job, after all?

'OK,' he said, sitting up and nodding to himself. He had to take control of this situation, and as far as he could see, there was only one way to do it. 'You're right. We'll have to get away, as far away as possible. Somewhere where we can get married and you can have the baby, and I'll just have to get a job, any job, and . . . and . . . we'll find somewhere to live – it will probably just be, I don't know, a room somewhere.'

'I don't care!' Chrissie's eyes were bright with tears in the moonlight. 'I don't care where I have to live, as long as it's with you. Let's do it, Phil. Let's go away together. Soon, as soon as we can, before Freda tells my mum and dad. I'll bring my savings book. Mum and Dad have put some money away for me every birthday. I don't know how much,' she admitted, 'but it'll help, won't it?'

'Yeah. Of course it will,' he said.

'We won't need much,' she went on, sounding almost excited now. 'Just as long as we're together, we'll manage somehow, won't we.'

He hugged her close in the cold winter air. He loved her, he was responsible for her, and however scared he was, he knew he had to try to reassure her that everything was going to be OK. For the moment, he had to put aside the reality of how ridiculous their plan really was, and pretend to join in with her childlike excitement of this so-unrealistic dream, this idea of being together for ever in some faraway place without a name, where lack of money wouldn't matter, where they'd live on bread and soup – and love – and let the world go hang.

'So let's both go and get a bag packed,' Philip said, getting to his feet and pulling Chrissie up beside him. It didn't feel real, of course. It just felt like they were planning a holiday. 'Don't pack too much: you might have to carry it for a long while. Just what fits into … maybe your school bag. I'll get some food out of the larder after Mum and Dad have gone to bed. Wait till your family are all asleep, then put all your warmest clothes on, your big coat and warm boots, make sure you don't wake them up! Meet me back down here as soon as you're ready.'

'*Tonight?*' she gasped.

'Yes, tonight.' He heard the wobble in his own voice and forced himself to stand up straighter and collect himself. 'It has to be tonight, Chris, or else Freda's going to snitch. Come on – we'll be all right. Together, for ever, OK?'

She nodded. 'OK,' she whispered.

'Don't forget, we need to travel light.' He smiled. 'Travelling light, like that Cliff Richard song you like.'

She gave a nervous little laugh, and he kissed her, tasting the salt from the sea breeze and her own tears, feeling the cold of her cheeks, wanting nothing more than to keep her warm and safe for ever.

'I'll look after you from now on,' he promised her as they turned, ready to hurry back inside their own homes. 'It'll just be you and me.'

'And the baby,' she reminded him, putting a hand on her stomach – still so completely flat, she couldn't have believed it if she hadn't already missed two of her monthlies, and been sick five mornings in a row.

'And the baby – of course!' he said quickly. He had no idea what to do with a baby, could barely remember his little brothers being born, let alone his mother being pregnant with them. Babies belonged to the mysterious world that women kept to themselves. He'd been brought up to believe the man of the house was merely expected to provide the income, and beyond that, get involved as little as possible. He was aware that this wasn't good enough; that he'd like to be a different type of father, but he had no idea how. 'I'll look after you *both*,' he said firmly.

He'd have to make it happen. Somehow.

Tuesday 23 October

Last night's drizzle cleared up by dawn, and now I'm sitting on the bench on the decking outside, watching Charlie playing down by the rock pools, probably making up his own little adventures as he jumps from rock to rock, clutching something he's made from LEGO in one hand and putting things in his bucket from time to time.

Sara comes out and stands by the rail at the edge of the decking, smiling as she, too, watches Charlie. I move up the bench to make room for her, and she comes to join me, holding her face up to the sun.

'It's a beautiful morning, isn't it?' she says.

'Yes. I wonder how many more days like this we can hope for. I'm glad it's so nice for Charlie, anyway – for his school holiday.'

'Me too. I love watching him when he's playing like this,' she says. 'Especially knowing he'll soon be back at school again until Christmas. And then in the spring, there'll be another birthday, and he'll be another year older – another year closer to growing up, making his own way in the world ...'

'Oh, I think you've got quite a few years yet before you need to worry about that!' I say, laughing.

'Yes – sorry!' She turns and smiles at me. 'I'm being a bit maudlin, aren't I. And it's a nice sunny day, too nice to mope.'

'There's been no more news about Pumpkin yet, I take it?' I ask tentatively.

'Not yet. And Charlie keeps wanting to go out all the time, calling for him in the woods and down the lane. But I've told him we just need to wait to hear from Luke again now.'

'Yes, I think that's sensible.'

For a few moments we sit in silence together, watching Charlie playing, and watching the sea, the endless motion of the waves rippling onto the shore, the sunshine dappling the water with dancing diamonds of light. It's almost hypnotic. It's a calm day, approaching high tide, and there's hardly a breath of wind to disturb us, nobody around for miles, the only sound that of a seagull crying high in the blue sky above us.

Sara suddenly seems to take a deep breath.

'I . . . wanted to talk to you about something, actually,' she says.

I look at her, but wait for her to carry on – which eventually she does, slowly, quietly.

'I've been wanting to tell you for a few days now. The thing is, I haven't told anyone yet, and it's just . . . a bit hard to actually come out and say it.'

But instead of coming out and saying it, she falls silent again, looking down at her feet.

'Would it help if we do it over a cup of tea?' I ask her, and I'm glad this makes her laugh.

'Strangely enough, that's what my mum always used to say! It doesn't matter what might have happened – the house could be burning down, or the country could have been invaded by aliens – she'd still have asked who wanted a cup of tea. I love it!'

'Would you like one, then?' I persist, smiling back at her. 'If it'll help?'

'Maybe after I've told you, otherwise I might just put it off again—' she begins.

But just at that moment, her phone starts to ring. She looks at the caller display, and gasps out loud.

'It's Luke,' she mouths to me as she answers the call, a little breathlessly: 'Hello?'

And now she's just nodding, saying 'Yes', and 'Right' and 'Thank you' into her phone, and wiping her eyes at the same time.

I'm practically rigid with concern. Is it bad news? I've moved closer and put an arm around her, and now she turns to me, thank goodness, she's smiling through the tears.

'He's just on his way to Lina's place to pick Pumpkin up! She managed to get him back indoors this morning.'

'Oh, thank God!' I give her a hug. 'I'm *so* pleased.'

'Yes. Oh, I just hope the stupid woman doesn't let him escape again now, before Luke gets there.'

'I'm sure she won't,' I try to reassure her. 'Is he going to call again when he's got Pumpkin?'

'Yes. And – all being well – he'll take him back to the surgery, so the vet can check him over and check the microchip. It's just standard procedure, he said.'

'Fair enough.'

She doesn't refer any more to whatever it was she wanted to tell me, and I decide not to remind her. If it's something that's going to be difficult to talk about – as she implied – she won't want it to spoil her more optimistic mood. We've both forgotten about having a cup of tea now, too, and we spend the next few minutes simply enjoying a chat about Pumpkin and how lovely it's going to be when he's back home again. But as we pause for breath and turn our faces back up to the sun, she suddenly says:

'Oh, I forgot to ask how the meeting went last night. The Historical Society?'

'Well . . .' I feel the heat coming to my face just thinking about it – the way it ended. 'It was OK, but – look, if I tell you what happened, promise you won't laugh?'

'Of course I won't laugh. Why would I?'

'Because I've made an idiot of myself,' I say.

'OK, we all do that occasionally, don't we?' She waits, but I don't quite know how to start. 'What happened, Joy?' she encourages me. 'I *won't* laugh, I promise.'

'Well, I thought someone – a man at the Historical Society . . . I thought he was interested in me,' I manage to blurt out.

'The one you told me about? Howard, wasn't it?'

I just nod.

'And . . . were you interested back?' she asks gently.

'I'm a married woman, Sara!' I protest, conscious that I'm sounding like a Victorian lady having a fit of the vapours. And, more to the point, I'm aware that I'm not protesting to Sara, I'm reminding *myself*.

'I know,' she says. 'But when you're on a diet, you can still lust after chocolate eclairs in the cake shop, can't you? It doesn't mean you're going to eat one.'

I burst out laughing at this, and then abruptly stop.

'Look, I'm sixty-five, for God's sake,' I say. 'It wasn't a question of *lusting*. It was just . . . nice to think someone had actually noticed me.'

'I get that, Joy, I really do. Especially if Terry's . . . not taking as much interest in you as you'd like at the moment. And anyway, I don't actually think there's much harm in a little bit of innocent flirtation, whether you're married or not – and no matter how old you are.'

'Maybe not. But I got it all wrong anyway. He wasn't interested in me at all. Only to help him organise the meetings of the bloody society and try to attract new members. I thought he was asking me out for a drink – as in, you know . . . ' I'm blushing even more now. I can't even look at her. 'As in a date, or something. And I panicked. It's one thing to fantasise about someone liking you, wanting to . . . take you out, or whatever, but it's another thing to contemplate it actually happening. I panicked, and he said he only meant talking about the bloody society's programme and bloody membership over a drink.'

I wouldn't have blamed her if she'd burst out laughing, but she doesn't.

'Poor you,' she says. 'It must have been embarrassing. But—' she reaches out for my hand now '—have you thought that perhaps he *did* really want to take you out for a drink – as in a date – but as soon as he saw he'd panicked you, he backtracked and pretended it was just to talk about the society?'

'No.' I shake my head. 'No, and why would he? How ridiculous of me to even *think* such a thing. Look at me – dumpy, old and grey – as well as married.'

'Joy, you're lovely. You don't look anywhere near your age. Is *he* old and grey himself?'

'Well.' I shrug, trying not to blush again. 'He's just normal, you know, for his age. OK, perhaps he *doesn't* quite look sixty-five, but—'

'But he's just a nice, pleasant guy who you enjoyed chatting to. And why shouldn't that continue, now you've got the awkwardness out of the way, and he knows you're not up for anything more?'

'Because it would *always* be awkward now! I really couldn't face him again, Sara. I feel a complete idiot. Like . . . like a teenager who's shown herself up in front of the whole class.'

'Just brazen it out, love,' she says. 'I would! He'll respect you for it.'

'I don't care whether he does or not. I never want to see him again. I'm not going back.'

'Ah, come on. I can't believe how upset you're getting about this. I'm not being funny, but presumably you've got a lot of life experience behind you by now, a lot of ups and downs and ... and hurts of various magnitudes. Why let a little social faux pas like this get the better of you? I know you feel embarrassed at the moment, but if you go straight back next week, face him – get it over with – I'm sure it'll settle down again. You might even find you can laugh about it together eventually.'

'Huh! I don't think so.'

'Well, see how you feel by next week. You were enjoying the meetings until this happened. You seemed quite excited after the first one. Look, why don't you concentrate instead on what you've managed to find out from the meetings – about Angel Cove, and Freda's sister? Come on, bring me up to date – I'm really interested.'

'OK,' I agree. I look up at her and try to smile. 'Sorry. I'm a silly old fool, aren't I?'

'No. You're just a human being!' she says, smiling back. 'We all do silly things, whatever our age.'

'I suppose so. Thank God for other women. We're so much better at understanding each other, aren't we? Men are just useless.'

'You can say that again!'

I don't know if Sara's really as interested in hearing about what I found out last night as she says, or if she's just looking for something to keep her from thinking about Pumpkin until Luke calls again. But perhaps she's right, and it'll stop me thinking too much about Howard, too.

'Well, Freda did start talking about her sister again last night,' I tell her. 'It was quite funny really. One of the other ladies happened to tell us she and her husband used to *canoodle* on the beach here at Angel Cove—'

'*Canoodle!*' Sara says, laughing.

'Yes! And Freda then said that's what Chrissie did: she canoodled on the beach with Philip – the boy who lived next-door – and it led to a lot of trouble – pretty obvious what that meant – but they ended up getting married.'

'Ah; so that's when she was a bridesmaid.'

'Yes. She seemed to feel guilty about her sister in some way. She said she should have helped her, and said something about being jealous. It was obviously upsetting her, and I didn't want to make things worse by asking any more questions.'

'No, of course not. Did she say Chrissie was older than her?'

'No: quite a bit younger, apparently but one of the other ladies told me she died of cancer some years ago.'

'Oh, that's sad. I expect you'd have liked to meet her. Did she live in your cottage, or mine?'

'Yours. Philip lived in mine. And I was told he's probably still alive, and living somewhere in the area.'

'Oh! Are you going to try to find him?'

'I don't know. I think I might just forget about the whole thing. I don't really know why I wanted to find out about them.'

'Yes, you do,' she says. 'It's because they lived in these cottages, and it's interesting to know what their story is. What's wrong with that?' She gives me a look. 'You're just saying that because you don't want to be involved in the Historical Society any more! But surely, you've got enough information now to try to track down this Philip, haven't you? Even if you *don't* ever go back to the meetings – which would be a shame, if you ask me,' she adds with a smile.

'I suppose so,' I say. 'Apparently Philip might be living in one of those complexes for the elderly.'

'Sheltered accommodation? My mum used to live in one of those, in Plymouth. You could google *apartments for the elderly* – or *sheltered accommodation – near me*. It shouldn't be too difficult.'

'You sound more excited about it than me!' I comment, laughing.

'Well, it'd be interesting for both of us, wouldn't it, to find out about the couple who lived here in our cottages and fell in love? I'd love to know their story.'

'Yes. Me too,' I admit. I give her a smile as I get to my feet. 'OK. Thanks for listening, Sara. And . . . for the encouragement. You're right: I'll go home and start googling for Philip.'

Later

In fact, it doesn't take me long at all to find out where Philip Sutton lives. There only appear to be two sheltered complexes for the elderly listed online in the local area: one about two miles from the other side of Bierleigh, and one in a neighbouring village, Ferndell. I call the first one, Adelphi Park, but the manager tells me they don't have anyone by the name of Sutton living there. I then try Goldcrest Lodge in Ferndell. The manager here seems reluctant to tell me whether Mr Sutton lives there, but she rather gives the game away by saying, 'Can I ask whether Philip is a personal friend of yours?' So I take a chance, and type a short letter to Mr Philip Sutton, care of Goldcrest Lodge, explaining that I've found out that I live in his old house, also mentioning that I know his sister-in-law, through the Historical Society.

'I wondered if you'd be willing to have a short chat with me about your early life at Angel Cove?' I write. 'I promise not to take up too much of your time, but, of course, if you'd rather not, I quite understand.' And I add my phone number.

After printing this off, I get distracted by some emails, and by lunchtime I'm still wasting time reading some posts on the Bierleigh Facebook group, from people complaining about dog walkers who don't clear up their pets' mess. I get up to consider what to have for lunch, when I notice an ancient-looking white Fiat pull up outside Sara's house, and Luke jumping out of the car, reaching into the back seat and picking up a cat carrier.

I'm too excited to think – until it's too late – about being polite and not interfering. I'm out of my front door and running down the path to meet him at exactly the same time as Sara bursts out of her own door.

'Pumpkin!' she squeals, grabbing the cage out of Luke's hands and turning to take it straight inside. Then she stops, turns and says, awkwardly, 'Sorry – thank you, Luke. I . . . really appreciate it. I suppose you . . . I mean, would you like a coffee or anything?'

Charlie's now followed Sara out of the house and is literally jumping from foot to foot with excitement, asking for Pumpkin to be brought inside and let out of the cage.

'Yes, all right, Charlie,' she laughs. 'Just make sure all the windows and doors are closed, please. I don't want him getting out again yet!' She turns back to Luke; I can see she's making an effort to be nice – she's obviously so relieved and grateful. 'Come in, Luke. And you, Joy – come and join the celebration!'

Once we're all in the sitting room, with Pumpkin purring on Charlie's lap, Luke – who seems to have got over his own awkwardness around Sara – starts to tell us what happened when he went to Lina's place today.

'The thing is, of course, that she doesn't think the way you or I might do,' he begins.

'That's fairly clear,' Sara says crossly.

He nods. 'I completely understand how you must feel, believe me. But I've now managed to have a word with Lina's carer, Amy—'

'Her *carer*?'

'Yes. She was there when I went today, and we had a chat outside, after I'd got Pumpkin safely into the car. She told me Lina's only been living independently for a few months. She does have learning difficulties. She was living with a member of her family before, but she's now been given this flat: it's the ground floor of one of those semi-detached houses that were converted into maisonettes. Apparently, she manages pretty well on her own, but Amy calls to check on her every day.'

'How old is she – Lina?' I ask. For some reason I've got the impression she's very young, but I'm surprised when Luke says:

'Oh, middle-aged. I'd guess well into her fifties, although she's quite childlike.' He shrugs. 'Amy said Lina had genuinely believed Pumpkin was a stray and thought she could keep him. She'd called him Bobby. Amy was having trouble making her understand that she should have taken him to the vet's, and she was about to call in and tell us about the situation herself, when that neighbour saw Lina with Pumpkin and told us anyway. She says Lina feels really upset and guilty about it now that she understands.'

'So I guess it wasn't really her fault,' I concede.

'No, not really,' Luke agrees. 'Even today, I think she was genuinely frightened that she was going to get into trouble. I had to promise her nobody was angry or upset with her. And she cried her eyes out when I picked Pumpkin up to put him in the travelling cage. She asked me to say sorry to you – his *proper mummy*, she said – and tell you she didn't mean to upset you or Charlie. "But I'm going to miss Bobby now – I mean Pumpkin," she said. "I'm going to miss him ever so much." She actually sat down on the floor next to Pumpkin, and put her arms round him – like a little girl.' He sighs. 'It was … quite emotional, to be honest.'

I must admit I've got a lump in my throat.

Luke looks at Sara and adds quietly, 'But I realise that none of this will make you feel any better about it.'

I smile. I can't help myself. He just seems … so *nice*. So sympathetic and understanding – exactly how I would expect a fellow nurse to be, whether it's humans or animals they're caring for. I guess I still don't really know him, but it's odd that despite having been friends with him for so long, and despite how happy she is now he's found Pumpkin for her, Sara still doesn't seem very pleased to be in his company.

'Well,' she manages to say, after a moment, 'I suppose I can understand, now. And the main thing is, he's back.'

'Yes, definitely.' Luke pauses, then goes on: 'Lina did say she's always wanted a cat, and now she's got a flat of her own, she thought she could have one. But because she made such a bad mistake with Pumpkin, she doesn't think she ought to have one any more.' He shrugs. 'I don't know. I very nearly suggested she could look into adopting a rescue cat. But I'm going to talk to Amy again first – see if she thinks Lina really understands how to look after one, long term. If she thinks it'll be OK, I could take Lina to the pet shelter myself to choose one.'

'That's nice of you,' I say. 'You're obviously a cat lover.'

'I had a cat myself till recently. Furr-o.' He gives a little shrug. 'He was an Egyptian Mau, and his previous owners had called him that as a kind of play on words: *Pharoah*. I suppose they thought it was funny. To be honest it seemed a bit silly to me, but I couldn't change it. He wouldn't have liked that.'

I laugh. I like people who treat their pets as friends, and respect their feelings. I can see why he works as a veterinary nurse.

'You haven't got Furr-o any more?' I ask sympathetically.

'No. He was quite an old boy, even when I adopted him. Died of old age at sixteen. I might get another cat eventually, but as I was moving, it wasn't a good time.'

'No, I suppose not.'

'Well,' Luke goes on, 'I'd better get back to work; I've overrun my lunch break.' He gets to his feet and looks at Sara, who looks down at the floor. 'I'm really glad it's worked out OK,' he says. 'I don't think Pumpkin will wander off again, you know. He's probably learned his lesson.'

'Thanks again,' Sara says.

'Yes, thanks, Luke,' I agree. Not that Pumpkin's my cat, or anything, but I just feel like Luke deserves double the thanks, and Sara – even though I know how grateful she is – seems a bit lukewarm with hers.

'Thank you *loads* and *loads*, Luke!' chimes in another little voice – and we all look at Charlie, who's still cuddling his cat and stroking his little head. 'I missed Pumpkin *so* much and I'm *so* happy he's back!'

'What a relief,' I say to Sara after Luke's driven off.

'Yes!' She laughs as Pumpkin jumps from Charlie's lap to hers and starts to purr. 'Well, at least *one* thing in my life is back on track now.'

'Perhaps the good-luck angel of Angel Cove is giving you a look-in, eh?'

'Mm,' she says, looking away as she strokes Pumpkin distractedly. 'Perhaps.'

Friday 26 October

It's nearly the end of October, and as if to make the point that we can forget summer ever happened now and start preparing for winter, it's pouring with rain. I stay in the house all morning, and I'm just putting some washing in the tumble dryer when I hear my phone ringing in the bedroom where I've left it on charge. I manage to get to it just before the call goes to voicemail.

'Hello, is that Joy Vincent?' I don't recognise the caller's voice, but his tone is deep and pleasant, probably that of someone a little older than myself. Somehow, he doesn't sound like a cold-caller, but of course, we're primed, these days, to be suspicious.

'Um – who's this?'

'This is Philip Sutton.' As I start with surprise, he pauses, then goes on: 'I *am* speaking to Joy Vincent, am I?'

'Yes, yes. I'm sorry, Mr Sutton.'

'Call me Philip,' he says, laughing. 'It's the modern thing to do, isn't it – so I'm told. People don't seem to bother with formalities now.'

'Thank you, Philip.' I sit down on the bed, beginning to feel a little spark of excitement. 'I hope you didn't mind me writing to you out of the blue like that.'

'Not at all, Joy. I was fascinated by your letter. I can't remember the last time anyone was interested in hearing about my past life.'

'It probably seems a bit odd,' I say. 'But I found out about you through Freda, you see. I was trying to research the origins of the name of Angel Cove—'

'The old legend about the angel!' He laughs again. 'Oh yes. I could tell you a little story about that.'

'I'd love to hear it.' I smile. He sounds nice.

'Poor old Freda,' he goes on. 'How is she?'

'I don't know her very well,' I admit. 'But obviously, she gets quite confused, so I wasn't sure what to make of the things she was saying.'

'Yes, I know she's gone badly downhill, poor thing. I can't manage to get to see her these days, sadly.'

He doesn't explain why, and I don't like to ask. Perhaps he'll tell me more when – if – I get to speak to him in person. Which we haven't discussed yet, and there's now an uncomfortable pause, and I'm wondering if he's just going to say goodbye. So I rush on a bit awkwardly:

'Um, so how would you feel about me coming to see you for more of a chat? I know it's a bit of a cheek – you don't know me – but—'

'Well, of course I'd like you to come and see me!' he says at once. 'I wouldn't have called you otherwise! I can't wait to meet you. I'm just as fascinated by the fact that you live in my old house, as you seem to be to hear my story.'

'That's really kind of you,' I begin, but he interrupts me at once.

'Not at all. I hardly get any visitors these days, apart from the warden of this prison facility I live in – checking up on me to make sure I'm still alive!'

'Ah, don't say that!' I laugh. Margaret at the Historical Society told me Philip would be about seventy-seven or seventy-eight now, but he certainly doesn't sound his age. I wonder why he's chosen to move into sheltered accommodation. Perhaps he has some health issues, or maybe he just didn't like living on his own. 'Well, when would be convenient for you?'

'Whenever you like. I don't exactly have a diary packed with commitments,' he says lightly. 'How about Monday morning? Is that too soon?'

'No, that'd be great. Thanks so much, Philip. I really look forward to meeting you.'

'Likewise, Joy. Just press the button for visitors when you get to the front door here, and tell the old bat in charge that you're here to see me. I'll let her know to expect you. That'll start all the tongues wagging!'

I'm smiling to myself as I go back to the washing, feeling ridiculously pleased. I've got something to put in my diary! Something to look forward to. A reason to get in my car and go somewhere, and someone different to talk to. In fact, I'm so pleased about it that I give Sara a quick call to tell her.

'Oh, that's great!' she says, as soon as I've said that Philip called me. 'Actually, Joy, why don't you pop over, if you're not busy? You can tell me about it while we have a quick cup of coffee – or tea.'

'Are you sure? You're not doing something with Charlie?'

'Not at the moment. He's working on his fourth or fifth painting of the day; he's happy.'

Sara's opened her back door so that I can rush straight in, but the jacket I've slipped on over my clothes is drenched anyway. When it rains heavily, down here on the Devon coast, it really means it; the clouds open and empty themselves as if God has pulled a plug up in heaven. My hair, luckily, is short enough for me to be able to shake it, like a dog, and Sara and I are laughing as I peel off my jacket. Charlie's watching me, smiling, as he sits at the kitchen table with his paints, and I chat to him while the kettle's boiling.

'These are fabulous, Charlie,' I tell him, looking at the pictures he's painted today. One is of the beach and sea outside, the rain portrayed not by straight lines of grey or blue paint in the way I imagine most children might do, but by brush streaks of water overlaying the scene. Then there's a realistic picture of this house, with himself and his mum smiling on the doorstep. And two different pictures of Pumpkin, one showing him in a street, looking frightened, and another where he's curled up, contented, in his own bed – as he is now.

'Let's go and sit in the living room, Joy,' Sara suggests when she's finished making the tea. 'Are you all right there, Charlie, or do you want to watch something on the TV?'

'I'll just finish this picture,' he says, already concentrating on his next masterpiece.

'So tell me what Philip Sutton said,' she encourages me as soon as we're sitting down. 'Was he OK about talking to you?'

'Yes, he seemed quite keen. I got the impression he's lonely. He's invited me to go and see him on Monday.'

We chat for a while about what I'm going to ask Philip, what I'm hoping to find out about. Then we go on to talk some more about Charlie's pleasure at having Pumpkin home again. And then – just as I've finished my tea and I'm about to get up and go – Sara says, her voice suddenly sounding a bit shaky:

'Well, I never did get around to ... what I wanted to tell you, did I.'

'Oh – no, you didn't. We got sidetracked by Pumpkin coming home. And, well, I thought I should wait until you were ready to bring it up again.'

She shakes her head. 'I'll probably never really feel ready. But I do want to tell you. I need to tell someone, because until I say it out loud, it isn't going to feel real.' She takes a deep breath, and then comes straight out with it. 'The thing is – I'm pregnant.'

'Oh!' Of course, given the circumstances, I don't know whether I should be pleased for her or not. I watch her expression, hoping for a clue, but what I wasn't anticipating was to see a tear roll down her cheek, swiftly followed by more, which she tries hastily to wipe away with the back of her hand.

'Oh, for God's sake!' she splutters, sounding angry with herself. 'I wanted to tell you *without* getting all emotional like this! It's just—'

I jump up and go to put my arms round her. 'Don't apologise. I quite understand. It must have been hard, finding out, after . . . being on your own like this.'

'Yes.' She nods, wipes her tears again and sits up straight, making a visible effort to control herself. 'It was. So ironic, too. At one time this would have been so exactly what I wanted. But now . . .'

'How far along are you?' I ask her gently.

'About eight weeks, I think.' She drops her head. 'I feel really stupid; I only started to realise it about a week ago. I knew I was late, but I just put it down to, you know, the situation. The move. The stress.' She shrugs and sighs again. 'Well, perhaps I did suspect, but I didn't want to believe it.'

'You didn't feel sick, at all? Or any other symptoms, apart from being late?'

'No. But I didn't with Charlie, either. I seem to be lucky in that respect.' She sighs. 'If not in any other.'

'Ah, don't say that.' I smile down at her. 'I know it must be a shock, but—'

'But you probably think I'm being ungrateful. You must think it's terrible of me, not to be happy that I'm having another baby, when you couldn't have any yourself.'

'I don't think that, at all,' I tell her emphatically. 'Don't forget I've been a nurse all my working life. I've counselled lots of girls and women who found themselves pregnant unexpectedly, and I would never have dreamed of letting my own circumstances influence anything I said to them.'

'Of course you wouldn't. I'm sorry. I didn't mean anything—'

'I know you didn't, love.' I wait for a moment before going on. 'I presume it's definite? I mean, you've done a test?'

'Yes,' she says, nodding. 'I did two, just to make sure! Positive.'

I hesitate, unsure whether I know her well enough yet to ask. I think we've become pretty close in a relatively short time, but I don't want to cause offence. 'Have you decided,' I go on, trying to phrase it as delicately as I can, 'what you're going to do?'

'You mean whether I'll keep it? Yes, I'll have to. I can't ... my conscience wouldn't let me do anything else.' She gives a little smile. 'I was brought up a Catholic. I haven't really kept my faith, but, well, when you've grown up on warnings about sin and damnation, it gets kind of ingrained into your psyche, never really leaves you, even if you choose not to believe in it any more.'

'I can understand that.' We're both quiet for a moment, then I add: 'What does Rob say?'

She blinks. 'Rob? I haven't told him.'

'Oh.'

I'm just wondering how to point out that she'll need to do so, obviously, and perhaps sooner would be better than later, when she suddenly stands up, so that she's facing away from me. Making it easier. So I'm already hit by the realisation of what she's going to tell me, before she even begins to utter the words:

'It isn't Rob's.'

'Right.'

'It's someone else's. A mistake. A really, really stupid mistake.'

'Ah, I see.' Poor Sara. She probably ran into the arms of another man to console herself because of Rob and his girl-friend. Who could blame her? It's the most understandable thing in the world. 'Have you told *him*, then – Mr Mistake? Or shouldn't I ask?'

She turns back. 'You're not shocked? I'm still married, after all.'

'Your husband doesn't seem to think you are, though, does he? You're separated, and *of course* I'm not shocked, Sara, don't be silly! But you do need to tell him, don't you – the father. He needs to know.'

'I don't want to.' She scowls. I'm surprised. Whoever he is, wouldn't she want his support – emotional, at least, and hopefully financial too, in due course? 'He won't be interested,' she goes on. 'This is *my* mistake, and it'll be *my* baby. I don't need Luke to get involved.'

'*Luke*,' I say softly. 'Ah.'

Now I understand; it all makes sense – their embarrassment at meeting again, and realising they've both moved to the same area. The awkwardness between them. But – I frown to myself, looking back at her, puzzled. It doesn't really explain her antagonism – an antagonism he doesn't seem to return. But I get the feeling she might not want to say any more. She gets to her feet, wiping a hand across her eyes.

'I'm going to have another cup of tea,' she says. 'I feel like I need it. Want one?'

'Let me make it. I'll go and fill the kettle, shall I? I pause and add, 'I presume this is why you've been drinking decaf coffee and tea?'

'Yes. Mostly herbal teas. But only since I realised I was pregnant. I hope I haven't done the baby any harm before then. I *was* drinking tea, and coffee, and the odd glass of wine. I wasn't *trying* to get pregnant, you see, so—'

'I'm sure a few caffeinated drinks before you realised won't have harmed the baby,' I reassure her.

'Thanks, Joy.' She rubs her tummy, looking down at herself as if she's still trying to believe it's true. 'I feel bad for thinking about the baby as a problem, a nuisance, something that shouldn't have happened. I don't want to . . . hurt it. I don't want to cause it harm.'

'I know. Of course you don't.'

'And sorry for blubbing. I'm OK, really. I'll be fine. I'll just have to . . . get on with it.'

'I'm sure you *will* be fine. You're a coper – I can tell.'

I go through to the kitchen and make the tea, while having a quick chat to Charlie, who's still busy with his painting. Sara and I sit in silence in the living room while we drink it.

'Well, look,' I say eventually, as I don't know what more I can do, 'if you need someone to talk to about this, any time at all, you know I'll always listen. I understand it's difficult for you, but really you should . . . perhaps . . . think about telling Luke.'

'Maybe,' she says quickly. 'But not yet. I've barely even got my own head around it yet.'

'OK. Well—'

I'm just about to say I'd better go, when there's a shout from the kitchen.

'Mum! I've spilt my water all over my painting!'

She manages a short little laugh. 'All right, Charlie, I'm coming. Sorry, Joy. I was going to explain . . . about Luke—'

'You don't have to,' I tell her firmly. 'Go and see to Charlie. I'll leave you to it. We'll catch up again when you're feeling more like it, OK?'

'Thanks,' she says. 'Charlie! Grab the sponge from by the sink. Oh dear,' she adds with a ghost of a smile to me, 'I hope I can save his painting!'

But as I follow her back through the kitchen – where Charlie's frantically dabbing at what is, in fact, just a tiny drop of water on the very edge of his painting – I can't help thinking that it's easier to save a painting than it is to save her little family's happiness. I wonder whether a new baby will do it – or not.

Monday 29 October

The rain carried on all weekend, streaking down like needles from the sky, hiding the horizon, turning our view of the sea and sky into one great blurry murky cloud. Much as I love every season here, there's no denying a wet weekend at this time of year is probably the dreariest thing that can happen. Even a thunderstorm is better – more exciting, seeing the dark clouds roll in and watching the lightning over the sea – and at least they don't carry on relentlessly like this for hour after soggy, grey hour.

I think even Terry was fed up with the rain by yesterday. He was more restless than usual, getting up from his chair, putting his laptop down, walking to the window and staring out of it. I kept trying to initiate a conversation, keeping the tone light, asking if he'd like to watch a film, or play a game of cards if he'd finished his work. But he just sighed and said he needed to get on.

'Is something wrong, Terry?' I asked him, deciding to try a different approach. 'I know you keep saying you're just busy, but is anything worrying you?'

For a moment, I actually thought he was going to open up and confide something to me. He stood there with his back to me, staring out at the rain, seeming to think it over for a moment or two before suddenly shaking his head and saying no, nothing was wrong, he was just tired because he's been so busy.

The thing is, I'm tired, too. Tired of worrying about it, trying to get through to him, trying to work him out. Tired of feeling hurt and bewildered by the way he's behaving, wondering if it's my fault, whether, in fact, I do really need to find myself more *little hobbies*, when all I want is to spend an occasional half-hour or so with my husband. It's not too much to ask, is it? But I can't carry on bashing my head against a brick wall.

This morning the sun's trying its best to make an appearance through the clouds, although everywhere is still wet from yesterday's heavy rain, huge puddles filling every dip in the lane, every strip of hedgerow slick with red mud.

I'm going to Ferndell today to meet Philip Sutton. The sunshine is warming me through the car windows as I navigate the country lanes, the radio playing old rock music. Ferndell's only about three miles from Bierleigh by road. In fact, it's more direct to walk there through the footpaths, but the last thing I wanted to do was arrive at Philip's place with muddy boots when he's being kind enough to invite me.

My satnav brings me to Goldcrest Lodge easily enough. The building is painted a light gold colour that makes it looks quite pretty in the pale wintery sunshine. I park in the car park and walk up to the main entrance, where, as Philip instructed me, I press the button for visitors and explain who I'm here to see. The door opens with a loud buzz, and the heat from inside hits me as I walk into the lobby.

'Mr Sutton is expecting you, Mrs Vincent,' says a woman approaching me as I enter. She's proudly wearing a name badge proclaiming her to be *Janet Bull, Warden.* 'His apartment is number nineteen. Ground floor, obviously.'

'Thank you,' I say, heading in the direction she's pointing, and wondering why it's *obvious*. 'I left the door ajar for you when I checked on him this morning,' she calls after me. 'To save him the trouble.'

Save him the trouble? The trouble of opening his own door? I get the impression, already, that Janet Bull's a bit too interfering. I thought these 'sheltered' places were supposed to be for independent living, with just a bit of help at hand if it's needed. I walk down the corridor, stripping off my coat as I go. The heat in here is blistering. Hopefully the residents have thermostats in their own flats, or they'll all be comatose. Perhaps that's the idea!

When I reach number nineteen, I ring the doorbell, out of politeness, despite the door being ajar.

'Hello, Philip! It's Joy Vincent,' I call through the gap.

'Come in, Joy,' he calls back. 'I'm just getting the kettle on.'

I push the door open and walk into a small hallway. A door on my right is open to a living room, and from what I presume to be the kitchen beyond, I can hear a clatter of cups.

'Tea or coffee?' Philip's voice calls as I walk into the lounge. No carpet or rugs, I notice – just a vinyl floor covering, one of the nice, expensive ones that manages not to feel as cold and hard as bare concrete. Unusual, though, I'd have thought, for the home of an elderly person. Otherwise it's a pleasant room, light and airy with lots of space, and a window with a view downhill to the little stream that runs nearby.

'Coffee, please, Philip. Milk, no sugar, thank you,' I say, walking towards the sound of his voice. There's no door here – just an arch-shaped entrance into the kitchen area. And as soon as I step through, I understand everything. Why Janet Bull seemed so interfering but is probably just caring and protective; why Philip's apartment is so uncluttered, why there aren't any carpets, why the cooker, and the kitchen units and cupboards, are all at waist level; and why Philip is 'obviously' on the ground floor. There's a lift in the building, of course, but in the event of a fire that wouldn't be safe. He's a wheelchair user.

'I'm sorry,' I say, as he looks round from stirring the coffees and sees me hesitating in the doorway. 'I didn't realise . . .'

'Oh, nothing for you to be sorry about!' he laughs. 'My fault, I never think to mention it to people. I always forget it can make people feel uncomfortable.'

'No, not at all, it's just that I understand now why the warden left your door open!' I say with a chuckle.

'She's an old bat!' He laughs. 'She means well, but she forgets I'm quite capable of getting myself around. That was the whole point of having this place adapted for me before I moved in. Anyway, I'm pleased to meet you, Joy. Go and sit down, I'll bring the coffee.'

'Let me take the cups for you,' I offer, but he's already lifting the tray off the low worktop and fitting it across the armrests of his wheelchair with a click.

'All mod cons!' he says as he follows me into the living room, where he puts the tray on the coffee table. He lifts himself out of his wheelchair with the help of a frame next to one of the armchairs, and lowers himself back down with a sigh. 'Nice to have a change of seat,' he jokes, and he pulls a light blanket over his legs. 'One leg amputated below the knee,' he confirms with a smile, seeing that I couldn't help noticing. 'Diabetes.'

'Peripheral arterial disease?'

'Yes.' He gives me a look of understanding. 'Of course, you said you were a nurse?'

'Until very recently, actually. Only retired last month.'

'Ah, I see.' He nods, takes a sip of his coffee, and then sits up straighter, obviously deciding to change the subject. 'Anyway, so you're living in Smugglers' Cottages!'

'Yes. Number one.'

'My old house,' he says, smiling. 'Such memories.'

'I was hoping you'd say that. I'll be honest, Philip: originally, I was just trying to find out about the legend – the Angel of the Cove. But when I learned through Freda, and her friends, that you used to live in my house, well, obviously I'd *love* to hear about your memories of living there, Philip. So would my neighbour in number two.'

'Ah, Chrissie's family's house,' he says. He sips his coffee again, gazing across the room at the sunlight streaming through the window, a faraway expression in his eyes. 'My little Chrissie. My sweetheart. My dear love.'

Unexpectedly, I feel quite choked with emotion. After all this time, even now she's gone, he still calls her his sweetheart, his voice still softening over her name.

'Freda mentioned your wedding,' I remind him, as he appears to be lost in thought.

'Yes,' he says. 'Nineteen sixty. Sometimes it only feels like yesterday – but also, strangely, it could have been another planet. Everything's changed so much in the intervening years.'

'I know. I'm not much younger than you,' I say, smiling.

'I'm seventy-six,' he says, as if to correct me. He doesn't look it. He's still got a surprising amount of steel-grey hair, cropped short to his head, dark blue eyes and a smile that softens the lines of his face. 'Chrissie would have been seventy-three now.'

'So you were neighbours, down at Angel Cove?' I encourage him.

'Angel Cove.' He sighs and shakes his head. 'I'm sorry, I don't think I can help you about the legend. As far as I know, people have believed in the angel for ever – including my parents.' He gives a little chuckle now, as if at some private joke, and then smiles at me and goes on: 'But yes, I lived there with my family. Mum, Dad, and two younger brothers – twins. One dead now, the other one living overseas.'

'Quite a family, in such a small house.'

'It was fine, we boys shared the bigger bedroom – the twins slept in the same bed till they got too big,' he laughs. 'Then all our beds were shoved up together, we had to climb over each other to get in and out.'

'Sounds like fun.'

He shrugs. 'I was never as close to the twins as they were to each other. I was closer to Chrissie.'

'Even when you were kids?'

'Oh yes. From when she was knee-high to a grasshopper. I looked after her. I loved her.'

'And she had an older sister, of course. Freda.'

'Freda was ten when Chrissie was born. Had her nose put out of joint! They didn't used to get on. People said she was an old maid because she didn't get married – people were cruel. Nobody talked about lesbians back then, did they. It was whispered about, laughed about, but nobody showed any understanding. Looking back, I'm glad she had Doris. Glad she had a chance to live with somebody she loved. But . . . ' He hesitated, then went on, his smile slipping: 'She wasn't very understanding, at first, about Chrissie and me.'

'Freda said something, when we were talking at the historical meeting, about being jealous of the two of you, getting married. "Always the bridesmaid, never the bride", she said.'

'I know.' He nods. 'I realise that, realised it at the time, too, I think. But I hated her for what she said to Chrissie, when Chrissie was asking for her advice. She was her big sister! She should have helped her, when Chrissie confided in her, not called her names.' He sits back in his chair, takes a last mouthful of his coffee and puts the cup down. 'If she'd helped – if she'd just been kind to Chrissie, when we found out she was pregnant – and tried to talk to their parents for her, well, we might not have had to do what we did.'

I don't know what he's referring to, of course – about what they did – but I don't want to break the spell, while he's reminiscing, staring across at the view from the window again, seeming to have almost forgotten that I'm there. But, a moment later, he suddenly seems to come back into the here and now, turning to give me a little grin, so that I get a glimpse of the cheeky young man he might have once been.

'Actually,' he says, 'd'you know what, Joy? Looking back now, remembering what happened, knowing how it all turned out, I don't think I'd have wanted it any other way. No. I wouldn't go back and change a thing.'

February 1960:
Sunday, close to midnight

Philip could see Chrissie was shivering even before she reached the spot on the beach where he was waiting for her. She couldn't have been cold – she was wearing her warmest clothes, her big coat, her boots, hat, scarf and gloves, just as he'd told her to – so he knew she was shaking with fear.

'Don't be scared,' he whispered, putting his arm around her and hoping his voice didn't betray his own fear.

'I was so terrified Freda was going to hear me getting up,' she whispered back. 'I had to creep around the bedroom getting dressed in the dark. She kept grunting in her sleep and I was sure she'd suddenly sit up and shout out to Mum.'

'I know. I thought the twins were never going to stop talking and joking around, and go to sleep,' he agreed. 'I'm not going to miss sharing a room with *them*.'

He glanced down at Chrissie, wondering if the reality of what they were doing was finally hitting home with her, as it was with him. Leaving home. Possibly never coming back. Having each other, but nobody else. He'd been so determined, felt so strong and brave, while he was secretly packing his bags. But now, out on the beach, under the brooding night sky, he felt less sure. And he was just as nervous as Chrissie, that they'd suddenly see her kitchen light turn on, and her father silhouetted in the doorway.

'Quick,' she said, her teeth chattering. 'Let's get going, in case they wake up and notice we're gone. We need to run. We've got to get as far as we can before—'

'It's OK, we're not running anywhere,' he said, leading her down the beach. 'Give me your bag.'

'Where's yours?' she said, looking in surprise at his lack of luggage.

'In the boat already. We're taking the boat, Chris. It's the only way.'

'Your dad's boat?' she gasped. 'No, come on, we can't! It's *stealing.*'

'We can. We have to.'

He was forcing himself to sound calm. He didn't want Chrissie to know about the hours that evening that he'd spent arguing with himself about it, tormented by indecision, sick at heart at the thought of the damage he was going to do. Taking his father's livelihood, destroying his family, cutting ties with them for ever, because this wasn't something that they'd ever be able to forgive. And weighing it all up against the probability, if they stayed, of Chrissie's parents sending her away, making her give up the baby, refusing to let them see each other any more. It was no good; he didn't like what he was doing, but he had to put Chrissie first. He'd got her into this mess; he had to protect her now. And anyway, it wasn't the only theft he was guilty of. He'd also emptied the tin where his mum kept the housekeeping money. Knowing how little she had to manage on every week, he felt hot and weak with shame at the thought of this, but how on earth else were he and Chrissie going to live until he could get a job?

'Come on. It'll be OK,' he said. He grasped her hand firmly and led her towards the shadowy shape of the little fishing boat moored at the sheltered end of the beach, away from the rocks.

'Where are we going to sail to, though?' she asked in a frightened little whisper.

'France. I heard somewhere that girls can get married at fifteen in France.'

'Are you sure?' Chrissie shivered even more.

'Well, that was what I heard,' Philip said. He didn't really know much about France, of course, apart from what he'd been taught at school. Neither of them had ever been abroad – nor had anybody in either of their families, or even anybody they knew. 'Anyway, even if we *can't* get married there, we can live together and nobody will know we're not married. But I really want us to get married, Chris. That's how it should be. We should be married, before the baby comes.'

'Well . . .' He could see her wavering. They were at the water's edge now, and although he understood her doubts, he needed her to agree, to be prepared to get into the boat and go, before it was too late.

'Look,' he said gently, 'if we *can* get married in France, perhaps we'll be able to come back again. If we come back and show our parents we're married, there'll be nothing they can do about it.'

He didn't like lying to her. If he ever came back from France, his parents would probably get him locked up for stealing the boat, never mind getting Chrissie pregnant while she was under-age – married or not. But he knew that if she believed they might actually be able to return one day, that this might not be goodbye to her family for ever, the whole thing might feel less frightening for her.

'OK,' she said, her voice almost drowned out by the sound of the waves. 'But . . . the sea looks ever so rough, Phil.'

'It seems worse because it's night-time, and it's cold,' he said. 'You trust me, don't you?'

'Yes, 'course I do.'

Philip was a competent sailor. He'd been going to sea with his father and uncle ever since he was a little boy, and during recent years he'd often taken the boat out on his own. He knew all about the tides and the local hazards of submerged rocks and dangerous currents. Their family boat was small but sturdy, and Philip was easily as strong as his father, if not stronger.

He settled Chrissie into the boat, covering her carefully with an oilskin over the top of her coat.

'How long will it take to get to France?' she asked.

'Um, probably a few hours,' he said, hoping he sounded surer than he felt. He'd studied the map, the charts, he knew where he was heading, which direction to take, and how many nautical miles it was. He just didn't want to estimate a length of time that might prove to be completely unrealistic if conditions changed during the crossing. 'Why don't you snuggle down and try to get some sleep?'

'I won't be able to,' she protested. 'I'm too nervous.'

Philip started the motor, and they both looked back at their cottages. He half expected the noise of the engine to wake their parents; that at any minute he'd see a light go on in a window, or see one of their parents running out of their door, waving their arms, demanding that they came back. But nothing happened. The little boat, its chugging muffled by the density of the clouds hanging low over the sea, quickly powered away from the beach, away from Smugglers' Cottages – gradually looking smaller and smaller in the distance – and finally, out of Angel Cove altogether and onto the open water.

He glanced at Chrissie and saw that, despite what she'd said, her eyes were beginning to close as she sat, huddled warmly and rocked by the motion of the waves. She must have been exhausted from all the worry and stress, he thought, as he watched her with a mixture of tenderness and anxiety.

She slept on for hours, through the bouncing of the boat as, further out to sea, the waves got bigger and wilder. She even stayed asleep when seawater began to splash over the side of the boat, and when, later, it started to rain – light, sleety drizzle at first, being swept into their faces by the cold wind blowing down the English Channel from the Atlantic beyond, carrying the little boat steadily off course, despite the best efforts of its capable but under-experienced young captain.

Philip sat as close to her as he could, trying to shelter her with his body as he did his best to steer the boat through the darkness. Chrissie slept on, unawares, and he liked to think she might be dreaming of something happy – perhaps of being on a fairground ride with her friends from school – and that she might not wake up until the storm had passed, and he'd never have to tell her how scared he was becoming.

It was the thunder and lightning that finally did wake her. And she stared at Philip in shock to hear him swearing out loud, shouting into the heavens that he was an idiot. Telling her in a shaking voice about the one thing he'd forgotten – stupid, stupid fool that he was, for putting both their lives in such danger. He'd forgotten the cardinal rule his father had drummed into him: never believe the fuel gauge. On a small boat like this, the gauge wasn't reliable, it could show a full tank when it was actually nowhere near full. His father never left the tank full while the boat was moored; he always filled it before setting off. Philip *knew* that; he'd been taught that, ever since his father first started taking him out to sea. How the hell had he forgotten it today, of all days, when it mattered more than ever?

They were going to be cast adrift in the middle of a storm. And it was all because of his own stupid haste to run away, like a pathetic, frightened baby, instead of being a man and facing the consequences, facing Chrissie's parents and standing firm by her side as he knew in his heart he should have done.

Chrissie was clinging to him now, as the thunder crashed above them, the rain pelted down and the boat rocked frantically from side to side. And – coward that he now recognised himself to be – Philip covered his face with his hands and cried.

Monday 29 October

Philip's staring at the floor, his face creased in distress, his hands clenched. The memory of that night in the boat with Chrissie must be terrible for him. I'm beginning to wish I hadn't asked him to talk to me.

'I'm sorry,' I say quietly. 'This must be awful for you to remember.'

He looks up at me as if he'd forgotten I'm here, shaking his head as he focuses on me sitting next to him and looking around, reminding himself where he is. Finally, he gives himself a little shake and says:

'Not at all. I said I'd tell you about what happened, didn't I.'

'But it must have been so scary! Out on the sea in the darkness, with a storm raging – and for God's sake, you were both only kids!'

'Yes, we were,' he agrees. 'We thought we were grown-up at the time, but looking back, of course we were just silly children, running away.'

'What happened? How did you survive?' I ask gently – but he's resting his head on his hand, now, and trying to smother a yawn. He's had enough. It must have taken it out of him – recalling that dreadful night.

'Would you mind if I tell you the rest another time?' he says.

'Of course. If you're sure you don't mind me coming back again?'

'I'd like it very much if you would.'

'When would suit you?' I ask, automatically looking at the calendar in my phone, even though I know I've got nothing planned for the foreseeable future.

'How about Saturday?' he suggests. 'I don't tend to see anyone at weekends. Not that I get many visitors anyway! But weekends ... well, somehow, they seem that little bit lonelier, when other people here are seeing their families.'

I have to bite my tongue to stop myself saying that it can be lonely at weekends too, when the person you live with is completely ignoring you. But how can I even think of feeling sorry for myself? At least my husband is still alive. I'm sure Philip would give anything to have his Chrissie, his *sweetheart*, back with him.

'Yes, Saturday would be fine,' I agree, and I tell him I'll see myself out, as frankly, he looks completely shattered.

'Say hello to Freda from me, when you see her at your society,' he calls after me. 'If she still manages to remember who I am.'

'I will.'

It's not till I'm leaving, that I remember – I said I wasn't going back to the Historical Society, didn't I. The meeting's tonight. I'm going to have to decide pretty quickly whether I can face it – face Howard – or not!

Pumpkin's lying on Sara's front doorstep as I pull up outside Smugglers' Cottages. He looks so contented there in the pale wintry sunshine, I find myself smiling, wanting to go and stroke him, but at the same time not wanting to disturb him. Until I met Pumpkin, I'd managed to put out of my mind my disappointment at not being able to have a cat. It's such a shame, especially now I'm not working. A pet would be such company for me. Then, out of nowhere, as I open my front door I have a sudden thought. Why shouldn't I get a dog? Terry has no problems with dogs, in fact, he's always liked them – his family had dogs when he was a kid. We've never had one since we've been together, because we've always both worked full-time, so it wouldn't have been fair. But now? What's stopping us? I could take a dog on lovely long walks, and looking after it would give me a new interest in life. I decide I'm going to talk to him about it.

Then I stop the thought instantly, remembering how difficult it's been to talk to him lately – how silent and distracted and ... just *different* he's been. I can't imagine how I can raise the subject of something as important as getting a dog with him, the way he is at the moment. He'll either just nod dismissively and tell me to go ahead, it'll be good for me to have *something else to keep me occupied*. Or he'll just turn on his laptop and say he's too busy to chat. And yet talking things over was always something Terry and I were so good at.

We were in our twenties when we met, and both living in Exeter. I was sharing a flat with two girlfriends, colleagues from the hospital where I'd started work after finishing my training. Terry lived on the same street. Three years older than me, and a chartered accountant, he'd already managed to acquire a flat of his own. We used to see each other in the street, and sometimes in the same pubs and bars of the city, and one morning when I was waiting at the bus stop in the rain, he pulled up in his car and offered me a lift. It went from there. He seemed so much more grown-up, sensible and serious than the junior doctors I normally dated, but we had fun, too. I always thought we complemented each other: I talked to him about things that annoyed me, he calmed me down; he talked to me about things he brooded over, I cheered him up. It wasn't long before I moved in with him. Then we bought a house together. And eventually we moved here, to

Angel Cove, and it was never going to be anything other than Happy Ever After. Until now.

I have some lunch and go for a short walk along the beach and up onto Harry's Plain – on my own, as Sara's busy working. I stroll back slowly, trying to make up my mind about this evening – the Historical Society meeting. I know Sara advised me to just *brazen it out* with Howard Hardcastle, and although I'm not sure I actually can, I'm beginning to wonder if it would really be so much worse than yet another evening sitting in silence, watching Terry glued to his laptop, not liking to interrupt him, even to ask his opinion about getting a dog. Despite everything I've said about never going back, I think I need a break from that – from the endless worry about what's wrong with Terry, what's going on, what he's not telling me.

So when the time comes, I do, after all, end up getting myself ready and leaving Terry his note and his usual plated meal, and I set off a bit early to make sure I've gone before he comes home. Of course, when I get to the village hall I don't want to go in, because I'm so early and I know Howard will probably be the only one here. This is ridiculous! I sit in the car, pretending to be sending a message on my phone, but really, I'm giving myself a stern lecture. It goes something like this:

What the hell is the matter with you? Are you a woman or a mouse? You used to be a sensible, intelligent, professional person who spoke her mind and took no nonsense from anyone. Look at you now – cowering in your own car like a pathetic schoolgirl, scared to face someone just because you embarrassed yourself, scared to face your own husband when you should be demanding answers from him! And what happened to your sense of humour – did you leave it behind when you retired? Why are you taking yourself so seriously these days? Can't you laugh off a bit of embarrassment? Get inside that hall and stop being so wet!

I get out of the car, slamming the door, and march into the hall, where – sure enough – Howard is on his own, arranging the chairs. I walk straight up to him, giving him what must probably look like a completely manic grin as he turns round and sees me, smiling a little nervously.

'Hello, Howard, how are you?' I boom, stumbling a little over the triple 'H', and aware that the volume of my voice matches the craziness of my smile. Without waiting for a response, I plough straight on without so much as a verbal full stop: 'Look, I just want to say something, get it out of the way, you know, before the meeting.'

'OK,' he says, looking even more nervous.

My courage is starting to fail me now, but I take a deep breath and rush on:

'I'm sorry for the misunderstanding last week. My fault entirely. I stupidly imagined that, in asking me to go for a drink, you were showing some kind of interest in me personally. Obviously, that was ridiculous; I must have been having a momentary lapse of sanity. So I just want to apologise for embarrassing us both. Can we start again and pretend that conversation never happened?'

I don't quite know how I managed to get all that out with barely even a pause for breath, let alone all the stammering and blushing nonsense I seem to have got into recently.

'OK,' he says slowly. So slowly that the O comes several long seconds before the K, making me think it's just an exclamation of distress, an 'Oh!' at the very idea of starting again with me. Then he starts to smile, and I feel the muscles of my face – taut from the effort of the fixed grin – relax slightly in relief. 'OK,' he says again. 'Of course I'm happy to start again, Joy. And to forget that conversation, if you like.'

'Oh, good. Thank you,' I begin, but he interrupts me:

'But I'd still be really grateful if you'd meet me at some point to discuss ideas for the society, if you'd like to?'

'Oh, well, yes, of course, if you think I might be able to help.'

'Definitely. Thank you.'

He's smiling widely now. Beaming. I smile back, finally feeling glad I forced myself to say my piece. It was worth it, worth going through those few minutes of further embarrassment, to get it over with so that we can both go back to normal, to being sensible adults together, and hopefully, going forward, friends.

'Good. Well—' I'm just about to launch into telling him about my meeting with Philip Sutton last week, when he holds up a hand to stop me, and adds in a quieter voice, still smiling:

'But just so you know, if you *weren't* married, I *would* be interested in you personally too.'

Wednesday 31 October

Sara's laughing so hard, I'm worried she's going to hurt herself.

'What on earth did you say to that?' she demands, wiping her eyes.

'Well, what *could* I say?' I laugh too. 'I think he was teasing, really – just trying to make me smile. Trying to lighten the tone, because it was pretty obvious how awkward I felt, making that little speech!'

'Joy, I'm sure he probably *does* like you – fancy you—'

'Don't say that! You'll start me off again, getting all embarrassed and not wanting to see him.'

'If you'd let me finish, I was going to say that he probably fancies you, but he knows you're married so he won't make a move on you.'

I shake my head. '*Make a move? Fancy me?* For God's sake, I'm sixty-five, I've been married for ever, I left that kind of vocabulary behind about forty years ago!'

'Ah, Joy, never say never!' She laughs again. 'I'm *joking*, love! Seriously, I think it's good that you've had that conversation with Howard, and yes, good that he said what he did, too. Best to get it all out in the open. You've got an admirer, Joy. Lucky you! I'm quite envious!'

'Huh. Well, I suppose it's nice to think there's *one* man, at least, who likes me. Even if my husband's being . . . well, whatever.'

'I know. You must be feeling neglected, hon,' she says sympathetically.

She takes a sip of her fruit tea and we sit in silence for a few minutes. I didn't see Sara at all yesterday, but when she saw me outside this afternoon, she asked me in to tell her about Monday night's meeting. And as soon as I started on the conversation with Howard, she closed her laptop and put the kettle on.

'I can finish that work this evening,' she said firmly. I know she doesn't mind having some work to do after Charlie's in bed. She says it keeps her from having to sit on her own with the TV, thinking too much about things.

'So, how did the rest of the meeting go?' she asks now, grinning at me. 'After you'd got that bit over with?'

'Oh, it was fairly quiet, actually. Freda wasn't there – she had a cold, apparently, so the ladies who bring her thought she'd better stay at home. We talked about fashions through the ages. It was quite interesting, especially when old Saul started describing his long Y-front underpants . . .'

Sara chuckles. 'I bet that got all the old ladies going!'

'Margaret told him not to be disgusting!' I say, laughing. 'But no, apart from that, there wasn't really anything to report. I hate to say it, but to be honest I only went to the meeting to avoid trying again to talk to Terry.'

'I don't blame you. Just try and do your own thing, Joy, until he's ready to talk to you,' she advises.

'Yes, I suppose that's best. Although I'd *like* to discuss the idea of getting a dog, that's the thing—'

'Oh!' she says. 'I didn't know you were planning—'

'We're not,' I say quickly. 'I just thought about it for the first time, yesterday. It was just a fleeting idea. I started wondering about it, and thinking of talking to Terry, but . . . well, it's probably not a good idea at the moment. I'll wait till—'

Till what? I think, with a sigh. Till he goes back to how he used to be? But what if he doesn't?

'I'll probably just forget it,' I end abruptly. 'Probably a silly idea.' I look back at Sara, give her a smile and change the subject. 'Anyway, how are you? And . . . oh, sorry, isn't it time you were going to pick up Charlie?' I add, suddenly noticing the time.

'He's on a play date with his new friend, Max,' she says happily. 'And I'm . . . OK, thanks.' She pauses, looks down, and adds quietly, 'I was thinking this morning that I ought to be doing something – about the baby. Going to the doctor. Making it official.'

I nod. 'Yes, you need to register for antenatal care. Sorry,' I add quickly. 'I don't mean to . . . act like a nurse.'

She smiles. 'But you *are* still a nurse, at heart, I'm sure. And honestly, I'm grateful. I do need to . . . well, to start taking on-board that this is real. A real baby, growing inside me, not just . . . a mistake. *I* made the mistake, but I don't want to label him – or her – that way. I need to start looking after him.'

'I think that will come naturally to you, now you're accepting it. You're already a mum, and your instincts will kick in again.'

'I know.' She shifts in her chair. 'Now . . . would you like another tea or anything, Joy? Because if you've got time, I want to tell you about it. About Luke. I want to explain.'

I shake my head at the tea. 'Are you *sure* I'm not keeping you from your work? And, well, are you sure you want to tell me? It's none of my business, really.'

'I do want to, if you don't mind? Charlie's having his tea with Max and they're apparently dressing up for Halloween later and having some fun with some other children in their street. Max's mum has kindly offered to take Charlie with them. So I can carry on working later, until he gets home.'

'Ah, that's nice for him! Well, OK,' I agree, 'if you want to talk, I'll listen, of course.'

'It's not a long story, really,' she says. 'That night – when I met up with Luke – I was out for a farewell drink with some girlfriends, before the move down here from Plymouth. When I told Rob a couple of my friends had suggested it, he insisted I should go. He said I should have a good time, and he'd make sure he was home early to do Charlie's tea and put him to bed. Well, I suppose it helped to ease his conscience,' she adds, scowling.

'So did you just bump into Luke by chance when you were out?'

'Yes. He was in the bar we went to. I hadn't seen him for years. I did used to think about him sometimes, and wonder what he was doing, but I wasn't curious enough to call him, or look him up on Facebook or anything. But it was nice to see him that night; we caught up a bit, he told me he'd been single for a few years, after breaking up with someone. And he said he'd chucked in his old job and gone back to college, to study veterinary nursing, something he'd always wanted to do. Well, you know what it's like with the loud music in a noisy bar – or maybe you don't.'

I smile at this. She must think I'm too old to have ever gone to bars or clubs and enjoyed myself!

'I do remember,' I tell her.

'Well, I didn't hear – or I just didn't appreciate – that he'd actually already qualified. And he certainly didn't tell me he'd also already accepted a position at this vet's in Bierleigh and had arranged to move down here. I didn't realise that *he* was out for farewell drinks with friends that night, too. We must have both moved here from Plymouth round about the same time.'

'That really is a coincidence. Are you *sure* it wasn't engineered?'

'To be honest, it couldn't have been. There wouldn't have been time for him to find a job vacancy down here, be interviewed, get somewhere to live – no, it really was a coincidence.'

'So it was obviously embarrassing for both of you to meet up the way you did, then,' I sympathise.

'Yes. Especially as I'd just begun to suspect that I might be pregnant. What an idiot I was, sleeping with him that night. I'd confided in him, you see: all about my marriage breakdown. I suppose I just wanted some sympathy. We always used to get on so well together, and during all those years that we were such good friends, I ... actually kind of loved him, you know? In a platonic way, of course. Not the way I loved Rob. That was ... everything all the songs are written about: love at first sight. Bells, rainbows, shooting stars! We got married within months of meeting, we were so besotted with each other, it was so perfect. And even after he told me about Jade, I still loved him. I was mortally wounded by what he was doing, but I couldn't stop loving him.'

I feel sorry for her, of course, hearing her talking like this. But still, the cynical side of me – the side that comes with age, and experience of life, from talking to lots of hurt, damaged people and learning some truths about relationships – can't help but wonder: How much of her love for that man was really a romantic fantasy? Let's be honest, no relationship can ever really be *perfect*. Especially as she and Rob didn't even seem to know each other for very long before committing to each other for life. But of course, I don't say anything.

'There came a point, that evening – a couple of drinks in,' Sara goes on, 'when I made a conscious decision that if Luke was up for it, so was I. Why shouldn't I have some fun too? Why should I stay faithful, when Rob was leaving me for someone else? I'd always found Luke attractive, as well as being good company, and that evening, I remembered how much I'd always liked his smile. And how he had ... such kind eyes. He always used to have this way of looking at me and listening to me as if he was really interested. Like he really cared.' She laughs. '*Beer goggles*, they call it.

I suppose that was what made *him* seem to be attracted to *me* that night, too. Anyway, we spent the rest of the evening together, and yes, we went back to his place. I messaged Rob to say I was staying overnight with one of my girlfriends. And—' she sighs and shakes her head '—I never even gave a thought to the fact that I'd come off the Pill. Rob and I had been sleeping in separate rooms since his big revelation about Jade, so it hadn't exactly been necessary.'

'I suppose it hit you afterwards? In the morning?' I suggest.

'No, not even then. I didn't think about it until I started to worry that I was late. That sounds mad, doesn't it? But I had so much else on my mind – the separation, the move, Charlie settling at school ...'

'Yes, of course.'

'But he – Luke – must have just *presumed* I was on the Pill. He never asked.'

'I see.'

'Yes.' She pulls a face. 'And the point is, Joy, the reason I might have *expected* him to think of asking about it, was that he'd been telling me during the evening that he doesn't want children.'

'Oh.' I reach out for her hand. I get it now, of course.

'It was,' she goes on quietly, 'apparently the reason he'd split up with his ex. He said she'd started wanting marriage and kids, and he didn't.'

'So that's why you don't want to tell him – about the baby.'

'No point, is there? He won't be interested. And anyway, we were both so embarrassed that morning, when we'd sobered up. It felt ... oh, I know this sounds really gross, but I felt like I'd just had sex with my brother – not that I've got one!'

I laugh at this. I could imagine it, somehow. 'Yes, I suppose – because you'd been such close friends when you were kids – it must have felt really weird.'

'It did. So we made a kind of pact, to pretend it hadn't happened, and that we'd never mention it, if we ever met up again. To be fair, I don't think either of us really *expected* to meet up again, and certainly not so soon, and . . . finding ourselves living in such close proximity. I felt so annoyed about it – about having to face him – I suppose I took it out on him.'

'But he *has* helped you with Pumpkin,' I can't help pointing out.

She gives a little snort of laughter. 'Oh, well, that makes it all OK, then, doesn't it!'

'Sorry. Do you think you're *starting* to feel a little happier about the baby now, though? Now you're getting over the shock?'

'I've got mixed feelings. I always did want another baby, but not like this, obviously. On my own, and the father being someone who won't even want anything to do with it.' She pauses, then gives me a smile and says: 'I'm sure I will love it, though – if I can get past the regret about how it started. Thanks for listening, Joy. I know there was no need to explain all this to you, but I wanted to. I suppose I just needed to confide in someone.'

'Well, as I've said before, any time you want to talk, you know where I am.'

And I'm not going to say this, of course, but I'm not really the person she needs to be confiding in, am I?

Friday 2 November

'Are you going to the firework display up on Harry's Plain tomorrow evening?' Sara asks me this morning.

To be honest I hadn't even noticed it was November already. It's funny how that happens when you're not at work any more. The days, weeks and months all roll into one. Sometimes I have no idea whether it's Tuesday or Wednesday or Thursday. During the first couple of weeks of my retirement, I loved the fact that my life was no longer dictated by my appointment diary. Now, although it's still very liberating to have no fixed routines to keep to, it can also feel slightly bewildering.

'Oh, Terry and I haven't been to that for years,' I say. 'It used to be fun when we were younger – we'd meet a few friends from the village and watch the fireworks together. But now, well . . .'

'I suppose there's a limit to how many fireworks displays you can enjoy,' she says lightly with a smile.

I feel a bit relieved that she seems to understand. If she'd wanted me to go along to keep her and Charlie company, I would have done, of course. I hesitate. Although she's right, I'm not in much of a hurry to stand in the cold watching a few fireworks, I suppose it would be more fun with an excited little boy. But she's already going on to say:

'On the other hand, Joy, if you just want to watch a little bonfire that I'm planning to light on the beach for Charlie and Max this evening, while they hold some sparklers and I let off just a couple of cheap fireworks ... you could watch from your window if you like?'

'Oh, Sara, yes that would be lovely!' I exclaim. 'But of course, I'll come outside and watch with you, if that's OK? I was just thinking it *would* be more fun to watch it with children. Unless it's raining, of course!'

'I hope not. If it's raining, we'll probably do it on a different day! Yes, do come and join us – and Terry, if he'd like to? The heat from the fire will keep us warm, not that it'll last long! I'm lighting it in an old metal dustbin. Rob always used to use it when we had fires, and I brought it with me. So it'll be safe.'

'Has Charlie made a Guy?' I ask her.

'A what?' she says – and I laugh.

'A Guy Fawkes – you know, to burn on the bonfire.' I stare at her. 'Please don't tell me children don't do that any more? Don't you even know what it is?'

'Oh yes, a Guy – of course I know,' she says, the light dawning in her eyes. 'My dad did help me make one once.'

'Only once?' I squawk in surprise.

'Yes. We didn't usually even have a bonfire. Halloween was starting to take over, really, when I was a child. We did normally go to the firework display in the local park, though. My parents told me how kids used to knock on doors and ask for "a penny for the Guy"! I can't imagine that happening now. It's ... well, it's like sending your kids out begging really, isn't it?'

'No!' I protest. 'It was just a bit of fun, that's all, and as kids, we used to work hard making our Guys look realistic. Asking our fathers for old shirts and socks and trousers, stuffing them with rolled up newspaper ...' I sigh, then add, suddenly feeling indignant about it, 'And anyway, what's all the Halloween stuff about, if it isn't begging too? Isn't *that* sending your kids from door to door asking for sweets and treats?'

'I suppose you're right!' Sara says, laughing. 'Halloween has completely taken over from Guy Fawkes, now, hasn't it. But ... you know what? Talking to you about it now, I think making a Guy would be brilliant. Charlie and Max would love doing it, if there's enough time, after school. And if I can find any suitable old clothes I don't mind being burnt!'

'I've got an old shirt that's got paint on it, if you want it. And Terry's put a pair of his old jeans out for recycling: I'll grab those, they're really too bad for recycling anyway. And we've got a stack of old newspaper they can use for stuffing.' I'm suddenly feeling strangely enthusiastic about this. It's bringing back such memories from my childhood, when my cousin Pauline and I used to work on the Guy together and collect wood for the bonfire. I haven't thought about it for years! 'I'll help them, if they'd like me to,' I add. 'We'll just need some string to tie up the ankles of the trousers and the wrists of the shirt.'

'You're really getting into this, aren't you, Joy!' Sara says.

'Yes, I suppose I am!' I smile at her. 'Reliving my childhood. Seriously, send the pair of them in to me when they get home, and we'll make the Guy together. You come too, of course – unless it gives you a chance to stay and get some more work done.'

'I might come with them – thanks. I'll look forward to it!'

They come in soon after they're home from school, Sara bringing an old pillow case for the Guy's head and a pair of socks for his feet.

'I've got a horrible old pair of gloves somewhere,' I say. 'For his hands. Now, we used to buy cardboard masks for Guy Fawkes' face, but I'm sure nobody makes those now, so how about you boys make one out of cardboard?'

Sara goes back for an empty cereal box to cut up and Charlie and Max proceed to design a face for Guy Fawkes while Sara and I start screwing up newspaper for stuffing.

'Poor Mr Guy hasn't got any shoes!' Max points out sadly.

Sara smothers a giggle. 'He's not going to be cold, Max. He's going on the bonfire!'

'Why does he get burned?' Charlie asks innocently.

I hesitate to answer. It feels like a gruesome story to tell seven-year-olds. But I'm obviously underestimating them!

'You remember, Charlie,' Max says. 'We learned about that at school. Guy Fawkes tried to burn down the Houses of Parliament, so—'

'Oh yes! And they caught him and they killed him! Ha! Serves him right!'

'Yeah! They threw him on a fire and burned him to bits!' Max joins in, and the two of them jump around the room, shouting excitedly about setting Guy Fawkes on fire and watching him burn.

'Actually they *hanged* him,' Sara corrects them. 'But the tradition to burn him was because that's what he wanted to do to the government, you see? Bloodthirsty little tykes, aren't they – kids,' she adds to me with a casual shrug. 'All right, boys, calm down now, we're in Joy's house, behave yourselves.'

'Sorry, Joy,' they chorus, grinning at me.

'It's fine,' I tell them, laughing. 'But come on now, help us stuff these clothes or he's not going to be much of a Guy. I wonder if I can find him an old hat ... '

By the time Terry comes home, we're all in our warm coats, hats and gloves and Mr Fawkes is sitting comfortably on the 'bonfire' in Sara's old dustbin, down on the beach. The two boys are almost frantic with excitement and I'm happy to see Sara's pretty excited herself, joining in with their laughter as they skip around chanting, 'Remember, remember, the fifth of November' at the tops of their voices.

'What's going on?' Terry asks, looking bewildered.

'We're having a mini bonfire night,' I explain.

'Guy Fawkes is going to get burned!' the boys shout. 'And we're having sparklers and a rocket!'

'You're welcome to join us, Terry,' Sara says. 'If you'd like to. It won't last long. We're going to the display tomorrow evening for their real bonfire night treat.'

'It's not the fifth of November yet, is it?' Terry asks, looking surprised.

'No, but it all has to be at the weekend, really, so the kids can stay up late,' I explain. 'Come and join us, Terry. We can have dinner afterwards.'

'Well, I've got a lot of . . .' he begins, looking down at the laptop case in his hand.

I turn away, sighing. The words 'suit yourself' die on my lips. I can't be bothered.

'But if it's just for a little while,' he goes on suddenly, making me almost gasp with surprise as I swing back to look at him again, 'why not?' He smiles down at Charlie and Max. 'Give me two minutes to change out of my work clothes and I'll join you outside. Save me a sparkler, boys!'

'Wow,' I mouth to Sara.

She smiles at me. 'Perhaps it reminds him of his childhood too?' she whispers. 'Right, boys, you stay on the decking with Joy and Terry, and don't come any closer to the fire, understand?'

'Yay!' Charlie shouts. 'Light it now, Mum. Burn Mister Guy Fawkes all up, go on!'

'Who's that?' Max says quietly, and we all turn to look towards the side of the house, where there's a dark shadow of someone approaching, tentatively, looking apologetic.

'I did try ringing the doorbell,' he says. 'I don't want to intrude, but—'

'It's the man who found Pumpkin!' Charlie says excitedly. 'Mummy, it's the man who—'

'Yes. Hello, Luke,' Sara says quietly.

'I just thought I'd pop round to see how Pumpkin's settled down,' he says. 'And, well, to make sure you're aware about fireworks this weekend and keeping him indoors.'

'Of course I'm aware,' she says shortly. 'He's indoors and he's fine. We're having our own fireworks, so obviously—'

'Can Luke stay for the fireworks?' Charlie yells. 'Can he stay and watch Guy Fawkes burn? We made him ourselves,' he adds to Luke. 'I drew his face. Max cut it out.'

'It's very good,' Luke says. 'But I won't intrude—'

'*Please*,' Charlie says, his little face pink with excitement. 'Please, Mummy, can he stay? He can have a sparkler, he can have one of mine, I don't mind. He *did* find Pumpkin for us.'

'Well,' Sara says, 'OK. If you want to, Luke. Don't feel obligated.'

'Thank you,' Luke says. 'I can light the fireworks for you, if you like?'

'It's fine, I can do it. You can stay on the decking with the boys.'

Terry comes out to join us at the same time, bringing with him some plastic cups, a bottle of lemonade and some cans of beer.

'Refreshments,' he tells everyone. 'Thought I'd better contribute something – although I see I've already donated my old jeans.' He laughs – actually laughs. I haven't seen him this relaxed for weeks. 'Help yourself, everyone. I'll get a bottle of wine, too.'

'Don't worry with that, Terry, I'll just have a lemonade shandy,' I tell him. 'Thank you.'

'What about you, Sara? Would you like some wine?' he asks.

'I'll just have lemonade,' Sara says quickly. 'Thanks, Terry.'

'This is Luke,' Charlie tells him importantly. 'He found Pumpkin, so he's our friend.'

'Pleased to meet you, Luke,' Terry says. 'Have a beer?'

'Well, only half a cup, then, thank you. I'm driving.' He smiles. 'This is nice.'

Sara's still doing her best to ignore him. She's handed the kids their sparklers, with which they're happily writing in the air, and now she's down on the beach, lighting the bonfire, setting the rocket and the other couple of fireworks ready to launch.

'Bye, Mr Fawkes!' Charlie and Max shout together as the flames start to lick around his legs. 'Serves you right!'

'Sweet innocence of childhood – what happened to it?' Terry whispers to me, laughing.

I can barely answer. Because he's poured us both a beer and he's got an arm loosely around my shoulders, while we watch the fireworks lighting up the sky and reflecting in the calm, dark water of the sea behind. And I'm wondering if all my worries about him were just a figment of my imagination. Because this evening, suddenly everything – the glow of the fire, the excited shrieks of the children, the strange little furtive looks Luke's giving Sara, and Terry's arm, warm and comforting around my shoulders – it all feels just perfect.

Saturday 3 November

I suppose the nature of perfection is that it's fleeting. And sure enough, by the time the fireworks were over, our Guy was burnt to ashes and we'd helped Sara tidy up a bit, it had started to drizzle with rain. Luke said good night and took his leave, Max's father arrived to take him home, Charlie was sent in to get ready for bed, and Terry and I went indoors, where he immediately got his laptop out and settled back down to work.

'It's twenty past eight, Tel,' I said, shaking my head at him. 'And we've still got to have dinner. Can't you just have a night off?'

'I've had a little while *off*, as you put it,' he said, a note of irritation in his voice. 'I've just got to—'

I felt so disappointed I could hardly speak. Had I really imagined things were going to change, just because of an hour or so where he actually relaxed and seemed like his old self? I'd had, in the back of my mind, the idea of broaching the subject of getting a dog with him when we were back indoors; of sitting down and discussing it together, perhaps starting to get excited about the idea and discussing types of dogs. But the stress and anxiety were back on his face already, and looking at him frowning over his spreadsheets, I forgot my frustration about the lack of time he spends with me, and suddenly began to feel really worried.

'Terry, you look exhausted,' I told him gently. 'You're overdoing it, you know that.'

'No, I'm not,' he responded.

'Well, in that case, I'm worried you might be ill. Perhaps you should see the doctor for a check-up.'

'No!' He turned to me with a flash of annoyance. 'I don't need to see the bloody doctor. It's bad enough living with a bloody nurse, nagging me all the time.'

His voice was so sharp, his tone so cross, I actually had to blink back tears. It was so unlike him. I'm certain, now, that I haven't been imagining anything. There's something going on, something he refuses to talk to me about. I was going to ask him next whether there was a problem with the business, something serious that he's really worried about, but I could see the situation would escalate into an even worse argument if I asked any more questions. I just broke some eggs into the frying pan, put some baked beans into the microwave, and snapped back that it was too late to cook a proper meal. And I don't think either of us enjoyed it anyway.

This morning, as soon as we wake up, Terry does at least apologise. It seems pretty genuine: he claims he'd had a headache and was just tired out from a busy week – although you'd never have known it when we were outside watching the fireworks.

'I still shouldn't have snapped at you. You know I didn't mean it,' he says, giving me a quick hug.

Personally, I've always thought I *didn't mean it* to be a pretty weak excuse. If you don't mean things, you shouldn't say them – it's an excuse for toddlers, not people who are old enough to understand how much words can hurt. But I'm still feeling too shaken by his outburst, the ferocity of it, to do anything other than shrug an acceptance of his apology. Do I have to walk on eggshells now, avoiding making any comment at all about his work, or any mention of my worries about his health, in case, God forbid, I should sound like a *bloody nurse* again?

'I'm going out this morning,' I tell him after breakfast, determined not to be childish enough to add *not that you'd care*.

'For a walk with Sara?' he asks.

'No. I'm going back to—' I stop, suddenly aware that I haven't even told Terry about Philip yet. The realisation of this just adds to my despair about how few proper conversations we have now. 'I'm visiting someone who used to live here, in this house,' I explain. 'I found out about him through the Historical Society.'

'Oh, that sounds interesting,' he says. I can tell he's making an effort to say the right thing, but his phone is in his hand and it's quite clear he's itching to open it. 'Will you be all right? Visiting some strange guy, I mean. On your own.'

I laugh. 'He's seventy-six and in a wheelchair, Terry.' I don't bother to mention the fact that I've already visited Philip before. 'He lives in an apartment for the elderly, in Ferndell. I'll be back by lunchtime.'

'OK. Have fun.'

I'm not going to make any sarcastic response. And I'm not going to worry about it any more. Well, that's what I'm telling myself, anyway.

Janet Bull, the warden of Goldcrest Lodge, recognises me when I arrive, and ushers me towards Philip's apartment with a majestic sweep of her arm. Again, she's left his front door ajar for me. Philip looks a lot perkier than when I left him last time, smiling and telling me the kettle's on. I've brought a pack of shortbread biscuits with me, and you'd have thought I was the last of the big spenders, the way he lavishes thanks on me as he puts them on a plate.

We make polite conversation while he makes the coffee. He tells me about his visits to the communal lounge here, and laughs as he assures me the organised 'sing-song' sessions and beetle drives that take place there are as dire as they sound.

'I haven't been living here very long,' he explains. 'My operation was only earlier this year, and afterwards I decided it would help me to be independent if I moved into somewhere like this and had it adapted for me. I've made a couple of friends here, though. It's quite nice really – I'm being unfair. A lot of the other residents are much older than me so they probably love the "old-time music hall" evenings!'

'Yes, you're probably just a spring chicken compared with some of them!' I agree. 'Maybe you should request some rock 'n' roll sessions!'

We're laughing together as we go to sit in the lounge.

'Now then: where did we get to before?' he asks once we're finally sipping our coffee and enjoying the biscuits. 'I think I was telling you about my attempt to elope to France with my Chrissie, wasn't I?'

'Yes. And about running out of fuel while you were out at sea.'

He nods. 'What a young idiot I was,' he reflects, shaking his head and giving a little chuckle. 'I don't know how I ever thought that plan was going to work, even if I hadn't forgotten about the fuel.'

'We don't think logically when we're young, do we? And desperate things call for desperate measures,' I say.

'Yes. And I did love her *so* desperately.'

I feel a pang of sympathy for him: for the young man he was, and the older, wiser, but less able person he is now. Still, he has his memories – as we all do.

'So . . . what happened?' I prompt him, as he seems to be drifting off into those memories now and forgetting I'm here. 'How did you and Chrissie make it back?'

'Oh, the lifeboat rescued us eventually. I don't think I quite appreciated, back then, how much we owed the RNLI our lives,' he reflects. 'Chrissie wasn't at all well. She was vomiting repeatedly – because of the pregnancy, of course, to say nothing of the way the boat was being tossed about in the storm – so she was getting really weak. She passed out a couple of times and I was terrified she was dying. I didn't know what to do. I remember I kept trying to make her drink; fortunately, I'd taken plenty of water on-board, as well as some orange juice I'd nicked from home. I think I just kept trying to reassure her it was going to be OK, even though I had no idea whether it really would be. We were drifting further out to sea, and further along the coast, but I was panicking so much I no longer had a clear idea of our position.'

'It must have been so frightening,' I say. 'Out there in the dark on your own, and you were both so young!'

'Young and stupid,' he agrees. 'Yes, it was – terrifying. I can still remember the fear I felt that night, as if it was yesterday. The worst thing was knowing it was all my own fault. I was crying like a baby. And Chrissie – when she was conscious –was hallucinating.'

'Oh, God, poor girl.' I can't even begin to imagine it. Fifteen, pregnant, lost at sea and being ill. 'And poor you – you wouldn't have had a clue how to help her.'

'No. I didn't.' He sighs and hangs his head for a moment. 'I'd put her in terrible danger, and it wasn't until that point that I realised it. I think, up till then, I'd almost thought of it as a kind of adventure – a romantic adventure. I imagined I was saving her, but in reality, I was just trying to save my own skin.'

'Ah, you're being hard on yourself,' I tell him gently. 'You were young and in love, and scared of the consequences. How did you know Chrissie was hallucinating? What was she saying?'

'Oh, she was rambling about seeing angels. At least, that was what I thought at the time. She kept sitting up and pointing out into the darkness, through the rain, and muttering about an angel. It wasn't until after it was all over that she explained.'

'Explained what?'

'She'd believed she saw the angel of Angel Cove,' he says, quite matter-of-factly. 'However much I tried to make her understand she'd been hallucinating – that she'd been ill, dehydrated, her brain playing tricks on her – she was convinced, that night, that she'd seen the Angel of the Cove, and that he directed the lifeboat crew to us and got us safely home. Even after we were rescued, she talked about it – the angel saving our lives.' He pauses and smiles, nodding to himself. 'In fact, it was another angel altogether.'

February 1960:
Early hours of Monday morning

It was probably the howling of the wind that woke Freda initially. She'd been dreaming that she was getting married, a recurring dream for her, but one that always ended badly. She'd be dressed all in white, with the requisite veil and bouquet, and would be walking down the aisle on her father's arm, her family and friends all there in the church, but nobody waiting for her at the altar apart from the vicar. When they reached the vicar, he always had his back to her, but then he'd turn round and his face would be hideously deformed by an incontinent anger. He'd begin to shout at her, proclaiming her to be a sexual deviant who would burn in hell. The dream normally concluded with her turning and running from the church in tears, but on this occasion she somehow woke herself up while the vicar was still ranting, and she found herself sitting up in bed, crying.

As she slowly tried to calm herself down, she glanced across at the other bed. Chrissie seemed to still be sleeping soundly, despite the disturbance of Freda's nightmare. *How could she sleep at night*, Freda asked herself bitterly, *considering what she's told me*? Stupid, stupid girl – she'd had everything going for her: young, pretty and clever too. And yes, madly in love with the boy next door. Her life could have been perfect. If she'd only waited until she was old enough to marry Philip, they could no doubt have had several beautiful children and lived happily ever after, while she, the 'ugly' big sister of the fairy tales, would always be the sad and lonely, resentful old spinster. She and her girlfriend would always have to hide the true nature of their relationship, never able to declare their feelings publicly to the world in a ceremony like the one she dreamed of.

But now, her little sister had thrown all that good fortune down the drain by getting pregnant at fifteen – *fifteen!* – and ruining everything for herself. Their parents would never agree to them getting married. The baby would be taken away from her and given up for adoption. She'd probably never get over it, and meanwhile Philip would probably find someone else. Freda sighed with exasperation. She knew she should have been kinder, tried to be more helpful when Chrissie had confided in her, but her own shock and distress had taken over. Despite their differences, despite the age gap, despite her own unforgiveable jealousy, she loved Chrissie, and hated to see her frightened and unhappy.

She got out of bed and padded across the room to head downstairs for a glass of water. She'd probably have trouble getting back to sleep again now, as usual. As she passed the end of her sister's bed, she realised how quietly she seemed to be breathing – almost as if she wasn't breathing at all. Freda stopped, feeling guilty now. What a terrible thing to imagine – her sister not breathing! She was overcome with a sudden surge of protectiveness. If anything bad ever happened to Chrissie, she thought with a dreadful pang, how would she be able to forgive herself for the awful jealous thoughts she so often harboured?

'Are you awake, Chris?' she whispered in the darkness.

No reply. Still no sound of her breathing. Freda squeezed herself down the narrow gap between their two single beds and leaned closer. It took her a couple more moments to realise that there was no head on the pillow; that the bulge beneath the eiderdown that she'd taken to be Chrissie, huddled underneath for warmth, was, in fact, made up of her rolled-up nightie and dressing gown.

She straightened up, blinking with shock. *Calm down*, she told herself. *You probably woke her up with your mutterings during your nightmare. She's probably just gone downstairs for a drink herself.*

But why would she take off her night clothes and leave them in the bed like that – bundled up to make a body-shaped bulge under the covers?

Shivering with fear as much as with the icy cold of the bedroom, Freda pulled her own dressing gown off its hook behind the bedroom door, and slipping it on as she went, flew across the landing and down the stairs, into the living room, where she put on the light as she whispered her sister's name. Nobody there. Nobody in the kitchen either. She threw open the back door and stared out into the blackness of the stormy night, and suddenly her fear gave way to a surge of irritation as she guessed what might be happening here. That sneaky young madam was out here somewhere in the dark, kissing and carrying on with that Philip next door. As if it wasn't bad enough that she was already in the family way! And here was Freda feeling sorry for her, worried about her, guilty about her! Well, she'd put a stop to this nonsense. She took her father's big torch down from the shelf, marched outside with it, and went down onto the windswept beach. Shivering in her nightdress and dressing gown, her bare feet freezing on the cold wet sand, she was nevertheless burning with righteous indignation. How dare Chrissie get pregnant, come to Freda expecting help and sympathy, and then *continue* to sneak around at night having illicit meetings with that boy! She shone the torch along the breakwater, expecting at any moment to see movement, the two young lovers she so envied and so resented being disturbed in their lovemaking.

But she didn't see anyone. Instead, having walked the whole width of the cove, along the inky-dark water's edge where the waves were crashing, she suddenly became aware that something was missing. It took her a few moments to realise what it was – but when she did, she was so shaken, so alarmed, she dropped the torch on her foot and burst into tears. She turned and hobbled back to the house, the sore foot hindering her progress, and ran into the kitchen. Thanking God for the fact that she'd persuaded her father to join the twentieth century and get a telephone installed, she grabbed the receiver and dialled 999.

'Coastguard, please!' she sobbed, and, trying to keep her voice as quiet as she could, she tearfully, breathlessly, told the sympathetic-sounding man who answered that she needed a lifeboat sent out, quickly, urgently, to find Philip's father's boat; to find her little sister and bring her safely back.

She knew she'd have to wake up her parents. And they'd have to alert Philip's parents' too. But she wanted to be able to tell her mum and dad she'd done everything she could, before they came downstairs and began to panic. She was panicking enough herself, but she needed to calm down. Chrissie was in trouble. Chrissie needed her. She'd let her down already – she hadn't helped, when she'd asked her to – and now she and that stupid boy had taken matters into their own hands, in the most dangerous way imaginable, on a cold February night with a storm brewing.

Oh, God! she prayed as she stood in the darkness of the kitchen, taking deep breaths, waiting for the coastguard to tell her he'd alerted the RNLI station at Dartmouth. *God, please, please bring them back safely. I promise, I PROMISE I'll never be jealous of*

Chrissie again, I'll never be unkind to her again, I'll do whatever she needs me to do, I'll help her keep the baby, I'll tell Mum and Dad, I'll look after her for the rest of my life if need be! Just bring her back!

Saturday 3 November

'Poor Freda!' I shake my head at Philip. 'So she was actually the "angel" you referred to – the one who was responsible for you both getting safely back. She must have been beside herself with worry about you both.'

'Yes, of course. Well, about Chrissie, anyway!' he says with a smile. 'Neither of us appreciated at the time, of course – we were too young and too wrapped up in our own selfish feelings – that Freda actually adored her. She'd always come across as such a grump, and yes, always seemed so jealous of Chrissie. But we came to understand, as we got older. When she moved in with Doris, about a year after Chrissie and I got married, it finally dawned on us – what she'd tried to hide, all those years, because her parents probably would have found it hard to accept. She and Doris made a great show of having decided to live together because neither of them had been able to find a man. I never knew whether their parents really believed it, but if they'd suspected the truth, they'd have preferred to go along with the subterfuge. In those days, it was still important to people in quiet villages like Bierleigh to avoid scandal.'

'Yes. I do remember what it was like! I lived in Exeter, but even there in the city there was a lot of hypocrisy. Things did start to change gradually, though, didn't they, during the course of the sixties.'

'They did. But of course, homosexuality was still illegal until nineteen-sixty-seven. I think gay women were pretty much ignored by the law, but it was definitely still a social taboo to be a gay woman. I think Freda and Doris could actually have lost their jobs – they were both teachers – if they'd admitted openly to being gay.'

'It seems quite incredible now, doesn't it?' I reflect. 'It was such a relatively short time ago.'

'It was a different world back then, wasn't it? And, of course, the whole point was that there was still a lot of social stigma attached to being an unmarried mother, too.'

'But you did end up getting married, after all, you and Chrissie. How did that come about?'

Philip glances at the clock on the wall, and I immediately feel guilty for having kept him talking for so long.

'I'm sorry,' I say quickly. 'Look, it's nearly lunchtime already; shall we leave the last part of your story till another time?'

'The next part,' he corrects me with a grin. 'Hopefully not the last part!'

We both laugh, and he goes on, sounding a bit sheepish: 'Well, to be honest, I'm enjoying your visits so much, I've been rather hoping you'd say you'll come back again.'

'Of course I will. And, of course, I'm still waiting to hear what happened about the angel. I mean the angel of Angel Cove – about Chrissie thinking she saw it. Freda still remembers that – she mentioned it the first time I met her at the Historical Society.'

'Oh, she would do, of course,' he says, grinning again. 'The angel became part of their family folklore. So: next week. Any day apart from Friday would be OK for me. My friend Arthur here, who still drives, has offered to take me into Dartmouth then, for a little shopping trip. If I can pluck up the courage to get in the car with him! He's a little bit erratic, if you know what I mean, on the roads.' He glances at me and shrugs. 'I'm waiting for the DVLA to decide if I'd be OK to drive – if I get a car adapted for me, I mean – but these things take time. Anyway, how about Thursday? Are you free then?'

'Thursday would be good for me, Philip. Good luck with Arthur's driving!' I hesitate, and then add quickly: 'I could always take you shopping, if you'd like me to?'

He shakes his head. 'No, no, I'm fine, Joy, thanks. I get my main weekly shop delivered, not that I need a lot, just for me. And Arthur likes to take me out occasionally for these little outings. Don't worry, I'm probably exaggerating about his driving. He stays on the road most of the time!'

I head straight home, and Sara sees me from her window as I pull up outside. She gives me a wave and opens her front door.

'How did it go this morning with Philip?' she asks. I'd reminded her last night that I'd be seeing him today, and she's following his story with almost as much excitement as I am. 'Come in out of the cold for a few minutes,' she adds as I start to tell her about it.

She sits listening, spellbound, as I describe how Freda discovered her little sister missing and called the coastguard.

'So they got back safely?' she says.

'Well, they must have done – they did get married eventually! He's going to tell me more next time.'

'So her parents must have agreed to them marrying, in the end. After she was sixteen.'

'Yes. I get the impression from Philip that Freda might have had something to do with that, too.'

'It sounds as though she always regretted not helping when Chrissie confided in her about the pregnancy.'

'I know.' I pause, thinking back to the first time I met Freda at the Historical Society. 'And I think she still does. Despite her dementia, that's something she still seems to remember clearly. It was quite sweet, though, the way Philip referred to Freda as being the "real" angel who saved him and Chrissie from the sea that night.'

'So at least they seem to have been reconciled afterwards.' She smiles. 'But we still don't know any more about the angel itself – why the cove got its name.'

'Sadly, no. Philip doesn't seem to know the answer to that himself. But I'm so hooked on their story now – his and Chrissie's – that I keep forgetting that was what I wanted to find out about originally!'

'Me too. I can't wait to hear the next instalment! It's like following a series,' she says.

'Thanks again for last night, by the way,' I say. 'It was lovely. Charlie looked so happy with his friend.'

She smiles. 'Yes, Max is a nice boy, and it's really helped Charlie settle down, now he's got a friend. He still looks forward to his weekends with Rob, of course. Apparently, Rob's going to take him ice-skating next time. I wonder if it'll get hard for him eventually, thinking of things to do, how to entertain him.'

'In a small flat, yes, I guess so.'

'But they'll be moving before long – Rob and Jade. It seems they've found a house they want to buy. Quite a big one, with a garden. Sounds a lot like the one we used to have, actually.'

She's trying to sound flippant when she says this, but I'm not fooled. It feels unfair; I don't blame her. But she knows she was, really, entitled to stay in the marital home while Charlie's young, and she's told me Rob was surprised she decided against that. I was surprised too, but she explained when she first arrived here that she didn't want to live in that house any more, that she'd always feel somehow beholden to Rob if she did, and she'd made up her mind to start living as independently as she could right away. I admire her for that decision, but I can't help wondering if she might regret it now. Now that – with the benefit of Jade's proceeds from selling her own previous home – the pair of them can afford a big house.

'But you're happy here, or as happy as you can be, in the circumstances, aren't you?' I point out gently.

'Yes, of course I am,' she says in her characteristically determined tone. 'Or I would be,' she adds more quietly, 'if it weren't for the worry about the baby.'

'Of course.' To be honest, it's easy to forget about her being pregnant. She seems as fit and well as ever, and she barely mentions it, so it's only when I notice her drinking fruit tea that I remember.

'I ... still haven't told Rob. Or Charlie,' she adds. 'I'm putting it off for as long as I can. I have no idea how to tell either of them.'

'I'm sure when the time comes, you'll know how to,' I suggest. 'And how to tell Luke, too,' I add. 'It was nice of him to come round last night, wasn't it? To make sure Pumpkin was OK?'

Although I'm not altogether sure that was the only reason he called!

'I suppose so,' she says. She shrugs and changes the subject. 'I was glad Terry joined us, too. He looked quite relaxed.'

'Yes.' I sigh. 'He was. But as soon as we went back indoors, he got straight back on his laptop, looking as stressed as ever.'

I don't tell her how he snapped at me. I'm trying my best to forget it.

'Have you actually spelled it out to him: how upset and worried he's making you?'

'Huh. That's easier said than done, when he won't talk to me properly, and won't listen when I talk to him.'

'Write him a letter, then.'

I stare at her. Write a letter? To my husband, because we can't even talk to each other?

'Seriously,' she says. 'Why not? Or write it in an email, if he won't take his eyes off his laptop. Spell it out in black and white.'

'Perhaps you're right,' I say a little doubtfully. Then I look back at her and smile. 'Perhaps that's how you should tell Luke, too – about the baby. If you don't want to talk to him.'

She laughs. 'Maybe I will. See, we've helped each other already.'

'Yes, perhaps we both need someone to give us a push in the right direction.'

'Ooh, don't talk about *pushing* yet!' she groans. 'I can't believe I'm going to have to go through all that again in June!'

'You've got a due date now? You've seen a doctor, or a midwife?'

'Yes. I went to the antenatal clinic down at the village surgery, and yes, they've estimated my due date as the sixth of June, but, of course, I'll be having a scan at twelve weeks, to confirm that.'

'June's a nice time of year to have a baby,' I say encouragingly.

'Mm. If only it wasn't ... *his*.'

'He might surprise you. I mean, even if he *didn't* want children, he ought to at least take an interest, now it's happened, and give you some support. He seems ... well, too nice ... not to want to do that, at least. He was so kind and helpful, wasn't he – getting this little one back for you.'

I point down at Pumpkin, who's asleep in his bed, snoring gently, and Sara smiles.

'Perhaps he prefers cats to women, Joy, that's all I can say.'

I think it's a good sign, for both of us, that we manage to laugh together at this.

This evening, while Terry's working, I stand at the back door, watching the fireworks in the distance. Sara's taken Charlie to the organised display up on Harry's Plain, but I think everyone in the village seems to be letting fireworks off tonight too, as they're lighting up the sky in all directions. I guess it's because it's a dry evening and people don't want to wait till the fifth, in case it rains again. For such a small population, Bierleigh seems to have a disproportionate number of pyromaniacs. Thank goodness Pumpkin's safely home: Sara will, of course, have kept him indoors again tonight, but how awful it would have been if we'd had to picture him, still out there lost somewhere, scared out of his life by all the explosions and flashing lights. I wonder if my dog will be scared, too ... if I get one. I stop the thought quickly. I can't start imagining myself with a dog before I've even broached the subject with Terry, never mind choosing one!

I tried twice, this afternoon, to write him an email, and twice I deleted it. I tried writing an old-fashioned letter instead, in case that felt more natural, but I ended up throwing it away. It felt silly. We've never written each other letters, never had to – we've always been together. After I'd given up, I just sat and watched him for a while, pretending to be watching the TV. He was looking at his laptop but not really doing anything, just staring at it, and then sighing, like he was too exhausted to even think straight.

You need a break, I wanted to tell him. And it was quite painful to realise that I didn't feel able to. I didn't even feel able to show my husband I was concerned about him, any more. How has it come to this?

Monday 5 November

It's possible that by now Terry might remember that I go out on Monday evenings, but I prefer to go through the same routine of leaving a note along with his dinner. I suppose I'm being old-fashioned; probably I should just let him get his own dinner on Monday nights – it wouldn't hurt him. But I'm conscious that I've got all the time in the world to do what I want, now, whereas he's still working hard. Whether that's his own choice or not feels irrelevant. It was *my* own choice to retire, after all. I don't want him ever to be able to say I didn't do my bit; that I made things any harder for him.

There's a full house tonight at the society meeting, including Annie French, who hasn't been at the previous meetings I've attended because she was in hospital. Judging from the animated chatter coming from all four ladies when I arrive, a few minutes late this time, she's holding court, relating her experiences at the hands of the NHS.

'I kept telling the consultant it wasn't my guts, but he wouldn't believe me,' she's complaining loudly, to sympathetic tuts of concern from the others. 'He had me carried off for one of those *procedures*, as they call it, where they ...' She looks around, notices that Howard and David appear to be listening, leans closer to the other women and drops her voice a couple of decibels. 'You know,' she goes on, every word still carrying right across the hall, 'that *procedure* where they put a camera up you.'

'*Up* you?' squawks Margaret.

'Yes. You know. Up your ar—'

'Right, everyone! Shall we start the meeting?' Howard interrupts in the nick of time.

I exchange a grin with him as I sit in the empty chair at the end of the row, next to old Saul, who says, 'Hello, my lovely,' to me in the manner of someone addressing a favourite grandchild. I suppose at his age, everyone seems like a kid.

Howard's still trying to get everyone's attention. I watch him for a moment as he picks up a small pile of photos from the table next to him. He's a nice guy, I remind myself, just a nice guy, that's all. I've read too much into the attention he was paying me. He's probably simply glad to have someone the same age as him here, and anyway, as Sara said, what harm is there in a little bit of attention? I'm not going to feel embarrassed about it any more.

'Now then,' he's saying, holding up the pile of photos to show us. 'Annie has kindly brought in these pictures of the village; they were her late father's and she's only just come across them in her attic.'

'My son brought them down from the attic for me,' Annie says. 'I wanted the attic cleared out, see? Because the thing is, you don't want to leave a load of old junk up there, for your family to have to sort out after you pop your clogs. I thought I was going to pop my clogs when I was in hospital, I can tell you. I thought I was a goner, especially when they said they were going to stick that camera—'

'Yes, well, we're all glad you're OK now, Annie,' Howard says quickly. 'And thank you for lending us the photos. I'm going to pass them around for you all to look at. As you'll see, Annie's parents lived in Briar Cottage at the lower end of Fore Street—'

'Until me and my four sisters came along,' Annie interrupts. 'Then they needed more space, of course. So they moved to the house where I live now. Being the eldest, and being as they had no sons, I inherited the house, see.'

'Yes, it was like that, years ago, wasn't it?' Howard comments as he passes half the pile of photos to me at my end of the semicircle, and one half to David at the other end. 'All about primogeniture, and, of course, no kind of equality for women whatsoever. Perhaps we can talk this evening about your experiences of that, ladies? As you outnumber us men here! If you had children, did you still go out to work, or were you expected to be housewives for the rest of your lives?'

There's a general hubbub of excited conversation about this, which Howard tries valiantly to control, but one voice rises above all the others – and I'm surprised to realise it's Freda's.

'Never had any children. That was the trouble. No children. I'd have liked to have had children,' she says, loudly and plaintively.

Everyone else has fallen silent, looking at her, unsure quite what to say to this.

'Well, you didn't have a husband, Freda, did you,' Grace says. 'So, unfortunately—'

'No, husband, no children,' Freda responds more quietly. 'But I had my Doris. My friend. Where's Doris?' She looks around, suddenly looking panic-struck. 'Why didn't Doris come?'

'She's gone, Freda, love,' Grace reminds her.

'Gone where? Is she coming back? Has she gone home?'

'Oh dear,' Grace says to the rest of us, looking distressed. 'Can we talk about the photos instead?'

Everyone quickly rallies to this suggestion. I pass some of the photos along the row, and flick through the rest with Saul, sitting next to me. They're mostly pictures of various ancestors of Annie's family, posing in front of their cottage or outside the pub and the village shops.

But Freda isn't taking any notice of the photos. She's still staring blankly across the hall, looking worried.

'No children,' she mutters again. 'That's the trouble, no children. Still, I had my niece. My sister's little girl, that was lovely. Pretty little girl, isn't she?' Freda moves swiftly from past tense to present, looking around at us all, seemingly unsure again of where she is – in time as well as in place. 'Where is she? Where's my little angel? Such a pretty little thing.'

'All right, Freda dear.' Margaret tries to soothe her. 'Come on, let's look at these nice pictures Annie's brought along.' She shoves a picture of a man in a suit standing next to a penny-farthing bicycle in front of Freda's eyes. 'Look at this old-fashioned bike! No cars in the village in those days, eh?'

Fortunately this seems to catch Freda's attention and she takes the photo out of Margaret's hands, studying the image intently for a few moments, before handing it back and returning to her usual quiet manner. We carry on passing the photos between us, and then resume the discussion about women's place in society when we were all younger. It's interesting to hear the different stories. The older ladies all remember how they were expected to leave their jobs as soon as they became pregnant, and in some cases, even as soon as they got married.

'To be fair, though,' says Margaret, – although none of the rest of us seem to agree that it *was* fair! – 'the housework was so much harder in those days. The cleaning, washing and shopping took up our whole time. We wouldn't have had time to go out to work.'

'So the men should have helped with the housework, shouldn't they?' Annie retorts. 'But they'd been brought up to think it wasn't their job. My Fred used to come home from work and expect his slippers and newspaper to be waiting for him, and his dinner on the table ten minutes later. He wasn't the nasty sort,' she adds quickly. 'He was just a normal man, and I didn't really think anything of it. It was his job to earn the money, and mine to look after everything else. Including the three kids!'

'Looking back, though, Annie, do you wish things had been different?' Howard asks her.

'You're bloody right I do!' she says, hooting with laughter. 'You know what I wish? I wish I'd gone to college and trained as a vet. I always loved animals, and I was good at science at school. I'm sure I could've done it. But I left school at fifteen, went to work on the farm, married Fred when I was seventeen, and had my first boy, Douglas, six months later.' She gives another cackle of laughter. 'Had to get married, we did. Served me right, didn't it! Still, it was OK, really. Lots of people in the same boat in those days – no Pill or anything like that, see?'

I feel sad, though, thinking about Annie and her unfulfilled ambition. How many other women through the ages might have lived and died without ever doing what they really wanted with their lives? I might not have been blessed with children, but at least I had an interesting career that I loved.

'You're right, it is sad,' Howard says when I express this view to him during the tea break. 'But thank God, things are better for women now. I've got two daughters; they've both got kids of their own, but one daughter's a doctor and the other's a pilot.'

'Wow. Good for them. I presume their husbands – partners – must play their parts.'

'Up to a point, but, of course, they're busy in their own jobs too. Fortunately, they can afford to pay for childcare, and help in the home, where necessary.'

'So maybe society hasn't really changed that much. Women just work, to pay for their freedom to work!'

He gives a rueful smile. 'You could have a point. Or you could just be being a bit cynical!' He takes a sip of his coffee and changes the subject. 'How's your research about the Angel of the Cove going?'

'I haven't really got anywhere with that. But I *have* met up with Philip – Freda's brother-in-law – twice now. He's been telling me the story of how he and Chrissie, Freda's little sister, tried to run away to sea. It's been fascinating.'

'Have you talked to Freda about it?' he asks.

'No. I don't like to, to be honest. I'm too worried about upsetting her. It's obvious, from the flashbacks she has, that she remembers some painful things about that time.' I hesitate, and then go on: 'She mentioned her sister's little girl tonight, didn't she. Called her "my angel". I guess this was the baby Chrissie was expecting when they tried to run away. I'm hoping Philip will tell me more about her next time I see him.'

'Sounds interesting. Keep me updated!' he says. 'And how about we have that chat about membership, and future meetings, one evening this week? Can you make Friday, or Saturday?'

'Yes, OK. Let's say Friday, then, shall we?'

When Howard suggests we get back to our talk, the ladies of the group are still energetically discussing the missed opportunities of their lives. He bravely decides to turn up the heat by mentioning the point I'd just made.

'Do you think, in fact,' he asks the members when they've all sat themselves back down, 'that women haven't really gained much by becoming more financially independent, because they now have to spend a lot of that extra money on childcare?'

'But they're happier!' Grace responds fiercely. 'Try telling my daughter she should go back to being a stay-at-home mother! Why should she? Why shouldn't her lazy lump of a husband look after the kids instead?'

It may not be strictly a 'historical' discussion but it's lively and fun. I'm glad I've joined this group, glad I decided to face Howard again after my faux pas. It's good to have a new interest, making friends, talking to different people. I'm even looking forward to talking with Howard about how to encourage new members and come up with some different ideas for meetings. In fact, it's exactly what I needed – and much as I hate to say it, what Terry keeps telling me I needed: a new interest.

He even looks up from his laptop when I get home and asks if I had a good evening. So perhaps he's glad I joined the group, too. Perhaps, I tell myself sternly as I go to make us both a cup of tea, I'm imagining the problems in our marriage. That's my trouble: too much time on my hands, for imagining things.

Tuesday 6 November

By half past eleven this morning I've already been for a walk, the housework and washing are so up to date I could get a prize for the cleanest home in Devon. I've got enough shopping in to last us through a siege, and I feel too restless to spend another day just reading or browsing the internet. I know Sara's under pressure with a work deadline so I'm not going to disturb her. It's a damp, cloudy day, not a day for being outdoors, and not a day, either, for standing at the window watching the sea, which is what I'm doing at the moment.

'I think I'll go for a drive,' I say out loud to myself.

I'm going to get in the car and head off, with no idea where, and for no other reason than for something to do. And if that seems sad, then I'm going to make sure it isn't. I'll make sure it cheers me up. Perhaps I'll head across Dartmoor and admire the autumn scenery.

I drive through Bierleigh and out up to the main road, away from the coast, following my nose, my instincts, from a lifetime of living in this part of Devon, and head north towards Dartmoor. As the distant horizon begins to change to a hazy line of purple, I feel my heart lift. Much as I love the sea, the moor always holds a fascination too, a sense of being at one with nature. It commands respect, because up here, weather conditions can change in seconds, rain clouds or fog can descend suddenly out of a beautiful, sunny sky, leaving inexperienced hikers lost and completely vulnerable to the elements. There's something raw and awe-inspiring about the way the road snakes across a vast, empty landscape where outcrops of rock suddenly loom towards the heavens. I'm not hiking today, I'm staying in the car – I haven't even got my walking boots with me, or any provisions. Today I've just come for a change of scenery, and more time to think.

When I reach a particularly high part of the moor where I can see for miles into the purple distance, I pull over for a while to enjoy the view. I'm miles away, thinking back over the years when Terry and I used to come up here sometimes at weekends for picnics, when there's suddenly a movement against the car window on the passenger side, the sound of a snort making me almost jump out of my skin. I turn to see two of the little Dartmoor ponies with their noses pressed up against the window. I laugh, my worries forgotten, and watch as they slowly amble off again to rejoin their family further up on the moor. My stomach rumbles, and I realise it's nearly one o'clock. I start the engine again, turn on the satnav and confirm that, as I'd guessed, I'm only about a mile from Two Bridges where I might as well pull in and have a bite to eat at the pub.

At first, pulling into the car park here and walking into the pub on my own feels a bit odd. But once I'm inside and settled at a table I decide I don't mind it at all, having a solo lunch. In fact, I quite like being out on my own, enjoying the weather, the scenery, seeing the ponies. And perhaps Sara might like to come up here with me sometimes. After a hearty ploughman's lunch, I get back in the car and follow my nose again, taking a different road but heading vaguely back towards the edge of the moor. I haven't driven too much further when I suddenly come across a sign that makes me stop in surprise.

SOUTH DEVON PET SANCTUARY. PLEASE DRIVE CAREFULLY.

The sign is fixed to a tree trunk at the junction with a narrow lane leading past a couple of isolated houses, and I've never seen it before. Out of sheer curiosity, I turn into the lane, which gives me no option but to drive carefully, because it's full of dips and bumpy bits of rock. I navigate a sharp bend and continue across a little hump-back bridge over a stream, and finally the lane runs out in a windswept car park beside a small, squat stone building with a green door and a large sign on the wall repeating the words: SOUTH DEVON PET SANCTUARY.

I park the car and, purely out of curiosity, head for the door, where another smaller sign reads: PLEASE REPORT TO RECEPTION. Inside, I'm surprised to find a reasonably modern interior. To one side, a few chairs surround a coffee table bearing copies of cat and dog magazines and healthcare leaflets, while within a glass-screened area to the other side I can see a desk with phones and a computer, and shelves with rows of files. There's a window in the glass screen, with a counter behind it and the sign RECEPTION above it, in case anyone was in any doubt, and a bell to ring for attention. I ring it, and after a minute a tall woman with shockingly red hair, wearing a matching red jumper that looks as if several cats have pulled out almost every thread of it, bustles into the reception area through a back door and gives me a beaming smile.

'Hello! You found us, then?'

'Well, yes, it seems so!' Slightly confused, I wonder whether she thinks I'm someone who she's been expecting, but she goes on cheerfully:

'Lots of people just find us as they're passing by and come in on impulse.'

'Yes, that's exactly what I've done,' I agree.

'We're an adoption centre, if you're interested in acquiring a pet,' she tells me. 'Want to come and see our current guests?'

I smile. 'I'd love to, but I'm afraid I won't be adopting. I'd love a cat, but my husband wouldn't. And ...' I tail off, remembering I still haven't even felt able to discuss with him the idea of a dog.

She shrugs. 'Well, you're welcome to visit them, anyway.' She heads towards the back door again, turning to look back over her shoulder. 'Coming? I'm Merry, by the way.'

It takes me a moment to realise this is her name, rather than her disposition, so I'm trying not to laugh out loud as I respond, 'Nice to meet you, Merry. I'm Joy.' What a jolly, happy pair we should make together! I follow her through the door and out to another building, where the sound of meows greets us as soon as we enter.

'All right, my lovelies!' Merry calls out cheerfully. 'Got a visitor for you. Hope you've all got your tails and whiskers looking nice and spruce.'

We walk up and down the aisle between the enclosures, Merry pointing out each occupant, telling me their names and their temperaments.

'Want to see the dogs now?' she asks.

'OK, thank you, why not!'

She leads me outside and across a wide area of grass to yet another building. I can hear the dogs barking and whining as we approach. When we go inside, they all start to run about in their enclosure, noses sniffing, eyes bright with excitement, tails wagging frantically.

'Oh my God, how does anyone ever choose between them?' I ask, bending down and reaching in to stroke a particularly insistent cocker spaniel on his nose. 'They're all so gorgeous.'

'People usually say they just fall in love with one, and know it's the right choice,' she says, smiling. 'Are you tempted?'

'To adopt one? Oh, I'd love to.' I straighten up from stroking the little spaniel. 'To be honest,' I tell her, 'I've thought for a while about getting a dog, but I haven't really had a chance to discuss it with my husband yet.'

'Of course,' Merry says. 'You both need to be on-board with it, obviously. Nobody should adopt an animal unless they're totally committed. Bring your husband with you another day, if he's interested. Retired, are you? Dogs are good for your health – nice long walks in the countryside.'

'Yes. I think I'd really like that. I will talk to him about it.'

'OK. Well, you know where we are, now. And here's our phone number.' She passes me a card.

When I leave the centre, I'm smiling and walking with a spring in my step, imagining myself with a little furry friend to take out for walks, to look after and love and talk to when I'm at home on my own. I'd have to make sure any dog we adopt is used to cats, so that it doesn't chase Pumpkin. And at least, now I've met Luke, I've got a friendly contact at the local vet's whenever I need any advice.

Almost as if I've conjured him up by thinking about him, I'm just crossing the car park when Luke himself pulls in, gets out of his car and gives me a wave.

'Hello, Joy!' he calls in surprise. 'What are you doing here? Decided to adopt a cat just to upset your husband?' He laughs, and I pretend to find it funny too.

'No, although I am considering getting a dog,' I tell him. 'But, in fact, I was just out for a drive, and found this place by accident.'

'And Merry talked you into it? She's good at that!'

'She didn't, to be fair – but I'm not ready yet. Terry and I need to discuss it first, obviously.'

'Yes. Well it'd be great if you do.'

'Are you here for one of the animals?' I ask him.

'No, we're not the local vet's, here. I do like visiting, though!' He smiles. 'I've just sneaked a long lunch break so that I can talk to Merry about Lina.'

'Oh, right! Have you spoken to the carer, then? Does she think Lina would be OK to adopt a cat?'

'Yes!' He smiles. 'Amy thinks it would work well, as long as the cat's an adult, with an easy temperament and no particular problems to complicate its care. I'm going to ask Merry to look out for any suitable candidates. If we can settle on one or two possibilities, I'll bring Lina here to see them.'

'Ah, good, that's kind of you. And it'll be nice to think of her having a cat of her own.'

'Yes, it will. Well, good to see you, Joy. No doubt I'll bump into you again.' He starts to walk towards the door of the centre, then stops suddenly, turns and walks back to me. 'I hope you don't mind me asking,' he says in a very quiet voice, 'but I know you're good friends with Sara, so I just wondered: is she all right, do you think?'

He goes a bit red, just saying her name, and immediately looks down at his shoes.

'It's just ... I've known her for ages, you see,' he goes on. 'We were good friends years ago, and ... well, we met up again recently.'

He pauses now, shifting uncomfortably, and I say – because I actually feel a bit sorry for him now:

'Yes, she did say she's known you since school.'

I'm certainly not going to tell him she's poured out the rest of the story to me!

He nods. 'We always got on well. But she's seemed a bit off with me since we've both been living down here. It was a surprise, of course – a coincidence – both of us moving here. And I know, obviously, she was upset and worried about Pumpkin. But now . . . now I've helped to get him back for her . . . well, it still feels really awkward between us. I still felt it when I came the other evening, even though she invited me to stay and watch the fireworks. And, well, I don't quite know how to put that right.'

'Oh.' I'm not sure what to say to this. To be honest, I can't believe he's asking me! He must *know* why it's awkward between the two of them, unless he's suffering from some odd kind of permanent post-coital amnesia!

'Well,' I manage to say, 'I haven't actually known Sara for very long. But, as you know, she's been through a really tough time, with her marriage ending, and having to start again on her own in a new house, with her little boy . . . '

'Of course, absolutely, I get that. I get that she'll be stressed, and unhappy – of course. And I'd like to think I could try to help her in any way I can, seeing as we've both moved into the same area.' He ducks his head, looking away again. 'Well, I suppose, understandably, she's just sick of men in general.'

'Have you asked her?' I say, deciding to be more direct. 'Asked her whether there's anything wrong?'

'Well, no, I haven't. I felt a bit awkward about approaching the subject, to be honest.' He gives a self-deprecatory little laugh that isn't really a laugh, and adds, 'I hope you didn't mind me asking.'

'No, of course not. But I think it's Sara you should be asking.'

'Yes. Perhaps I should. Thank you.'

We say goodbye and I walk back to my car. I'm beginning to think that, however nice Luke seems, he can't be terribly bright. He can't possibly be unaware of why Sara feels uncomfortable around him; he quite obviously feels the same, with all his blushing and stammering! Has he forgotten they promised never to mention that night they spent together, is that it? And has it honestly not occurred to him that neither of them discussed contraception? That she could be pregnant?

Honestly, men can be unbelievably dense at times. But then, why would that still surprise me?

Wednesday 7 November

I made up my mind to discuss the dog idea with Terry yesterday evening, whether he wanted to talk or not. To be honest, it was good to talk to him about something that didn't involve delving any further into what's wrong with him, or with our marriage.

'I went for a drive on Dartmoor,' I told him while we were eating dinner. It's the one time I can be fairly sure he won't be distracted by anything on his phone or laptop. 'And I happened to come across a pet sanctuary up there. I've never noticed it before.'

'Oh, really?' he said.

'I had a look around,' I went on, 'and it occurred to me—'

'I can't have a cat, Joy, you know that.'

'I know. But . . . I've been thinking: why not a dog?'

He blinked in surprise. 'I didn't know you were thinking about getting a dog.'

'Well, I wasn't. It's only recently occurred to me, but I didn't think seriously about it until I looked around the centre today. There are so many dogs there, needing someone to adopt them.'

'You're right, actually,' he said, nodding slowly. 'That *could* be a good idea. I think you need something like this. A dog would be company for you, and it would give you more encouragement to go for walks.'

I was pleased and surprised that he seemed to agree so quickly. We went on to talk for a while about what type of dog would be suitable. And although we haven't made any decisions yet, I'm singing to myself this morning as I tidy the kitchen, thinking about the possibilities.

I mention it to Sara today when we both happen to be going out to the recycling bins at the same time.

'How exciting!' she says. 'That'll be lovely for you, Joy. I'm glad Terry's agreed.'

'I'm going to make sure we choose a dog that's used to cats,' I tell her. 'That's a priority. Pumpkin was here first, after all!'

She smiles. 'Dogs and cats often get along fine together, though. When I was a kid, we had one of each, and it was so sweet to see them snuggled up together.'

'Well, fingers crossed!' I hesitate, wondering for a moment whether I ought to mention it or not, before ploughing on: 'And I bumped into Luke at the pet sanctuary.'

'Oh.'

'He said Lina's carer has agreed she should be fine to have a cat of her own, as long as it's an adult one with a calm nature. He's going to take her there to choose one, once they've found a couple of suitable options.'

'That's good.'

'And he asked after you,' I add.

'After Pumpkin, I suppose.'

'No. Specifically you. He . . . ' I hesitate again. I don't think it'd be helpful to tell her he'd wondered what was wrong with her. 'He wondered how you were,' I finish instead.

I watch her face. She's gone from looking completely impassive, to blinking and turning slightly pink – whether with surprise or annoyance, it's hard to tell.

'Well, he only saw me on Friday evening when he watched the fireworks with us!' she says. 'He didn't bother to ask how I was then, he said he was just concerned about Pumpkin. And anyway,' she goes on, seeming to become more indignant the more she thinks about it, 'it's a bit late to start wondering how I am *now*, isn't it! If he'd really been interested in my welfare, he'd have asked at some point, even if not till afterwards, whether I was on the Pill!'

I'm not about to point out that, on her own admission, this somewhat vital question had also slipped her own mind, so it seems a bit unfair just to blame Luke!

'Well, anyway,' I say. 'He seemed worried about you. As a friend, he said.'

She just shrugs, and I decide it's time to change the subject.

'Typical November weather today, isn't it – damp and dreary.'

'Yes. Shall we tog ourselves up and go for a walk? I've caught up with the work, I could spare an hour or so.'

'That'd be good,' I agree. 'Let's head up to Harry's Plain and I'll show you the path down the other side – not the one into the village – one that goes down to the next bay. It's a slightly longer walk.'

'That sounds great.'

'Get your walking boots on, then – it'll be muddy,' I warn her, as we walk back up the beach together. 'See you in five minutes?'

I'm ready and waiting outside for Sara within a couple of minutes, and I have to smile when I see her waving goodbye to Pumpkin, who's watching her from the kitchen windowsill as she locks her back door.

We walk slowly, across the rocks and up the path to Harry's Plain. We stop on top of the plain and look out across the cove from above – as always, the view warms my heart and reminds me of how lucky I am to live here. As we walk on, down Old Harry's Staircase, across the fields, through the thicket and out the other side, eventually hitting the coast again at Redland Bay, I talk to Sara some more about my ideas on the proposed dog.

'I think an adult dog will be best,' I tell her. 'We're a bit past the stage of starting with a puppy. And probably not too big – we've got to think ahead. We might get old and frail and a big dog might be too much for us.'

'Old and frail?' Sara laughs. 'Look at you, striding up and down these hills. You're fitter than I am!'

'Well, if we got a young dog, it could live until we're eighty,' I point out, and she laughs again before conceding that I'm just trying to be sensible.

'I'm really pleased you've got something nice to look forward to.'

She tucks her arm through mine and we walk on for a while, neither of us talking, until eventually, we stop for a breather on the beach at Redland Bay. It's a quiet, rocky beach and there's nobody here, nothing but the sound of the waves lapping the shore and the seagulls crying as they swoop and dive above.

At the other end of the beach, we turn to head back. As we climb the footpath to take us away from the coast again, the sun suddenly comes out from behind the bank of murky, grey clouds. We stop to watch the sunshine over the sea, and Sara gasps as she notices the light picking out a dark shadow close to the rocks at the edge of the bay.

'Is that something under the water, there?' she says, shading her eyes and pointing.

'Yes. A shipwreck. There have been a lot of wrecks along here, over the years. This stretch of coast isn't nearly as safe as Angel Cove.'

'No. Those rocks look pretty hazardous.'

'So are the currents. I wouldn't want to swim here.'

She shudders. 'I'm glad we're at Angel Cove.'

'Me too,' I agree.

As we walk back to Smugglers' Cottages, Sara asks me about this week's Historical Society meeting. She's particularly interested when I describe the conversations we had about women's rights — or lack of them — in the past, and laughs out loud about Annie describing her hospital experience, and Howard's attempts to stop her giving us all too much information about it.

'But nothing from Freda this time? About the Angel of the Cove?' she asks.

'No. She did get upset, though, about the fact that she never had any children. Oh, and she mentioned her niece: Chrissie's baby. Called her "my little angel".'

'Ah. I wonder what happened to that baby. Where she is now. Doesn't Philip mention her?'

'He hasn't so far — only in passing.' I pause, and then add, half to myself: 'I do wonder if she's still alive. Surely if she was, she'd be looking after her father, now that he's disabled? Or at least visiting him.'

'Perhaps she lives too far away.'

'Yes, I suppose so. Anyway, I guess he'll come to that soon. I'm going back to see him again tomorrow.'

'Oh, good. I'm looking forward to the next part of his story,' Sara says.

I smile. The truth is, I'm looking forward to my visits to Philip a lot myself, too. I obviously still don't know him terribly well, but we seem to get along together, and I'm really grateful to him for sharing his memories with me. I've found myself thinking about him while I'm at home on my own: thinking about him living here with his family, in my house, going out fishing from this beach with his father. Being with his childhood sweetheart next door, playing with her on the beach when they were still children. Perhaps it's doing him some good, too – talking about it all, after so long. Reliving all those precious memories.

Thursday 8 November

To my surprise, Sara knocks on my door this morning as soon as she's back from taking Charlie to school.

'Could I ask you a favour, Joy?' she says.

'Of course you can, love. What is it?'

'I wondered if you'd mind looking after Charlie for me tomorrow evening? It'll probably only be for a little while.'

'Oh, I'd love to, any time! I hope you're going out somewhere nice? With a friend?'

She pulls a face and looks down at her feet. 'No. In fact, I'm meeting Luke. He called last night.'

'Did he?' I try to sound surprised, and not to smile to myself. So it seems Luke actually took my advice!

'Yes. I was pretty taken aback when he suggested meeting up. To be honest, I nearly said no, but – well, you're quite right: I do need to talk to him, don't I. I need to get it over with – telling him about the baby. So I might as well take the opportunity.'

'Good. Yes, grasp the nettle, otherwise you might keep putting it off. And I'll really look forward to sitting with Charlie. Tell him to choose his favourite bedtime story for me to read him.'

'I will. I'm sure he'll look forward to it too. Thanks, Joy, I do appreciate it.'

An hour or so later, I'm back at Goldcrest Lodge with Philip again. I feel like we're getting to know each other a little more now, and instead of going straight into talking about his and Chrissie's story from 1960, we chat a little about our current lives. He tells me some more about his move into Goldcrest Lodge, earlier this year, after the surgery to his leg.

'I'd moved back to Bierleigh after Chrissie passed away,' he explains. 'I'd felt the need to return to my roots, while I was getting used to ... being without her. But after the operation, it was difficult. I had stairs in my house, and steps up to the front door, and, well, the way I see it, there's no point clinging on to a place that doesn't work for you any more. And it's nice here. Janet's all right really, she doesn't mind me calling her the prison officer, and she does a lot to help us old crocks when we need it.'

'You're definitely not my idea of an old crock!' I retort. 'And I bet you don't need much help, either.'

'No, I try to be as independent as possible. I'll be glad to get back to driving, though. I prefer not to let Arthur drive me too far!'

I smile. Despite what Philip says about his friend's driving, I expect the two of them enjoy their jaunts out together. But I can see Philip doesn't want to talk too much about his own circumstances, as he changes the subject now, asking about my job at the surgery and what I've been doing since I retired.

'It's helped a lot, having a new friend and neighbour next door,' I explain after I've tried, without much success, to articulate my mixed feelings about retirement. 'Her name's Sara. It must seem so strange to you: hearing me talking about our houses, when they used to be yours and Chrissie's.'

'A long time ago now!' He says. 'Have they changed much – Smugglers' Cottages?'

'Well, ours has probably changed the most: we had an extension built, at the side. Number two probably wouldn't look much different to you. When were you last at Angel Cove?'

'Oh, many years ago now. We moved away from the area early in the sixties, rented a farm cottage in one of the villages up in North Devon. I worked on the farm; it was the only way to keep a roof over our heads – we were so young, and we had no money.'

'But you were a fisherman.'

He laughs. 'I *was*. But we needed to move away, to find somewhere with living accommodation that went with the job. We couldn't find anywhere to rent – even if we could have afforded to – around Bierleigh. And there wasn't room for me, Chrissie and the baby to stay indefinitely in either of our parents' cottages. You know how small the rooms are.'

'Yes. That's why we had the extension,' I agree.

'Exactly. My house was already overcrowded, with my two brothers. And it wasn't fair to impose on Chrissie's parents for ever, either, even though it was a bit less crowded after Freda moved out.'

'Did she move out soon after you got married?'

He nods. 'After the baby was born. That's when she moved in with Doris, in Bierleigh.'

'So you and Chrissie were able to take over the second bedroom.'

'Yes.' He pauses. 'In fact, we took over the room straight after we got married. She slept on the sofa.'

'Oh!' I find myself wondering whose suggestion this was – for Freda, the older, apparently resentful sister, to give up her bedroom for the teenage newly-weds. Presumably her parents pushed her into it. But it was surprising that the parents were so accommodating too, considering what Chrissie and Philip had got up to – stealing the fishing boat, running away to sea, worrying the life out of everyone!

'Freda insisted,' Philip says, watching my face, seeming to realise what I'm thinking. 'She thought it was only right.'

'Well, that was good of her. Considering how she'd felt before; what you told me she'd said to Chrissie . . .'

'Yes.' He chuckles. 'But she changed, completely, after we tried to run away. And a lot of what happened afterwards was thanks to the Angel of the Cove.'

February 1960

They were all huddled together in Chrissie's parents' kitchen: Freda, her parents, Philip's parents and his brothers, having all finally fallen silent after their initial outbursts of shock, anger, fear and distress. Freda's mother, Nora, and Philip's mother, Betty, were sitting at the table, holding on to each other, both dabbing their eyes with their hankies and swallowing back sobs, while their two husbands marched back and forth across the room, stopping every few minutes to stare out of the window yet again. Philip's young brothers, who'd just turned fourteen, were both white-faced with shock, their thin, gawky bodies barely covered by their worn and outgrown pyjamas, shivering violently in the cold kitchen, having been woken from their sleep and trying to make sense of what was going on. Looking at them with more compassion than she normally felt, Freda went upstairs and brought them down the two blankets from her own bed, then lit the gas in the oven and left it open to warm up the room. She'd made everyone strong, sweet tea for the shock as soon as she'd explained what had happened to her own parents first, and then knocked at Number One cottage to wake up Philip's family.

'Come and wait with us,' she'd told them, trying to sound

braver, more in control, than she felt. 'If there's any news, it's our phone they'll be ringing.'

'Why would they *do* such a stupid thing?' her own mother cried out now, setting Philip's mother off crying again. It seemed to be all she could say.

Freda had to turn away, shoving a fist against her mouth to stop herself from blurting out that Chrissie had done it because she was desperate; because she was pregnant, and she was too scared to tell her mother; that she'd run away because her big sister *wouldn't help her*!

It was another hour, another long hour of waiting, and crying, and pacing, before the phone finally rang, and Freda, having jumped to grab the receiver off the hook, turned to tell the others in the room:

'They've been found. The lifeboat's bringing them back.'

'Are they OK? Did they say whether they're both all right?' her mother asked.

'Yes. Both alive and well. Chrissie's just . . . seasick, they said.'

As she said this, Freda sat down abruptly and burst into tears – tears not just of relief, but of shame too. Her little sister wasn't just seasick, she was sure of that. She'd heard her being sick every morning for the past week, and had already been starting to suspect what it meant, even before Chrissie had come to her, asking for the help that wasn't forthcoming. No wonder she was sick *now*, having been out at sea all night in a storm!

Unable to sit still for long, she got up, lit the gas under the kettle again to make more tea and, taking a deep breath, turned to face her mother. The least she could do to help Chrissie now was to save her having to break the news later on. And if it meant Philip's parents finding out at the same time, that was all well and good.

'Mum,' she said, her voice quavering slightly, 'There's something you ought to know. Chrissie's . . . she told me she's—'

But just at that moment the kitchen door was flung open and there was a shout from outside, where the two fathers had gone to pace up and down on the beach, puffing on their cigarettes and staring out at sea.

'They're on their way! The lifeboat – we can see its lights – it's definitely the lifeboat – it's heading into the cove now!'

And for the next little while there was a pandemonium of action as they all ran outside to see the lights steadily approaching, then rushed around hugging each other and crying openly in relief, and finally ran back into their own houses to prepare warm clothes, blankets and hot drinks for their returning children and the rescuers.

'Lucky you made the call, miss,' one of the lifeboat crew said quietly to Freda as she handed him a mug of hot tea, gushing her thanks all over again. 'Thank you' and 'Thank God' were the only words anyone from the two families seemed to be capable of uttering, from the moment Philip was helped out of the lifeboat, and Chrissie was carried out in the arms of a crew member – shockingly white, confused and muttering incoherently about an angel. They were now all in Freda's family's living room, being debriefed by the crew. 'Your sister's been very sick,' he went on. 'She's dehydrated and weak. Give her plenty of water to drink, but just in little sips through a straw, so she doesn't bring it up again. But you might be advised to call her a doctor.'

'Thank you,' she said yet again. 'I will.'

She went into the kitchen to make the call. She and her mother had already taken Chrissie up to her bed, where Freda could hear her, tossing and turning and still muttering deliriously in her sleep. When she came off the phone, the first signs of daylight were appearing above the horizon. The lifeboat crew were setting off again and Philip's family was preparing to return to their own house. She watched Philip as he staggered upright, his father and one of his young brothers holding him up. His legs were shaking, his face was grey with exhaustion and he was hanging his head, trying to hide his tears.

'Let's talk about all this in the morning – I mean later, when everybody's caught up on their sleep,' Philip's father said.

'Yes,' Freda's father agreed. 'I can't even think straight at the moment, Jack.'

Freda wondered what the talk would involve. How were the young couple going to be punished? She presumed they'd be dealt with pretty severely, despite the fact that all their parents could think about right now was their relief at seeing them safely returned. Their anger would be sure to resurface as soon as everyone had settled down, especially because of Philip's father's boat – his livelihood. Although it had been recovered, it had been badly damaged by the storm.

'Philip,' Freda said softly, catching hold of the young man's arm as he was being guided out through the kitchen. She hadn't had a chance to talk to him yet. 'Are you OK, really? Is Chrissie going to be OK?'

He looked up at her, his eyes bleak with tiredness and stress. 'I hope so,' he muttered.

She knew he probably hadn't forgiven her for not having offered any help or sympathy. She didn't blame him. But she wanted to make amends now. She wanted his forgiveness and, most of all, Chrissie's.

'What was Chrissie saying – about an angel?' she asked him quietly.

'She was hallucinating. She thought she'd seen the Angel of the Cove.'

She saw the two mothers exchange a look.

'The Angel of the Cove?' Betty whispered.

'It was just a hallucination, Mum,' Philip said with a sigh. 'Can I go to bed now?'

But Freda suddenly knew, now, how she might be able to help. She knew, as soon as she'd seen that look pass between her mother and Philip's mother, that the way to help her sister and Philip and make up for her past unkindness lay with the angel of Angel Cove.

'So what *did* she do?' I ask, as Philip's stopped talking now, and is staring at the floor, a half-smile on his lips, seemingly lost in his memories. 'What was it about the angel that Freda said, or did, to help you and Chrissie?'

For a few moments I think he's not going to reply; that he's tired himself out again, that recalling the physical and emotional strain of that dreadful night has taken its toll and he's not going to be able to tell me any more today. I ask him if he'd like me to make some more coffee, but he shakes his head, so I just sit and wait until he's ready.

'I found out all of that from Freda, of course,' he says eventually, looking back up at me. 'Everything that happened that night, while we were lost out at sea. She told us afterwards, after things had finally calmed down, how she'd woken up and found Chrissie's bed empty, and then realised the boat was missing, and called the coastguard.'

'She saved your lives.'

He smiles. 'Probably. Of course, we might have been found anyway, when daylight came. The English Channel's not exactly a quiet backwater! But we might also have been mown down in the dark by a bigger ship. Or we might have died of exposure or been washed overboard. And yes, Chrissie needed a doctor, she was badly dehydrated.'

'But she came through it OK?'

'She was young and strong. The doctor said she just needed fluids and rest.'

'But I'm itching to know how the Angel of the Cove came into it,' I say again. 'How did Freda use it to help you and Chrissie?'

He laughs. 'Ah, well you see, Joy, the story of the angel had been handed down the generations. To both our mothers, mine and Chrissie's, it was almost part of their religion. They'd both grown up in the area, and lived most of their lives at Angel Cove. So they'd gone through life with the idea of the angel firmly implanted into their psyches. Any mention of it, and you could almost expect to see them cross themselves!'

'They really believed in it – the legend?'

'Of course they did. Our fathers teased them about it, but, to be honest, I think they were just as much in awe of the whole thing, too. Especially my dad; being a fisherman, he was pretty sure the angel was protecting him every time he went out in his boat.'

'Yes, I've heard tales about it being impossible to drown at the cove.'

'Exactly.' His eyes twinkle. 'Our generation scoffed at it, of course. Thought it was superstitious nonsense.'

'Well, at the end of the day, you and Chrissie *didn't* drown!' I smile back at him, and then go on cautiously, almost holding my breath: 'But your parents never mentioned knowing how the legend of the angel started in the first place?'

'No, they didn't, unfortunately. I think our parents just accepted the angel was some kind of eternal entity that had always been there, hovering over the cove.'

'So I suppose your parents chose to believe it was the Angel of the Cove, looking over you, that kept you safe that night?'

'Yes.' He nods. 'Especially because Chrissie kept saying she'd seen it. And, because Freda backed her up.'

I blink in surprise. 'Backed her up? But she wasn't out there with you!'

'No, but you see, when Chrissie was feeling better, and was out of bed, we all gathered again in her house for the . . . telling-off we were bound to get from our parents. And she was *still* insisting she'd seen the angel, that it wasn't an hallucination, that she was sure the angel had saved us.'

'Hallucinations can seem so real, people do completely believe in them.'

'Yes. Especially when someone's *schooled* them to continue believing.'

'Oh!' I chuckle, beginning to understand. 'Freda encouraged Chrissie to keep talking about the angel, to convince your mothers you'd both really been rescued by it?'

'Yes. Once Chrissie was feeling better, she knew, of course, that she hadn't really seen an angel, but Freda prompted her to keep to the story. Not only that, Freda added a cunning little postscript of her own. She announced that, as we were helped out of the lifeboat, as she watched Chrissie being carried up the beach, she herself saw the angel, leaning over us both, protecting us with its wings!' He shakes his head, laughing. 'How the dickens our parents fell for that one, I'll never understand, but they did. Chrissie's mother actually fell to her knees to thank God for sending the angel to save her daughter, and my own mum started singing a hymn at the top of her voice – that old seafarers' hymn about saving the lives of those in trouble at sea. It was . . . uncanny . . . how easily they were convinced about, frankly, a lot of nonsense!'

'Freda just wanted to make up for what she'd done,' I muse. 'How she thought she'd let Chrissie down.'

'And for her jealousy,' he says, nodding sadly. 'She admitted it, you know, in later years – after she was settled with Doris, and happier herself. She considered her jealousy of her sister to have been her greatest sin.'

'Poor Freda. From what I've heard her say, she still thinks that.'

We're both silent with our thoughts for a moment, then I ask: 'So, *were* you punished for running away? For taking the boat?'

'Yes, but not as severely as we might have been, if everyone hadn't been consumed with the business of worshipping the angel!' he says. 'Dad missed a week's work while the boat was repaired, and afterwards I had to work without pay, to cover the cost of the repairs. And Chrissie—'

'Yes, what happened when her parents found out about the pregnancy?'

'Strangely enough, it turned out her mother already suspected.'

'Not so strange, really,' I say. 'Mothers do tend to notice their daughters exhibiting signs of morning sickness.'

'I suppose so. Anyway, Freda took care of that, too. Had a quiet word with their mum, who then had a surprisingly quiet word with Chrissie before they faced her dad together. Chrissie said her mum had been more hurt than angry, about the fact that she'd been too scared to tell her. She might have been strict, but she was more understanding than we realised. My own father gave me a clout, called me a bloody idiot, reminded me of Chrissie's age – as if I could ever forget – and asked why I couldn't have *kept it in my pants for a few more months*, or failing that, at least have asked him how to get hold of contraceptives. But Chrissie's punishment, really, was the fact that she had to leave school.'

'That was sad for her. But her parents obviously agreed to you and Chrissie getting married.'

'They not only agreed, they told us we had no option! The two families had a crisis meeting and our parents basically took over. They arranged the wedding for the week after Chrissie's sixteenth birthday. I think Chrissie's father would have held a shotgun to my head if such things were still allowed. Not that I needed any encouragement. It was what we both wanted anyway.'

'You must have been surprised, though? That they didn't, after all, send Chrissie away to have the baby adopted, or anything like that?'

'You're right, we were surprised. But again, I think it definitely helped that everything, in their minds, was now tied up with the Angel of the Cove. Chrissie's mum, in particular, seemed convinced the angel had *blessed our union*. We might have laughed at them, in any other circumstances, but believe me, we were grateful to that so-called angel for the rest of our lives!'

'Ah, so everything turned out happily.'

'Yes,' he says. He smiles, but then falls silent again.

'And the baby? You said it was a little girl?'

'Yes.' He looks away, over at the window. 'Do you mind if we call it a day now, Joy? All this chatting and reminiscing fair wears me out. Not used to it.'

'Of course, I'm sorry, Philip. I didn't mean to tire you so much.'

'Not at all. I really enjoy telling you about our story. It just gets a bit ... overwhelming. But you'll come again, won't you?'

'Of course I will, as long as you'd like me to.'

Perhaps he can't face talking about his daughter. I wonder if it's a painful subject. I do hope not, it would be so sad if something awful happened at the end of this story. Perhaps next time I'd better wait and see if he brings up the subject or not. I don't want to pressure him into discussing anything he'd prefer not to. We make our next date and I leave him alone with his memories again.

Friday 9 November

I'm sitting down with my lunchtime sandwich today when I hear my phone ringing in the kitchen. By the time I get to it, I've missed the call ... but the display tells me it was Luke. I hesitate before returning the call. I can't imagine what he wants to talk to me about – unless it's something to do with the pet sanctuary; perhaps he's found a suitable cat for Lina and just thought it would be nice to let me know? Or ... perhaps it's even that he's seen a really, really cute dog there and thinks I'd be mad to miss it!

But when I call him back, he sounds hesitant, almost nervous.

'Hope you don't mind me calling you, Joy. It's just a quick question – I'm on my lunch break ...'

'Of course I don't mind. Is everything all right?'

'Well, I think so. I mean, I'm not sure. Sorry.' He pauses, and then goes on in a rush: 'It's about Sara.'

'Right,' I say, my heart sinking. I don't know what's coming, but I'm pretty sure I don't want to get involved in it.

'I've arranged to meet her tonight,' he says.

'Yes. I know, she's asked me to sit with Charlie.'

'Right. Well, it's just ... I arranged to meet her because of what you said. That I ought to talk to her myself, ask her if everything's all right between us.'

'OK.'

'But, I know this sounds pathetic, Joy, but I'm nervous about it. I'm sorry, there isn't really anyone else I can ask about this, so I . . . I hope you don't mind.'

'Mind what?' He's lost me now. He sounds like he's all over the place, to be honest.

'Um, mind if I ask you: has she talked to you about me at all?'

'Well, only that you were old friends,' I say.

He drops his voice a little, and I imagine him eating his lunch at work, surrounded by colleagues.

'Has she mentioned anything . . . um, anything that happened? Between me and her?'

I'm *not* being drawn into this! I can't believe he really wants to discuss his sex life with me!

'No,' I say a bit abruptly.

'Right. Of course, she wouldn't have . . . I'm sorry, Joy. Sorry to ask. It's just, the thing is, I really like her, you see. I've always really liked her, but now she's not with her husband, to be honest I was hoping . . . but now, I don't know how to . . . and it's going to be difficult to . . . and she might not want to . . .'

'Luke,' I say firmly, trying to be gentle but struggling with my impatience. I mean, it's lovely – and in the circumstances, very reassuring – to hear how much he likes her, but this is ridiculous! 'I'm afraid you're not making very much sense. And I'm sorry to say this again, but: you're talking to the wrong person.' *And if you babble on as incoherently as this with Sara tonight, it's not exactly going to get you anywhere*, I feel like saying.

'I know. Sorry to have bothered you. I'm just feeling a little bit desperate. Tonight might be my only chance to say something, and I don't want to blow it, you see.'

'I see. But I don't think I can help, I'm afraid,' I say. For God's sake, he's a grown man, sounding like a gibbering, overgrown schoolboy. At this rate, I'd give his so-called *only chance* about as much likelihood of success as a snowman on a bonfire.

But then I remember just how childish and pathetic *I* must have sounded, when I bleated to Sara about my embarrassing faux pas with Howard Hardcastle. And I'm supposed to be a mature woman with a bit more sense, even further beyond the silly, dithering stage of life than Luke ought to be! Who am I to talk?

'Look, Luke,' I interrupt him in the middle of his stammering attempt to thank me and say goodbye, 'whatever you do, tonight, just don't carry on like you're doing now, being all awkward and embarrassed. If you *really* want some advice – from a woman's point of view – just try to forget your own feelings, and remember how vulnerable *Sara's* feeling at the moment. She's been putting on a good front, but the separation from her husband is still very recent, and very raw. I doubt she'll want anything from any man just now apart from friendship, and perhaps some . . . support. It might be best not to talk at all. Just listen. Hear what *she* has to say.' I pause. When he hears what she does, in fact, have to say, he might completely forget about everything else! Especially if it's true that he doesn't want children. 'Just listen, and be kind,' I say. 'We tend to like that.'

'Thank you,' he says. He clears his throat, and says, in something close to his normal voice, 'That's good advice. I hope you won't tell Sara I called you?'

'Of course I won't.'

I feel strangely conflicted after we hang up. He's seemed, all along, such a decent young man to me – a bit hopeless, but decent. And I've suspected all along that despite Sara's discomfiture about finding herself living close to him, and despite her shock at finding herself pregnant by someone who professes not to want children, she actually likes him more than she's admitting. But she's obviously not ready for a relationship – it's far too soon. And whether he wanted to be a father or not, he's soon going to be one. If he isn't already babbling incoherently to her as soon as they start to talk tonight, he probably will be when she drops *that* little bombshell and – who knows? – he might run a mile.

I go next door a bit early this evening to look after Charlie, and even before Sara's gone out, he and I are on our second game of Snap and we've chosen two stories to read together. He's had a bath and is in his pyjamas, his hair smelling of strawberry shampoo, and has his favourite toy tiger tucked under one arm as he sits next to me on the sofa.

'Are you sure you'll be all right?' Sara asks anxiously.

'Yes, Mummy,' Charlie says, although the question was obviously aimed at me. 'We'll be fine. Have a nice time!'

She laughs and bends down to kiss him good night and remind him to be good.

'Just call me if you need me to come back,' she says quietly to me. 'I won't be late.'

'You can be as late as you like. As Charlie says, we'll be fine.'

She's dressed in an uncharacteristically understated way, with no discernable make-up and wearing jeans and a plain grey jumper. I know she's not particularly looking forward to this evening. It's going to be awkward for both of them, and I think she'd back out if I gave her the slightest excuse.

Charlie behaves perfectly. I read him the first story downstairs, and the second one after he's cleaned his teeth and got into bed – after which I don't hear another sound from him. When I check him a little later, he's fast asleep, one arm on the pillow, his hand resting on his tiger. I stand for a moment, gazing down at him, before I suddenly become aware that my phone's warbling away downstairs. I smile to myself, imagining Sara calling to make sure everything's all right, even though she hasn't even been gone very long yet. But when I get back downstairs and check the missed call display, it's not Sara's name that comes up at all. It's Howard's.

'Oh, God!' I say when I call him back. 'I'm *so* sorry! I didn't forget, honestly – it's just, something came up unexpectedly, something I've had to do for a friend, and I haven't had a chance to call you to explain—'

'You forgot,' he overrules me mildly. 'You double-booked, didn't you! Don't worry,' he goes on, laughing, as I start to splutter another apology. 'I'll forgive you. Is it worth trying for another date, or are you just trying to let me down gently?'

'Don't be daft!' I'm laughing with him now. 'Of course we'll make another date. Whenever. Tomorrow if you like. I'm really sorry, Howard. I promise I won't stand you up again.'

'It's just as well I know we're only meeting to talk about the Historical Society,' he says. 'If I was really hoping for a romantic evening, I'd be crying into my beer now! Yes, let's make it tomorrow night, then – same place, same time. Hopefully that won't be long enough off for you to forget about it.'

'Ouch!' I chuckle. 'I deserved that.'

'Actually,' he goes on more quietly, 'it's probably fortunate we didn't try to have our discussion in here tonight. There's a couple at the next table having a furious row. Can you hear them?'

'No . . .' I begin. But the next minute, I assume he must be holding the phone away from himself, towards the offending couple, because yes, I can hear raised voices all right now. And I recognise one of them only too well. It's Sara's; and although I can't make out what she's saying, because of the general chatter going on in the background – the pub noises of clinking glasses and orders being called to the bar staff – I can tell perfectly well that she's having the rant of a lifetime.

'Oh dear!' I mutter.

'Sorry?' says Howard.

'Um . . . it sounds a bit fraught, doesn't it?'

'Yes . . . lovers' tiff, I presume,' he says mildly.

If only he knew.

It's not even nine o'clock when Sara arrives home. She throws her car keys on the table and sits down, her expression giving nothing away.

'Has Charlie been OK?' she asks after a moment.

'Yes, as good as gold. Hasn't even stirred since he went to bed.'

'Thank you, Joy. Would you like a coffee or anything before you go?'

I feel a bit like I'm being dismissed.

'No, I'm fine, thanks.' I get to my feet but my curiosity gets the better of me. I just can't restrain myself from asking, 'So, did it go OK with Luke?'

Instead of answering straight away, Sara leans back in her chair, closes her eyes and sighs.

'I seem to have made a complete arse of myself,' she says eventually.

'What? Why?'

'Because I've got it all completely wrong.'

Again I wait for her to go on, but she still sits there with her head back and her eyes closed. Perhaps I should just go. If she doesn't want to talk about it, that's fair enough. But as I start to walk towards the door, as I open my mouth to say goodbye, she suddenly bursts out, all in a rush:

'I told him about the baby straight away. Almost as soon as I sat down. Before I'd even got my coat off. I had to, Joy. I was so stressed about telling him, I just blurted it out: "I'm pregnant, and I'm sorry, but it's yours." And honestly, Joy, have you ever seen

206

someone's face literally drain of colour? I was worried he was going to faint.'

'But what did he say – once he'd calmed down?'

'That was the trouble. He didn't really calm down! I could see he was trying to. He was asking me questions: when I'd found out, how I felt and whether I was ... going to keep it. Whether I'd told Charlie, or Rob. Then he went and got us both a drink, and he just sat there, staring at me, with this shocked look on his face, and I suddenly got really cross with him. I said it was all right, he didn't have to pretend to be interested, I'd known perfectly well he *wouldn't* be interested. I was only telling him because it was his right to know, I didn't want anything from him, he'd already told me he never wanted children ...'

She pauses, and I wait. I obviously can't tell her I heard some of this rant of hers on Howard's phone call!

'And then he just put a hand on my arm and said, really quietly, "I didn't say I never wanted children, Sara. I said I'd left my ex because I didn't want children *with her.*"'

'Oh!' I can't think what else to say. 'Oh, I see.'

'Yes. It pretty much knocked the wind out of my sails,' she says, with a sigh. 'He said Rona – his ex – was getting really broody, wanting to get married and have babies, and he realised he just wasn't committed enough to her. Didn't love her enough,' she adds quietly. 'He felt really bad, but knew he had to be honest with her – and with himself – and let her find someone else, while there was still time for her.' She pauses, and then adds quietly: 'I'd completely misunderstood.'

'He did the decent thing, then, really. So ... how does he feel about *your* baby?'

'Well obviously, I told him I still didn't expect anything from him. Let's face it, if he didn't want kids with the woman that he'd been in a serious relationship with, he won't want one with me, when all we had was a . . . ' She looks down again, going a bit red. 'Let's face it, a one-night stand. But he did at least say he'd like to be involved – if it's all right with me, he said. He's promised to contribute financially, but he said he doesn't want me to think he'll just be a *chequebook father.*'

'Well, that's nice, isn't it?'

'I suppose so. I don't really know what that means. Whether he'll want to . . . see the child occasionally, or whether he just feels he ought to take some kind of responsibility. We didn't go into it any more than that. I think he needs a bit of time to process the shock, to be honest. So we just finished our drinks and said good night, pretty much!'

Poor Luke. After all that angst about whether to talk about his feelings for her, he never got the chance.

'So nothing was said about . . . the night in question, I presume?'

'Well.' She looks a bit sheepish. 'He did just say – as we were leaving – that he was sorry it had been so awkward, coming face to face with each other down here, but he'd respected my wish not to mention what happened that night.' She meets my eyes and adds, quietly: 'He says he still thinks of me as his best friend and . . . and he's sorry if I blame him for what happened between us. Sorry if I feel like it's ruined our friendship. Sorry if he's done anything to hurt me.'

'Oh, Sara.' Got to hand it to the guy: he's learning fast. Nothing like an apology – even if there's nothing really to apologise for – for melting a woman's heart!

'And he did ask if we could meet up again soon,' Sara adds.

'That would be good, wouldn't it? Perhaps you'll both feel calmer after a few days and can have a better talk about it all.'

'Yes.' Finally, she gives me a smile. 'I think it'll be good to do that. Oh, look, I'm sorry, Joy, I've kept you sitting here while I whine on – are you sure you won't have a cup of coffee? Or a drink?'

'No, I'll get back, thanks. I enjoyed looking after Charlie tonight, though – so please let me do it again. When you fix another meeting with Luke. Soon.'

'Thanks.' She returns my smile, a little sheepishly. 'And you're right. I will. Soon.'

Saturday 10 November

'Going out tonight?' Terry asks, looking me up and down. I'm surprised he's noticed, but I'm wearing one of my nicer jumpers and smartish jeans, instead of the ones I've taken to slopping around at home in.

'Yes. With . . . a friend from the Historical Society.'

I don't know why I feel reluctant to admit it's a man. It's not as if there's anything wrong with meeting Howard to talk about ideas for the society's programme and membership.

'Well, that's nice,' he says, surprisingly warmly. 'I'm glad you're making friends there, Joy. Are you going into Dartmouth, having a meal out somewhere?'

'Oh, no, nothing like that. Just a drink at the Angel.'

'Well, let me give you a lift. So you can relax and have a couple of glasses. You can call me when you're ready to come back.'

'It's fine. I was just going to walk,' I say. 'I thought you'd be busy, anyway.' I manage not to add anything sarcastic like *as usual*. It's nice of him to offer.

'It's horrible out there,' he says, shaking his head. 'Cold and wet. Come on, get in the car – it won't take two minutes to drop you up to the village.'

'Oh, well, OK, thank you.'

I grab my bag and pull on my shoes and jacket, as he stands waiting patiently by the door, passing his car keys from hand to hand and humming a little tune to himself. It occurs to me that he actually looks quite cheerful.

'Thanks,' I say again as he pulls up outside the Angel. 'There's a portion of lasagne left from last night, in the fridge, and I've already done some carrots and—'

'It's fine, Joy. You shouldn't have to worry about doing my dinner if you're going out.' He leans across to give me a peck on the cheek. 'Have a nice evening, and don't forget to call me when you want picking up.'

I don't know what's happened to Terry all of a sudden. But whatever it is, I'm liking the result!

'Hello, Joy.' Howard's already sitting at a quiet table away from the bar. He gets up as I come in and gives me a smile. 'Glad you remembered, this time!'

'All right,' I say ruefully. 'Apologies again for last night. It was a bit of an emergency. My neighbour—'

'I'm only teasing. What would you like to drink?'

'I'll have a glass of Merlot, please. I haven't got to drive – my husband's giving me a lift.' It feels nice to be able to say this: as if things were normal between me and Terry, as if he was – like he used to be – a nice, attentive husband, instead of one who ignores me.

Howard puts the drink in front of me on the table and we get straight down to business.

'Right, so: to attract new members,' he begins. 'What I'm thinking is, we need to start off by producing a proper programme of our meetings. Plan them, give them interesting titles and publish the schedule, perhaps a month or so ahead, on the local Facebook group.'

'Yes, that makes sense,' I agree. 'And perhaps we could produce a paper copy too, as an advert to put in places like the library noticeboard, and maybe a couple of the shop windows.'

'Good thinking. And I wondered about a half-page advert in the *Bierleigh Bulletin*.'

The *Bierleigh Bulletin*, the monthly village newsletter that gets delivered to every home in the area, is normally, to be honest, about as riveting a read as the back of a cereal packet. But it *is* where every social activity in the village tends to be announced. The church fete, the school concert, the vicarage garden party and the Women's Institute's garden-produce sale on the village green are all announced in its pages, in generous inches of bold type, exclamation marks and promises of wondrous raffle prizes.

'That's a good idea,' I agree.

Howard scribbles some notes on the pad he's got in front of him on the table, takes a mouthful of beer from his pint mug and puts it back down with a thump as he continues excitedly:

'Maybe we could take the opportunity to suggest a free try-out session for potential new members?'

'Yes. And we do need to make sure we attract younger, working people as well as retirees.' I think this over for a minute before tentatively suggesting: 'Should we meet in *here*, perhaps, instead of in the village hall?'

'Here? What, in the function room at the back, you mean?'

'Well, why not? It would save any of us having to make tea and coffee; we can all buy our own at the bar. And if people prefer to get a beer or glass of wine, that's available too.'

He looks at me thoughtfully over his glasses, nodding his head slowly.

'Actually, Joy, I think that could work. I don't know what the existing members would think about it, though. Some of them are a bit ... well ... '

'Set in their ways?'

'Mm.' He laughs. 'But bless them, we wouldn't want to upset them.'

'No, of course not. And anyway, it would be a shame to completely change the ... *ambiance* ... of the meetings. They're so friendly and informal at the moment; that's what I liked about it when I joined. You're right to say we need to organise a programme, to attract new people, but—'

'But we don't want to go too formal. And I think the pub setting would help with that. So, let's put it to the membership.'

'Take a vote?'

'Yes.' He scribbles some more on his pad. 'Now: we need to get some ideas for the first few weeks of meetings that we're going to schedule and advertise.'

'I've been thinking about that,' I tell him. 'How about the subject of street names? The origins of the older ones – I think that's quite fascinating. For instance, Dobbins Lane. Who's that named after? Or Goose Green Cut? And – everyone's favourite, around here – Stinkditch Lane!'

'That would be really interesting,' he agrees. 'And the attraction of it is that everyone who lives in the roads we talk about, will want to come. But ... who's going to research the origins?'

'We are – the current members! You can announce it to the group at the next meeting. See if any of them already know where some of the names come from. And we can all do our bit, online or in the library. I bet we can gather information about at least half a dozen roads, between us. Then we present our findings to prospective new members.'

'Great!' He almost spits out a mouthful of beer in his excitement. 'And it'll give our existing members something to do, too.'

'If they want to,' I caution him.

'Fair enough. Well, that's one thing for the programme. What else can we come up with? How about the actual houses in the village? The oldest ones, anyway. I'm sure there must be some history available for places like Longstomps Cottage, and – well, the vicarage. And Bierleigh House, of course.'

'Are you sure that hasn't already been done? At meetings before we both joined, I mean.'

He shrugs. 'Probably, but new members would be interested, and some of our current members might like to share what they know.'

'Good point.' I take a gulp of wine and I'm surprised to see I've nearly finished the glassful. 'Let me get you another drink,' I suggest, getting to my feet. At the rate I'm knocking it back, I'm going to need a couple of packets of crisps or nuts too, to soak it up. But I'm enjoying myself. It's been a while since I've been out for an evening, having a drink and a chat in the pub. The last time would have been my retirement celebration back in September. I definitely need to get out more – with Terry or without him.

'Thanks,' Howard says, as I return from the bar with another beer for him and another red wine for myself, plus some snacks for us both. He smiles up at me. 'This is nice. Thanks for coming tonight, Joy. It's good to have an evening out, somewhere other than at the village hall on Monday evenings.'

'Yes, it is,' I agree. I sit down and open a packet of crisps. I don't want to say too much more on the subject, don't want him to know how emotionally needy I seem to have become. Instead, I return to the real purpose of our meeting. We discuss having an evening where we all simply display any old photos we have, and perhaps old artefacts too, and talk to any new members about them.

'I know for a fact that David collects old maps, for instance,' Howard says.

'Oh, that *would* be interesting,' I agree through a mouthful of crisps.

I think we're getting a bit loud, in our excitement. A couple of people nearby have turned to smile at us. Well, at least we're not having a rant at each other, like a certain couple last night.

'It was my neighbour,' I say out loud without realising I was going to.

'Sorry?'

'The couple arguing in the pub last night – it was my neighbour and her ... friend. I was looking after her son and – oh, sorry, I don't know why I told you that.' I look at my glass – half empty again already – and push it a little way away from me across the table. 'Drinking too fast,' I mutter.

'It's all right,' he says quietly. 'Don't worry, I won't tell anyone.'

'What – that I can't hold my drink?' I giggle.

'No. About your neighbour. I hope she's OK, though. It sounded quite ... heated. So she's the one who had an emergency?'

'Yes. But it's all right. Emergency over.' I stuff some more crisps into my mouth. I really do need to slow down. Have I really become so unused to social drinking that I'm gabbling like this after only a glass and a half of wine?

'Good,' he says. 'Well, another idea for a meeting: how about we schedule one about Angel Cove, and your angel?'

'But I haven't been able to find anything out! How can we have a meeting about it?'

'Well, OK, you might not have found anything out about the angel, but you surely know quite a lot about the cove itself. About your homes – Smugglers' Cottages. You've been living there a long time yourself, and you've found out a bit about the people who lived there before – Philip and Chrissie – haven't you? Would Philip mind, do you think, if you told his story?'

'I don't know. I wouldn't like to presume. I still hardly know him, really. I could ask, but he hasn't even finished telling me his story yet, and it seems ... very personal. And I think I'd have to ask Freda, too, if I could get her to understand. She was involved in what happened, and she obviously still finds it quite painful to remember, even if she does get confused about it.'

'Yes, fair enough. But either way, the cove itself would be an interesting topic for one of the meetings. If you'd be happy to lead it?'

'Yes, OK.'

'Have you got any photos from years ago, by any chance?'

'Well, yes, but hardly anything has changed down there!'

We both laugh.

'That's surely part of its charm,' he points out.

'It is.'

I sit back and look around the bar. It's such a nice pub. Such a lovely village. And I do think I live in one of the most beautiful and unspoilt little places in the world. How did I get to be so lucky? Why do I ever waste my time complaining because my life – OK, my marriage – might not be absolutely, completely perfect? I look across the table at Howard. He's smiling as he looks through the notes he's made, obviously pleased with the discussion we've had and the plans we've made. I don't think I ever needed to be worried about him. He's on his own, a widower, and he probably gets lonely. I should welcome his friendship. And this revamp of the Historical Society could be just what I need to open up more new friendships, new interests. I'm going to embrace the opportunity, get involved and start appreciating what I've got.

Howard and I chat a bit more. I sip the rest of my wine slowly, we finish off the crisps and peanuts between us, and when I notice, with surprise, that it's nearly ten o'clock, I give Terry a call to come and pick me up.

'I'll wait for him outside,' I tell Howard. 'I think it's stopped raining now.'

He insists – despite me arguing that it's not necessary – on waiting with me until Terry arrives, and as the car pulls up he gives me a little wave and walks off towards his street.

'You didn't mention your friend was male!' Terry says, as he waits to start the car while I do up my seat belt.

'Didn't I?' I avoid meeting his eyes. 'Why – does it matter? We were just meeting to discuss a membership drive for the Historical Society and—'

He puts a hand over mine, and when I look up, he's giving me a gentle smile.

'Of course it doesn't matter, Joy. I'm glad you're making new friends, regardless of who they are. You don't have to keep your friend a secret from me just because he's a bloke. That's not how we've ever been with each other, is it?'

I shake my head, but can't find the words to reply. What's happened, suddenly, to make Terry look so calm and relaxed? He's smiling and cheerful and seems to be taking an interest in me, and in my friends. He's . . . like the old Terry again. I'd like to ask him why – what's changed – but I don't. I remember how different he'd seemed on the night of Sara's fireworks too, and how short-lived that was. I'm too nervous that this time, again, it isn't going to last. So I just smile and nod, and enjoy having a pleasant chat with him – while I can.

Monday 12 November

Yesterday morning, Terry pretty much acted like Mr Perfect Husband. Instead of working, he went outside and cleaned both cars, then came in and asked if I'd like him to put the Hoover round. He sang to himself while he was hoovering; then, while I was sitting at my laptop this afternoon reading Howard's email, inviting me to comment on his draft of an advert to go in the *Bierleigh Bulletin*, Terry brought me a cup of coffee and asked if I was OK as I was frowning in concentration.

'I'm fine, thanks, Terry.' I smiled up at him. 'You seem happy!'

'Well, what have I got to be unhappy about?'

I shook my head. 'I don't know. But ... I think you *were*. Recently.'

'No, not at all. Just busy,' he said. 'Things have settled down a bit now.'

'Well, I'm glad,' I said.

I got up to have to have a look in the fridge, to decide what to do about dinner – whether to have a roast or not, whether to have it a lunchtime or wait till the evening – and I suddenly decided to test out this sudden new atmosphere of cheerfulness a bit further.

'Do you fancy having Sunday lunch at the pub?'

Terry looked back at me, smiling. 'OK, why not?'

Perhaps I've finally got my husband back.

It was a bright day, with a brisk, cold breeze off the sea, carrying with it the tang of salt and seaweed. It felt strange, being out together again. I think Terry must have felt it, too, as for a while neither of us seemed to know what to talk about; but once we started, it was as if we were catching up on months of missing conversation. I told him a lot more about the Historical Society, making him laugh about the members' average age, and nod with sympathy about their various ailments. After we were settled at a table in the pub, I told him more about my meetings with Philip Sutton, and Terry listened, wide-eyed with interest, as I described what I'd heard so far about the story of his teenage romance with Chrissie and their attempt to run away to sea.

'And this is the couple who lived in Smugglers' Cottages?' he said. 'I know you were visiting him but I didn't realise you were unearthing their story.'

I swallowed and fiddled with my menu. 'You haven't exactly been easy to talk to recently.'

'I know. I'm sorry.'

I didn't want to push it. Didn't want to spoil our first time out together for months with an argument, or another inquest into what had been going on with him. So instead, we turned to other things we hadn't discussed for ages: whether we needed to paint the walls of the spare bedroom or get a new TV, whether Sara would agree, or be able to afford, to share the cost of having the decking painted in the spring; when we needed to renew the car insurance; and the importance of moving some of our savings to an ISA.

'I really enjoyed today, Terry,' I said after we'd been back at home for a while, and had sat in companionable silence, watching an old film on TV. I got up to pull the curtains against the early dusk, and stood for a moment as I did so, looking out at the sun setting into the sea, casting its orange glow over the water. 'Aren't we lucky?' I added. 'So lucky to live here.'

He came up behind me and put his arms around me.

'We certainly are,' he agreed. 'I wouldn't ever want to be anywhere else.'

Maybe it's all going to be OK now. Maybe I just need to give him time and he'll explain everything when he's ready.

This afternoon, Max has come back to play with Charlie again. The two boys seem to be inseparable now. I watch them running around on the beach; it's cold and damp out there but they don't seem to notice it. I'm just about to turn away when Sara appears outside and taps on my back door.

'Luke's here,' she says when I open the door. 'He's got something to tell us both, about Lina.'

Luke's standing behind her. He gives me a smile but shakes his head when I ask if he wants to come in.

'I've got to get back to work, Joy, but I wanted you both to hear the news. I took Lina to the pet sanctuary yesterday and she's chosen herself a cat.'

'Well, that's *excellent* news. What sort of cat is it?' I ask.

'A three-year-old tabby called Bella. She's very quiet and calm; her previous owner was a woman on her own who's had to downsize to a flat where pets aren't allowed. She's apparently really glad Bella's going to a nice quiet home, and she's asked Lina's permission to call on her occasionally, to see her. I'm taking Lina shopping this Saturday, for all the things she's going to need, then we'll go on to pick Bella up. Amy's going to help Lina get used to Bella's routine and make sure she keeps her indoors until she's got settled in her new home. So it all looks good.'

'I'm really pleased for her,' I say. 'Thanks for letting us know.'

'It was nice of him,' I comment to Sara after he's gone, 'to come and tell us about that.'

'Yes.' She gives a little shrug. 'But I can't imagine why he didn't just call me, instead of taking time out of work to drive down here specially.'

I have to almost bite my tongue to stop myself saying, *Can you really not imagine why?!* I'm not sure if she doesn't realise at all, or whether she just doesn't want to acknowledge it to herself yet.

'Are you going to your Historical Society meeting tonight?' Terry asks me while I'm dishing up the dinner.

I'm still having trouble getting used to him being home this early. Chatting together while I cook; talking about what I've been doing, sounding genuinely interested, without the peculiar emphasis he seemed to have before about me keeping myself busy. We've chatted some more about the dog, and although he still seems keen, he doesn't seem to want to be tied down to a date to go and look at them together, so I'm not pushing it. The only thing we're still not talking about is his work. It seems to be a closed subject, together with the whole question of why he needed to work flat out every hour of every day for all those weeks, and why it's suddenly now all back to normal.

'Oh yes, I have to go to the meetings: I think I'm the membership committee now!' I joke. And then, because things *are* better between us, and it seems only right to ask, I add: 'If that's OK with you? If you don't mind being on your own?'

'Don't be silly,' he laughs. Then he goes on, more seriously: 'I've left *you* to your own devices enough recently, haven't I? Far more than I should have done.'

'Yes.' I hesitate; but I've got to be fair about this, if we're ever going to work it out, get to the bottom of it. 'But in a way, it did give me the push I needed, to find things of my own to do. Joining a group, making friends, finding new interests. You were right about that.'

'But we should also still be doing things together. And I've been too busy for that. I *am* sorry, Joy. I'm going to make it up to you.'

'Good, I should hope so!' I say, with a smile – but the truth is, I'm only half-joking. Of course I'm glad if everything's now back to normal, if he's ready to spend more time with me, talk to me, be generally nicer. But should I really be so prepared to just move on – forgive some of the quite snappy and unpleasant things he's said to me over the course of the last couple of months and pretend nothing happened? Well, I will; for now. But, to be honest, I'm still not sure that *I've just been busy* is quite enough, long term, of an explanation. I'm still waiting.

The meeting tonight is quite formal really, for a change. Howard and I present our suggestions about future meetings to the rest of the members – all six of them – and tell them we need to take a vote. It goes quite well really, considering Grace and Annie vote both ways – to move our meetings to the pub *and* to stay at the village hall – because they can't make up their minds, so their votes have to be discounted. Saul votes twice for the pub because he's so keen on it; and Margaret spends a good ten minutes telling everyone she never sets foot in the Angel or any other pub because she doesn't drink alcohol and pretty much thinks they're dens of iniquity. This leads to David losing his patience with her and telling her even Jesus liked a drop of wine, but if she doesn't want to, it's up to her, she can have tea or fruit juice in the pub but it's hardly good Christian behaviour to lecture other people about what they like to drink.

Howard and I raise our eyebrows at each other, half expecting Margaret to take offence, as well she might. I think David was at fault too, for calling her out on it in front of everyone. Margaret has gone very red and very quiet. But, after a few minutes, she stands up and issues an apology to everyone.

'Thank you, David,' she says in her quiet, rather formal manner, 'for pointing out my lack of tolerance, in view of which I've decided to vote for the pub, in accordance with the majority's wish, to show I regret the way I spoke to you all.'

We all try to express our appreciation of her apology and I tell her I'm sure no offence has been taken. She's all right really, and usually quite a kind person, but just a bit old-fashioned. Meanwhile poor Freda can't vote at all; she's under the impression it's a general election and keeps asking who the Labour candidate is. So, in the end, all the votes that are actually legitimately cast are for moving the meetings to the pub.

As for the plans Howard and I came up with for increasing the membership, everyone seems to be in favour.

'I'm hoping someone new might take over from me as treasurer,' David says, to everyone's surprise. There's nothing much to do, of course, with only eight current members. 'If we become a bigger organisation, it's going to become very onerous,' he says. 'I might have to learn how to use Excel spreadsheets.'

It doesn't seem to take a lot to get him stressed, sadly.

'I'm going to invite my neighbours to join,' Grace says excitedly. 'They're a young couple, only in their fifties.'

'Good. It's about time we had some young people in the society,' says Annie French. 'Some nice young men would cheer things up a bit!'

'You cheeky thing!' says Grace, laughing.

'Well, we're putting our advert in the next edition of the *Bierleigh Bulletin*,' says Howard. 'And we'll be asking if some of you would like to act as "guides" when we have the exhibition of photos and artefacts. We think we should make the first meeting or two of the new year open to the public, so if people find it interesting, they might join us, there and then. We'd like you all to be thinking about street names; tell me if you've got any knowledge of the history of any of them, or the history of any of the old houses. And Joy's agreed to giving us a talk about Angel Cove at one of the meetings.'

I take a deep breath at the thought of this. I have no idea, yet, how I'm going to fill a whole evening about the Cove. I know Howard thinks I should ask Philip if I can tell his story, but I wonder if perhaps he could be persuaded to come and talk at the meeting himself, telling everyone about his memories of the Cove when he was growing up. I guess I could broach the subject when I see him this week.

Thursday 15 November

I'm getting in the car this morning to drive up to Ferndell for my morning with Philip, when Sara comes out of her door with a bag of rubbish for the bin. I haven't seen her for a few days; the weather's been dire, and she's been busy with her work.

'Hiya!' she calls out. She sounds so different these days – so cheerful but in a more natural, less forceful manner than when I first met her. It's really nice to hear. 'How are you, Joy? What's the latest from the Historical Society?'

I tell her quickly about the vote, the fracas with Margaret about drinking and how Saul's already planning his beer order at the bar for when we start meeting at the pub. She laughs and says she'd love to meet some of these people she's now heard so much about.

'I'd really like to come to the talk you're going to do about Angel Cove,' she says. 'If I can get a babysitter, of course.'

'It won't be till after Christmas; that's when we're changing the venue,' I explain. 'But I could always ask Terry if he wouldn't mind sitting with Charlie, any time I can't. I might not have wanted to ask him before, but he seems . . . much more like his old self, now.'

'I'm glad about that,' she says. 'And I'll bear it in mind – thanks, Joy. In fact, I wondered if you'd be able to sit with Charlie again for a little while on Saturday evening? Only if it's convenient, obviously. I mean, if you and Terry were planning—'

I laugh. 'Of course I'll sit with Charlie. Terry and I don't do anything special on Saturday nights. I presume you've arranged another meeting with Luke?'

'Yes. He called me last night and asked if we could *try again* – as he put it – now that he's got over the shock. He said he wants to talk to me about it all more calmly, and he didn't want to leave it too long.'

'That sounds sensible.'

'I agreed to Saturday, because it's supposed to be Charlie's weekend with Rob, so I wouldn't have to bother you to babysit. But Rob called after I'd finished talking to Luke, asking to change his weekend. Apparently he's got a bad cold,' she adds, raising her eyebrows and shaking her head. 'He *says* it's because he doesn't want Charlie to catch it. But, honestly, Joy, he sounded so full of self-pity, you'd have thought he was dying of the bubonic plague. What the hell does he think *I* have to do if I get a cold? We mothers just have to carry on regardless. Maybe next time I don't feel well, I'll call Rob and suggest he takes Charlie for a whole week.'

It's unusual to hear her sound so scathing about Rob, apart from when she's describing the way he left her for Jade. She normally sounds more loyal than he deserves her to be, in my opinion. Perhaps she's beginning to see the light!

'It's fine, Sara,' I soothe her. 'I'm more than happy to sit with Charlie again.'

'Thanks. I know he'll be pleased.'

As I drive into Ferndell, I realise I'm going to miss our weekly meetings, once Philip's finished telling me his story. But perhaps, if he enjoys my visits as he says he does, they won't need to stop. I already think of him as a friend.

'Come in, Joy, the door's unlocked,' he calls as usual when I tap on his door.

By the time I join him in the kitchen, he's stirring two mugs of coffee, and he's already arranged slices of a delicious-looking fruitcake on a plate.

'You shouldn't have gone to that trouble,' I chide him.

'No trouble. Got it with my shopping delivery yesterday.' He turns and gives me a grin. 'I prefer to rely on the deliveries than on Arthur driving me into Dartmouth. Nearly drove us off the road on the way back, once. I was lucky my half-dozen eggs came through it unscathed – and me, come to that.'

I laugh, but I do feel slightly concerned at the thought of this chap still being let loose on the roads.

'He's told me his son thinks he should give his licence up,' Philip goes on, as if I've spoken my thoughts aloud. 'He's right, really. Shame, though. That'll be the end of our little outings together.'

'Well, I've been meaning to suggest this to you, Philip, but I wasn't sure how you'd feel about it ... whether you feel you know me well enough, really. But if you'd like me to, I'd love to pick you up sometimes and take you out for a drive.'

We're in the lounge now, ready to sit down, and he seems so startled by my suggestion, he almost overbalances in his manoeuvre from wheelchair to armchair, and I grab his arm quickly to save him from falling.

'Thanks,' he grunts, obviously not used to needing help, and feeling embarrassed. 'And thanks for the offer, too. But you don't need to feel sorry for me. I'm quite happy here, with the supermarket deliveries.'

'Oh, Philip, I'm sorry, I didn't mean any offence. Of course you're fine. I realise you don't need my help, but – well, I've been enjoying your company these past few weeks. And I thought you might like a trip back to Angel Cove one day, that's all.

To see your old house. As ... a thank you, for sharing your story with me.'

He nods to himself for a moment, then looks back up at me.

'No, it's me that should say sorry; sorry for biting your head off like that, when you're being so good as to offer me a trip out. It's just that I don't like to think people are feeling sorry for me. I don't need help, I've got everything I need and I'm really quite content.'

'I know; and hopefully you'll soon be driving again. Look, let's just forget it for the moment and enjoy our coffee and cake, shall we?'

'Definitely. Here.' He passes me a plate. 'Help yourself. If we don't eat it soon, it'll get cooked, it's so bloody hot in these apartments. I think Janet wants all us residents to be constantly falling asleep. It'd make her life easier, I suppose!'

I laugh. I'm glad he's back to his usual jokey self. I feel bad for letting him think I was being sorry for him when, in fact, all I want to do is continue our friendship.

'Where did we get to last time?' he asks me, as he sips his coffee.

'Well, you told me how Freda convinced her parents, and yours, that the Angel of the Cove was involved in your rescue.'

'Ah, yes.' He smiles. 'Good old angel! Saved us both from drowning, apparently. Never mind the real heroes – the RNLI.'

'Quite!' I agree. 'You and Chrissie were none the worse for your experience that night, though? Apart from Chrissie being dehydrated.'

'We were damned lucky,' he says seriously. 'Stupid fool that I was, putting her in danger like that. The storm, the dark, the fear of being thrown overboard and never found – I had nightmares for months. So did poor Chrissie. Even though our parents were almost too relieved that we survived to be angry for long, my father lost his temper with me all over again when I admitted I'd set off without refuelling. I think, in his eyes, that was almost the worst thing I'd done – ignoring all his training. Perhaps I never really was cut out to be a fisherman after all.'

'But you took to farming? After you moved?' I'm trying to avoid asking directly about his daughter again. Hoping it might just come up as we chat.

'Oh, yes. It was a good life, actually. The farm we lived and worked on was primarily a sheep farm. I enjoyed working with the animals out in the open air. In springtime, the lambing season was the highlight. That never lost its magic. And the sheepdogs, they were the most intelligent dogs you'd ever meet. We grew some crops, too, mostly vegetables: cabbage, leeks, swede. They had to be planted, tended and harvested. It was a busy life, but it kept us fit.'

'I can imagine! Did Chrissie work on the farm too?'

'Oh, no. She was too busy in the house.'

'You wouldn't have had all the labour-saving devices we have today.'

'No, we certainly didn't. And it was just a little cottage, but there was always work to do. It was difficult to heat, you see – solid stone walls – and it used to get damp. Chrissie would have to make up a fire every morning and evening, sometimes even in the summer, just to keep it dry indoors, and to get the washing dry, when the weather outside was bad. Our cottage had a little garden, where she grew our own vegetables, ones we didn't grow on the farm, and she kept chickens, too. We had lovely fresh eggs every day,' he remembers with a smile. He pauses, swallows the last of his coffee, then goes on: 'And of course, she had the baby to look after.'

Ah. I feel a rush of relief. He's talking quite happily about their baby – smiling, with a faraway look of pleasure in his eyes at his memories. Nothing too awful could have happened.

'So you only had the one child – you and Chrissie?' I ask. 'A daughter, you said?'

'Yes.' He nods. 'Our little angel.'

'Oh – Freda mentioned her, when she was . . . a bit confused. *My niece – my little angel*, she said. I did wonder—'

'Whether she'd got it right?' He laughs. 'Well, it's what we always all called her – our little angel. She had the most beautiful golden blonde hair. As she got bigger, she wore it long, and she loved people to brush it for her. Freda and Doris used to come and stay with us during their holidays from the school. It was a squash, in our little cottage, but we used to have such a lovely time together. Freda adored our little angel.'

'I could tell that,' I say, remembering the look on Freda's face when she spoke about her. 'She must have been a lovely little girl.'

'Yes. She was.' For a while, Philip doesn't say any more. He looks out of the window, still smiling faintly to himself, and I'm just about to move the conversation on, he looks back at me and says, 'She did have a few problems, though, as she grew up.'

He doesn't enlarge on this, so I just ask, casually, 'But she's . . . OK now? Grown up and happy?'

'Yes,' he says again. 'She's happy.'

And finally he starts to explain.

August 1960

Philip had to pinch himself sometimes to believe how much better everything had turned out than he'd anticipated. His wedding to Chrissie, which took place as soon as legally possible, after her sixteenth birthday at the beginning of May, had been a quiet one. Chrissie – who was normally small and slim – was unable to hide her then six-month pregnancy, even by holding her hand-picked bouquet of spring flowers in front of the tent-shaped wedding dress her mother had made on her old sewing-machine. A cream-coloured dress, not white. It wouldn't be right, her mother had said, to wear white – the colour of purity – when the opposite was so blatantly obvious.

Despite this, and other frequently uttered tight-lipped comments of disapproval, their parents had accepted the situation and ignored the stares and knowing looks of some of the local people. When Chrissie's mother was out shopping in the village one day shortly before the wedding and overheard two well-known gossips tittle-tattling about her daughter, she rounded on them, telling them to mind their own business and adding that if they *really* wanted something to talk about, they might like to know that the Angel of the Cove had blessed the two young lovers and their coming child. Whether or not the gossiping women believed this or not, she told her family with satisfaction when she returned home, it certainly shut them up!

Freda had been Chrissie's only bridesmaid, and Philip, unable to choose between his twin brothers, broke with tradition and asked his own father to be his best man, which Jack accepted with great pride. There were no wedding photos – nobody in the family had a camera – and no reception, it being understood that going for a drink at the Angel would only invite more stares and more gossip; so both families simply retired quietly to Smugglers' Cottages, where Chrissie's mother made sandwiches, and Freda, in a gesture of her new kindness and generosity towards them, had made a rich fruitcake which she'd iced with the couple's names.

And now they were still living in Chrissie's parents' house, and sharing a bedroom – the sisters' single beds pushed together – thanks to Freda insisting on sleeping on the sofa. Philip was still working for his father, and often thought that it was part of his punishment for the night when he took the boat that he now found it difficult to be out at sea without feeling sick, because of the memories of that terrible time in the storm. He kept his sickness to himself. It had to be endured; he had to work, to help, to repay his father for his own stupidity. Meanwhile Chrissie, waiting for her due date, with no schooling and no job, was helping her mother with the housework, washing and cooking. They both felt that the least they could do in return for the forgiveness and grudging understanding they'd been given, was to work hard without complaint.

It was ten days after the date Chrissie had been given for the baby's arrival when she woke up in the middle of the night with cramping pains.

'Do you think this is it?' she asked Philip, having nudged him awake. 'The baby?'

'Well, it had better be,' he joked to hide his nervousness. 'It can't stay in there for ever!'

Despite the many conversations they'd had about this moment, Philip was overcome with the jitters now, and couldn't remember what he was supposed to do.

'Shall I make you a cup of tea?' he suggested.

'No!' Chrissie was pacing the bedroom – not that there was enough space in the little room to take more than a few steps – holding her back with one hand and rubbing her stomach with the other. 'I want my mum!'

Secretly relieved, Philip knocked on the door of his parents-in-law's bedroom, and Chrissie's mother, Nora, came out in her nightie and dressing gown, her hair in rollers.

'I think she needs to go to hospital now,' he said, his voice shaking.

'No hurry, lad,' Nora said, laughing. 'First babies take a long time. Anyway, I don't know why she couldn't have had the baby at home, like I had both of mine. Midwives know best.'

'The doctor said she has to go to hospital,' Philip reminded her. 'Because she's ... only young, and she's not very big, and it's her first—'

'I know, I know. Well, it's too soon to call the ambulance yet.' As neither family owned a car, it was normal practice to call an ambulance to take an expectant mother to hospital, and Philip was all for doing it straight away, and getting Chrissie into the safe hands of the professionals. But Nora was having none of it. 'Let's have a look at you,' she told her daughter. 'Lie down on the bed for me, there's a good girl. How often are the pains coming? Out of the room, now, Philip – this is no place for a man.'

Philip waited downstairs, frightened and uncertain, as the minutes and hours ticked by. Every now and then he'd hear Chrissie start to make those animal groaning noises again, and her mother telling her everything was all right, but he wasn't reassured. It was morning now, and Chrissie's groans and cries were getting louder, the episodes getting closer and closer together. Surely by now he should be calling the ambulance?

Chrissie's father had gone to work, looking relieved to escape the drama, but Freda was on holiday from the school and seemed as uncertain as Philip about what to do. Eventually, having made yet another cup of tea that nobody wanted, she went upstairs to see if she could help. Two minutes later, she flew back down the stairs, her face white.

'Call the ambulance! Now! Quick!' she gasped.

'What's happened?' Philip said. 'Is it . . . is the baby coming?'

'Just make the call, Philip, or give me the phone and I'll do it.'

The rest of the morning was a blur. In the ambulance, with Chrissie thrashing on the narrow bunk, screaming, her face contorted beyond all recognition, while Philip tried to tell her everything would be OK, they were going to hospital now and she'd be looked after there. Speeding off up the lane, leaving Nora and Freda standing on the cottage doorstep, holding each other's arms. 'She'll be fine, Philip,' Nora had said – despite the panic in her own voice – as his precious Chrissie had been carried into the ambulance in agony. 'Remember, this baby has been blessed by the angel.'

At the hospital, he was shooed away impatiently to the waiting room with those same words again: *No place for a man.*

'We'll look after her now,' said a senior-looking midwife. 'We'll call you when Baby's here.'

It was at least another hour – a long, terrible hour or more of sitting waiting, staring at posters on the waiting room walls, of nodding at the other anxious fathers-to-be who were enduring the same wait, and seeing two of them called by the nurse with the longed-for words: *It's a boy!* or *It's a girl!* He didn't care which his own baby was. He just wanted his turn to come. He wanted Chrissie to be all right, to be out of pain, for it all to be over. He wasn't sure if he was more scared now, than he'd been that night in the boat. He'd just resorted to mouthing a silent prayer for help, to the God he wasn't even sure he still believed in, when – finally! – a nurse opened the waiting-room door again and called his name.

'You've got a lovely little daughter, Mr Sutton!' she told him, and he promptly burst into tears.

Chrissie looked exhausted as she cradled the baby – so tired, he was frightened she was about to drop her. He bent over her, kissed her gently and took the baby out of her arms.

'She's beautiful,' he murmured, not wanting to admit he was alarmed by the slightly squashed look of his little daughter's head.

'Your wife had to have forceps,' the nurse who'd brought him to Chrissie's bedside told him. He had no idea what that meant, and didn't like to ask. 'She's had to have quite a few stitches but she'll be fine.'

'Is the baby all right?' he asked, stroking the little pink cheeks, the perfect tiny hands, the fuzz of pale golden hair on her soft little head.

'She's fine, just a bit squashed by the forceps, that's all.' The nurse dropped her voice. 'She's a big baby, she was too big for your wife to push out on her own, you understand? Baby's head got stuck. She needed a little bit of help, that's all. Have you got a name for her yet, Mr Sutton?'

'Yes.' He smiled down at Chrissie, who managed a weak little smile back. They'd spent months talking about names, eventually having decided, in honour of their mothers' certainty about it, to name the child – if it was a girl – Angela, after the Angel of the

Cove. The nearest similar alternative they could come up with for a boy was Andrew. But Chrissie had seemed quite sure the baby was going to be a girl.

'I do like Angela, but ...' Chrissie had said, just a few weeks earlier, and he'd laughed at her, teasing her for seeming to be suddenly changing her mind again.

'But what?' he'd said.

'But can we maybe make it a bit different, a bit more special? There are a lot of Angelas around.'

And so, they'd agreed.

'She's going to be called Angelina,' he told the nurse now. 'It's like Angela, but more special.'

'That's lovely,' the nurse said. 'Now, we're going to take Angelina into the nursery, so Mum can get some sleep. You can come back at visiting time this evening,' she added, dismissing Philip as she took the baby out of his arms.

'Will you be all right?' he asked, bending over Chrissie again to kiss her goodbye. 'I don't know if I can get back this evening – the buses don't run late enough. But I'll come back tomorrow. I'll come back every day. Dad said I could have some time off.'

'It's all right, Phil. I just want to sleep.'

All the way back to Bierleigh on the bus, Philip was smiling to himself, finally able to relax, too happy for his own exhaustion and hunger to hit him until he was home, enjoying a celebratory cup of tea with his family.

'We've got a baby girl. Angelina. A perfect, beautiful little baby girl!' he kept repeating. Trying to make himself believe it. He couldn't help wondering if the Angel of the Cove really *had* blessed them, after all. It all seemed so much more than he deserved.

Thursday 15 November

I feel so relieved to hear everything was OK, I can hardly speak. Philip's story of his daughter's birth has had me sitting on the edge of my chair. Things were so different, of course, back in the 1960s. There's no way, now, that a mother, especially a young, petite teenage mum, would be allowed to labour for so long, with the baby's head stuck in the birth canal, before some kind of intervention – forceps or even a Caesarean. And no way her poor partner would be banished from the delivery room, either!

'Thank God they were both all right,' I tell Philip. 'It could have been so much worse! Chrissie's mother should have—'

'Called the ambulance sooner. And the forceps should have been used sooner.' He pauses, nodding. 'We realised that later, of course.'

'Later?' I look at his face. His expression hasn't changed. I don't want to ask.

'Later,' he repeats. 'As Angelina got bigger. As she started to miss the "developmental milestones", as they called it at the baby clinic. She was always behind where they expected her to be. She crawled later, walked later, talked later, took longer to stop needing nappies. At first, they kept reassuring us it didn't matter. "All babies are different, she'll soon catch up." And she was so perfect in every other way: such a beautiful little girl, so good, so happy, so eager to please everyone. That was what made it so hard.'

'Made what hard?' I encourage him, although already, the answer is becoming far too clear.

'Finding out, the way we did,' he says quietly. 'When she'd been at school a little while, her teacher said we ought to have her properly assessed. So our doctor got us an appointment at the hospital, with a paediatrician. He asked lots of questions, talked to Angelina herself, tested her on all sorts of things she didn't understand and couldn't manage, until I got cross because she was getting upset. I said: "She's just a late developer, isn't she? She'll catch up." And the consultant just stared back at me. "You do realise, don't you," he said, "that your child is brain damaged?"'

'Oh, God. How unbelievably insensitive!'

'Yes, it was. But I suppose we'd been fooling ourselves. We should have realised. Her birth was traumatic, she didn't get enough oxygen during the delivery. It should have been obvious there would be problems. We just hadn't wanted to face it.'

'But now you *did* have to. That must have been so awful for you both. Such a shock.'

To my surprise, he smiles and gives a little shrug. 'Well, it was, at the time – hearing those words. But do you know what? I think we were both too young and inexperienced to realise fully what it meant for Angelina, for her future life. We loved her anyway, obviously, she was such a happy child and . . . she just kept working at things until she could manage them. She never let her difficulties frustrate her or get her down. So we didn't, either.'

'And how serious were the difficulties?'

'Well, she was transferred to a special school. But there were a lot of kids there far worse off than she was. The school was good for her; the teachers were patient and persistent, and so was she.

So, step by step, she made progress. Once she'd grasped some-thing, that was it: it just took her a long while to grasp things in the first place.'

'You must have been proud of her.'

'Still am,' he says firmly, and I allow myself a little sigh of relief. She's still with us, somewhere, anyway.

'What happened when she grew up – left school?' I ask.

'Well, work was difficult. She had a variety of jobs, but most of them were quite a struggle. It took her so long to learn how to do things, you see. And she was always such a home-loving girl, it suited her better, in the end, to stay at home with us, on the farm, helping with the animals. She was happy there. The farmer and all the farmhands loved her too. Everyone knew her as our little angel, even when she was grown up. She was so much like Chrissie, with her lovely blonde hair.' He closes his eyes for a moment, then goes on suddenly, quickly, as if the words are hurting him: 'When Chrissie died, I moved back to Bierleigh. We'd bought our cottage from the farmer by then, so I was able to sell it and get a nice little house here for myself and Angelina. We settled down in the new house, she seemed happy, made some friends. And I think that started her feeling like she wanted more independence. She used to say it was about time she lived on her own, it was what other girls – other women – did. I didn't like the idea; I doubted she could manage. But then I had my own problem.' He points to his leg. 'And everything seemed to happen all at once. I needed to move to somewhere like this, and although Angelina could have come with me, she wanted to stay in Bierleigh, and she was determined to try living independently. We talked to Social Services and finally they found her a little flat – a maisonette – and arranged for a carer to call every day and make sure she could cope.'

'And has that worked out all right?'

'Yes.' He smiles. 'She's only been there a few months but she's doing fine, by all accounts. She struggles a bit to make phone calls – gets flustered – but if I call her, she'll answer. She loves having her own place. She does her own housework and cooking; Chrissie taught her to cook when she was younger, but the carer makes sure she's coping, and not doing anything dangerous. She's got a little garden, which she mostly takes care of herself too. The latest thing is, she wants a cat! And Amy, her carer, apparently seems to think she'd be capable of looking after one, so she's—'

'*Amy?*' I sit up straight. 'Did you say her carer's name is Amy?'

'Yes. Nice young woman, and very fond of Angelina.'

'And she's getting a cat?'

'Apparently there was an unfortunate incident; she tried to adopt a cat that she thought was a stray, but it actually belonged to someone else. She was so upset—'

'*Angelina,*' I repeat, smiling now. 'Do you call her Lina for short, by any chance?'

He laughs. 'No, but she's taken to calling herself that! She thinks it sounds more modern. I suppose it's all part of this new, independent life she's leading, and I'm pleased for her, really pleased. I won't be here for ever to take care of her, after all, so—'

'I know who she is,' I interrupt him excitedly. 'I knew about the cat: he was my neighbour's, I was helping to find him. And the vet nurse, Luke, was helping too, and he's already taken Lina – Angelina – to the pet sanctuary to choose a cat. They're picking it up at the weekend. So, she's your daughter – what a coincidence!'

'Yes, it is!' he responds, smiling in surprise. Then his smile drops. 'Unfortunately, since she moved into the flat, I've only seen her a couple of times – when Arthur's offered to drive me into Bierleigh. I don't really like him driving me down those narrow lanes too often.'

'But *I* can take you to visit her now, Philip! If you'd like me to, of course,' I add quickly. 'I know you prefer to be independent—'

'Like my daughter, eh?' he says ruefully. 'No, I'm sorry I was rude to you earlier, Joy. I've got used to trying to manage things on my own, but you're right: there are things I can't do at the moment, and I'd be a stupid, stubborn old bugger if I didn't accept the occasional offer of help. It would be *wonderful* to be able to go to Bierleigh and see Angelina occasionally – it's so nice to think that you know her—'

'Oh, I haven't actually met her,' I explain quickly. 'It's just – I know about her because of the cat. But I'd love to meet her, if you'd let me take you to visit her.'

'Then thank you, yes, I'll accept. And you were right, too: I'd love to take a trip to Angel Cove, and see our old homes. It's kind of you to offer. I just wish there was something I could do for you, in return.'

'You've done so much already, telling me your story. But, actually,' I go on, 'I think there could be! You know I told you I've got involved with planning the meetings of the Historical Society? Well, I wonder if you'd mind . . .'

Parts of his story might be too personal to share. But, on the other hand, he might not mind me telling some of it. Or perhaps he'd even prefer to tell it himself. And by the time we're saying goodbye again, that's exactly what he's agreed to do.

Friday 16 November

'Fancy a walk?' Sara asks me when she spots me outside this morning.

It's really cold out here, despite the occasional glimmer of some weak and watery sunshine, between the clouds, and while I've been sweeping sand off the decking – an almost daily task here – I'm thinking that maybe it's time to put covers over the wooden outdoor furniture now, until the spring.

'Yes, a walk would be nice.' I smile at her. 'As long as you can spare the time?'

'I'm up to date. Starting on a new book tomorrow, so I'm free at the moment.'

We decide to walk through the woods opposite our houses this time, heading away from the coast. The path is a gentle one, curving its way slowly up the incline, the ground soft but fairly dry, thick with fallen leaves and bracken. We stop from time to time to watch a squirrel scurrying up a tree, or listen to a woodpecker drilling away loudly above us.

'Have you thought any more about getting a dog?' she asks.

'Yes, actually Terry and I have talked about it quite a bit.'

'What sort of dog will you be looking for?'

'Oh.' I shrug, smiling to myself. 'A sad one, I think.'

'A *sad* one?' She laughs. 'Why?'

'Well, I rather like the idea of giving a home to a poor, sad little thing who's had a bit of an upsetting time.'

'That's nice. But surely it applies to all the dogs in the shelter, doesn't it?'

'Not necessarily. Merry said some of them come from good, loving homes but their owners either pass away, or move abroad with their jobs, or they get a new partner who doesn't like dogs – oh, all sorts of reasons. But Terry and I think we'd like to adopt a middle-aged or elderly dog who perhaps hasn't had much fun in life, and give him a nice "retirement". We don't want a puppy, at our age, and besides, puppies get adopted quickly. It's the older ones who get left *on the shelf.*'

'On the shelf – that does sound sad!' She turns to look at me. 'I'm glad things are a bit better between you and Terry now. It sounds like you've been making decisions together over this.'

'Yes, we have.' I hesitate. 'We've talked about the dog idea quite a lot,' I go on. 'But he doesn't seem keen when I suggest going to look at them, at the rescue centre.'

'Sometimes men just don't like being rushed,' she says, laughing. 'Maybe at the weekend, if you say you're going back on your own to look at the dogs, he'll just decide to come with you? He won't want to be left out.'

'Yes, perhaps I'll try that,' I agree.

We walk on together in a companionable silence, puffing a little as the path begins to climb more steeply, and after a few more minutes the trees begin to thin out, and when we arrive at the top of the incline, our path meets a firmer track, with a wooden signpost pointing us back towards Bierleigh in one direction, and Ferndell in the other.

'Ferndell's further inland, isn't it?' Sara says. 'I've never actually been there.'

'Oh, it's a nice little village, even smaller than Bierleigh,' I tell her. 'It's where Philip Sutton lives, in fact – in the complex for the elderly there.'

'Yes, of course. You drive there though, don't you, when you go to see him?'

'I do. But it's actually much more direct to walk, on this path, than it is to follow the road from Bierleigh all the way round. Do you want to carry on there now? We're halfway already; it'll only take about another fifteen minutes. There's not much there apart from a church and a pub, the Spotted Cow.' I check my watch. 'We could have a quick coffee – sorry, a soft drink or something – in the pub, if you've got time?'

'That sounds perfect. Lead on!'

I'm thinking again, as we set off along the track towards Ferndell, how cheerful Sara seems these days. Charlie's much more settled at school, Pumpkin's safe again and doesn't seem inclined to stray far from home, and, surprisingly, she doesn't mention Rob so much now, apart from in reference to Charlie's weekends with him. It's almost too much to hope for, but perhaps Angel Cove is beginning to work its magic on her.

It's downhill the rest of the way to Ferndell so we step it out pretty briskly.

'So what do you think?' I ask Sara as we finish our stroll through the village – it takes only a few minutes – and head for the Spotted Cow.

'Well, it's very pretty, and very small,' she says. 'And just one little shop!'

'Yes, the people here come into Bierleigh or go to Dartmouth for their shopping. And for the doctor's. And the school. And pretty much everything, really.'

'Well, it's nice but I wouldn't choose to live here. I prefer Angel Cove. I think I'd miss the sea, now, if I had to live anywhere else.'

'Yes. Me too,' I agree with a smile.

We push the pub door open and head for the bar to order a coffee and a fruit juice. Once we're sitting at one of the tables, Sara asks me what Philip talked to me about yesterday, and listens in silence as I describe the traumatic day of the baby's birth; but she actually sits up in surprise when I get to the part where I realised that baby is Lina.

'Oh, what a coincidence,' she says.

'Well, I should really have guessed while he was describing her difficulties as a little girl. I didn't even make the connection when he said they'd called her Angelina. It was when he mentioned her carer's name – Amy – it suddenly all fell into place.'

'*Angelina,*' Sara says thoughtfully. 'Such a pretty name. How very moving it is, that they named her after the Angel of the Cove.'

'Yes. And strange, really, considering neither of them believed there was really an angel at all, let alone that he was responsible for saving their lives.'

'I bet their parents – well, their mothers – were pleased with the choice of name, though.'

'Yes, I expect they were!' I smile, thinking about this, imagining the two mothers who believed so sincerely in the legend of the angel that they surely would have thought it only right and proper that their granddaughter was named after him.

'It's so sad, his only daughter having those problems,' Sara says.

I hesitate. 'Well, it must have been a shock, the way they were given the prognosis when she was a child,' I agree. 'But apparently Angelina's always been a lovely, happy person, and Philip is so proud of her: of the person she is, what she's achieved, how she was determined to become more independent. I'm going to take Philip to visit her. I'm looking forward to meeting her myself, now that I've heard so much about her.'

She nods. 'I shouldn't have judged her so harshly for taking Pumpkin, I realise that now. She obviously didn't mean any harm to him.'

'But you were distraught with worry about Pumpkin. I didn't blame you for being cross about it.'

'Well, I'm really glad she's getting a cat of her own now.'

'Me too.'

This evening, I initiate another conversation with Terry about the dog. He's in a good mood again, asking me about my day as if he's really interested, without any sarcastic comments about me not having enough to do. He doesn't even get his laptop out at all, and apart from one brief call, even his phone stays silent. Remembering Sara's suggestion, I tell him I'm thinking of going back to the pet sanctuary at the weekend to look at the dogs. I even add that I'll probably register officially to adopt, so that we can move on with it as soon as we find a suitable one.

'Oh.' He looks a bit surprised. 'Already?'

'Well, why not? What are we waiting for? If we're both agreed it's what we want.'

'Yes, sure. Well, have a look at the dogs, of course. But I didn't think we'd be rushing into actually getting one yet.'

I look at him suspiciously. 'You're changing your mind, aren't you?'

'No, I'm not, not at all. I just thought ... well, is it the best time to be getting a dog? I mean, we're just going into the coldest time of year—'

'What's that got to do with it?'

'—and Christmas will be coming up. You'll be busy.'

I stare at him, now totally confused. 'Busy? Terry, I'm retired now! If Christmas ever *has* made me busy – which it hasn't, particularly, as there's always just been the two of us here – then this is going to be the *least* busy Christmas of my life! How is having a dog going to make any difference?'

'Well, you know what they say. A dog is for life, not just for Christmas.'

'It's still only the middle of November!'

'Yes.' He pauses, and I sense that he's struggling for more excuses. 'And honestly, Joy, I'm not against the dog idea at all, I just don't want to rush into it.'

'Fine!' I resort to a sulky shrug. 'Well, let me know when you're ready to come with me to the shelter, won't you.'

He gives me a sad, regretful kind of look. 'I will come,' he says quietly. 'I promise.'

'OK,' I say, a little more calmly.

I admit I'm quite tempted to snap back that he can just forget it, I'll go on my own, like I seem to be doing everything else on my own these days. But I don't, because it's not really true any more. And because of that sad, regretful look. It's caught me, strangely, like something sharp caught in my throat. Things seem to be better between us now, and if Terry's agreed to the dog idea in principle but just doesn't want to rush into it, for some odd reason of his own, well, I don't want to risk throwing our relationship off-kilter all over again. I'll just have to be patient.

To change the subject completely, I remind him about tomorrow evening, when I've promised to look after Charlie again.

'Oh yes, of course.' Terry smiles at me. 'It's nice that you're helping Sara out like that. Did you say she's meeting her friend again? Luke – the guy who was here for the fireworks?'

'Yes.'

I haven't told Terry about her pregnancy yet. Or anything much about Luke, other than that he's an old friend of hers. But he's obviously thought about it, because he adds now:

'Do you think he's hoping for more than friendship? I mean,

I doubt she's ready for anything more yet, is she. I hope he realises that.'

'Well, he seems like a really genuine guy,' I say. 'Not the type to mess her about. And they've known each other since they were toddlers.' I hesitate, but although it's really nice that Terry's showing such concern for Sara, I still don't feel it's right to share her news until she tells me she's ready. She'll obviously want to tell Rob, and Charlie, first.

All the same, I know perfectly well, of course, that Luke *is* hoping for more than just friendship – and was, even before he knew about the baby. And it's pretty obvious, whatever she says, that Sara likes him too. He was her childhood sweetheart, after all, and her first proper boyfriend too. But, as Terry quite rightly says, it's probably far too soon for her to be thinking in terms of another relationship with anybody right now. Anybody apart from Charlie and her new baby.

Saturday 17 November

I call Howard this morning. I was going to wait until Monday's meeting to tell him my news about Philip, but I suddenly decide it's not something, yet, to talk about in front of everyone else. Or more particularly, in front of Freda.

'Guess what?' I say as soon as he answers. 'Philip has not only agreed to me telling his story at the meeting we're planning about Angel Cove, he's offered to come and tell it himself!'

'Oh, that's great!' he says. 'Well done. Will he be able to get a lift from Ferndell, do you think? Otherwise I'd be happy to go and pick him up.'

'No, I'll do that. I'm going to be picking him up for a drive back to Bierleigh from time to time anyway. I've found out his daughter's living in Bier Road.'

'Really? That was a surprise, wasn't it? How did you find that out?'

'It came out during his story. She's only been living there a few months. But Philip would like to come and visit Smugglers' Cottages one day, too – to see his old house – and I'd like to take him for the occasional drive, anyway. He's pretty lonely, although he never admits it.' I pause, then go on quickly: 'There's just one thing, though.'

'We need to talk to Freda,' he said.

'Yes, we do need to talk to her. But I don't think she'll mind about the story being told, because it'll be her own brother-in-law telling it. It won't be until after Christmas, anyway, will it. And by then, they'll have reconnected with each other – hopefully – because that's another visit that I'm going to try to set up for him.'

'Ah, that'll be nice for them both, won't it. It's good of you, Joy.'

'Not at all. I've been enjoying Philip's company, and the memories he's shared with me, so it seems like the least I can do, really.'

'Well, I think his talk will be a fantastic attraction for the new year's programme at the society.'

'I just wish I could have found out more about the Angel of the Cove,' I say. 'But I think that's proving to be impossible, sadly. I think the legend must be so old, nobody's going to know how it started.'

'It seems that way, doesn't it?' Howard agrees.

I don't say this to him, but, in fact, I've been so taken up with Philip's own story of the angel: how Chrissie thought she'd seen it while she was ill out on the sea that awful night, how Freda used it to persuade Chrissie's parents to let them get married – and, most of all, how her mother believed the baby, Angelina, was blessed by the angel – that I've almost given up caring about the origins of the legend. It's sad but true: we might never know.

Terry's been doing jobs around the house today, whistling to himself while he worked. This evening he even offers to cook dinner, but I have to remind him that I need to have something quick because of babysitting this evening.

'I can do quick!' he responds, laughing. 'Cheese and mushroom omelette coming up, madam.'

I'm still feeling stunned by Terry's different attitude when I go next door later.

'He even offered to come in with me tonight,' I tell her. 'Just *to keep me company*, he said.'

'Well, he'd have been welcome to, obviously.'

'Sure, but I hardly need him with me, just to look after Charlie for a couple of hours. And anyway why – all of a sudden, after weeks, months, of hardly even speaking to me, much less wanting to spend any time with me – does he suddenly seem to be unable to let me out of his sight? It's bizarre.'

'You know what I think?' she says, grinning. 'I think he's jealous. Jealous of Handsome Howard. Seeing you meeting another man, he's suddenly realised his behaviour might have been pushing you into someone else's arms.'

'Oh, don't be ridiculous!' I laugh. 'Terry's never been like that. He's not the jealous type. Now: is Charlie ready for bed, or do you want me to—'

'He's in his bedroom, getting into his PJs, Joy. But as it's Saturday, I usually let him stay up a bit later – I hope that's OK with you?'

'Of course! Go on – go and enjoy your evening,' I tell her.

'Hmm. I don't know whether I'm going to enjoy it. Now he's had time to think things over, Luke might have decided being a daddy isn't on his agenda after all and he's getting the next flight out of the country!'

'Who's getting a flight out of the country?' squawks Charlie as he rushes into the room, in his jungle-themed pyjamas, his hair sticking up and his toy tiger under his arm.

'Nobody, Charlie,' Sara says, grabbing hold of him for a hug. 'Now, be a good boy for Joy, and you go straight to bed when she tells you to, OK?'

'What – without cleaning my teeth?' he challenges her cheekily, and she shakes her head at him, smiling.

'You know what I mean. Night, night, Charlie-bear.' She kisses him and then heads for the door. 'Thanks, Joy.'

'No problem. Have a nice time,' I say with a wink, and she pulls a face as she leaves.

'Mummy didn't look very happy about going out with her friend, did she?' Charlie says thoughtfully. 'Perhaps she didn't really want to go.'

'Oh, I'm sure she did,' I reassure him. 'Now: are we going to play Snap again, or shall we get your LEGO out? Or start on the stories already?'

The evening passes quickly, but even so, it's much longer this time, after settling Charlie in bed, before I hear Sara's car pull up outside. She comes in looking pink-cheeked from the chill of the night air, with a smile playing about her lips as she asks if Charlie's been good.

'So how did it go?' I ask, since she seems to be deliberately keeping me in suspense, fussing with her coat and shoes, going upstairs to look at Charlie, coming back down and fiddling with her phone, offering me coffee, picking up cushions and putting them down again. 'What did he say? I hope he's got over the shock now?'

'Yes, he seems to have,' she says. 'He did say he was sorry he hadn't thought – that night – to check with me about whether I was on the Pill or anything. Which, of course, I have to admit was my fault as much as his – more than his, really! And anyway, as I told him, I'm happy about it. Happy about having the baby, now I've got used to the idea.'

'So how does he feel about it now that *he's* got a bit more used to it?'

'He's fine about it.' She looks up at me, and there's a softness in her expression that I've only seen before when she's talking about Charlie. 'He wants to be a part of this baby's life,' she goes on quietly. 'But only if I'm happy with that.'

'And are you?'

'Yes.' She sounds surprisingly sure. 'Well, what could be more natural? He's the father, and after all, we've known each other all our lives, we always got along well – apart from this recent … misunderstanding. So I'm pleased to think he's going to take an interest in the baby, and be a bit of support.'

'Yes. Well, *I'm* pleased, too: pleased for you. Glad it's all worked out OK between the two of you now. I must say I always thought he seemed a nice guy.'

'Yes, I know.' She chuckles, and then adds, 'And you're right. He is. A good friend. I'm glad we've sorted things out between us.'

I can't help giving her a hug as I get up to leave.

'Thanks again for tonight,' she says after we break apart.

'You're always welcome. Let me know when you want to meet up with him again!'

'Well, he did ask if he could come with me when I have the twelve-week scan. I've got the appointment already: it's the week after next, on the Wednesday afternoon. Charlie will be at school, but it'd be nice to know if you're around, just in case I'm not back in time to pick him up.'

'Absolutely; I'll put it in my diary. Are you happy about that – Luke going with you?'

'Yes.' She nods slowly. 'Yes, I think it'll be nice, actually. Nice to have a friend with me. I would have asked you to come with me, otherwise, Joy,' she adds quickly. 'I hope you don't think I wouldn't have … '

'Don't be silly, I'm not offended! Of course Luke should go with you. As you say, it's only natural, he's the father. As well as being a friend,' I add quickly, since she seems very keen to make this clear: a friend. Nothing more. Of course not.

When I get back indoors, Terry's watching TV, a glass of wine on the table beside him, looking completely relaxed. No laptop open, no phone in his hand. I stand for a moment, just looking at him, enjoying the sight of my old Terry, back to normal.

'Want a glass of wine?' he asks, jumping up and going to get the bottle.

'Thanks.' I sit down next to him on the sofa. 'Terry, how about we go out for Sunday lunch again tomorrow? We could go to Two Bridges. I went there on my own the other week and I realised it's been ages since we've done that together – driven across Dartmoor ...'

And perhaps I could accidentally on purpose turn off towards the pet sanctuary afterwards, I'm thinking.

'Yes, that'd be nice,' he agrees.

And immediately my little plot loses its appeal and I feel guilty for even considering it. He's being nice. He's being his old, kind, agreeable self and I'm not going to spoil it for the sake of looking at dogs a bit sooner than he wants to. I call the pub and book a table for lunch tomorrow, and I'm looking forward to it already. Life's looking good again. I'd be mad to rock the boat.

Monday 19 November

'Did I ever tell you,' Sara says this morning as we're having one of our customary chats outside on the decking, 'about the time I stalked Jade – Rob's girlfriend?'

'You what? *Stalked* her?' This has come completely out of the blue, after we'd been talking about what she's thinking of buying Charlie for Christmas. 'No, you didn't!'

She looks away from me, out to sea, with a sigh. 'Well, when I first suspected something was going on, I looked Jade up on Facebook. Her profile picture made her easy to recognise: she has bright red hair, very long, very striking. Well, on Thursday afternoons, Rob always worked late at the school where they both work – he ran an art club for the kids – so I knew he wouldn't be coming out at three thirty, but Jade presumably still would. I arranged for Charlie to be picked up from *his* school by a friend's mum, and I drove to Rob's school, parked a little way down the road, got out of the car and watched for Jade coming out of the school gate. I even followed her for a few yards before I suddenly came to my senses and realised I was behaving like an idiot. I got back in my car and cried all the way home.'

'But why did you want to see her?' I ask. I can't really see how that would have helped her.

She shrugs. 'I just felt I had to. To see what I was up against, I suppose.'

'And?'

'And she was stunning. Short dress, high heels, figure like an hourglass—'

'How very predictable!'

'Yes. But at the time, I felt totally belittled, even by the sight of her. I felt old and ... kind of *mumsy* compared with her. It made me want to give up.'

'Poor you, I can imagine. But you *were* a mum. His child's mum! How's he going to feel if Jade has a child one day, do you think? Will he ditch *her* for a younger, more glamorous model?'

'I don't know. I don't really care any more. I don't even know, now, why I thought I still loved him. He cheated on me, hurt me and tried to tell me he still loved me but wanted to be with someone else instead. I realise now that I was stupid to even listen to all that crap.'

'No, not stupid,' I say. 'You were probably in shock, in a way.'

'Well, I'm going to shock him back, soon,' she says, an edge of determination in her voice now, 'when I tell him about the baby. I've been wondering how he's going to take the news, and I'm pretty sure he won't like it.'

'It won't be any of his business!' I protest.

'Exactly.' She smiles. 'And he won't like that. And it bloody well serves him right.'

Terry's home early from work again, before I've even prepared dinner, let alone got myself ready to go out to my meeting. He helps with the dinner, humming to himself cheerfully.

'Shall I give you a lift up to the village?' he asks after we've eaten.

'No need. Honestly, I quite like the walk.'

'It's freezing out!'

'OK, I'll take my car then. Thanks, Terry, but honestly, you don't have to offer to take me. It's not as if we have a drink at the meetings. It might be different after Christmas, if we change the venue to the Angel!' I stop, suddenly having a thought. 'Would *you* like to join, Tel? Now that you ... don't seem quite so busy ... and you're coming home earlier? I think you might enjoy it.'

He gives me a long look, as if he's considering it. 'I might, perhaps, one day. Although I think, when I've retired, we should still have some separate interests. It's not good for a couple to do everything together after retirement, so they say. I'll have to think about what I'd really like to do.'

'You're actually talking about retirement?' I say, my voice coming out as an incredulous squawk.

'Well, I'll have to one day, won't I!' he says, shrugging and laughing it off.

'Seriously: is this something you've started to plan for now? When are you thinking – soon? Next year?'

He hesitates again, then turns away, but I can see him still smiling, like he's pleased with himself. 'I'll let you know when I decide,' he says.

Howard's chatting excitedly to David when I arrive at the village hall. I join them, and quickly learn that they've now reached agreement with the landlord of the Angel about having our future meetings there after the Christmas break.

'Because we're a non-profit organisation, and we're part of the community, we're not going to be charged for using their function room,' David explains, 'as long as it's always on a Monday evening. They don't tend to get bookings for Mondays. In fact, Frank, the landlord, is pleased to hear about our membership drive. The more people we bring to the meetings, the more drinks they're going to have during the break – and afterwards. Some of the members might even want to eat in the pub before the meetings sometimes. So it's all good for Frank.'

'That's great,' I say. 'And on the subject of meals: do you normally do anything at Christmas, for the members?'

Howard and David look at each other in surprise, before turning back to me, shaking their heads.

'Nobody's ever suggested doing anything special – not since I've been coming, anyway,' says David. 'And Howard, to be fair, hasn't been here as long as me.'

The other ladies have all been arriving and taking their seats as we've been talking, and Howard now turns to face them, clapping his hands to get their attention.

'Hello, everyone, good evening!' he says. 'Now then: Joy's just asked me whether we've ever done anything special, as a society, at Christmas time, and whether we should do something this year.'

'Went to the Angel after a meeting once,' Saul says. 'When old Harry Tomkins was still alive. That was a night, all right. Neither of us could remember how we got home afterwards.' He pauses, frowning to himself. 'Not sure whether that was Christmas or not. Or whether it was a meeting of this club or something else, to be fair.'

'What sort of thing are you thinking about doing?' Grace asks, pointedly ignoring Saul's reminiscences. 'I could bring in some of my homemade mince pies if you like.'

'You normally burn them,' Margaret reminds her a little unkindly.

'I could bring in a bottle of whisky,' Saul offers, perking up. 'If you pay me for it.'

Howard turns to me. 'Did you have anything particular in mind, Joy?'

'I was thinking, actually, of us all having a table in the pub for a meal together. It wouldn't have to be expensive,' I add quickly.

'They always have a set meal on offer at Christmas time. You can either choose two courses or three. And pay for your own drinks if you want them.'

'That sounds lovely,' says Annie.

'Yes, I'd like that,' Grace agrees. 'It'd be nice, wouldn't it, Freda? Having a Christmas dinner together?'

'Christmas?' Freda echoes. 'Is it Christmas today?'

'Not yet, love. Next month.'

'I think that'd be good,' David says, and Howard nods in agreement. Saul's still muttering on about whisky. I doubt he'd actually manage more than one drink, at his age, before passing out!

'We'd probably have to book fairly soon,' I warn them all. 'Everyone gets Christmas outings arranged really early these days, and the Angel is popular with people from outside the area too. But Mondays might not be so busy. How about I pop in there after the meeting tonight and see if we can reserve a table for the last Monday before Christmas?'

'That's Christmas Eve,' Howard warns me, looking at the calendar on his phone.

'Oh. Maybe the week before, then. The seventeenth. That's exactly four weeks off,' I realise, feeling slightly startled. How did Christmas start to loom so close without me noticing?

'Well, if we're too late to book, we could always do it in the new year instead,' David suggests. 'As we'll be meeting at the pub then anyway.'

'I suppose so. If necessary.'

But I really hope it can be for Christmas. It'd be nice to have a Christmas night out with these new friends. I'm going to find it strange this year, not having the annual meal out with my surgery colleagues that we always had, one evening after we finished work. We used to have a Christmas tree in the waiting room, too, and there were lots of cards from patients, occasionally boxes of biscuits or chocolates to share. The receptionists would wear Father Christmas hats, we took mince pies and other goodies in to share at lunchtime, and the doctors gave all the staff presents. It was a busy time of year for us with all the usual coughs and colds, chest infections, flu and other seasonal problems like norovirus, but somehow it was always a happy and fun time too.

The rest of this evening passes uneventfully. Everyone seems to be on a high, talking about our change of venue, the idea of having a meal together, and all the plans for welcoming new members with an interesting programme. It's not until after tea and coffee that we even get down to chatting about tonight's proposed topic, which is transport. It proves to be quite a hilarious subject, listening to Saul describing how, years ago, he had to walk everywhere or drive the tractor.

'I nicked a bike once,' he admits, to tuts of disapproval from Margaret. 'I had a date with a lass from Ferndell, and I didn't want to turn up on the tractor. It would've cramped my style. I set off to walk, but I was going to be late, so I nicked this bike from outside the shop. It was a girl's bike, and too small for me, but I didn't care. Well, I met my girlfriend at the Spotted Cow, left the bike outside the pub and when we went back outside afterwards, it had gone. Someone *else* had nicked it!'

'Did the real owner ever get it back?' Annie asks, sounding worried.

'Oh yes. Turned out it was her brother who'd found the bike, he rode it home and got the blame from his dad for taking it!'

Margaret starts to ask whether Saul ever confessed to his crime, but luckily Grace is already recounting another story, about hitching a lift on a hay-wain, and Annie goes on to bemoan the fact that the bus from Bierleigh to Dartmouth now only runs twice a day, whereas when she was young it was apparently a regular service and only cost threepence and halfpenny all the way into town.

'I wonder what sort of stories we're going to be treated to at this dinner, once they've all had a drink or two!' Howard jokes to me as we leave the hall at the end of the meeting. 'I'll walk down to the pub with you,' he adds. 'If we can book the table now, we'll pick up a copy of the menu for the set meal.'

Terry's watching TV when I arrive home. He looks up at me, smiling, and offers to make a cup of tea. While the kettle's boiling, I tell him about the meal I've just successfully booked, and then go on to chat about tonight's meeting. We laugh together about Saul's bike story. And it occurs to me: I'm the happiest, now, that I've been since the day I retired.

Friday 23 November

I didn't visit Philip yesterday as planned; he'd called me the previous day to say he hoped I wouldn't mind postponing, as one of the other residents at Goldcrest Lodge had an eightieth birthday celebration planned for yesterday in the communal lounge, and as he'd been invited, he felt he ought to go.

'I expect it'll be exhausting,' he said, his voice dripping with sarcasm. 'You know – a rave-up with disco lights, everyone dancing to reggae music, boozing and snogging in corners. And there's only so much fun I can have on one day, so—'

I chuckled. 'How about I come on Friday instead, then? How about I pick you up and take you to visit Lina – Angelina?'

'Oh, are you sure?' His voice brightened considerably. 'That would be wonderful, Joy. Thank you!'

I considered suggesting we tie it in with a visit to Smugglers' Cottages too, but on second thoughts, decided to leave that till another time. The way Philip was joking about the eightieth birthday *rave-up* didn't fool me. He actually does get tired, and I'd like to think he could spend as long as he wants with his daughter – and as long as he wants, another time, visiting his old home. But on the other hand ...

'How about we pop in to see Freda, too?' I asked him. 'Her care home is in Bierleigh, and I doubt whether we'd be able to spend very long with her. She might be ... a bit confused by us visiting.'

'Yes, she probably will,' he agreed. 'But it's a nice idea. Yes, if you don't mind. I'll call the care home and make sure it's OK.'

It's all been agreed, and I've arranged to pick Philip up from Goldcrest Lodge at ten o'clock this morning. I'd been a bit worried about getting him into the car, but he's obviously used to it from his outings with his mad-driver friend, and manoeuvres himself without much difficulty out of his wheelchair and into the passenger seat. We've brought the walking frame with us as well as the wheelchair, in case he needs it where we're going, but I'm pretty sure the care home has a ramp for wheelchairs, and fortunately Lina's flat is on ground level.

The meeting with Freda at her care home is as short as I thought it would be. She seems to recognise Philip at first, but then becomes confused and upset, asking why Chrissie isn't with him, and finally decides he isn't Philip at all but one of his brothers.

'I thought I heard you were dead,' she says bluntly.

'Not yet, thanks to God,' Philip says calmly. 'Every day's a gift, right, Freda?'

'I don't know what you're talking about. What are you doing here? Who is this man?' she asks, turning to me, her voice quivering with anxiety.

One of the carers approaches, putting an arm around Freda's shoulders.

'Don't be like that, Freda, these nice people have come to see you,' the carer says gently. 'This is your brother-in-law Philip, remember?'

She stares at him again. 'Where's Chrissie?'

'It's OK,' Philip tells the carer. 'I think we'll go — it's only upsetting her.' He smiles at Freda. 'I'm glad to have seen you, my lovely, even if maybe it wasn't such a good idea to come.'

'You're welcome to try again,' the carer says as we turn to leave. 'She's normally quite happy in her own little way.'

'Thank you. I might; but I think ... possibly I'd prefer to think of her *being* happy in her own way, rather than turning up to confuse and upset her.'

'Are you OK?' I ask him gently as we return to the car.

'Yes, of course,' he says. 'It's sad, Joy, but it's no good trying to force something. I'm glad we tried – thank you – and glad I've seen her again. But ... well, I think, unless *she* seemed to be benefiting from me visiting her, I might prefer to hang on to my memories of Freda as she was. When she was happy, with Doris.'

Our second visit is far more successful. Lina's pink-cheeked with excitement and beaming from ear to ear when she opens her door to us. She must be in her late fifties, but looks younger, her hair still very fair, her eyes blue like her father's.

'I've shut Bella in the kitchen until I close the front door,' she tells us importantly before we're even over the threshold. 'I have to be very careful that she doesn't run out until she knows her way around. Hello, Dad,' she adds almost as an afterthought – as if she sees him every day.

'Hello, my angel,' Philip says. 'This is Joy. She's my very kind friend, who—'

'Hello, Joy. I know who you are.' She smiles at me. 'You live next door to Pumpkin, don't you? Please come in.'

Once the front door is duly closed and I'm helping Philip carefully along the narrow hallway with his walking frame, she points us towards her lounge and says:

'Please go through and sit down. I'm going to make tea.'

'I'll come and help you,' I offer, but she insists firmly that she knows quite well how to make tea and only needs me to tell her who wants milk or sugar. The tea, when it arrives, is perfect and by now, I have Bella purring on my lap.

'I'm managing very well, aren't I, Dad?' Lina says, as she puts a plate of biscuits next to Philip, her eyes full of hope for his approval. 'Amy says I'm managing very well.'

'You certainly are, love.' His voice sounds a little shaky. 'I'm so proud of you.'

Her smile lights up the room, making her look even younger.

'I'm looking after Bella very well, too, aren't I, Joy?'

'You must be, Lina! She looks the picture of health. Well done.'

'Please will you tell Sara that I'm looking after her very well? I'm not making mistakes like I did with Pumpkin.'

'Of course I will. She'll be as pleased about it as I am.'

Still beaming with pleasure, she begins to tell her father about her everyday routine, explaining what she does from the moment she wakes up and feeds Bella, to what she has for her breakfast, how she plans, with Amy's help, what to buy from the shops and how to cook her meals. Her pride at her own achievement, at living independently like this for the first time in her life, is so touching, neither Philip nor I can speak for a moment.

'I have to admit, I was worried at first,' Philip tells her after he's taken a sip of his tea, 'when you said you wanted to live on your own. But I'm so impressed, Angelina – sorry, *Lina*! You're doing brilliantly. I'm really happy for you.'

'I'm happy for you too, Dad, because you don't have to look after me or worry about me any more,' she says. 'And you're being looked after too, so it's like in the stories you used to read me, isn't it?'

'Is it?' He smiles at her. 'How?'

'It's what they used to say at the end. You know: *Happy Ever After.*'

This afternoon, I'm setting off to Bierleigh to get a couple of things from the shops when Sara catches me up.

'Collecting Charlie from school,' she explains. 'I'm trying, now, *not* to take the car unless it's raining. It's too easy to get into the habit.'

'Well, at least it's dry today,' I agree. Cold, with a gloomy grey sky and a calm, flat, grey sea – but dry. We walk on together, and I tell her about my morning's visits with Philip.

'Seen any more of Luke since Saturday?' I ask her when we briefly run out of conversation.

'Um ... yes, actually he popped round yesterday after he finished work.' She frowns and shrugs. 'I don't really know why he came, to be honest.'

Yes, you do! I want to protest, but, of course, I don't.

'Charlie seems to like him,' I say, trying to keep my voice neutral.

'Yes, he does. In fact, Luke helped him with a LEGO ship he's been struggling to make. He now thinks Luke's *brilliant*, of course!' She laughs. 'Well, anyone who's got a clue about these complicated LEGO kits is brilliant to Charlie. I'm hopeless – I haven't got the patience.'

We're nearing the village now, and just as I'm thinking she seems to be in a very thoughtful mood today, Sara suddenly turns to me and asks:

'When you married Terry, Joy, did you have a hen weekend?'

I look at her in surprise.

'What a funny question!' I laugh. 'Well, not a weekend, as such. We didn't tend to do that so much, back then. I just had a night out – a bit of a pub crawl – with a crowd of my girlfriends. Why do you ask?'

'I just wondered if you played any silly games. It's what happens at a lot of hen weekends now. There's one where the bride has to answer a list of questions about her husband-to-be. Her friends have got the answers from him beforehand, and if she gets any wrong, she gets teased, has to pay a forfeit or drink a shot, something like that.'

'Sounds like fun,' I say, although to be honest, I think it sounds like a particularly masochistic kind of hell. And I have no idea where this is leading. 'Did you play that game at your hen weekend, then?'

'Yes.' She gives an awkward little laugh. 'I've never forgotten it. The humiliation.'

'Because you got one wrong?'

'No.' There's a pause, and she kicks a couple of pebbles into the road, quite viciously, as if whatever happened back then was their fault. 'I couldn't answer any of them.'

I laugh out loud, but she doesn't join in. It really must have upset her.

'Well, they probably chose deliberately difficult questions!' I say, although I still can't understand why she's suddenly brought this up. 'I suppose that's the idea of the game – to try to catch you out. That's what they think makes it funny?'

'It wasn't funny,' she retorts. 'It was really embarrassing. I think my friends actually thought so too, even if they pretended to find it amusing. I didn't even know Rob's favourite colour. I didn't know if he'd ever had a pet. I didn't know how many cousins he had.'

'Well, that could be a tricky one,' I suggest, trying to help.

'He only had one! One cousin, that I didn't even know about. He'd had a cat and two dogs during his childhood and I didn't know *that*. His favourite colour was red, and I'd never asked, he'd never told me.'

'Well, perhaps he wouldn't have known the answers to the same questions about *you*.'

'You're right. I asked him, afterwards. He could only answer one. Slightly better than me, but still – *he* thought it was hilarious.

He persuaded me it didn't matter – he said we knew all we needed to know about each other, that we were in love, we were soulmates, a perfect match. But . . . ' She takes a deep breath, almost gasping, as if it's hurting her. 'But that was nonsense, wasn't it, Joy? The fact was, we didn't know each other at all. We were so carried away, so absolutely stupidly besotted, we got married without even knowing each other.'

And I understand, now, how this has come up. She's been thinking about her marriage, about her relationship with Rob – about the fact that she always believed they were *soulmates*. She's finally realising that perhaps it wasn't completely true. And – as I put a hand on her arm to comfort her, without saying anything because, quite honestly, what is there to say? – I'm sure she realises, too, that if she were asked those questions about *Luke*, she'd have got them all right, with no trouble at all.

Monday 26 November

'Do you realise,' Sara says this morning when we're walking on the beach together, wrapped up against the cold but enjoying some winter sunshine, 'One month from today, it'll be Boxing Day. Then Christmas will be all over for another year!'

'Oh, stop it. I can't even believe it's nearly December, never mind Christmas!' I groan. 'We were talking about it at the Historical Society meeting last week; we've decided to have a Christmas meal together at the Angel.'

'That'll be nice, won't it?'

'Yes.' I sigh. 'Don't get me wrong, I've always loved Christmas time: the lights and decorations everywhere, Christmas carols being played, children getting excited and the lovely family service at the village church ...' I laugh, and admit, 'It's the only time Terry and I set foot inside there. I like the traditions, and the way people seem nicer to each other, but not the commercialism of it all and the way the shops are so full of Christmas tack these days.'

'From September onwards,' Sara agrees. She looks at me carefully and goes on: 'Is it ... a lonely time for you and Terry? Not having a family?'

'Maybe, although I've never really thought of it that way. In the past, I always had a really busy time at work during the build-up to Christmas. So I never minded Christmas itself being just me and Terry. I think he felt the same way, too, as he had lots of social engagements himself, through his work, in the lead-up to the actual day.'

'But it'll be different this year.'

'Yes. No frantic busy-ness, or that excitement that comes from working with other people.'

'It's the same for me, in a way, working at home, for myself.'

'But I'm sure Charlie makes it fun!'

'Of course. But this'll be the first Christmas without Rob.'

'Oh, Sara, of course it will, I wasn't thinking. *You're* the one who's going to find it strange, and different, this year – much more so than me.'

'We both will,' she corrects me with a little smile. She pauses for a moment, standing still at the water's edge, watching the waves roll in. The stiff breeze off the sea makes me shiver, despite the sunshine, despite my thick coat, boots and gloves, but nevertheless it's good to be outside, breathing in the tang of salt and seaweed. 'That's why I've brought the subject up, Joy. I wondered whether you and Terry would like to come and share Christmas Day with Charlie and me? Only if you want to, of course,' she adds quickly. 'If you both want to.'

'Oh!' I turn to look at her in surprise. 'Oh my goodness, I don't know what to say . . .'

'Well, you don't need to answer straight away. You've got nearly a month to think about it!' she teases.

'No, I'd love to, Sara. I mean, I'm sure Terry will say the same, but obviously I'll have to ask him. It's just . . .' I swallow, feeling stupidly overcome with emotion. 'We've never been invited anywhere for Christmas Day before.'

'Never?' She looks almost as overcome as I am, by the thought of this. 'Not even years ago?'

'No. When our parents were still alive, we were always the ones who hosted them at Christmas. And between the two of us we only ever had one sibling – Terry's brother – but he and his wife live in the far north of Scotland, and Lizzie, the wife, has a huge extended family up there, so they always spend Christmas with them. We were invited once or twice, years ago, but it's such a long trip to make when you have to come back for work after a couple of days. To be honest, we don't really see them now. We just send cards. It's sad, but—'

'But that's what happens, isn't it, when families don't live close to each other. And of course, your cousin – the one you were so close to – lives even further away.'

'Australia.' I nod. 'Well, as far as I know she's still there, anyway.'

I'm struck by such a sudden longing to know where Pauline is, such a terrible sense of loss for not knowing, for not having done anything about it, that for a moment I can't even speak. How did I let this happen – this lack of contact, this careless loss of our closeness? How did we *both* let it happen?

'Well, look,' Sara says gently, 'I haven't got any family nearby either. And on Boxing Day, Charlie's going to Rob's. So I'm sure he'd love it if you and Terry wanted to come to us for Christmas Day.'

'Well, in that case, *you* must come to *us* on Boxing Day! You definitely can't spend the day all on your own.'

'I'm getting used to it now.'

'Maybe you are, but not at Christmas!' I say firmly. 'I'm sure Terry will agree.'

It's nice to be able to say that now. Only a week or so ago, I'd have been wondering whether he'd even take a day off work for Christmas!

'Well, talk it all over with him, Joy,' Sara says. 'But it *would* be lovely to spend time with you over the holiday, if you're both up for it.'

We stroll on along the beach, turning our faces up to the wintery sunshine. Angel Head looms in front of us, looking dark and somehow forbidding against the pale sky, and I find myself wondering if that was how it looked on that cold, dark day in February of 1960, when Philip and Chrissie were huddled together on the big flat rock here, discussing her pregnancy and what they were going to do about it.

'I wish I believed in the Angel of the Cove,' I say, smiling at Sara. 'Like Philip's mum, and Chrissie's, did. Believing the baby was blessed by an angel! It's such a nice idea – having an angel here, protecting us . . .'

'Maybe it *is* true,' she says, smiling back. 'Who knows!'

At the end of the beach, we turn to walk back. We're both quiet for a while, before Sara suddenly takes a deep breath and announces: 'I told Rob. About the baby. I told him when he brought Charlie back last night. Asked him to stay a little while so I could talk to him while Charlie got ready for bed.'

'Oh! What did he say?'

'Well, I think – when I said I wanted to talk to him about something important – he was probably expecting trouble. Probably thought I was going to want more money for Charlie, or to discuss his access arrangements – make his life difficult in some way. When I said I was pregnant, he nearly fell over. It hadn't occurred to me that he might think I was implying it was his! That just shows how self-centred he is, doesn't it? We weren't even sleeping together any more, and yet he still seemed to assume he was responsible.'

'So what did he say when you explained whose it was?' I ask her. I'm thinking, again, how differently she's talking about Rob now.

'Oh, I didn't tell him *whose* it is – why should I? Just that it definitely isn't his; I reminded him it would be a physical impossibility anyway. I'm sure he'll put two and two together eventually, as Luke's going to be involved when the baby arrives. But for now, he can wonder about it as much as he likes.' She chuckles. 'He kept looking at me, after I told him – like he couldn't believe it. Couldn't believe that another guy would have wanted me.'

'Or that *you* would dare to want someone else, instead of him?'

'Mm. You could be right. Well, he knows now. I've asked him not to mention it to Charlie until I think the time's right to tell him myself first. He's promised not to; and I do trust him on that one. I don't think he'd ever do anything to upset Charlie.'

'So when do you think you'll tell Charlie?'

'I thought perhaps just after Christmas. When all the excitement's over; things sometimes feel a bit flat then, don't they? I hope he's going to be pleased. It'll be awkward – explaining about Luke.'

'He'll probably take it on-board better than you think. Especially if he gets used to Luke being around *before* you tell him. Sees him as Mummy's special friend.'

'Yes. That's what I'm going to do. I've decided, if Luke wants to, that I might start including him in things with me and Charlie sometimes – at weekends and so on. It'll be good for Charlie to have another man around, anyway, when he's not with his dad.'

'Good idea.'

I manage to keep a straight face, but inside me I'm smiling at her. I don't think she's realised it yet, herself. She's still far too cautious, she was hurt far too much by Rob, to admit to having any feelings about someone else yet. But I think it's quite possible she was always in love with Luke, probably even since they were children together, without even realising that it *was* love. Not that kind of desperate passion, mad head-over-heels hurry to be together, that so often breaks down at the first hurdle of life's challenges; but the slow burn of a love that can turn into caring for someone genuinely and lastingly, no matter what. She's already seen the light, as far as Rob's concerned, and given time, I think she might eventually be glad that losing him helped her to find Luke again.

The Historical Society members are full of excitement this evening when we hand out the menus for the Christmas meal.

'I'll be having turkey, and Christmas pudding,' Grace says immediately, passing the menu on to Annie. 'It's not a Christmas meal if you don't have turkey and pudd.'

'Well, *I* can't have Christmas pudd,' Annie says. 'My guts won't stand for it. I'll be in and out of the toilet as soon as—'

'Well, there are three other dessert options, Annie,' I point out quickly. 'How about the sherry trifle? Or the passionfruit and mango cheesecake? That sounds delicious, doesn't it?'

'What's in it?' she says with a sniff.

'Passionfruit and mango,' Saul mutters, sounding exasperated. 'Pass the menu on, can't you, my lovely, while you make your bloody mind up?'

'All right, all right, man. Patience is a virtue!' Annie shoots back. 'I'll have turkey, and the festive apple and mincemeat tart. With custard. Thanks, Joy.'

I'm smiling to myself as I write down their choices. Margaret is aghast by the mention of so much alcohol on the menu: white wine in the cream sauce with the salmon; port in the cranberry sauce for the turkey; even the vegetarian option includes figs doused in apricot brandy. There's sherry in the trifle, and of course, brandy in the Christmas pudding.

'There's no consideration for teetotallers,' she complains. 'Or people with an alcohol intolerance.'

'There's a note on the bottom of the menu,' I point out, 'saying that if we give them notice when I hand in our orders, they can adapt most of the dishes to cater for all dietary requirements.'

'Ah. Good.' She nods in satisfaction.

'So what would you like, Margaret? And what alcohol would you want to be left out?'

'I'll have the boozy Christmas pie with Guinness for my main course,' she says, 'and the sherry trifle.'

'With no ... er ... Guinness and no sherry?'

'What? No, of course I want the Guinness and the sherry. *I'm* not teetotal! I don't like drinking alcohol but there's nothing wrong with having a bit in your food, is there? I just don't agree with people being force-fed it against their will!'

'They can force-feed me as much alcohol as they like,' Saul cackles. He grabs the menu and gives it a cursory look. 'Boozy pie, and Christmas pud for me. Can I order my beer to go with it?'

'No, Saul, I'm afraid you'll have to order that yourself at the table,' I tell him. 'Can someone please help Freda to choose her meal?'

Freda looks up at the mention of her name.

'Is it time for lunch?' she says, looking around. 'Is it fish and chips today?'

'No, lovely,' Grace tells her. 'We've got to choose our dinners for our Christmas meal. Would you like me to read them out for you?'

'Is it Christmas today? Where's the Christmas tree?'

Grace looks back at me sadly. 'I think we'll just get her the turkey and pud,' she says. 'I know she likes those.'

'OK. Thanks, Grace.'

David, Howard and I write down our own orders, and things go back to being what passes for normal for our group, until, during the tea break, I approach Freda to ask her about Philip's talk.

'We're having a meeting soon all about Angel Cove,' I tell her. 'And Philip – your brother-in-law, Chrissie's husband – has offered to come along that evening and tell his story.'

'Chrissie? My little sister,' she says. 'I was her bridesmaid.'

'Yes, that's right.' This was never going to be easy, but I know I've got to do my best to get her agreement, even though, by the time the meeting in question comes around, she'll have forgotten all about it again. 'And Philip came to see you last week at your home – remember?'

'Philip.' She shakes her head, sadly. 'He died.'

'It was his brother who died, Freda. But Philip – he wants to talk to our group about when you all lived at Angel Cove. Your family, and his. How he and Chrissie tried to go off to France in his dad's boat, and—'

'And Chrissie saw the angel,' she says, suddenly looking me straight in the eye, all signs of confusion gone. 'She saw the Angel of the Cove. She was lucky to see it, wasn't she? So lucky, she named the baby after it. Our little angel. Where is she? Where's my little angel? Such lovely blonde hair, she had. I used to go to visit her with Doris.'

'Oh, Freda, Angelina's living here in Bierleigh now!' I'm so pleased she suddenly remembers as much as this – however briefly it might last – that my eyes are filling with tears. 'Philip and I saw her just the other day. Philip wants to tell everyone the story – what happened with him and Chrissie and the Angel of the Cove. Is that all right with you?'

'What?' Her eyes have clouded over again. 'What story? What are you talking about? Where's my dinner? Is it Christmas?'

I swallow hard and have to look away. 'Don't worry, Freda. Look, here's Margaret with your cup of tea. Chocolate chip biscuits today, isn't that nice?'

I think I need to keep mentioning Philip's talk every time I see her, until the day it happens. And even then, I don't know how much she'll understand on the evening itself. As long as it doesn't upset her – that's the only thing that really matters. And then it occurs to me: the one thing that Philip and I haven't tried is to take

276

Angelina to visit Freda. I doubt Lina's even seen her aunt since she's been back living in Bierleigh. Surely Freda will recognise her *little angel*. If it brings them even a few moments of pleasure, it's got to be worth a try, hasn't it?

A week later: Monday 3 December

It's been a roller coaster of a weekend. On Friday evening, Terry and I watched a film together on TV, with a glass of wine each and a bar of my favourite chocolate that he'd picked up for me on his way home from work. It was a simple enough situation, but so different from how things were, only very recently. I didn't really want to spoil it, but I'd reached the point where I simply couldn't help asking, as the film ended and I drained my wine glass before going to put the kettle on:

'Are you *ever* going to tell me, Terry? Tell me exactly what's been going on during the last couple of months?'

'Yes,' he said, looking up at me, his voice suddenly serious. 'I was always going to tell you, Joy. I just couldn't, until ... well, until I was sure. And then I thought I'd wait till there was a good moment. Christmas, perhaps. But maybe you're right, maybe this is as good a time as any.'

'OK,' I said, a little warily. 'So shall I make us both a cup of tea before we start this conversation?'

'No,' he said. 'Never mind the tea. Pour us both another glass of wine instead.'

I felt ridiculously nervous as I sat back down, sipping the wine and waiting for Terry to speak again. And when he did, I nearly dropped my glass in surprise.

'Well, as you've already gathered,' he began, 'I'm retiring soon. It's because David and I are selling the business.'

'You're *what*?!' I gasped. 'Selling the—?'

David, the other partner in the company, is about the same age as Terry, and I've always had the impression both of them would work until they dropped.

Terry laughed. 'Yes, I knew you'd be shocked. Well, Dave's got a few health issues now; he gets tired, and when he started talking about retiring, I didn't really want to go on without him. Then, out of the blue, we got a takeover bid from Mount and Amos.'

I know the name well. They're a much bigger, very successful accountancy firm with several branches. But I couldn't believe Terry's kept all this quiet from me!

'The negotiations went on for so long,' he said, 'I didn't want to say anything to you until it was definite. Dave and I thought so many times that the whole deal might collapse. It was really stressful: all the extra work involved, the endless meetings with Mount and Amos, then dealing with correspondence to and from the solicitor, and of course, having to catch up with the work I didn't have time to do during the day. I was worried that if it all fell through, and I hadn't kept on top of all the accounts in the meantime, I'd lose clients.'

I took another gulp of my wine. I was too shocked to even respond.

'Even when we were virtually ready to sign contracts, we hit more problems,' Terry went on. 'Mount and Amos were refusing to commit to keeping on all of our existing staff – which we'd insisted all along was non-negotiable. It was getting ridiculous: we had meeting after meeting, with and without the solicitors, all sorts of compromises being suggested but Dave and I were determined to stick to our guns. I honestly thought we'd have to pull out of the deal after all. But, well to cut a long story short, in the end, they relented.' He stopped, took a mouthful of his own wine, then went on: 'I know I've been unbearable to live with, Joy, but the one thing I was determined about was that I didn't want you having to share the worry of it all, just as you'd got rid of all the stress of your own job! I thought it would only be a short while before everything was signed and sealed, and I'd be able to tell you. But, unfortunately, it went on longer than I anticipated. I was so exhausted by it all, I couldn't sleep, couldn't think about anything else, and I knew you were getting annoyed, but—'

'*Worried*, Terry,' I corrected him. 'Yes, I was annoyed at times, but mostly I was just worried about you. I couldn't understand what was wrong. But it's all sorted now? The takeover's definite?'

'Yes. Contracts signed, all the staff told, every last detail sorted. Mount and Amos take over in January. Just in time,' he added, almost to himself, raising his eyes to the ceiling.

'Just in time for what?' I asked.

'Well, for New Year,' he said quickly. 'For Christmas, as far as I'm concerned. I'm retiring on Christmas Eve.'

We were both silent for a moment, then I raised what was left of my glass of wine to him and said:

'Well, here's to that! I honestly thought this day would never come!'

'Cheers!' He laughed, raising his glass and finishing off his own wine. 'Me too, for a while.'

Then he got up and walked across the room to me, put his arms around me and slowly, gently, kissed me.

'I'm so sorry,' he said. 'I should have told you – I realise that now, now I can finally think straight and understand how horrible it's been for you. I just wanted you to keep busy so you didn't notice how stressed and shattered I was by it all.'

'But of *course* I noticed! I didn't know what to think – whether you were ill, or if you'd started finding me boring now that I've retired, or if you were having an affair.'

'Don't be ridiculous,' he retorted softly. 'You could never be boring. I could never want anyone else. But I couldn't have blamed you if *you'd* been so fed up with me that you'd looked elsewhere. At that handsome Howard you met for drinks at the Angel, for instance . . . ?'

And I just had to laugh. If only he knew the ridiculous embarrassment I'd gone through about Howard when I first met him, he might not joke about it! But fortunately, by now, it's not something I cringe about any more. And I felt far too happy to care.

And now it's December, and Christmas is fast approaching, whether I'm ready for it or not. All the shops in the village are lit up and tinselled, the windows full of Christmas gifts, Christmas food, Christmas cards, Christmas decorations. Terry and I usually only buy one present each: for each other. But this year, since he's agreed it would be lovely to spend the time with Sara and Charlie over the holiday, we went to Totnes together on Saturday for a shopping trip. The shops are all so quaint there, and so full of things you never find anywhere else, and we bought bagfuls of gifts for them both. I can't remember when we last went shopping together. When I was at work, I did the food shopping at the Co-op in Bierleigh on my way home, and often popped in to the greengrocer's and the butcher's at weekends, but that was about it. I used the internet for anything else I wanted. But Saturday was fun. It reminded me of the sort of fun we used to have together when we were younger, which just goes to show how much things have suddenly improved between us. We seemed to spend the day laughing together. We sang along with carol singers in the street, bought freshly made mince pies from a market stall and ate them while wandering around the other stalls, and finished off with lunch at the big pub on the way back to the car park.

'I'm so glad you had a nice time,' Sara says when I tell her about it this morning.

She looked so cold when I saw her coming back from walking Charlie to school – December seems to have brought with it a sudden, icy feel to the weather – that I've invited her in for a cup of hot chocolate and a toasted teacake.

'Hot chocolate hasn't got much caffeine in it,' I reassured her. 'And an occasional treat won't hurt you – or the baby.'

She looks cheerful today – I'd actually say really happy. Perhaps I do too. I certainly feel brighter, more enthusiastic about things, than I have for a while.

'So you're saying Terry's going to *retire*?' she squawks when I tell her the latest news. I haven't had a chance until now, because of being out with Terry on Saturday. Then on Sunday, Charlie's friend Max came to play – and so did Luke! I saw, or rather, heard – his old car arriving outside and Luke going into the house, so I stayed away, letting them enjoy some time together.

'I bet you didn't see that coming!' she goes on now, shaking her head at me in surprise.

'You're dead right, I didn't.' I'm still not sure I can believe it, even now. 'But it was even more of a shock to hear about the sale of the business.'

'I'm sure it was.' She gives me a sympathetic look. 'Are you ... a little bit hurt that he's taken so long to confide in you?'

'I was at first. But when he explained how it's all been really uncertain, with so many ups and downs in the negotiations, such a lot of work to sort out the terms of the takeover and so many times he thought the whole deal was going to collapse, I did understand. He was totally exhausted, and the light at the end of the tunnel kept threatening to go out completely. But thank God, it didn't.'

'And he seems happy about it all, now?'

'He's absolutely over the moon! He says he's "relieved to the point of euphoria". No wonder he's seemed so different, so happy, recently!'

'So what's Terry going to do to *keep himself occupied*?' she says, giving me a grin. She knows quite well how much that phrase was irritating me before!

'He doesn't know. He hasn't exactly had a chance to decide yet! But we *will* have a dog to walk—'

'Oh!' she squeals, but I stop her quickly, going on: 'He's still saying not till after Christmas. I don't understand why, but just between you and me, I think there's something else going on, something else he isn't telling me about.'

'Oh, I hope not,' she says, her smile dropping. 'Another secret? Are you worried about what it might be?'

'No. Actually ...' I shrug. 'I know I shouldn't presume, but I think it might be something to do with my Christmas present.'

'Ooh! What – you think he might be buying you a dog in secret?'

'Well, it has occurred to me, yes. He's been kind of smiling to himself whenever Christmas is mentioned. There's obviously something going on, and I think it must be something nice. I hope so, anyway!'

'He might be planning to whisk you away somewhere – on a romantic break in the countryside to spend Christmas at a hotel with a roaring log fire and massive, massive Christmas tree, and turkey and tinsel ... oh, how lovely that would be, Joy!'

I'm laughing now. 'No, it's nothing like that – he's said several times how much he's looking forward to seeing you and Charlie over Christmas. Anyway, I'm not sure I'd like it. I'm fairly traditional about Christmas, really.'

'Well, it is lovely that he's planning something special for you,' she says. 'Or – at least – that you think he is!'

'Yes. I hope I'm not going to be disappointed, after all this!'

But I don't, really, want to try to guess what it is. I don't want to spoil it.

Wednesday 5 December

This afternoon, Sara and Luke are going to the hospital for her first pregnancy scan. She gives me a call to make sure I'll be around in case she's late home to collect Charlie.

'Don't worry, I haven't forgotten,' I reassure her. 'Are you excited?'

'I feel a bit nervous, to be honest,' she says. 'About whether everything's all right, you know.'

'You haven't got any worries, have you? Any worrying symptoms?'

'No, not at all. But it's just nice to have that reassurance, isn't it?'

'Of course. Is Luke picking you up to take you to the hospital?'

'Yes.' I can hear the smile in her voice. 'He's taken the afternoon off work, specially. And I've asked him to come back for dinner tonight.' She pauses, then adds, as if she's making an excuse for it: 'I like him spending time with Charlie.'

'Yes. Charlie seems to get on well with him. That's good. As you said, good for him to have another man around sometimes.'

I wonder how long it'll be before she can bring herself to admit she likes having Luke around herself, too!

At three o'clock, Sara and Luke aren't back from the hospital, so I make my way down to the school in plenty of time to collect Charlie. He comes out of his classroom laughing, chasing after Max, while a couple of other boys run beside them. It's so nice to see him happy.

'Where's Mum?' he asks in surprise when he sees me waiting for him.

'She's ... at an appointment. She told you, didn't she – that I might be meeting you?'

'Oh yes!' He grins. 'I forgot. What's an *appointment*? She said she had to go to a meeting.'

'Yes, that's right. Meeting, appointment – same thing,' I say, smiling down at him. 'Now, come on, do your coat up properly, Charlie, it's freezing cold!'

He chats away to me as we walk home, telling me things about maths and history that I'm sure I didn't know at his age, and just as we're approaching Angel Cove there's a bleep on my phone and a message from Sara:

> On our way back now, sorry for delay, hope
> Charlie's OK. Tell you more when I see you!

I've only just got him settled at my kitchen table with a drink and slice of cake when Luke's car pulls up outside.

'Oh good, Luke's here too!' Charlie says, jumping up and looking out of the window. 'I like Luke, he's cool. He tells me lots of stuff about animals.'

Sara has a look about her as she comes in. I can only say she's positively glowing, but at the same time, looking ... kind of shell-shocked. Luke looks slightly paler than usual and keeps blinking, as if he's not sure where he is.

'How did your *meeting* go?' I ask her. She follows me into the kitchen as I go to make tea, and pulls the door closed behind her.

'It's twins,' she says in a kind of strangled gasp. 'Twins! Two little shapes on the screen – it was quite clear – the sonographer said there's absolutely no doubt about it.'

'Oh my goodness!' I grab hold of her in a hug, partly because I'm so excited, but partly because she looks like she might faint. 'Are you ... I mean, I know it must be a shock, and it'll be hard work ... but are you pleased about it?'

'I don't really know how I feel yet,' she admits. 'I'm relieved everything seems to be OK, but I can't quite grasp the fact that there are going to be *two* of them!'

'How about Luke?'

'I think he was even more shocked than me. That's why we were a bit held up. We had to go to the coffee shop at the hospital, get him a cup of strong tea and let him have a little break so he was calmed down enough to drive back!'

I laugh. 'Oh, Sara, I know it must have been a surprise, but won't it be lovely? You'll have Charlie to help – he'll love it, and at least he's old enough to do a lot for himself now. Imagine if he'd been younger – still a toddler, not even at school yet.'

She shudders, then laughs along with me.

'I know. And I'm ... excited, really. As you know, I always did want another child and now, well, double the pleasure, as they say. Luke keeps on telling me how much he wants to help, too.'

'That's good.'

'Yes.' She meets my eyes. 'It definitely is.'

Back in the living room, while we drink tea and eat cake and listen to Charlie chatting away about school, Sara and Luke keep looking at each other and smiling. I can almost feel the air between them shimmering with the heat of their excitement.

'Sara's told me that the ... er ... meeting went well,' I say, giving Luke a little wink.

'Yes,' he says, and he takes a deep breath and manages to laugh. 'Um, very interesting!'

'Anyway,' Sara says, looking like she's trying to pull herself together – and nodding towards Charlie to warn us that his ears were probably flapping! 'Enough about my meeting. Any news from you, Joy? How was the Historical Society on Monday night?'

'Oh, we talked about our memories of the village shops over the years,' I say. 'And Freda mentioned Lina – Angelina – again. *Her little angel*, as she calls her. Margaret was just in the middle of a long story about how her mother used to send her to the butcher's for a pound of tripe and some pigs' trotters, when Freda interrupted her, saying Angelina refused to eat tripe when she was little. And everyone else said they didn't blame her, apart from Margaret who said there was nothing wrong with tripe and onions, it's a balanced meal.'

Sara and Luke are laughing at this, and I join in when Sara admits she doesn't even know what tripe actually is, and Luke has to tell her.

'Anyway,' I continue when we've all got over our disgust about eating tripe, 'it's surprising how often Freda does mention Lina. I've been wondering whether Lina would actually like to pay her aunt a visit, if I offer to go with her.'

'I'm surprised Philip hasn't suggested it before,' Luke comments.

'Well, Philip's had such a lot to contend with in recent months: his leg, the operation, getting used to being disabled and having to move into sheltered accommodation. And, at the same time, worrying about his daughter starting to live independently in Bierleigh, while it was difficult for him to even visit her. Unfortunately, I don't think Freda was at the top of his list of priorities, as he knew she was safe and being well cared for in her home. So when I took him to see her the other week, she didn't even recognise him, sadly.'

'That must have been disappointing for him,' Sara says. 'But how do you think Freda would react to a visit from Lina?'

'I really don't know. It could go either way,' I admit. 'But I think it would be good to try.'

We chat for a little longer about other things while we finish our tea, and as they start to get ready to leave, Charlie looks up at his mum and asks eagerly:

'Is Luke staying for dinner?'

'Yes,' Sara confirms. 'And it's sausages.'

'Yay!' he shouts. '*Two* good things! Can I have three sausages, Mum, and can I show Luke my new paints that Daddy bought me?'

'Wow, new paints!' Luke says with an engaging degree of enthusiasm. 'Yes, I'd like to see those, Charlie. And I'd love you to do me another new painting one day, when you've got time – if you'd like to? I can pin it to the noticeboard in my room at the vet's, with the one you did for me of Pumpkin.'

'Yes, I'll paint one of Mummy for you, shall I?' Charlie asks in all innocence.

Luke looks at Sara, grinning, and she actually blushes.

The three of them say goodbye and head off next door, and I'm still smiling to myself long after they've gone.

Later, while it's still on my mind, I call Philip and ask him if he'd like me to pick him up for his promised visit to Smugglers' Cottages on Saturday.

'And we can pop in and see Angelina again afterwards, if it wouldn't be too much for you?' I suggest. I'm hoping it won't be, now the excitement of the first visit is over.

'That would be wonderful, Joy, if you're sure you don't mind.'

'Terry and I will look forward to it,' I insist. 'And there's something else I wanted to suggest. Do you think Angelina might like to go and visit her Aunt Freda in the care home one day? I'd be happy to take her. But only if you think it would be a good idea, and wouldn't upset either of them.' I hesitate, then go on: 'Freda seems to remember *her little angel* so clearly for a minute or two whenever we talk at the Historical Society meetings.'

Philip seems to think about this for a moment.

'It's very kind of you to suggest it, Joy,' he says eventually. 'And I'm sure Angelina would be very excited at the idea of visiting Freda. I'm pretty sure it won't have crossed her mind; she tends to only be able to focus on one or two things at a time, and since she moved into her flat—'

'Of course, she'll have only had room in her mind for getting used to everything about that – and then having her cat!' I agree.

'But I think, now, she'd love to see her aunt. I don't know the answer to your question, though: whether it would upset either of them. Freda's deteriorated a lot since Angelina last saw her; she might find that distressing. And if Freda doesn't recognise her – like she didn't recognise me . . .'

'I know. It's a gamble, I suppose. If you'd rather just forget it . . .'

'No.' He clears his throat and then goes on firmly: 'I think it's a lovely idea. Freda's probably used to you now that she sees you every week, so I think it would be helpful if you were there with Angelina rather than me. And if it *does* give either of them a brief moment of pleasure, well, that would be wonderful, wouldn't it?'

We agree that he'll raise the subject with Lina when we call on her on Saturday. I hope I'm doing the right thing. I don't want to be too intrusive – they're not my family, and I haven't known any of them for very long.

'Do you think I'm interfering? Is it too much?' I ask Terry this evening over dinner.

He looks up at me, smiling, shaking his head.

'No,' he says quite firmly. 'I don't. I think you're just trying to be a good friend, helping out where you can. Trying to make people happy – how can that be wrong?'

Well, I hope he's right.

Saturday 8 December

Philip sits in his wheelchair, a blanket around him, another over his knees, gazing at the sea with a faraway look on his face.

'Are you sure you're warm enough, Philip?' Terry asks. 'We can go indoors whenever you want.'

Terry insisted on coming with me to Ferndell this morning, helping me to transfer Philip to the car and being available to help get him into the house. While I'm in the kitchen making coffee, he's sitting on the bench next to Philip's wheelchair, chatting to him about their respective lives here in this house. It's cold, but fortunately dry and bright today, and I've got the kitchen door open ready for them to come in whenever Philip's ready. He has his walking frame here, and Terry to help him.

'I never dreamt I'd ever be back here again,' Philip's saying.

'Has it changed much, from the outside?' Terry asks him.

Philip looks round at the house. 'No, not much at all, apart from your extension at the side, of course. Your neighbour's house looks *exactly* as it did when Chrissie's family lived there, though.'

'But maybe not for long!' I call out. 'Sara's thinking of having a similar extension built, in due course.'

She was only telling me this yesterday. The idea is so that the babies can have a room of their own, eventually. And they can all have a bit more space. Especially if ... well, I mustn't jump the gun, obviously, and I certainly wouldn't say this to Sara – but I wouldn't be surprised if, eventually, their little family might be joined permanently by the twins' father!

'They were small houses,' Philip says, nodding. 'Too small, really, for families, but that's how a lot of people lived back then.'

'Were you happy here, though?' Terry asks him as I carry three mugs of coffee outside on a tray and put them down on the table.

'Oh, yes. How could I not have been happy? With the sea at my doorstep, the love of my life living just next door – marrying her, having our baby daughter. What else in the world could I have wanted? It would have been greedy to ask for more.'

There's a lump in my throat, and as Terry turns to meet my eyes, I think I catch the glint of tears in his own.

'I'm glad you have those lovely memories,' I say.

Philip smiles at me. 'And I'm glad the old house has nice people like you two living here now. Making memories of your own.'

'Thank you.' I look up and add, 'Oh, and here's someone else to meet you. Philip, this is Sara, our neighbour who lives in ... Chrissie's house.'

'Hello, Sara.' Philip gives her a beaming smile. 'Is your little boy here? I've heard all about him.'

'Pleased to meet you, Philip.' She joins us on the bench. 'No, Charlie's with his dad this weekend. But I've told him about you, too. He's especially fascinated by the fact that you had twin brothers. I'm looking forward to his reaction when I tell him he's going to be big brother to twins himself!'

Philip chuckles. 'Well, I'm sure he'll be a nicer big brother than I was! I used to sulk about the fact that the twins were so close to each other that they didn't need me. I think, looking back, that it was really my own fault, because I spent all my time with a certain little girl from your house, instead of paying my brothers enough attention.' He closes his eyes for a moment, before going on, quietly: 'You know, sitting here, seeing the beach, listening to the sound of the sea, it's almost as if ... as if I was that young lad again, waiting right here for her to come out so I could chase her into the sea, play with her in the sand, search for shells and little fish with her in the rock pools ...'

'That's what Charlie likes doing,' Sara says.

'He'll have a lovely time growing up here, especially in the summer – swimming in the sea, playing with his friends ... and with his little brothers or sisters, of course,' Philips says. 'Tell him not to be jealous if they're especially close. Twins usually are. They'll still need their big brother. He'll be more important than ever. It's never good to be jealous, especially of your own siblings.'

I guess he's thinking of Freda now, as well as himself. When there's a break in the conversation, I remind him that we'll take him to see Lina again after lunch. His face lights up at the mention of her name. And we talk a lot more about Philip's life here. He tells us about his favourite places in the woods, where he and Chrissie used to climb the trees, build dens in the grassy hollows or play on fallen branches; how they used to race up and down the lane to Bierleigh and back on their bikes; and how he taught her to swim in the calm shallows of the cove. Eventually he says:

'Maybe you could help me indoors now, if that's OK? It is getting a bit nippy. And I'm looking forward to being nosy –'

'Having a look around the house?' Terry smiles at him. 'Of course: I'll show you around.'

'Well, around downstairs, anyway. I'm not expecting you to carry me upstairs!' Philip jokes.

'Luckily, we've even got a downstairs toilet these days,' I point out.

'Amazing. We thought we were the bees' knees, having one inside at all when I lived here!' he says.

He says goodbye to Sara and tells her he'd love to meet Charlie another time. Once Terry's helped him indoors, I make us all some lunch so that we've got plenty of time this afternoon for our visit to Lina. She's waiting for him at her front window as we pull up in the car, and this time the conversation between father and daughter is lively and spontaneous, as if they've never been separated, and the love in Philip's eyes as he finally hugs her goodbye is enough to get my eyes stinging again.

'I'll bring your dad again as often as I can,' I promise Lina. 'Or perhaps you'd like a little visit to him at *his* flat one day instead?'

She thinks about this seriously for a moment.

'Will Bella be all right if I leave her here on her own?' she says.

'Oh, yes, I'm sure she will. You leave her while you go shopping, don't you?' I remind her.

'Yes. But that only takes twenty minutes if I go to the butcher's or the greengrocer's, or thirty minutes if I go to the supermarket,' she says very seriously. 'Amy timed it. Amy says Bella is fine on her own.'

'Well, ask Amy what she thinks about you leaving Bella for an hour or so,' I suggest, keeping a straight face. It's nice that she's taking her cat-ownership so seriously. 'And if that goes OK, we can make it a bit longer the next time.'

'That would be nice,' she finally agrees solemnly, nodding her head. 'Thank you, Joy.'

'I'll give you a call in a couple of days,' Philip says, 'and ask you what Amy thinks about it.'

It's turned five o'clock by the time we've taken Philip back to Ferndell and stopped for another cup of tea with him. So it's not until we're heading home again in the car on our own that Terry and I finally get a chance to chat about the day's events.

'Phew. It makes you think, doesn't it?' he says softly, taking a hand briefly off the steering wheel to pat my knee.

'It does. And keep your hands on the wheel, if you don't mind – there's a double bend coming up!' I joke. Because if I don't joke, I'm afraid I'll cry. It's been an emotional day.

'We're so lucky, you and I,' he goes on after he's negotiated the bends. 'And maybe we don't appreciate it enough.'

'They're both happy in their own ways, though: Philip and Lina. And now we've promised to make this a frequent thing – bringing Philip back to Bierleigh, or taking Lina to visit him – they'll be even happier.'

'Yes. It's such a small thing to do, isn't it,' he agrees. 'Well done for . . . well, for finding out about them – all of them. It's so strange to think of them living in Smugglers' Cottages back then – Freda, too. What a shame her dementia's so advanced.'

'Yes.' I look out of the window, at the street lights, rooftops and church spire of Bierleigh coming into view down the hill, and add quietly: 'Do you know what Philip said to Freda, the other week when I took him to see her? *Every day's a gift*. It's so true, isn't it. Let's not waste a single day, in future, Tel. Especially now you're going to retire. Let's make the most of it, while we're both still, you know, relatively OK.'

'*Relatively?*' he retorts, and it breaks the spell, making us both laugh.

'Shall we stop off at the pub and see if we can get a table for dinner?' he suggests.

'On a Saturday evening in December?' I remind him. 'Nice idea, but no chance! Besides, I don't know about you, but I'm shattered. How about we pick up fish and chips from the chip shop and eat it at home?'

'Yes, that sounds nice,' he agrees. 'OK – home, then!' He taps the dashboard, as if to tell the car where to go.

'I think it already knows the way,' I joke.

And in the dark of the December evening, we head back along the so-familiar country lanes towards the coast, towards Bierleigh, towards Angel Cove, our home, our little sanctuary on the beach where we live, and love, and will, from now on, at least *try* to appreciate every day that we're still alive – and *relatively* OK!

Thursday 13 December

Sara and I are having a walk together today – up to Harry's Plain and across to the village and back. We haven't done this for a while; she's been busy, and the weather hasn't been very encouraging during the last few days. It's been cold and windy with sleet streaking down from the sky like icy needles blowing into our faces, but today it's dry, at least, with a pale, grey sky and a bleak-looking sun low down near the horizon. We're walking as fast as we can to try to keep warm, looking up at the bare branches of the trees around us and a couple of seagulls circling overhead. I pull my scarf closer around my neck. We're both looking forward to the hot chocolate we've promised ourselves in the teashop in Bierleigh. We can't really have a proper conversation until we've finally arrived, and have our drinks steaming on the table in front of us. And then I tell Sara my news.

'Terry told me something last night,' I say, smiling at her across the steam from my hot chocolate. 'Part of the secret – you know? – that I guessed he was keeping from me.'

'Ooh ... that sounds intriguing,' Sara says. 'Is it ... about the plan for a dog, by any chance?'

'Not exactly. But I do at least understand, now, why he's kept saying we can't do that yet.' I take a mouthful of my hot chocolate, wipe the foam from my mouth and sigh with pleasure. 'Mm, this is just what I needed – it's *so* cold out today, isn't it?'

'Don't change the subject!' Sara laughs. 'You're teasing me. I can tell from your face it's something exciting. Come on, what is it?'

'Well . . . you know I told you it'll be our fortieth wedding anniversary in the new year?'

'Your ruby one. Yes, it's in January, you said, I think?'

'Yes, the thirteenth. I didn't think we were going to do anything special to celebrate. I hardly liked to mention it to Terry, the way he was during the last couple of months. And it turns out, he *had* booked something – a special surprise – but when the takeover deal proved to be so complicated and so uncertain, he was really, really panicking that it all might have to be cancelled at the last minute – which just added to his stress and worries, as it might have been too late to get a refund—'

'So are you going to tell me what this special surprise is, or am I supposed to guess?' Sara demands impatiently.

'Sorry! Yes, it's a holiday. Terry says it's going to be our trip of a lifetime, Sara. He's booked it all – the flights, hotels, travel insurance and everything. Can you believe Terry's sorted all it all out on his own, without me knowing the first thing about it? I just can't get over it!'

'Wow, that's *really* exciting, Joy! You must be thrilled. No wonder he's had to catch up on so much work and stuff at home, if he was secretly booking all this while he was at work,' she goes on. 'But I'm so pleased for you. You deserve it, both of you.' Then she stops, frowning, and goes on: 'But you haven't told me where you're going, on this holiday.'

'I don't know! He says I've got to wait till Christmas Day to find out the rest.' I shrug, feeling a bit sheepish. 'It was *all* supposed to be a secret until Christmas. But – well, I started asking about the dog again – why he didn't want to get it until the new year. I suppose I was getting a bit impatient about it, and he just sighed and said he'd better explain. So, I feel bad about it now! He did say, though, that he'd started worrying that I might already have things in my diary for January – dates for the Historical Society and so on – and that if he didn't tell me about the trip, it could be difficult to cancel them. So he'd decided it was probably best that I know the dates, at least.'

'How lovely! And when you get back – he'll help you choose the dog?'

'Yes. He's promised. And he's right: I wouldn't want to have to put a dog into boarding kennels or whatever, almost as soon as we'd adopted it, that wouldn't have been fair.' I smile. 'We've both got so much to look forward to, Sara, haven't we? You, with your twins on the way.'

She rubs her flat tummy, and I smile. She's doing it instinctively, like so many other pregnant women I've seen before, in the course of my work. A gesture of protectiveness. *I'm looking after you, baby.*

'It's a coincidence, really, isn't it,' she muses. 'Philip having been the older brother – like Charlie's going to be – of twin siblings. And it's not as if naturally conceived twins are very common.'

'I know. It's like history repeating itself at Angel Cove – in Smugglers' Cottages.'

'It's nothing to do with the cottages or the Cove – or the angel, in case that's what you're thinking!' she says, laughing at me. 'These babies were conceived in Luke's flat in Plymouth!'

'Oh yes. That's a shame, I rather like the idea of the angel having a hand in things!'

'Well, anyway,' she says when we've both stopped laughing, 'Terry isn't the only one who's blabbed their secret a bit sooner than they intended.'

'What do you mean?' I ask. She's grinning into her chocolate.

'I told Charlie about the babies yesterday.'

'Oh my God!' I squeal. 'I thought you were going to wait till after Christmas!'

'I know, I know, but ... oh, it's just that Charlie's been mentioning brothers and sisters so much lately. His friend Max is one of four kids; he's got an older brother and two younger sisters. So, of course, Charlie feels a bit left out when he hears Max chatting away about things they do together as a family. A bit sad. And ... I just wanted to be able to tell him something nice; something exciting.'

'I bet he *was* excited!' I say, picturing his little face lighting up.

'Oh yes. He was almost beside himself with it. He couldn't wait to get to school this morning, to tell Max.' She smiles. 'He says he hopes at least *one* of the babies will be a boy, but he doesn't mind if it isn't, he'll love them both even if they're both girls. That made me laugh!'

'Ah, bless him. Did he ask about the twins' daddy?' I add quietly, remembering how Charlie had solemnly told me, during one of our very first conversations together, that *you have to have a man and a woman to make a baby.*

'Not till this morning. He must have been thinking about it overnight.' she chuckles. 'He asked whether his daddy sent me some seed in the post to make the babies! He doesn't *quite* understand the full picture yet, fortunately! I just said no, luckily for me, Luke had agreed to be the twins' daddy. He's fine with that, as I've already told him that I'd known Luke for a long time, since long before Charlie was born. And he thinks Luke's great. They were playing all sorts of games together yesterday afternoon and he was quite upset when he left after dinner.'

'So you didn't tell Charlie while Luke was still there?'

'Oh God no. Luke would have been dying of embarrassment,'

she says. 'But I'll call him later and give him the heads-up. Just in case Charlie starts asking him about his seed, when he comes round for Sunday dinner!'

'You're seeing him more often now, by the sound of it,' I say, trying to keep my voice quite neutral.

'Yes.' She manages to keep a straight face, but something in her eyes betrays her. 'It's good for Charlie, having him around. He won't replace Rob for him, obviously, but—'

'But Rob's not here.'

'Exactly.'

'And it's not exactly hurting *you*, having Luke around, either,' I tease her, and finally she grins and admits:

'No. It doesn't hurt me at all, strangely enough. I could even . . . perhaps . . . get used to it. As you've obviously realised already!'

I raise my mug of chocolate towards her and say, very softly, because with everything we've shared this morning, suddenly I feel ever so slightly emotional:

'Well, congratulations. On the twins, and on telling Charlie, and on . . . well, I'm going to say it, Sara: on you and Luke finding each other again, too. Cheers!'

'Cheers!' she agrees, chinking her mug against mine. 'Congrats to you, too, love, on getting everything straightened out with Terry. Nearly forty years of marriage,' she adds, shaking her head. 'How the hell have you managed it?'

'With difficulty, recently!'

She laughs, goes to take another sip of her chocolate and exclaims: 'Oh, damn, it's empty – I've drunk it all already.'

'Want another one?'

'No – thanks, but I really ought to get back to work. Otherwise I'll be up till midnight catching up again.'

'Of course.'

We head back to Angel Cove with our heads down against the

302

bitter cold wind blowing off the sea. The sky's darkened again while we've been in the café, and now there's a mixture of sleet and salty spray being blown into our faces. But I don't care how much it stings. Everything feels wonderful.

Monday 17 December

Terry and I took Lina to visit Philip yesterday. Philip had called me to say that Amy, Lina's carer, had been in touch, telling him Lina was worried about leaving Bella the cat for more than the usual half-hour or so but that Amy had reassured her that cats are independent creatures and Bella would probably spend the entire time outside and wouldn't even notice Lina wasn't there.

'But it's nice that she's being so caring and responsible,' Amy had said.

We arranged the visit for a Sunday because Terry had said he'd like to come with us. He likes Philip; I can imagine he might make a point of seeing more of him after he's retired.

'Thank you, Joy. Thank you, Terry. You are very kind,' Lina said in her usual polite, solemn manner as she got into the car.

She was on her best behaviour, quiet and a bit shy, on the drive to Ferndell and when we arrived at Goldcrest Lodge. But as soon as we were inside Philip's flat and she'd had a good look around, she threw her arms around him and said:

'This flat is very, very nice, Dad. It's almost as nice as my flat.'

'I'm glad you think so, sweetheart,' he said. 'I like it too. And it's especially nice now, with you here!'

'But why are there two bedrooms?' Lina went on, frowning. 'There's only one person living here, and that's you!'

'I know.' He looked down for a moment, then up and Terry and me, before looking back at Lina. 'It's ... just in case I get a visitor one day, who wants to stay overnight.'

Lina was still frowning, trying to work this out. She turned to me and asked:

'Are you going to stay here overnight one day, Joy?'

'I don't think so, Lina.'

'Will *you* stay overnight one day, Terry?' she asked him, and he laughed and said no, he didn't think it was likely.

'Lina, darling, I was thinking, when I bought the flat, that *you* might want to?' Philip told her finally. I sensed that he hadn't been sure whether to mention this yet; but his daughter was one step ahead!

'But I did tell you, didn't I, Dad, that I wanted to get a place of my own when you were moving here,' she said. 'I do miss you, Dad, but I wanted to be more grown up.'

'I know, sweetheart. But the room is here anyway, just in case you ever need it, OK?' He paused for a moment, then added: 'In fact, I was wondering about Christmas.'

'Christmas is coming!' she said, smiling with childlike enthusiasm.

'Yes. And we've always spent it together, haven't we, in the past.'

Her smile dropped. She obviously hadn't thought about this yet. Of course she wouldn't want to be on her own in her little flat over Christmas.

'I've got Bella now,' she said in a small voice. 'But I don't want *you* to be on your own at Christmas, Dad.' Then she brightened up suddenly and added: 'You can come and stay in *my* flat.'

'There's no room,' he said gently. 'And, it's fine for me to come for a visit, but I wouldn't be able to manage all day, and overnight, not without help. I'm too heavy for you. I have everything sorted out for me, here. The cooker, the toilet, the shower – all the rails and handles and things I need.'

Lina was quiet for a moment, thinking this over.

'If I come here for Christmas,' she said then, slowly, 'I'll have to bring Bella.'

'Yes, I've thought of that. Pets aren't usually allowed here, but I've had a word with—' Philip glanced at me and chuckled '—She Who Must Be Obeyed. And she says she'd be prepared to make an exception. We'd have to set up a litter tray, of course, because Bella won't be able to go outside. And she can have her own bed, her food dishes and toys here. What do you think?'

'I'm not sure,' Lina said, looking worried. 'I'll have to ask Amy if she thinks it would be all right.'

'Yes, of course,' Philip said. 'Talk to Amy about it.'

'I don't know whether Bella would like it,' Lina went on. 'She's got used to my flat now, and she likes going outside. I do keep her indoors at night, though,' she added quickly. 'That's what the lady at the cat shelter said. To keep her safe. I am looking after her properly.'

'I know you are,' Philip agreed. 'So, think it over. I think Bella's a very easy-going cat who won't mind a change of scenery, or being indoors, just for a couple of days. And I'd *really* like us to be together for Christmas, like we always used to be.'

'When Mum was alive,' Lina said, nodding. 'In the farm cottage.'

'Yes.'

Sensibly, Philip changed the subject then, leaving Lina to mull all this over in her own head without pressurising her. I hope, once she's discussed it with Amy – whose advice she obviously respects completely – she'll agree.

'If she does,' I told Philip quietly when we were getting ready to leave, 'Terry or I will bring her over to you on Christmas Eve and take her back after Boxing Day, or whenever she's ready, of course.'

He started to thank me but Terry and I both waved it aside. Making the short drive to Ferndell and back is such a small thing to do, for the reward of seeing father and daughter together for Christmas. I'm keeping my fingers crossed it all goes to plan.

Our next trip will be the one I've arranged for tomorrow: taking Lina to see her aunt at her care home. I don't want to leave it any closer to Christmas or we'll all be getting busy with preparations. I'm not sure whether that visit will be quite as happy as yesterday's; but Lina was keen to try, when Philip mentioned it to her. So I'm keen to try, too.

It's the Historical Society's Christmas meal this evening. It was all everyone could talk about at the meeting last Monday, despite the fact that poor Howard had planned for us to discuss 'Bierleigh Christmases through the ages'. Every time one of us mentioned the word 'Christmas', they were all off again, reminding each other which dinner they'd ordered for tonight and – in the case of the women – what they were going to wear for the event. I must admit, I'm quite excited myself. It'll be fun to celebrate with this little group of friends; I've become fond of them all in the short time I've known them.

Terry insists on dropping me off at the Angel, and although I'm early, three of the others are already here, sitting at our table. Howard's looking smart and festive in a bright red sweater; David, slightly uncomfortable, having decided on a shirt and tie; and Annie, resplendent in a shiny emerald-green blouse and flashing Father Christmas earrings.

'I'll take them out when everyone's seen them,' she says. 'They make my ears itch something terrible.'

The others arrive soon afterwards – all in happy party moods. Even Freda, who quite clearly isn't sure where she is, and why, is smiling vaguely around her.

'There's a Christmas tree in here!' she says in surprise as we all settle down.

'Yes, Freda – it's nearly Christmas,' Grace reminds her. Grace is wearing a white fluffy jumper bearing a logo of a reindeer with an enormous red nose. It's warm in the pub and she looks like she's already realised the jumper is going to make her too hot – the colour of her face matches the reindeer's nose.

'Look at the lovely lights on the tree,' Margaret encourages Freda. Margaret's the most overdressed of us all, in a sparkly silver dress that's perhaps more suitable for a cocktail party than a meal in a pub. 'Look at the pretty angel on top of the tree.'

'The Angel of the Cove,' Freda mutters wistfully. Her two good friends exchange weary looks. I guess they'd prefer not to be treated to another confused ramble about Chrissie and the angel, tonight of all nights.

'All right, dear,' Grace says. 'Have a little sip of your orange juice. Dinner will be here soon.'

'Perhaps it was true,' Freda says in response, looking back at Grace with a puzzled frown. 'I thought I made it up, to help my little sister. But perhaps there really was an angel?' There's a moment of silence while we're probably all wondering how best to respond in order to keep her calm, and then suddenly she lets out a yell, sounding scared out of her life: 'Who's *that*?'

We all turn round to follow her gaze. The apparition that's just entered the pub is certainly enough to terrify the faint-hearted, but fortunately everyone apart from Freda knows exactly who it is. Saul is dressed – or perhaps I should say half dressed – in a Father Christmas outfit at least two sizes too small for him. The trousers, held up by what appears to be some green garden twine, are straining so dangerously low around his hips I hardly dare think what might happen if he eats too much and needs to undo the string. The jacket is stretched over a grubby white shirt that's seen better days, its sleeves twice as long as the sleeves of the jacket. And the hat is so tight on his head that his face is already sweating profusely, so that the false beard has come unstuck and is hanging off one side of his mouth.

'Ho ho ho!' he bellows across the bar to us. 'Merry Christmas, everybody!'

With which he staggers towards us, falls against the table, crashes to the floor and passes out.

As I appear to be the only one with the modicum of basic medical knowledge required to understand right away that (a) he must already have had a drink or two somewhere else, probably with one of his mates, and (b) that, at his advanced age, it's more than likely he's fractured something in his fall – I'm calling an ambulance as soon as I've jumped up and put him in the recovery position. And I think I'll be going with him to hospital.

Shame. I was really looking forward to my turkey with all the trimmings.

Tuesday 18 December

'Oh no!' Sara says. She's come to see me this morning after dropping Charlie at school, with the sole intention of hearing all about the dinner last night. 'Oh, Joy, I'm so sorry you missed it! You were looking forward to it.'

'It's OK. I didn't miss it.' I smile at her. 'As soon as I called Terry to explain that I might be late back, and why, he told me he was going to drive straight to the pub himself, and he'd either go with Saul in the ambulance or, if the ambulance took too long to arrive, he'd drive him to hospital instead.'

She nodded. 'Ah, that was nice of him. You've got a good guy there, haven't you?'

'Yes.' I know it, obviously. I've always known it, but I think Terry's also doing his absolute best now to prove it – to make up for the last few months. 'He was there within five minutes, and it would have been quicker for him to drive Saul himself, but I didn't really want Saul moved from the recovery position until the paramedics arrived. He'd come round by now and was moaning like hell about the pain in the arm he'd fallen on. I was pretty sure his wrist was broken. Also, there was a chance he might pass out again, or vomit – it's ridiculous for a man of his age to drink so much alcohol, his system can't cope with it! Anyway, we were lucky; the ambulance didn't take long.'

'Hopefully he'll have learned his lesson now – about the alcohol,' she says.

'I doubt it! Oh, I know he's entitled to have a drop of something now and then – he's lived this long, he's still in amazingly good shape considering his age, and why shouldn't he enjoy himself? But he'd certainly had a lot more than a drop! Silly old man.'

'So, was his wrist broken?'

'Yes. He's got to go back to the hospital to have it plastered when the swelling's gone down – meanwhile he's in a sling. Terry said Saul was really apologetic and grateful – once he'd sobered up! Fortunately it's his left wrist – he's right-handed – but he's called his granddaughter in Torquay; he was going to stay with her over Christmas anyway, so she's taking him to her place right away. Otherwise he'd probably have hurt himself some more, trying to do things one-handed!'

'Well, I'm glad you didn't miss the meal,' she says. 'Tell me all about it.'

There wasn't much more to tell her, really – the excitement was all over once the ambulance had come and gone, and the whole thing had, unfortunately, left us all feeling a bit less festive. Poor Freda was particularly upset by it all. Grace and Margaret took her outside while it was all going on. She was getting confused about why the ambulance was there, imagining herself back in the middle of some previous disaster in her life – I wondered whether she was remembering the drama of poor Chrissie being taken off to hospital to have the baby. But she calmed down after the paramedics had gone, and then we all put on our party hats, pulled our crackers and agreed there was no reason for the rest of us not to still have a nice meal together. And we chatted about other things – what we were doing for Christmas, what our hopes for the new year were, and so on. We all managed to enjoy it, and Howard suggested we should definitely make it an annual event.

'That's good,' Sara says when I've finished relating this. She hesitates for a moment, and then says: 'Well, I might as well tell you: I had a bit of a drama myself last night.'

'Oh no, what happened?'

'It's OK. Everything's fine, as far as I'm concerned. But Rob turned up on my doorstep at about eight o'clock – after Charlie was asleep, fortunately – and demanded to talk to me.'

'*Demanded* to talk to you?' I repeat, frowning.

'Yes.' She raises her eyebrows at me. 'He was quite agitated. I told him to calm down first and made him a coffee.'

'So what was he agitated about?'

'In a word – me.' She shakes her head. 'I couldn't believe the cheek of him, Joy. It seems things aren't going so swimmingly with Jade now. It looks likely they won't even move into the dream home together after all.'

'Oh, really?' I'd like to say it serves him right, but I think I'd better keep quiet.

'Yes – shame, eh?' she says sarcastically. 'And surprise, surprise: he now thinks that perhaps he might have made a mistake.'

'He *surely* didn't say he now wants you back?'

'He did! And not only that – he made it sound like he was doing me a huge favour by suggesting it! "I must admit I'm not particularly happy about you having someone else's baby," he said, as if it's got anything whatsoever to do with him! "But I'd be prepared to forgive that, and take the child on. Let's just say we've both made mistakes. And it'll be better for the baby to have a father, after all."'

'What!' I exclaim. 'What a bloody nerve! How the hell did you respond to *that*?'

'I did consider throwing something at him,' she says, with a little snort of laughter. 'But no. I managed to hold on to my dignity. "The babies have got a father," I told him. "They won't need you in their lives, and neither will I. The only reason I need to see you or speak to you now is for Charlie's sake."'

'Well done, you,' I tell her.

'Yes, it was pretty satisfying. And his face was a picture! "*Babies?*" he said. "You're having twins? You're actually *with* their father?" I think he assumed the father was someone who wouldn't have anything further to do with me.' She stops and smiles. 'Well, to be fair I suppose I thought that myself to begin with, didn't I! But of course, it was great letting him think I was already in another relationship. Even if it's not exactly true.'

'Not exactly?' I say, smiling back at her.

She shrugs and looks down. 'Well, not really true yet, but, well – you know . . .'

Her cheeks have gone a bit pink.

'Yes, I know,' I say gently. 'But do you think Rob's going to keep pestering you now, if it's really over between him and Jade?'

'No.' She's actually giggling now. 'He started spluttering and stammering about how I'd be better off back with him, it would be better for Charlie, better for the babies – even suggesting we could buy the big house together, that he and Jade had been intending to share! I sat and listened to all this in silence until he'd run out of steam, then I just stood up and told him to piss off.'

'Ha! And how do you feel now?'

'Fantastic!' she laughs.

'Well, good for you,' I say firmly.

'Thanks, Joy.' She turns to gaze out of the window at the sea. 'Why the hell would Rob think I'd ever want him back in my life? He doesn't even know me any more. Everything I'm ever going to want is here, now.'

This afternoon when I go to pick up Lina for the prearranged visit to her Aunt Freda, Amy is there, and I'm grateful that she takes a couple of minutes before she leaves, to reassure Lina that Bella will be perfectly happy without her again for such a short while.

'And as I've already told your dad,' Amy goes on, 'I think the plan for Christmas is absolutely perfect. If ever there's a cat who won't blink an eyelid about being taken to a different flat and having a different routine for a few days, it's Bella.' She gives me a smile and adds, 'Honestly, Joy, that cat is the most laid-back feline I've ever met. I can't imagine anything ever worrying her, as long as she's got her food, her comfy bed, and she knows Lina is around for her.'

'She's the best cat in the world,' Lina says, smiling happily, and then adds quickly: 'Although I did love Pumpkin too; but he wasn't mine.'

It takes longer to say goodbye to Bella than it does to walk the short distance from Lina's flat to Freda's care home. Lina has insisted on walking.

'It's very kind of you to offer to drive, Joy,' she says in her usual serious tone, 'but I like walking and it keeps me fit.'

'That's true, Lina. Good for you.'

At Green Lawns Care Home, we're shown into the lounge and I find myself crossing my fingers, hoping this experience won't be a repeat of the last time I was here, with Philip. It will be sad and upsetting for Lina if Freda gets distressed again and doesn't recognise her. Freda's sitting in a high-back chair looking out over the gardens, and one of the carers moves two more chairs so that Lina and I can sit with her.

'Hello, Auntie Freda,' Lina says when Freda turns to look at us.

She says this completely calmly, with no show of excessive emotion. And somehow, that approach seems to work, because Freda looks back at her, completely unfazed, and simply replies:

'Hello, my little angel.'

I'm so relieved, and so astonished that she recognises Lina so instantly, that my eyes fill with tears and I have to look away. Lina herself doesn't seem in the least surprised, though, and the two of them proceed to have what almost passes for a normal conversation in the circumstances: both of them expressing interest in the colour of each other's cardigans, discussing the weather – Lina seeming unperturbed by the fact that Freda seems to think it's July – and what they've had for lunch. When Freda begins to talk about going out on her bicycle later on and meeting Doris at the cinema, Lina smiles and nods as if this is all absolutely fine.

'I've got a cat,' she tells Freda. 'Her name's Bella and she's the best cat in the world.'

'That's nice. I've got a dog,' Freda counters. 'Bilbo. He's a spaniel. I think he's asleep at the moment.'

'That's nice too,' Lina says calmly.

When her aunt asks if Lina's being a good girl and doing well at school, Lina looks puzzled for a moment; I'm just about to intervene, to help her out, when she shrugs, smiles, and says:

'I've left school now, Auntie Freda. But I'm still being good.'

'You always were a good girl, our little angel,' Freda says, reaching out and stroking her hand. She looks up at me and adds: 'Look after her, won't you.'

'Of course,' I say.

'She's Joy,' Lina tells Freda. 'She's my friend. She's very kind to me.'

'That's good.' Freda nods and, smiling happily to herself, closes her eyes.

'She wants to go to sleep,' Lina informs me. 'We should go now. Goodbye, Auntie Freda.'

'We'll come again,' I add.

Perhaps it's just been a good day for her – a better day than when Philip came to see her. Perhaps he should try again; maybe if he came with Lina, it would work better.

I call him, when I get home, to suggest it, and tell him how well the visit went.

'I'm so glad,' he says. 'I wonder if it's easier for someone with Lina's simplicity of expression, to get through to Freda.'

'Possibly. Even when Freda was saying she has a dog, and she was going out on her bike – drifting back in time, asking Lina how she's getting on at school – Lina just took it in her stride. I suppose she doesn't overthink things or feel awkward, the way we might do. But it was so moving to hear Freda straight away call her *my little angel*. As if Lina hasn't even changed, since she was a little girl.'

Philip gives a soft little laugh. 'She hasn't, much,' he says. 'She's still the same sweet, uncomplicated soul she was when she was knee-high to a grasshopper.'

'How lovely that is,' I say wistfully.

'I often used to think,' he goes on, 'that it would be easy to believe she really *was* blessed by an angel. Does that sound completely ridiculous?'

'No,' I assure him. 'It sounds totally logical, to me.'

Even Sara gets quite emotional when I describe the reunion between Lina and her aunt.

'It's so sad that Freda can't be with them over Christmas,' she says.

'It would be far too much for her. She can only tolerate visitors for a little while. Margaret and Grace – from the Historical Society – were saying that even her outings to the meetings are beginning to be too stressful for her. The Christmas meal certainly was – what with all the carry-on with Saul!'

'That's a shame. But I suppose it's inevitable – the deterioration,' she says with a sigh.

'Yes, sadly it is. But at least she's going to be seeing Lina regularly now. I'll make sure of that.'

'That's nice.' Sara nods. 'I can see that this is ... something you want to do, too. You like helping people, don't you. It's in your nature.'

'It was what I spent my working life doing, I suppose,' I say lightly. 'It gets into the blood! Anyway, how are you getting on with the Christmas preparations? Are you *sure* I can't do anything to help?'

She laughs. 'See, there you go again! No, as I've told you: Charlie breaks up from school tomorrow and I'm taking two weeks' holiday from work. He can help me put up some decorations, make the mince pies and ice the cake. He loves doing things like that with me.' She pauses, thinks for a moment, then nods and goes on: 'Although, actually – if you're free and you're sure you don't mind – perhaps you could have Charlie for a couple of hours on Saturday? While I go and pick up his present?'

'Of course. I'd love to.'

'I can only collect it at the weekend,' she explains. 'I'm buying it on eBay, and the seller works during the week.'

I'm intrigued now, of course, but before I can ask, she goes on, with a smile:

'It's what he wants: a keyboard. Second-hand, obviously, but only a year old and apparently completely OK. I'll check it, of course, before I pay. The seller says he bought it for his own son, who promptly got bored with it and has hardly used it. Kids!' she laughs. 'If Charlie does the same thing, I'll put it back on eBay next year!'

'I'm sure he'll be thrilled,' I say. 'He talks all the time about Max's keyboard.'

'Yes. I'm really glad I found one at such a reasonable price. Oh, Joy, I can't believe I'm actually looking forward to Christmas so much! After . . . everything . . . with Rob, the break-up, the move – I never would have thought that already, my life could have turned around like this. And so much of it has been because of you . . . '

'No it hasn't!' I laugh. 'It's because of Luke! And the twins!'

She automatically pats her stomach as she grins back at me.

'Well, yes. I guess they've had something to do with it, too. How did I get to be so lucky, after everything had gone so wrong?'

'It must be the Angel of the Cove,' I tease her.

And, for a moment, we look back at each other, almost wanting to believe it – before we both laugh the moment off.

As if!

Christmas Eve

Philip, Lina and I have decided between us to try visiting Freda again today. I drive up to Ferndell first, pick up Philip and he waits in the car while I collect Lina. She's standing by the front door waiting for us. I notice that her case is already packed ready for when we come back, as I've explained that we'll then pick up Bella and all her luggage and take them back to Philip's place for Christmas.

'Amy helped me get everything ready,' she says. 'But I'll have to put Bella in her travelling basket when we get back.'

'Don't worry, I'll help you.' I look at the mountain of Bella's paraphernalia that's piled up in Lina's hallway, ready for loading into the car later: her bed, blankets, food, dishes, litter tray, sack of litter, toys. It'll probably just about fit into my car, with Philip's wheelchair taking up the space of the boot!

It's only a one-minute drive to Freda's care home. Philip looks a little anxious as I help him out of the car and into the home.

'I'd hate to upset her again, especially after she got on so well with Lina,' he says quietly to me.

But he needn't have worried. Once again, Freda's immediate

attention is focused on her niece. She reaches out to hug her straight away, calling her *my little angel* and asking how she's getting on at school.

'Dad's here too, Auntie Freda,' she says, indicating Philip.

Freda turns to stare at him, frowning for a moment.

'You're the boy next door,' she says eventually. 'I thought you were dead.'

'That was my brother, Freda,' he explains again. 'I'm Philip, your brother-in-law. I married Chrissie.'

'Chrissie,' she whispers. 'My little sister. I was her bridesmaid.'

'That's right,' Philip encourages her. 'You wore a pink dress. You looked lovely.'

'I was jealous of her.' Her face crumples a little. 'I shouldn't have been jealous, she was my sister.'

'But, Freda, she loved you. She always loved you. And you made everything all right for us, didn't you? You said you saw the Angel of the Cove – that we'd been blessed. That our baby—' he smiles at his daughter '—our baby Angelina was blessed. We all loved you, Freda, dear. We still do.'

'Philip?' she says softly, realisation finally dawning. 'Philip, I'm sorry.'

'Nothing to be sorry for, my lovely,' he says, his voice choked with emotion. 'We're all fine, aren't we? We're all happy now, and isn't it marvellous that we're all together again?'

She nods, turning back to Lina, who's holding her hand and stroking it. Freda gives her a beaming smile before her eyes suddenly cloud with confusion again.

'I'd like to see my mother now,' she says calmly. 'And then I'd like to go to bed, please.'

'It's just her way of saying goodbye,' Lina explains to us matter-of-factly. 'She's tired.'

Philip and I are quiet at first as I drive us back to Ferndell. We've been back to Lina's flat to pick up the cat and load everything into the car, and Lina's now talking very softly to Bella on the back seat, telling her it's going to be Christmas tomorrow and that she'll be in a strange place but she, Lina, would be with her the whole time so she mustn't worry.

'Freda's deteriorated quite a lot,' Philip says eventually, with a sigh.

'But it was lovely that she did recognise you today. And you said exactly the right things to her. I think she understood – who you are, and that you love her. I know it's hard – so hard – for you to see her like that, but I think she seems content enough, in her way.'

'I hope so.'

'And she's being properly cared for. That's all we can do for her, Philip. Short visits occasionally, and don't take it personally if she forgets who you are again.'

'Yes. I know.' He smiles. 'You're very wise.'

'No, I'm not! If I'd really been wise . . .' I begin, and then shrug and shake my head as I indicate to pull into the Goldcrest Lodge car park. I'd been going to say that if I'd really been wise, I'd have trusted my husband when he was going through such a difficult time; trusted him and not automatically assumed it was all about me. But Philip and Lina don't need to hear all of that, and anyway I don't need to think about it any more.

I stay for a quick cup of coffee, long enough to see Lina – and Bella – settled in Philip's apartment, and to give them the gifts I've wrapped for them, to open the following morning. The latest book by Philip's favourite author (I checked on his bookshelves), and a warm scarf for Lina in her favourite shade of green.

'And here's yours,' Philip says, handing me a very obvious

bottle-shaped package. 'Sorry it's so unoriginal but I had to rely on my supermarket delivery! I hope you enjoy it.'

'I'm sure I will, thank you.' I lean down and give him a quick kiss on the cheek.

'And I've got something for you too!' Lina says, delving into her bag and pulling out a neatly wrapped box. 'Amy helped me choose it and wrap it up. It's a cat!' she adds, evidently far too excited not to spoil the surprise! 'Not a real one,' she goes on hastily. 'A china one, but it looks like Pumpkin, so I've got one the same for Sara.' She gets another, identical, parcel out of her bag. 'I wanted to give it to her because I'm sorry I thought Pumpkin was mine. Do you think she'll like it?'

'Lina, I'm sure she'll love it and treasure it,' I tell her. 'And I'll treasure mine, too.' I pull her towards me for a hug. 'It's so nice of you to think of us: thank you, love. Now, I need to get going, but I really hope you both have a really wonderful Christmas, and I'll be back the day after Boxing Day to take you home, Lina – OK?'

'And Bella,' she reminds me.

'And Bella, of course.'

I'm singing to myself as I drive home, the two identical, precious wrapped parcels on the seat beside me. *Driving home for Christmas*. Christmas – for the first time in God knows how many years – *not* spent quietly at home with just Terry and a seasonal film on TV, but with company. With an excited child. A proper Christmas. I can't wait!

Charlie's knocking on our door in the morning, almost as soon as we've finished breakfast. It's bitterly cold outside – just as Christmas is supposed to be – but with a blue sky, and winter sunshine sparkling on the sea.

'Father Christmas has been!' he says, his little face pink from excitement as well as from the cold wind. 'I've got a keyboard! An *actual keyboard*, like Max's.'

'Oh, that's great, Charlie!' Terry and I both exclaim together.

'When are you coming in to our house? Luke's already here. He came last night for dinner. I don't even know whether he went home,' he adds innocently. 'He was here at breakfast.'

I sense Terry grinning, next to me, and give him a nudge.

'Well, he probably wanted to be here early,' I say, 'to see what Father Christmas got you. Look, we've only just had our own breakfast, so we'll come in a little bit later, OK?'

I'm still recovering from the shock of Terry's present. Still recovering, in fact, when we finally go next door to join Sara and Luke.

'You're quiet,' Sara comments as I help her in the kitchen, turning the potatoes, checking the turkey. She's got the radio playing lovely Christmas songs, and we're both smiling as we listen to Charlie prattling away to Luke and Terry about his presents. 'Are you OK?'

'Yes – sorry. I was miles away.' I grin at her. 'About ten thousand miles away, in fact.'

'What—Oh!' She stops, her knife poised over a Brussels sprout. 'I'm sorry, Joy, I haven't even asked you yet: I presume Terry's told you, now? The destination – your special holiday?'

'My Christmas present, and fortieth anniversary present too, really! Yes. And it's still so ... well, it's so ... '

To my embarrassment, and Sara's horror, I'm crying – blubbing like a baby over the roast potatoes. She throws down the knife and grabs hold of me.

'What is it? Are you OK?'

'Yes!' I wipe my eyes, feeling a fool. 'Sorry, it's just that it's so wonderful, I'm so happy.' The tears are threatening again, and Sara holds me out at arm's length and tells me:

'Stop bloody crying, then, for God's sake, and tell me! I'm dying of suspense, here!'

'We're going to Australia, Sara. Brisbane. It's ... where Pauline lives – my cousin. Terry's found her! He ... even while everything was going on, all the worry about the takeover, all that extra work and responsibility, he was secretly looking for her, searching for leads on the internet, on social media – finding people who knew her, places she'd worked – and finally, finally, he's found her. She's married, she's got children, she's a grandmother. She's over the moon, she'd tried to find *me,* but she gave up in the end. Yes,' I go on, as Sara's frantically trying to interrupt to ask if we've already been in touch, 'yes, we've spoken on the phone already this morning – it's evening there – and well, we both cried, obviously! And I admitted *I'd* given up, too, on finding her.'

'But Terry didn't,' Sara says softly. 'He didn't give up, did he, Joy – because he knew how much it would mean to you, to be reunited with her. And he wanted you to be happy.'

'I know. I don't deserve him—' I start.

'Of course you bloody do, woman!' she retorts, laughing. 'You deserve *each other*, because you're both lovely people, and you've survived forty years together, and – oh, it's so perfect, I'm so happy for you! Come here, I've got to give you another hug, and I'm going to start bloody crying myself now. It's this pregnancy lark, my emotions are all over the place!'

'Well, I haven't got that excuse!'

'No, but you don't need any excuse. It's Christmas, and you're happy, and so am I – and we're both so very lucky, as it turns out, aren't we?'

'We are indeed,' I agree.

And as we rejoin the others in the living room, I glance up at the angel on the top of Sara's Christmas tree, and find myself grinning at it. The Angel of the Cove. Is there really anything in it, after all – that old story? Is it *really* lucky here, at the Cove? I never did find out the reason for the legend, after all. I've never considered myself superstitious, but who knows? Perhaps there really is some truth behind it, after all.

Monday 8 January

It's the new year's first meeting of the Bierleigh Historical Society this evening, and the first one being held in the new venue: the room at the Angel Inn. It's also the one where Philip and I are due to give our talk about Angel Cove. Howard decided to make this the first one because I'll be missing the next three meetings: Terry and I will be off to Australia this Friday. Our anniversary is on Thursday, and we're just going to celebrate with a quiet lunch together at the pub. The real celebration will be the holiday!

Terry's coming along to the meeting this evening, and so is Sara; Luke's going to sit with Charlie while she's out. I'm feeling nervous as I get changed ready for the meeting. I'm not used to speaking in public and I've already practised my talk twice in front of a mirror. Philip and I are going to take it in turns to talk, to share our memories of life at the Cove, and there will be photos on display for people to browse afterwards – Philip's, mine and those of other members who've lent their own pictures.

'I hope there'll be lots of potential new members turning up,' I say anxiously to Howard. We've arrived early, to get chairs arranged and lay out the photos on a table at the side of the room.

'Stop panicking, Joy!' he says gently, giving me a reassuring smile. 'There might be some new members, there might not. It's soon after Christmas, so some people might be away, and others might not want to come out in the cold and dark. I do hope our numbers are going to increase, but it might happen gradually. If tonight goes well, word will spread around the community ...'

'*If* tonight goes well,' I repeat, my voice shaking slightly.

'Just be yourself, love,' he says. 'It's just a friendly chat, right? Whoever turns up, remember they're just our friends and neighbours, not the royal family.'

I laugh. 'Right. Well, here's Terry – he's been to pick Philip up. And two friends of his from Goldcrest Lodge. Oh – I'll go and open the door wider, for him to get the wheelchair through.'

And, to be honest, I don't really have time, after that, to worry about my talk, because other people are arriving now. First the other members of the society turn up, some of them having brought friends and family members along for the occasion. Then there's a steady drift of other new people: faces I recognise from the shops and around the village. Sara arrives, and to our surprise so does Lina, accompanied by Amy.

'It's nice to see you both here!' I say, giving Lina a hug.

'I wanted to come,' Lina insists. 'Because you're talking, Joy, and so is my dad.'

'I understand her Auntie Freda won't be here?' Amy says quietly.

'No. Sadly, I don't think she'll be coming any more. Her friends here think the outings were getting a bit stressful for her, and frankly the only point of it was to give her a treat.'

'So there's no point at all if she's happier staying where she is,' Amy agrees.

By the time we're ready to start, every chair in the room has been taken, and Howard's gone into the bar to ask the manager if he can borrow a couple more. There's an excited hum of conversation, but everyone falls silent when Howard finally stands up at the front to welcome everyone and to introduce Philip and me.

'Here goes!' I mutter to Philip, who looks as nervous as me. But when I launch into the first part of my talk, giving a quick introduction, a description of Angel Cove and explaining how long I've lived there, I find I'm suddenly completely relaxed.

'And I'm going to hand over now,' I say, 'to someone who knows far more than I do about Angel Cove, having lived there with his family from the day he was born: Philip Sutton.'

Philip seems to have relaxed now too, and as he begins to tell the story of his childhood at Smugglers' Cottages, and how he used to play on the beach and in the woods with his sweetheart, Chrissie, I see Lina smiling happily back at him. I'm not sure how much of his story about the pair of them trying to run away to sea she's heard before, or how much of it she understands, but when he tells the audience that it all ended happily with the birth of their beautiful baby girl, Angelina, who he's proud to say is in the audience tonight and has been the blessing of his life, can't help calling out 'I love you, Dad!' And there are appreciative murmurs of 'Ah!' around the room.

'We called her Angelina because our mothers both believed we were – and *she* was – blessed by the Angel of the Cove,' Philip goes on. 'And do you know what? I think they might have been right.'

It's my cue to take over again.

'The Angel of the Cove!' I begin, smiling around at the audience. 'You know, although I've lived at the cove for so long, it's only recently that I've begun to wonder exactly how it got its name. Everyone around here seems to know there's a legend about an angel, and that there's a belief that the cove is lucky. Some even believe that swimming in the cove is lucky and that it's impossible to drown there! But it's strange; no matter how I tried, I haven't been able to find out how this legend began. In the end, I think we just have to accept that it's a nice name, and that the various myths have grown up *because* of the name, rather than there being any particular reason—'

'But ... excuse me, but there *is* a reason,' speaks up a rather apologetic voice from across the room. It's one of Philip's friends from Goldcrest Lodge. 'Sorry to butt in,' he goes on, 'but I know where the legend came from. My grandfather told me the story.'

The man falls silent, suddenly looking uncomfortable. Everyone has turned round to look at him, and there's an excited chorus of whispers in the room. I'm staring at him, staggered. This chap – who looks to be nearly as old as Saul, certainly at least in his nineties – actually knows the origin of the legend of the angel?

'Did you know about this?' I whisper to Philip.

'No, I didn't,' he replies. 'I don't even know him – Walter – very well. He just heard about tonight from my mate Arthur – he's the chap sitting next to him – and said he'd like to come along.'

I look back at Walter.

'That's very interesting,' I tell him. 'I'm sure we'd all like to hear all about it. Would you like to tell me more during the interval?'

'Happy to, miss,' he says. 'It's a right good story.'

I continue with my part of the talk, which suddenly seems tame and almost redundant compared with ... whatever it is Walter knows. And when we break for refreshments, I manage to get hold of Walter before he and Arthur wander into the bar.

'Can we sit somewhere quiet for a minute while you tell me what your grandfather told you?' I suggest. I'm thinking that what I'd really like – if Philip, and Howard, agree – is for this man to round off the evening by telling his granddad's story himself. But I need to make sure, first, that it isn't a lot of nonsense!

And ... when he's finished telling me ... I don't think it's non-sense at all. I think, in fact, that it's the answer we've all been looking for.

Walter

I was just a young boy, living in Bierleigh, when my grandfather told me about the Angel of the Cove. We used to go down to the cove on Sundays, like a lot of local people, to picnic on the beach and paddle in the sea. I remember seeing Mr and Mrs Jones who lived in Number One, Smugglers' Cottages, outside their cottage with their daughter Freda. She was just a baby then.

On this particular day, my grandad was talking to me about the original Smugglers' Cottages.

'There used to be a row of four old cottages there, when I was a boy – where the two houses are now,' he said. 'Tumbledown little ol' places, they were – abandoned, not fit for anyone to live in. We used to play in them when we were kids.'

'Why were they called *Smugglers' Cottages*?' I asked him.

My grandad laughed. 'Well, that's what they were, see? The smugglers used to use them, in the old days, way back before I was born – to hide their contraband under the floorboards, till they could move it on. My father told me about it.'

Of course, I found the whole idea of smugglers thrilling, so I asked my grandad to tell me more. He said his father had remembered smuggling still being rife along this coast when he was a young lad. Our coast was perfect for it, I reckon, because of being close to France and because we've got so many deep inlets and coves. Well, Bierleigh Cove – as Grandad said it was known back then – was apparently one of the smugglers' favourites. They especially liked to bring French brandy and wine over. Apparently, all the local people knew about it and a lot of them helped, too, by storing contraband in their homes. Even the minister used to be involved – hiding smuggled goods in the cellar under the chapel. My grandad wanted to know why there wasn't any smuggling going on in the area any more.

'People round here have had enough of it,' his father said, and he sat my grandad down and told him the story of the angel. So this was the story my grandad passed on to me. As a boy, I found it fascinating, of course. But when I grew up, I realised it was all nonsense, and that's why I've never really talked about it. Silly nonsense, believed by silly people, in my opinion – gossiped about over pints of ale in the pub. But . . . well, sorry. If I'd known you were all desperate to know, I would've told you about it sooner.

One dark, stormy night back in the early 1800s, two of the village's well-known smugglers were sailing back from France with their load of contraband brandy when their boat was blown off-course at the last moment, and dashed against the rocks – down beneath Harry's Plain. As you all know, it's a bad stretch of coast there; the currents are strong, too strong for the crew of a little sailing boat. There were plenty of shipwrecks down there, over the years, and sailors who survived those wrecks always claimed the devil himself – Old Harry – drove their boat onto the rocks and then ran off up Old Harry's Staircase.

Well, that particular night, there was nobody around to help the smugglers. Their accomplices were waiting down at Bierleigh Cove as usual, and because the weather was so bad, they took shelter in one of the abandoned cottages, biding their time during the delay by sampling some of the previous week's hidden brandy. When the sailboat broke up on the rocks, the two men were thrown out onto rocks themselves. Both of them were knocked unconscious, and they didn't remember any more about the incident, until they came to, hours later. They found themselves lying on the beach at Bierleigh Cove and – as the first man to regain consciousness put it – surrounded by a strange heavenly light. This man – my grandad said his name was Thomas somebody-or-other – was well known in the area. He was a 'rough diamond', he had a history of all kinds of lawbreaking. He was quite badly injured, but he managed to crawl across the sand to rouse his mate, and, according to them, they both watched in stunned silence as the 'heavenly light' shone down on them through the black, stormy night sky, before suddenly disappearing and leaving them in darkness.

By the time their accomplices had recovered from the effects of the French brandy and staggered out to find them, the sun was rising and Thomas and his mate were groaning from the pain of their broken bones, and muttering incoherently about being snatched from the jaws of death at the hands of Old Harry, and carried to safety by an angel of light.

Well, of course, everybody assumed they were hallucinating, but apparently, they stuck to their story, and they were so overcome by what they called this 'spiritual experience', that they both turned from their lives of crime and became model citizens. They started attending chapel regularly, working hard, raising families and giving to the poor. And they also went to great pains to dissuade their friends and neighbours from the dastardly trade of smuggling. Actually, when I started to read up on the history of smuggling, years later, I realised it was starting to die out in any case, over the following few decades, because the coastguard service was set up to stamp it out. And the government reduced excise duty, so in the end, smuggling wasn't really worth the risk any more.

So that was why people started to call Bierleigh Cove *Angel Cove* instead, and why the pub got named after the angel, and everyone started thinking it's a lucky place, where it's impossible to drown. I suppose you all think it's a nice enough story, and as a boy, when my grandad told me about it, I thought it was wonderful. But as I say, when I got a bit older, I started to think about it more logically and I reckon it was all just a hallucination, or a dream, those lads had that night. Still, if it turned them away from a life of crime, I suppose it wasn't such a bad thing. But how people have carried on believing in the angel, after all these years – well, that's beyond me. But I suppose some people will believe anything.

That's all I've got to say about it, really. Thank you …

Later

There's such a hubbub of excitement around the hall as Walter returns to his seat, that eventually Howard has to stand up and ask for quiet.

'Thank you, Walter,' he says. 'That was absolutely fascinating. I think I speak for everyone here when I say you've just solved a mystery for us all.'

'Didn't think it was that special,' Walter says with an awkward little shrug. 'Just a story, isn't it – just an old legend, really.'

'Yes, but—' I get to my feet and give him a smile '—the point is, Walter, nobody else – nobody apart from you – seems to have known how the legend started. And now we do. So yes, thank you for telling us your grandad's story, and even if there's no truth in it whatsoever, it means we can keep that old story alive, for future generations. Even if it *is* nonsense, it's still special, particularly to people like me who live at Angel Cove.'

'I agree. And I think,' Howard says, looking at his watch, 'unless anyone's got anything else to add about their memories of Angel Cove, that's pretty much taken us to the end of the meeting, folks. But please stay and look at the photographs if you'd like to, and if anyone who's new to us tonight would like to become a member, have a word with me or with David, our treasurer. Otherwise, of course the bar's still open if you'd like to linger for a while and chat with your friends over a drink or two.'

We all gradually drift into the bar. Everyone's still talking about the Legend of Angel Cove, and marvelling about the fact that the story's come out, so suddenly, so unexpectedly, after being lost to people's memories for so long.

'You must be thrilled!' Sara says. 'I know I am. I don't care whether the whole thing was made up by those smugglers, or just a dream, or whatever. It's such a great story.'

'And so nice to actually *know* it at last,' I agree.

'Not that it took anything away from your talk – or yours, Philip,' she adds, giving him a smile. 'Well done, both of you. You made it all so interesting. I noticed there was a queue of people waiting to sign up to become members, too.'

'Yes, Howard and David are looking really pleased,' I agree. 'Even Terry says he's going to join, now, when we come back from Australia! Oh – thanks, darling,' I add as Terry arrives back at our table with a tray full of drinks for us all. I look at his bottle of alcohol-free beer and go on, 'I'm happy to drive Philip home, if you'd like to have a proper drink? I don't mind having fruit juice.'

'Not at all,' he says at once. 'I'm happy to take Philip back, and anyway, you deserve this—' he plonks a large glass of Merlot in front of me '—after your star turn tonight!'

'The star turn was Walter,' I correct him, laughing.

'And regarding that . . . ' He sits down and takes a mouthful of his drink. 'I've been thinking about it. In fact, I did a quick spot of googling as Walter was finishing his talk.'

'Googling what?' Sara and I say at once.

'Well, Walter's probably right, that the bright light – what those guys described as an angel – was just some kind of hallucination. But I did wonder about . . . I don't know, I suppose some kind of

335

atmospheric phenomenon. And—' he waves his phone at us and taps it reverently, as if it's revealed the secrets of the universe to him '—I've actually found some references to something, something very rare called a "nocturnal sun" that's supposed to have occurred at various times throughout history. Scientists have been investigating it, and most now seem to believe it's actually nothing to do with the sun, but something bizarre happening in the earth's own atmosphere in certain conditions.'

We're all silent for a few minutes, sipping our drinks. I look from Terry to Sara, to Philip, and then around the bar at my friends from the Historical Society. I think about Philip and his pregnant teenage girlfriend, Chrissie, and their baby Angelina, who grew into the sweet-natured Lina who I've become so fond of. I think of Freda, who claimed to have seen the Angel just to help her little sister and convince their parents to allow them to marry.

'That's ... interesting, Tel,' I say, quietly. 'And I'm sure you're right that there could be a scientific explanation. But to be honest, I'd rather not know about it. I'd rather believe in the angel.'

'Me too,' Sara agrees at once. 'It's a much nicer story than some nocturnal phenomenon in the earth's atmosphere.'

Philip joins in. 'I agree. Despite everything my common sense tells me, I've always had a soft spot for the angel of the Cove.'

Terry smiles around at us. 'I thought you'd all say that,' he says, putting his phone down. 'And anyway, in these days of artificial light pollution, nobody would see a "nocturnal sun" any more, even if it were to occur.'

'Good!' I retort, and we all laugh.

Philip raises his glass, looking suddenly quite emotional.

'Here's to the angel,' he says. 'Through him, or her, I've met you – my new friends – and, in a funny kind of way, I've been able to reconnect with my Chrissie all over again by telling you our story.'

'To the Angel of the Cove!' we all chorus, raising our own glasses in response.

Philip has summed up how we all feel. Even if we know it can't be real, we like to imagine the angel is still out there, hovering over the sea, watching our beach and our waters, protecting us and everyone who visits our beautiful little corner of Devon. Perhaps the RNLI, who saved Philip and Chrissie that stormy night in 1960, is today's embodiment of the angel; their volunteers certainly do save lives, and, in my opinion, they deserve to wear haloes.

I'm so glad Walter decided to come along tonight and share his story with us. And I'm grateful, of course, now more than ever, for having the great good fortune to live where we do. Whether by an angel or by pure good luck, I think we have been truly blessed.

Epilogue

Six months later: Thursday 6 June

'It was my due date today,' Sara says thoughtfully, looking down at baby Oscar as she holds him against her shoulder to wind him after his feed.

'Only until you knew it was twins,' I say, smiling. 'Then we knew they'd come early, didn't we?'

The babies made their appearance at exactly thirty-seven weeks of Sara's pregnancy, on the sixteenth of May, but their birth weights were a nice healthy five pounds six ounces for Oscar and five pounds three for his sister Ava, who's currently sound asleep in the pram next to us on the decking. A boy and a girl – which was *super-brilliant*, according to big brother Charlie, who already absolutely adores them both and can't get enough of holding them and trying to make them smile.

'It's still far too early, Charlie,' Sara keeps telling him, but he's determined that he'll be the first person to elicit a smile and a laugh from *his* twins.

He's almost as proud of them as their dad is – although that would be a tough one to beat! Luke, who apparently cried buckets at the moments of both their births, could easily be mistaken for the first man in the world ever to have become a father. He's not just hands-on; it's almost as if he can hardly ever bear to be hands-off. He took two weeks off work when the babies arrived, and was so upset to be leaving them, and their mum, when it was time for him to return, that he's coming home every lunchtime just to see how they're doing.

He moved in with Sara towards the end of February; it was no surprise, of course, to anyone. In fact, Sara had started suggesting it to him over Christmas, and it was only because Luke was determined that she should be absolutely sure, that it took as long as it did. There's no talk yet of them getting married, but it wouldn't surprise me if that happens eventually – they seem so blissfully happy, and so well suited. It's not hard to see why they were best friends for so much of their earlier lives.

The babies are squeezed into their parents' bedroom for now, but plans are already drawn up for the extension. They want it to be built once things have settled down a bit. We've told them Charlie will be welcome to sleep at our place during the renovations if it makes life easier. And Terry's keen to help with any redecorating that might be needed once the building work is finished.

As we sit here in the sunshine, watching little Oscar's eyes gradually closing as Sara prepares to lay him in the pram next to his sister, there's a sudden greeting of excited *woofs* as Terry appears along the beach with Buster, our five-year-old rescue dog. Oscar's eyes fly open momentarily but Sara jiggles him gently back to sleep.

'Sorry!' Terry whispers, pulling Buster closer towards him.

'Don't be silly,' Sara says. 'They've got to get used to noise around them. Can't expect Charlie to creep around the house when they're asleep – or Pumpkin not to meow!'

'Did you have a good walk?' I ask Terry, and he nods enthusiastically as he starts to describe where he's been. Buster – a mixed breed who looks a bit like a cocker spaniel with some terrier in the mix – needs a couple of good walks a day, as well as runs on the beach, so I like to encourage Terry to take him out on his own sometimes. He's still working at finding his way around this strange thing called retirement. As well as the Historical Society, he's joined a golf club the other side of Bierleigh, and – after the fantastic time we had on our special anniversary trip in January – we're making plans for another holiday in the autumn. Probably somewhere in the UK, a self-catering place where dogs are welcome!

And, most importantly for me, I've finally been reunited with my cousin and childhood companion, Pauline. We both cried buckets when we first saw each other at Brisbane airport, where she'd come to meet us. And we must have asked each other about fifty times – before Terry, and Pauline's husband Steve, both begged us to stop – how on earth we'd managed to lose touch with each other. That reunion was the best present Terry could possibly have given me. After we'd spent a week with Pauline and Steve, meeting their daughter Lynne and their grandchildren, they came with us for the next leg of our trip, flying down to Sydney and staying in a wonderful waterfront hotel while we explored the sights of the city. Terry and I then said goodbye to them and we continued on our journey, taking another flight to Melbourne, and hiring a car to drive along the Great Ocean Road.

It was the most amazing trip, and saying goodbye to Pauline was made a lot less painful by the fact that she and Steve had already booked their flights to come and stay with us this Christmas! I find myself shivering with excitement already every time I think about it. It's hard to believe that it was only last September that I retired from my job at the surgery. Back then, I felt so lost and unsure, wondering how I'd fill my time, whether my new life would feel empty and unfulfilling. I couldn't have been more wrong. I've got so much to be grateful for now.

With the agreement of Walter, who still doesn't know what all the fuss was about, I spent a week or so back in the spring, writing up his great-grandfather's story and submitting it for publication in the *South Devon Gazette*. I've since been approached by the same local author who produced *Bierleigh Through the Ages* – the book I borrowed from the library last year – asking if he can include the story in a new edition he wants to bring out.

'Fame at last,' Terry teased me at the time. 'Perhaps this is your destiny for the next phase of your life – writing history books?'

'I don't think so!' I retorted. 'But I *am* more fascinated by local history than I ever imagined I'd be. In fact, you know, I think I might start researching Saul's family history next . . .'

That's if I have time, between walking Buster, helping Sara with the babies, sharing summer barbecues and picnics outside with her and Luke and Charlie. As well as visiting Philip, bringing him to Bierleigh regularly to see Lina, and through her, keeping updated about Freda, who sadly now seems to be peacefully, quietly, fading away from us. To say nothing, of course, of finally spending time with my husband, enjoying the freedom we both dreamed about during our years of working. Time together. Time spent at leisure, at our beautiful Angel Cove – watched over, I'm certain, whatever anyone else thinks – by our very own guardian angel.

As Sara often says, it must have been the angel who brought her and Luke back together again. That was no boring old atmospheric phenomenon! No: that was definitely the work of the Angel of the Cove.

Acknowledgments

With my grateful thanks to Anna Boatman and all the team at Piatkus, and to my agent Juliet Burton, for their help and support which has allowed me to concentrate on the part I love: writing the books.

And I'd also like to give a mention to the RNLI – Royal National Lifeboat Institution – as they play an important part in this book (referred to as 'the real angel' of the 1960 part of the story). These brave volunteers do an amazing job, saving lives at sea, and they rely on charitable donations to do so. Angels indeed.